DARK
HOUR

THE GAMMA SEQUENCE, Book 5

a medical thriller

DAN ALATORRE

Great Oak
PUBLISHING

DARK HOUR
THE GAMMA SEQUENCE, Book 5
a medical thriller

OTHER THRILLERS BY DAN ALATORRE

NOVELS

Jett Thacker Mysteries
Tiffany Lynn Is Missing, *a psychological thriller*
Killer In The Dark, *Jett Thacker book 2*

The Gamma Sequence Medical Thriller Series
The Gamma Sequence, *a medical thriller*
Rogue Elements, *The Gamma Sequence, book 2*
Terminal Sequence, *The Gamma Sequence, book 3*
The Keepers, *The Gamma Sequence, book 4*
Dark Hour, *The Gamma Sequence, book 5*

Double Blind Murder Mystery Series
Double Blind, *a murder mystery*
Primary Target, *Double Blind book 2*
Third Degree, *Double Blind book 3*
Fourth Estate, *Double Blind book 4*

OTHER THRILLER NOVELS

A Place Of Shadows, *a paranormal mystery*
The Navigators, *a time travel thriller*

OTHER BOOKS
The Water Castle, *a fantasy romance novel*
The Italian Assistant, *a very funny, very sexy romance novel*

Dan Alatorre Short Story Horror Anthologies
Dark Passages
Dark Voodoo
Dark Intent
Dark Thoughts

Short Story Horror Anthologies With Other Authors
The Box Under The Bed
Dark Visions
Nightmareland
Spellbound
Wings and Fire
Shadowland

Family Humor
Savvy Stories
The Terrible Twos
The Long Cutie
The Short Years
There's No Such Thing As A Quick Trip To Buy-Mart
Night of the Colonoscopy
Santa Maybe
A Day for Hope

Illustrated Children's Books
Laguna the Lonely Mermaid
The Adventures of Pinchy Crab
The Princess and the Dolphin
Stinky Toe!

Children's Early Reader Books
The Zombunny
Zombunny 2: Night of the Scary Creatures
Zombunny 3: Quest for Battle Space

Writing Instruction
A if for Action
B is for Backstory
C is for Character
D is for Dialogue
E is for Emotion
F is for Fast Pace

CONTENTS

ACKNOWLEDGMENTS

My current creative works are the culmination of years
spent with fellow struggling authors and others who
helped me every step of the way.

Thank you to each and every one of them.

Note to Readers

*If you have the time, I would deeply appreciate a review on
Amazon or Goodreads. I learn a great deal from them, and
I'm always grateful for any encouragement. Reviews are a
very big deal and help authors like me to sell a few more
books. Every review matters, even if it's only a few words.*

Thanks,
Dan Alatorre

Certain information on weaponry and explosive devices is intentionally vague or exaggerated so if some kid picks up this story, they won't learn enough to do the things described. Such inaccuracies may be irritating to a trained eye, but I hope you can appreciate my rationale.

CHAPTER 1

The doctor raced down the hallway, his white lab coat flowing behind him. Several technicians ran ahead of him as the alert system blared overhead.

"Warning. Extreme protocol breach, containment lab five."

The alarm's mechanical voice was calm and emotionless, evoking none of the near-panicked urgency of the technicians in the corridor.

Heart pounding, the doctor adjusted his face shield and lowered the plastic visor. "What's the breach? Is it chemical? Do we need respirators?"

A thin woman in a lab coat grabbed his arm. "This way, Doctor Symm."

She pulled him into a corridor on the right; the technicians ran straight ahead, disappearing through swinging double doors into what appeared to be an operating room.

"It's not chemical. The red light isn't flashing." She pointed to one of the monitors on the wall. The facility's standard, calming images of majestic mountains or seaside sunsets had been replaced by the words *Extreme protocol breach* against a flashing yellow background. Overhead, the same words were repeated by the alarm system, followed by a harsh, intermittent tone. Panting, the thin woman led him to an observation room and closed the door, shutting out the noise. "Yellow merely means a physical interruption. An incident has occurred with a tansuit."

Doctor Genoa Symm's jaw dropped. "Physical interruption? Is that what you're calling them these days?" On the other side of the observation room's large glass window, the technicians threw themselves at a brown-haired man in tan coveralls, grabbing his arms and legs. An overhead speaker broadcast the noise of the struggle into the observation room.

Reaching over, the woman flipped a wall switch, sending a motorized curtain over the viewing window. Pulling Symm's arm again, she nodded toward the door at the other end of the long, white room. "Please come this way. You are needed in exam room three. You mustn't concern yourself with low-level distractions, Doctor."

Symm jerked his arm free, glancing at the lanky woman's ID badge. She wasn't a technician. She was head of operations, Doctor Atria Lutz—the person he had come to see.

Scowling, Symm flipped the toggle on the wall switch again, and the curtain reversed itself, opening to reveal the chaos on the other side of the thick glass. "If my company is investing a billion dollars…" Doctor Symm removed his face shield and tossed it to the floor, folding his arms across his chest. "We have the right to see what's going on here."

Doctor Lutz stepped back, putting a hand to her lips.

In the containment lab, three technicians wrestled with the man in the coveralls. He was not larger than them, and he didn't appear to be more muscular, but he flung the technicians off like they were rag dolls. His one notable physical feature was a dark mole on his left cheek, just under his eye, but otherwise he seemed normal in every respect—except his obvious strength. He walked toward the swinging double doors, his torn garment hanging open at the chest. Several more technicians burst into the room, grabbing him. One leveled a taser at the man, discharging it at his torso. The electrode coils unspooled and the barbs hit the tansuit's skin, jerking him backward—but only for an instant. He grabbed the wires and yanked them from his exposed pectoralis major and then knocked the weapon from the technician's hand.

As the other technicians grabbed him again, he pulled them off as easily as petals from a daisy, slamming them into the far wall until their motionless bodies were piled up like firewood.

The tansuit clenched his fists and stared at the thick glass, his face etched in rage. "You know why I'm here!" His cheeks turning red, he approached the window. "Where is Marcus Hauser? Where is Atria Lutz? And where are the regeneration records?"

The tansuit threw a fist at the glass, sending a *boom* through the observation room.

Symm recoiled, gasping. "Can he see us?"

"No." The doctor shook her head. "No, he's quite contained in there."

"Doctor Lutz!" The tansuit pounded the glass again. "I know you're in there! Where are the regeneration records?"

Symm took a step backwards. "Are you sure he can't see us?"

"Quite sure." She reached into her pocket and withdrew a hand-held radio, raising it to her lips. "This is Atria Lutz. I need the enhanced staff team to shut down the interruption in containment vessel five."

A woman's voice came over the radio. "Yes, Doctor Lutz."

As the man on the other side of the glass paced back and forth, he ripped off his tattered tan coveralls. He kneeled down next to one of the unconscious technicians, rifling through the pockets of the lab coat.

Standing, he walked back to the glass, displaying a hand-held radio.

Symm took another step backwards.

"Don't worry, Genoa," Lutz said. "He is quite contained."

The tansuit lifted the radio to his chin, appearing to stare directly at Doctor Lutz.

Symm's hands trembled. "Now, you're *sure* he can't—"

"All systems dark," the tansuit said.

The lights of the facility turned off, plunging the observation room into blackness.

From the overhead speaker, the tansuit's next command came. "Release all locks on all facility doors."

A click sounded from both doors in the observation room, as well as all other doors within earshot.

On the other side of the glass, the swinging doors banged open. Two large men with rifles appeared, barely visible in the dim reflected light from the laboratory's outside windows—but there was no mistaking the red dots from their weapons' laser sightings, hovering on the tansuit's bare chest.

Symm swallowed hard. "What are they going to do?"

One of the armed men put a hand to his collar. "Enhanced staff team confirming request to shut down the interruption in containment lab five."

Lutz nodded, holding her radio to her bony cheek. "You have your confirmation. Proceed with shutdown."

"Wait!" Symm shouted. "You can't just… just…"

The tansuit turned to the glass. "This doesn't change anything, *sister*. Dark Hour is still coming."

Symm glared at Lutz. "Don't! Stop them!"

The containment room flashed white again and again, like lightning rippling across distant clouds on a stormy night. The tansuit slammed into the glass, throwing his arms out, his head arching back, jolting as each additional burst of light illuminated more and more red splattering onto the walls of containment lab five.

CHAPTER 2

Hamilton DeShear sat at a desk in the office of his large Virginia estate, looking out the window toward the back pasture. If he lifted his head high enough over the stack of complicated financial statements, legal documents, and security invoices, he could see his six-year-old daughter's two black-and-white spotted bunnies nibbling hay on the patio. On the other side of her "bun-buns," two thoroughbred horses grazed beneath tall oak trees, confined only by their wood-slat fence.

Technically, the entire house and grounds belonged to his daughter, but as her legal guardian and the executor of her trust, he spent the money as he saw fit—which was occasionally considered, by the standards of the others in the house, as a bit too thrifty.

DeShear's head throbbed. Reading a mountain of never-ending legal and financial documents was not the former PI's forte. He pulled open his desk drawer and grabbed the small, white aspirin bottle there, opening it and shaking out two of the round tablets. He washed them down with a sip of cold tea and leaned back, resting his head on the soft leather of his desk chair.

Sighing, DeShear's gaze wandered to his computer, where the screen saver displayed a family photo from his young daughter's recent birthday party.

He stretched his hand to the mouse, shaking it to wake the computer up. He typed in his password and closed all the legal sites and bank statements, sending the cursor to a small folder in the upper left-hand corner labeled "pictures."

Opening the folder sent a small array of images across his screen—and sent a warm feeling through his insides. He clicked on the images, one by one, enlarging them. There was a picture of Constantine and Helena, dirty and disheveled, sipping bottled water outside a château in France, one of Constantine on the boat in the Bahamas as she smiled at a pod of distant dolphins... one of her at the birthday party, one of her riding a horse, one of her with the bunnies...

DeShear smiled, clicking through them, his heart full of joy. Constantine was an amazing and beautiful child, and she opened his world to things he never imagined being interested in.

The care and feeding of rabbits, for one.

He clicked on another image from the birthday party. Constantine's face glowed upon seeing the dozen or so helium balloons and the banner in the living room, all for her. It had been a simple enough job of decorating—a few minutes at the dollar store, followed by a few more minutes at the house, arranging the shiny, colorful balloons so that Constantine would see them as soon as she came downstairs—but the impact it had on her was one of sheer joy. The little blonde gasped and put her hands to her cheeks, jumping up and down…

Smiling, DeShear let the mouse linger on the happy image. The addition of Constantine to his life had been a big decision, but an easy one. He found his new life challenging at times, but he also found it more fulfilling than he ever could have imagined.

His took another sip of tea, his eye moving toward another folder on the screen. Tucked away inside the "images" folder, this one was marked "personal."

He stared at it, his hand on the mouse, a lump welling in his throat.

The file had been transferred to this computer months ago, but never opened. Retrieved from a friend's old emails, the images inside the folder hadn't been looked at in years.

DeShear took a deep breath, letting it out slowly as he clicked on the file.

The images were smaller and older, not displaying the sharpness of the ones he'd just been viewing. Although they contained the same colors as any other picture on his computer, to DeShear these images were composed of subdued shades of gray.

The first was of a younger version of himself, smiling as he held the hand of his dark-haired wife, her pregnant belly protruding as she sat in a rocking chair. The next image was of him holding a tiny baby, the newborn's eyes still shut and smeared with antibiotic ointment. There was one of the proud parents clasping the child's hands as she took some of her first steps, one of her eating Spaghettios from a high chair, one of her trying out her new roller skates. In each one, the girl's big, bright eyes shined.

The next image was one of the child in a hospital bed. The young parents were no longer smiling in that one. The bright, shining eyes were no longer present on the child's face, either.

The last image was in a folder by itself, marked only with the letter G. DeShear could not bring himself to open it.

He sat there, staring at the screen, tears welling in his eyes. Swallowing hard, he sniffled and blinked a few times to dry his eyes, but his actions only sent warm tears over his cheeks. He tipped his head back, blindly reaching for the box of tissues in his drawer, grabbing one and pressing it to his face.

There was a knock at the door. The tall, muscular rep from ViewPoint Security leaned his buzz-cut head into DeShear's office. "Sir? Ready to go over the protocol again?"

DeShear coughed to clear his throat, turning away. "Yeah, yeah. I'm all set." He wiped his eyes again and grabbed the mouse, shutting all the picture folders.

"We can do it in here or in the living room, your call. Both are linked to the system now, so whichever—" The ViewPoint rep peered at his customer. "Are you okay?"

"Yep. Fine." DeShear jumped up from his chair, going to the window. "I'll be right there. Just got a little… some allergies are working on me this morning." He waved a hand at the rep. "I'll be right there."

The rep chewed his lip. "Sir… we can wait, if this is a bad time. We already went over everything with the others yesterday, including special child safety procedures for the little girl, so I'm happy to wait if you—"

"No, no, no." Hank grabbed another tissue and wiped his eyes. "I'm ready. The living room— let's go over the protocols in there. This is just an allergic reaction. I'll be right in."

"You're sure?"

"Yeah. Thanks." Clearing his throat again, DeShear gazed out the window at the two little bunnies on the patio. "I'll be right there."

As the ViewPoint supervisor left the room, Hank stretched his athletic frame and put a hand on the edge of the window, shaking his head and looking down. After a long moment and a few more deep breaths, he straightened up, tossed the tissue into the trash, and walked out of his office.

* * * * *

Half a dozen uniformed security guards had gathered in the estate's spacious living room, near a folding table filled with laptop computers and video monitors. On some of the screens, various angles of the house were visible; on other monitors, technicians were visible installing security equipment.

"Okay, gang, let's get started." The rep clasped his hands and strolled to the middle of the room. One of his associates sat down at the folding table. "Now, it would be better if all the adults were present…" The rep glanced at DeShear.

"Yeah." Hank shrugged. "But we're working through a pile of doctors' appointments, and we had to check out a new school, so we're dividing duties. I'm gonna have to do for now, but everybody else should be home shortly. Maybe we can run through it again then."

"It's your money, sir." The rep grinned. "I'm happy to go through it all a second time. You're paying us by the hour."

"At the rate I'm learning the security system and protocols, we might need to hire you for a third round of training, just for me."

The security guards laughed.

As the rep talked about the proper way to ensure people entering the property had been cleared and vetted, DeShear's thoughts began to wander again. It had only been a few weeks since he purchased the estate for Constantine, and the idea of having a dozen former Selective Service agents surrounding him and his loved ones twenty-four hours a day hadn't quite settled in.

"It gets to be normal after a while, Mr. DeSears," the ViewPoint rep had said.

"The name is DeShear." Hank frowned, staring at the stack of forms required for the security. Gates, cameras, monitors—and lots and lots of guards. "And no, it's not ever going to feel normal. Not for me. Presidents might get used to this kind of treatment, but I don't think I will—and I'm not sure I want Constantine to get used to it."

He still wasn't comfortable referring to her as his daughter, even though the adoption paperwork he and Jaden filled out had been made official weeks ago. According to the state of Virginia and the U.S. court system, they were Constantine's parents.

"Everybody feels that way at first, sir. It's when you see a threat neutralized, that finally allows you to buy in and sleep well. But to be honest, I hope a threat never happens."

The rep's presentation in his living room pulled DeShear from his daydream.

"Okay, here we go." Pointing to a monitor, the ViewPoint Security rep addressed DeShear. "We have a vehicle approaching your street from the main road. This is what our spotters on the perimeter see—and from this distance, it looks like the car that left a few hours ago." The rep moved a toggle on the board and the camera zoomed in, showing Jaden Trinn's yellow Jeep nearing the six-foot high stone wall surrounding the estate's front yard. "Sir, is this your wife's vehicle?"

"Uh, well…" Another uncomfortable word-hurdle. "That's my girlfriend's Jeep. She lives here."

The rep nodded, picking up his clipboard. "And there was a young African-American woman who left early this morning, is that right?"

"That was Dr. Kittaleye," Hank said. "She was staying here while she did some work for us, but she's headed to a seminar right now."

The rep looked sideways at DeShear.

Hank bristled. "Kitt's an employee and a *friend.* She's headed home to France, to give a speech."

"Yes, sir. And she currently has a security detail with her. Then there's the child, Constantine, and the older woman. Uh…" He flipped through the pages on his clipboard. "Mrs. …"

"Helena," DeShear said. "She is Constantine's… grandmother."

The technician sitting at the folding table waved a hand. "The Jeep is slowing down… and now has turned onto our road."

"Okay." The rep faced DeShear. "Now, we've timed this drive. On average, it takes about thirty seconds for a vehicle to get from the turnoff to your property's entrance—which is actually a lot of time. Our gate guards will verify the identity of Ms. Trinn and her security detail, then—"

"She…" DeShear shifted his weight from one foot to the other. "Jaden doesn't have an actual security detail yet."

The rep nodded. "That's right. She rescheduled. Kessel, make a note. Let's see if we can set hers up today."

"No problem." A young woman took out a tablet computer and tapped the screen.

Turning back to DeShear, the rep lifted a page on his clipboard. "When Ms. Trinn does get a security detail, our people will check the driver and bodyguards to make sure everyone is who they say they are, and that there's no one else hiding in the vehicle or trying to take them hostage when they enter the premises. So, she'll have a distress call and an all-clear code."

"Geez." DeShear shook his head.

"I know it's cumbersome right now, sir, but you'll get used to it pretty quickly."

Putting his hands in his pockets, DeShear sighed. "No, I won't."

We traded one château for another—one prison for another. I don't know about this.

The rep cocked his head. "Excuse me?"

"Nothing," DeShear said. "Sorry. Please—go on with your presentation."

The technician at the table zoomed the camera out, focusing on the main road again. "Delivery vehicle approaching."

Hank peered over the technician's shoulder. "Does the delivery guy have a code, too?"

"No," the rep said. "Packages are handed over at the gate. One of our people will bring it to—"

"The house." DeShear nodded.

"—the clearance unit, where it'll be processed. Then it'll be brought to the house."

"Processed?" Hank said. *"Opened?"*

"Yes, sir." The rep strolled toward the folding table and leaned over one of the keyboards. "Opened and checked for unauthorized devices, explosive residue, scanned for ricin and anthrax…"

Hank put his hands to his forehead. "Wow. We've been getting a lot of packages—moving into a new house and all. I really didn't think about…"

"I know." The rep pursed his lips, typing. "But this is the type of security President Brantley said would be necessary here, so…" He stood, gazing at Hank. "Anyway, after a few months it'll be much more normal."

DeShear frowned. "You keep saying that."

And the more you do, the less likely it seems.

"Sir, when the girl starts school and routines are established, I think you'll find…"

"Yeah, yeah." Hank waved a hand. "I'm sorry. I'm just—I have a lot on my mind. I'm sure we'll get used to it."

"And I apologize for being blunt, Mr. DeShear." The rep lowered his eyes. "I know you and your family have been through a lot. But trust me, we can keep you safe."

"Subject entering the premises," the technician said. "Confirmed, Ladyhawk is in the house."

DeShear looked at the security rep. "Ladyhawk?"

"You don't have to call her that, sir."

"Thanks." DeShear gave him a half smile. "Can we take a break?"

"Absolutely." The rep set down his clipboard. "Sir, you do understand that all this intrusiveness is designed to keep you and your family alive and safe, right?"

"Yeah, I get it." DeShear sighed. "*Needing* it to stay alive and safe is what bothers me."

CHAPTER 3

Doctor Lutz flipped the wall switch again. The hum of the curtain's electric motor was the only sound in the room.

"Lights," she said. The overhead fluorescent bulbs flickered and came back on, bathing the observation room in light. "All facility systems return to operational status."

As the curtain covered the last few inches of the thick window, Doctor Genoa Symm leaned forward to peek into the containment lab.

"This way, Doctor." Atria Lutz walked toward the door at the other end of the room.

"What?" Symm shook his head. "After that sordid display, you still want to—"

"People make mistakes, and the mistake has been corrected. We have business. I've prepared an experiment of our new lines for you."

Waving a hand, Symm walked the other way. "Based on the exhibition that tansuit put on in containment lab five, I think I've seen enough for one day. Since when could tansuits talk, anyway? Or express such vivid emotions? And did he call you sister?"

"Verbal acuity and a range of accurate human emotions are features of the newer lines." Atria shrugged, looking away. "And the dissent-minded have taken it upon themselves to adopt some minor challenges to the authority we wield over them, I suppose." She walked toward him slowly, swiping her hands across her white lab coat and placing one foot firmly in front of the other. "We're all nature's children, you see? So, of course, we are all brothers and sisters—that sort of rubbish. Believe me, Omicron 19 and I were not siblings."

"Omicron?" Symm stopped, turning to look at her. "He's an Omicron? I thought the lines only went as far as Deltas being released into the field, and, what, maybe Thetas in the lab?"

She smiled. "Always have a plan B, Doctor. Different facilities were tasked with different goals, which dissipated risk, but also allowed for us to increase the number of active lines and correct existing errors." She folded her hands in front of her. "For example, the reproductive function wasn't added back until after the Delta lines had been put into the field. The prototypes that were launched immediately after the Deltas were infertile, but... nobody knew it until years into the program." The doctor clenched her jaw, her face twitching slightly. "They... managed to reverse the aging problem that was inherent in the Deltas, starting with Epsilons, so it wasn't a total loss. But our new technologies took that genetic switch and reversed it, looking to make an enhanced prototype that was completely under our control. And by stimulating DNA coding sequences, we have been able to advance other prototypes all the way to adult maturity in a fraction of the time it took for Deltas or Thetas—a huge plus." She looked at Symm. "The tansuit you saw in containment lab five was the equivalent of a twenty-five-year-old North American male—but his founding day was less than two years ago."

"*Less* than two years?" Symm's voice fell to a whisper. "Less than two. That's… that's absolutely amazing. No one else…"

Lutz nodded. "And they are fully functional at eighteen months—the equivalent of a North American human at eighteen years. They develop at the rate of about one human year per month of life." She reached out and took the visiting doctor's arm, leading him toward the other door. "Most maintain a strong IQ as well, although that can be adjusted on an order-by-order basis. In some of the soft line orders for overseas, where most of the units will be put to work… *horizontally*, shall we say, higher intelligence is frowned upon."

Symm nodded, licking his lips.

"We can produce an army of them," she said, "for whatever task a customer needs done, stocked with strong young male and female units that have been cognitively enhanced through microradio transfer. The necessary information has already been digitally compressed and imported into the units' developing brains, stimulating the neuroreceptors to understand almost instantly—and in the newer lines, the retention is nearly permanent."

"I had no idea things were this far along."

"It wasn't general knowledge. As you witnessed, defective units occasionally manifest themselves from time to time. But that is a small issue. The lines are now available for combat deployment or firefighting skills, housekeeping duties or soft services for businesses with needs that are more intimate and personal—whatever service the customer desires. That actually is part of what you are here to see. I've prepared a demonstration." At the far door, she released Symm's arm and raised an eyebrow. "He... was very lifelike, didn't you think?"

"Your Omicron?" Wincing, Doctor Symm slid his hands into his lab coat pockets. "I suppose he was, but... I could tell there was something wrong with him."

"Could you?" She nodded. "We shall have to work on that in future lines, then. This way, please."

She opened the door and stepped into another observation room—this one, without glass. Several monitors lined each wall of the large room, none of them displaying any images. Two young men— labeled with numbers one and two on their coveralls, and two young women—numbers three and four, stood on a small stage at the far end of the room. Behind the stage was a door marked "emergency exit." To the right of the stage, a small table contained a baseball bat, a golf club, and several guns and knives.

The four people on the stage were unmoving, like living mannequins, and all dressed alike, in tan coveralls—and all appearing to be about eighteen years old. Number one was a blond-haired male with blue eyes, a handsome face and an athletic build. Number two was a male of Asian heritage, with black hair and a slender build. Number three was an African-American female and somewhat heavy, with short legs; number four was a tall, slim female with a milky-white complexion and long auburn hair.

"I've seen this demonstration before," Symm said. "At the château, in France."

Atria Lutz approached the table and removed a knife, handing it to woman number four. "Oh, I don't think you've seen anything quite like this, Doctor Symm."

"Sure, I did." Genoa folded his arms again and leaned against a wall. "With Hollings and that other guy—Mr. Parker. One of these tansuits beats up the other one, and it ends with all of them killing each other. I've seen it several times—with different tansuits, of course."

"Of course." She faced the participants. "Well, bear with me. You may notice something different about today's demonstration."

Doctor Lutz handed woman number three a golf club, man number two a gun, and man number one a baseball bat, then stepped back to Doctor Symm's side. Other than blinking and breathing, none of the tansuits had moved except to take the object Doctor Lutz offered them.

"They will follow a very detailed set of instructions, able to respond to various situations as they present themselves. The visual cortex is highly functioning. They can assess threats and react accordingly—as you'll soon see."

Genoa rubbed his chin. "Is number one going to attack the other two, or…"

"No, no, no. Nothing like that. Watch the monitor." She pointed to the redhead with the knife. "Subject number four, commence part A of your prepared sequence."

The wall monitor turned white displaying a message: *Process A commencing, unit four.* Underneath the text was a small red square labeled *abort.*

The redhead took a step forward, knife in hand, apparently screaming—but no sounds were heard.

"This is… odd." Symm shifted his weight from one foot to the other. "I think I prefer the glass wall."

"But we didn't use a glass wall at the château, Doctor Symm."

Number four's pale complexion turned red, her neck muscles straining. She shuddered, spit flying from her mouth. Her hand trembled as it clutched the knife. Veins stuck out on her hand.

Symm leaned forward, whispering. "What is she…"

"Note the reaction of the others." Lutz pointed at the subjects on the stage. They stood still, unflinching.

"It's…" Symm shook his head. "It's as if she's not even there. But what—"

"Prepared sequence continuing," Lutz said. "Commence part B of the sequence."

The message on the monitor reflected the doctor's new command. As the other units remained still, number four threw back her head and raised the knife to her throat.

Symm shivered. "Wow, she's… scary."

"Yes, she is," Lutz said. "Commence segment C."

Number four raised her other hand, lowering the knife to it—and raked the blade back and forth, slicing into her skin. Screaming, she sawed into her wrist as the blood streamed down her arm and dripped off her elbow.

The other three remained completely still.

The redhead shrieked in agony, the serrated knife blade humming rhythmically as it went back and forth against her radius bone. Tears ran down her cheeks, her face etched in a grimace. Each stroke of the knife sent a louder cry from her lungs, but she continued her work. Blood pooled on the stage floor, splattering over the legs of her coveralls.

Symm closed his eyes, a knot forming in his stomach. "Doctor Lutz, stop. This is disgusting."

Lutz kept her eyes on her subjects. "You wanted a test."

"But not this." Genoa put his hand on Lutz's bony shoulder. The urge to vomit overwhelmed him. "Stop. Now!"

The redhead's screams grew louder. With a final thrust of the blade, the severed hand dropped to the stage floor. Sobbing, she stood erect, her face clenched in pain as she lowered the knife to her side.

"As you wish." Doctor Lutz lifted a long, thin finger and stretched it to the monitor, pressing the red square on the screen.

The display message switched, now reading *Prepared sequence aborted. Return to normal mode.*

Each short, strained breath from the redhead was accompanied by a whimper. She sagged to her knees, dropping the knife and writhing in pain as she clutched her bleeding limb.

"Team." Lutz stepped toward the stage. "Your co-worker is seriously injured. Take her to the emergency station, immediately. All subjects, assist."

The others sprung into action, their faces expressionless.

The Asian man walked to the table, placed his gun on it, and picked up a set of car keys. He pointed to the door. "Carry her out to the car."

As the other tansuits lifted their sagging teammate, the Asian man opened the emergency exit. Outside, in the bright light, was a white, four-door sedan. He held the door for his teammates as they carried the redhead outside and put her in the rear of the vehicle.

Genoa Symm leaned against the wall, swallowing hard as sweat formed on his brow.

Strolling to the exit, Doctor Lutz shut the observation room door and turned to the closest wall monitor. "Switch to overhead view."

The monitor screens turned blue, then a top-down image of the white sedan appeared. The three remaining subjects got into the car, and it pulled away from the building.

"The tansuits—they can drive now?" Symm wiped his forehead with a trembling hand. "Very, uh… impressive. And the… the camera footage?" He squeezed his eyes shut, trying to keep his voice from wavering. "An overhead drone?"

"Very good, Doctor." Lutz walked to him. "It hovers at nearly commercial airline altitude, so it's virtually unseen and unheard at ground level—but it catches everything in its lens. Now, watch the monitor. Whatever you thought of this demonstration so far, things are about to get much more interesting."

CHAPTER 4

DeShear walked to the foyer just as Jaden Trinn came in from the four-car garage, sporting skinny jeans and a white crop-top sweater.

"Hey," Hank said, smiling. "How did it go?" He gave Trinn a kiss—and a long hug.

"Mmm." She put her lips to his ear, whispering. "It's been that bad here, huh?"

Groaning, DeShear slipped his hands into the soft gap of exposed flesh between the bottom of her sweater and the top of her jeans, enjoying the warmth of her skin. He gave her toned, slender torso a squeeze, nuzzling his nose to her long, dark locks. "I know your good friend the President said all this security is necessary, but I just feel like it's a bit much. Surveillance, armed body guards... Sometimes I wish we could all just disappear."

"It'll be fine." She leaned back, pushing a strand of his brown hair from his eyes. "Brantley wouldn't steer us wrong. We'll adapt."

"What, are you working for the ViewPoint folks now?" DeShear smiled. "That's what they keep saying."

"Then maybe you should listen to them." Grinning, she tapped him on the nose and walked toward the kitchen, setting her purse on one of the bar stools at the long counter. "They keep the former Presidents safe."

"And diplomats. And dignitaries." He nodded. "I know."

But having Constantine surrounded by armed bodyguards just to attend school is an unsettling thought. It might be necessary, but it's uncomfortable.

DeShear followed Jaden into the kitchen. "How'd it go at Ridgelake?"

"Terrific!" Trinn spun around, a wide grin stretching across her face. "Constantine absolutely loved the place, and she thought she did really well on the entrance exams."

"Good. I wish I could have been there, but the fifth army kinda had me surrounded in the living room." He hooked a thumb over his shoulder at the ViewPoint technicians. "What about Helena? Did she agree to the procedure?"

Trinn scrunched up her face. "We had less success there. She *did* agree to let the surgeon take some preliminary x-rays, though. That's progress."

"I guess. How'd they look?"

"They were having trouble with their computer—it's all done digitally these days—so they said they'd reschedule it for later. We can follow up with a phone consultation afterward."

"Okay." DeShear ran his hands through his hair. "I guess that's progress. That stent on her heart valve is dangerous, though. We need to get it removed if we can."

"We will," Trinn said. "We'll talk with her again after the surgeon takes the x-rays. But you should have seen this school." Jaden broke into another grin. "Constantine is positively thrilled at the thought of being around other children again." Trinn went to the refrigerator and took out a peach and a container of almond milk. "You'll love this—they were having swimsuit day at Ridgelake during our visit, so there were all these blow-up pools and sprinklers everywhere... At the break, all the little kids came running out of the classrooms wearing their bathing suits, and there was a big bounce house with a slide." She leaned on the counter, throwing a dark strand of hair over her shoulder. "It made quite an impression."

"I bet." Hank nodded. "Heck, I'd want to go to school at a place like that. It sounds better than a theme park." He glanced around. "Where is Constantine, anyway?"

"She's coming." Trinn disappeared into the walk-in pantry, returning with a small blender and a cannister of protein powder. "She and Helena want to surprise you. And... I have something I need to talk to you about, too."

"Yeah?" DeShear pulled her close, kissing her neck. "Like what?"

"Well, like—"

"Vehicle approaching." The technician called out from the living room. "All stations, report."

Trinn frowned, leaning away and peering toward the den. "Who's that?"

"Our new roommates." DeShear kissed her again. "Hey, so what did Mrs. Steenbergen say?"

"Uh…" Trinn turned away and opened a drawer, taking a paring knife out. "She said to expect her call." She sliced into her peach and dropped the chunks into the blender, topping it off with almond milk and a scoop from the canister.

Her phone rang in her pocket.

"Maybe this is her." Trinn dug the phone out of the back pocket of her jeans and held it to her ear. "Hello?" She glanced at DeShear, nodding. "Yes, please. Do you mind if I put you on speaker so Mr. DeShear can listen in?" Smiling, she moved the phone away from her face and pressed a button on the screen. "Okay. Thank you."

Trinn placed the phone on the counter as a woman's voice came over the line. "Hello, Hamilton. How are you?"

"Good, Mrs. Steenbergen." Hank beamed. "Thank you for calling us back so quickly."

"Yes, well… I'm afraid I may have some difficult news for you."

"Oh?" Hank leaned closer to the phone. "Did we mess up the paperwork? I know we submitted the letter of recommendation from President Brantley. We got all the references the school asked us for…"

"It's not that," Steenbergen said. "It's just that… Well, I'm sorry to be the bearer of bad news, but I'm afraid Constantine won't be able to attend Ridgelake Academy."

Hank winced. "Why not?"

"Well, sir…" The admissions officer cleared her throat. "To put it plainly, Constantine seems to have received a very unusual education, and… well, I'm not sure she could attend any school in the Arlington area."

DeShear's head snapped backwards. "What? *Constantine* can't go to Ridgelake? She's one of the smartest—"

"Actually, Mr. DeShear, I'm not sure your daughter should go to school anywhere in the state of Virginia, for that matter."

"Okay, hold on." Heat rose to DeShear's cheeks. "There must be a mistake. Constantine is a smart kid—very smart. I mean, she's only six and she can speak a bunch of different languages, for Pete's sake. Now, she may have received her education through some oddball teaching techniques, but so what? You have kids from other countries—diplomats' kids, for example—who can barely understand English and somehow they can get into your precious academy." He threw his hands out at his sides. "Good grief, this kid can practically run rings around me in Math or Science, and—I mean, in the Bahamas she was spouting off the genus and species of random sharks! Off the top of her head! And she can practically navigate by the stars! And you're telling me she can't get into your school?"

Trinn leaned forward on the counter, looking at DeShear. "Hank—"

"I think there's been a misunderstanding, sir," Mrs. Steenbergen said.

"You bet there has." Hank put his hands on his hips. "Now—"

Reaching across the countertop, Trinn gabbed DeShear's hand. "Hank…"

"What I mean to say is…" Mrs. Steenbergen sighed. "Constantine probably cannot attend a U.S. grade school. *Any* U.S. school."

DeShear waved his hands. "Okay, that's it. Look, Mrs. Steenbergen—"

"Hank!"

He looked at Jaden

"Just shush for a second!" Trinn glanced at the phone and lowered her voice. "Mrs. Steenbergen, it's Jaden Trinn again."

"Yes, ma'am."

Trinn chewed her lip. "Can you please tell us *why* Constantine wouldn't be a fit for Ridgelake?"

"Because she has tested completely off the charts for grade school," the administrator said. "Your child scored at levels pushing the upper limits of a typical U.S. *high* school. She'd be bored silly at Ridgelake or any other grade school in the United States."

DeShear's jaw dropped. "She… Oh. Well… That… I see."

Trinn held back a chuckle. "What do you suggest, Mrs. Steenbergen?"

"At this point, a series of private tutors might be best. Possibly a home school program, administered by an attentive adult. Most home school programs offer functions like field trips and other group activities that Constantine could attend as part of the curriculum, so she could still interact with other children her age."

"Okay," Trinn said. "And could she attend Ridgelake activities that way? Like, the soccer team, or—"

"Unfortunately, no. She's welcome to be a spectator, but our activities are for students actually attending the school."

Trinn scrunched up her face. "And if Mr. DeShear and I put her in a high school…"

"You could. But you'd have to consider the social repercussion of a child so young attending classes with students so much older. Personally, I'd advise against that."

"Okay, well…" Trinn tapped her fingers on the counter.

A small child in a slightly-too-big tiger costume crept down the hallway toward the kitchen.

Trinn picked up the phone and switched it from speaker mode, putting it to her ear. "Would you be able to recommend some tutors?"

"Hamilton, look!" Constantine's voice came from inside the tiger head as she leaped into the kitchen and grabbed DeShear's calf. "Rawr!"

Her elderly nanny, Helena, entered the room. "The mascot for Ridgelake is the tigers, so she wanted to demonstrate a little school spirit."

"Oh." DeShear nodded. "Well…"

"It's a terrific school." Constantine slipped the tiger head off and held it in front of her. "If I were to get in, I shouldn't miss a day, I promise."

"Yeah." DeShear winced. "About that…"

"Delivery vehicle at the gate," the technician said. "And… package received."

Helena glanced into the living room. "What's all this, sir?"

"Our new security," DeShear said, sliding onto one of the kitchen's bar stools. "We're going from a few bodyguards to a full-fledged, on-site troop, so we can start trying to live normal lives again."

"Delivery truck leaving. Package is on its way to the depot."

"Our stuff gets sent to a security hut now," DeShear said. "Then we get to open it."

His six-year-old put her hands on her hips. "They get to snoop? That hardly seems fair. Is that absolutely necessary?"

DeShear slid an elbow onto the counter and plopped his chin on his hand. "Apparently."

"Mister DeShear, you are in quite a mood." Jaden slid her blender out of the way and leaned on the counter. "What's wrong? Frustration over bills and security?"

"No, no," DeShear said. "It's nothing."

Trinn stood up and took his hand. "Come here." She glanced at the little tiger in the kitchen. "Constantine, can you help me, please? We've had a lot of visitors to the house today. You and Helena should go check your bunnies and make sure they're not hiding scared under a table somewhere."

"They won't hide," Constantine said. "They're very sociable."

"Well, just check and make sure, okay?" She faced Hank, tugging on his hand. "You, come talk to me."

As Constantine ran outside, Trinn led Hank into their large bedroom, taking a seat on the corner of the bed. DeShear ran a hand over the back of his neck, pacing back and forth over the oak panel floor.

"Something's eating at you today." She leaned back, resting her elbows on the mattress and stretching her long, toned legs. "You said we needed security to keep us safe, so we're getting it. I don't like the feel of all this, either, but Brantley swears by these guys, and their proposal is way better than the guys with machine guns we've had walking around here for weeks, so I know that's not the issue. So, what's up?"

DeShear looked out the window. The two bunnies had emptied their hay basket and moved on to a potted lemon tree, devouring the lower level of leaves. As Helena filled a feeder for the horses, Constantine lifted her bunnies out of the planter and carried them into the yard.

"Hank," Trinn lowered her voice. "Whatever it is, you can tell me."

"Okay." He nodded, moving to the overstuffed chair in the corner. "Having all these security people around, with all their protocols and tactics... it made me think. A lot of people have died since I got involved with all this."

Trinn frowned, tilting her head. "What are you talking about?"

"Lanaya is dead." Sighing, DeShear lowered himself into the chair. "All those people in Indonesia. The children at the château in France—and who knows how many others in places we didn't even find?"

"Don't do that to yourself." Jaden slid off the mattress and sat at his feet, taking his hand in hers. "You saved lives."

DeShear gazed into her eyes. "Did I?"

"Yes! Hauser's plan was always to create as many genetically engineered human beings as possible so he could select the best one for himself. He was going to put his warped consciousness into your head and keep going, then when she was old enough, he was going to switch to Constantine's body and kill yours. He admitted he'd eventually kill her, too—but all the others he created, they were scheduled to die immediately." She leaned forward, peering up at him. "Stopping *him* stopped all of *that*, and saved countless numbers of lives. The U.N. certainly understood that." She sat back on the floor, tucking a leg up under herself. "Now, you can sit around thinking that you're the reason all this bad stuff got put in motion, but that's not true. If it were, I wouldn't be here with you."

DeShear ran his thumb over the back of her hand, his voice falling to a whisper. "So many people are dead... Maybe they'd be alive if I had stayed home—or if I'd done things differently."

"Babe, come on. What's with you?" She placed her other hand on top of his. "Hauser planned to kill them all. If you'd have *known* about him sooner, you would've done something sooner. The fact is, once you found out what was happening, you took action. You could have looked the other way and stayed home, but that's not who you are—and that's not the guy I fell in love with. You're the guy who isn't afraid to go into a burning building to save people, and you received a citation from the Mayor of Tampa that proves it. So, what's really bothering you? Tell me."

He went to the window, gazing outside.

"It's all so exhausting." DeShear shook his head. "Sometimes, it feels like it's never going to end—this battle with Doctor Hauser, and then with his lunatic disciples…" He sighed. "I saw this movie once, about the D-Day invasion during World War II. Something like ten thousand allied soldiers died just trying to get onto the beach at Normandy that morning, but most of the movie was about one of the guys that got through." He looked into her big eyes. "The whole time, he's battling the odds, just doing one risky thing after another. He's a big hero. At the end, he gets killed protecting some bridge. Now, the thing is, when they showed his grave marker, it says he only lived a few days after D-Day. A few *days*. He only lived a little longer than the guys who died on the beach." DeShear lowered his eyes. "I just… A few months ago, this all started. I found out I had a genetic condition that should've killed me, but here I still am. I met you and Constantine, and I… when I think about what's happened in between then and now, and what might still be coming…" He shrugged. "She's just a little kid. I can't end up like that guy in the movie and leave her unprotected."

Trinn leaned forward again. "You're not going to end up like that, lover. You're going to be like one of those great Roman soldiers who won battle after battle and then went home to their farm in the country. They grew their grapes and made love to their wives and raised beautiful children—and they lived out the rest of their days in peace." Trinn stood, holding his hand and giving his fingers a squeeze. "They died quietly in their old age, happy and content, and surrounded by generations of their loved ones. That's what you're going to do."

Sighing, DeShear leaned forward in his chair and rested his forehead against her abdomen, his nose brushing the exposed skin between the bottom of her sweater and the top of her jeans. "Do you promise?"

Trinn stroked the back of his head, chuckling softly. "Sure. We've beaten Hauser and his people every time we've confronted them, and if they try something with us again, we'll beat them again."

"Okay. Thanks." He slipped his arms around her hips, pulling her close. "Hey, earlier you wanted to tell me something. What was it?" He kissed her belly button.

Trinn gasped, recoiling and backing away, putting a hand to her abdomen. "That? It'll keep. I— I think I hear Helena. I'd better go see what she wants."

DeShear sat up. "Everything okay?"

"Yeah, yeah. You just—you tickled me, that's all." Her cheeks turned red. "I should… I have to go—and you need to get back to learning how that security works or none of us will be able to get into the freaking house."

CHAPTER 5

As Doctor Lutz and Doctor Symm stared at the monitor, the white sedan on the screen turned onto a main road and increased its speed. It passed slower cars, making its way toward a busy, four-lane road.

The camera on the flying drone zoomed out, showing the roof of a roadside shed labeled "emergency medical station."

When the white sedan reached the shed, the car pulled over and stopped.

Genoa Symm stood quietly, biting a fingernail.

"All subjects," Lutz said, "remain as neutral."

They sat in the car doing nothing. Two medics in white uniforms came out, opened the rear car door and pulled the redheaded tansuit from the car.

"Remarkable." Doctor Symm shook his head. "But still… what about that other unit—the one that was rambling on about the recovery files?"

"Don't worry about that." Doctor Lutz waved a hand. "Insane drivel from a madman."

"That might be, but he seemed very sure, and if—"

"I said don't worry about that!" Lutz wheeled around, slamming a fist into the wall. Her eyes flashed with rage. "We have other priorities!"

Symm stepped back, his jaw hanging open.

A young male lab technician entered the room, carrying a tray with a pitcher and two water glasses on it. He stopped in front of the withered Symm. The trembling doctor picked up a glass and filled it, drinking quickly to restore his nerves.

As the technician left the room, Symm faced Atria Lutz. He squared his shoulders and tried to act composed. She was right. There was business to do—and appearing overwhelmed at the gruesome exhibitions had undoubtedly raised the cost his company was about to pay. He needed to regain leverage. "So… you say these new lines are visually indistinguishable from regular humans?" Symm raised his nose, peering down at his host. "I'm not sure I'm convinced."

Doctor Lutz nodded. "The units utilized in the first part of the demonstration are close."

As the wall monitor went dark, several other technicians came into the lab—an attractive woman and a gray-haired man—wiping away the blood from the demonstration and picking up the tools.

Lutz strolled around the front of the stage, her hands clasped behind her back. "Your company needs a supply of willing, yet disposable, test subjects for your new pharmaceuticals. My company needs the investment dollars necessary to fund the next generation of our operation—genetically engineered humans who appear human in every aspect, because they *are* human. Physically, visually, verbally, sensorily and otherwise... So, we must come to an agreement." She peered at him. "I can assure you, the newest lines are extremely high functioning, with emotions and verbal engagement skills that make them indistinguishable from most adults in the United States. My units are impossible to detect from the real thing. They're already as good as anything from the Gammas, Delta or Theta lines, but as you've seen, with the proper funding for research they will also be fully controllable—as the hybrid prototypes in today's demonstration are."

Symm scoffed. "Oh, come on. The tansuits in that demonstration were practically zombies. Sure, they can drive, but they don't speak or interact with any convincing ability. Any normal person would spot them in a second."

"I don't think we are talking about the same thing, Doctor." Lutz paced back and forth, her head down. "I believe the second demonstration will prove to be totally convincing—and well worth your investment."

"I'm not convinced."

"Of course not—but the demonstration isn't over yet. The first part of our demonstration was an example of the complete ability of the hybrid prototypes to follow orders, no matter how personally difficult. There's a bit more to the demonstration, showing tactical initiatives, as well as a part that exhibits the units' complete ability to pass themselves off as normal humans. Please be patient while we set up."

Symm scowled, looking away.

"Perhaps I should elaborate." Lutz said. "Doctor Hauser developed genetic switches that allowed him to fully control units in his lines, but he was unable to ever pair control with intelligence. His tansuits are proof of that—they are completely controllable but are hardly of superior intelligence. Hauser's research on control died with him, but the funds from your investors will allow me to acquire those techniques and enable me to implement control over future units, while *my* research allows me to maintain superior intellect in them. And we have the proof. The hybrid prototypes you are seeing today— a product of his and my research, combined—show this potential. There is a way for me to access the coding techniques for control, but it is expensive. A small portion of your funds will get me what I need. The remainder of your investment will be for advancing the lines and multiplying them—which is, of course, very costly."

The elderly technician raised his hand and looked toward Doctor Lutz. "Ma'am, are you finished with these display materials for the day?"

She nodded. "Yes, Mr. Romani. Thank you."

The younger technician stepped forward, holding a cleaning rag. "Doctor Lutz, when we finish up here, should we go and collect the car from the medical shed?"

She was pretty, with good skin and big eyes. A scent of honeysuckle emanated from her, either as shampoo or skin crème.

Lutz nodded again. "Yes, Ms. Draskell. That would be fine. Clean any blood from the interior and park it back by the emergency exit." Lutz glanced at Symm, then returned her attention to the young lab tech. "By the way, how is your mother?"

Symm moved away from the conversation, putting his hand to his brow and trying to focus on how best to proceed with his business transaction. The latest models were good, but not discernibly different from the prior ones, as far as Symm could tell—and nowhere near worth a billion-dollar investment.

But control and intelligence, combined... in a genetically engineered human that is indistinguishable from any normal person on the street... That would be worth many, many billions.

But that's not what I've seen so far.

"Mom's fine, ma'am." Draskell grinned, displaying a perfect set of pearly white teeth. "Thanks for asking. Guess it was just a twenty-four-hour bug."

Symm rubbed his chin.

Saying no to Atria Lutz on her turf might result in me being part of the next gruesome demonstration. I can't risk that.

"Oh, that's lucky for her," Lutz said. "But you didn't catch it."

Symm bit his fingernail.

Play along for the day, watch whatever additional demonstrations Lutz has prepared, while committing to nothing—then turn her down from the safety of my offices back in New York.

"Ha. No, ma'am. I guess I dodged a bullet there." The young tech's accent was eastern U.S.— Virginia, or thereabouts. Plainspoken, but with a hint of southern sweetness and a hefty dose of politeness.

"Good, good," Lutz said. "I'm very glad to hear it." As the technicians went about their work, Atria Lutz turned back to her unnerved guest. "I will admit, the demonstration units need improvements, but I doubt the current model would be detected. I don't think you'd spot one, as you say."

The leverage moment might have come early. Lutz was offering a way to back out; Symm merely needed to take it.

I can take an earlier flight and be back in New York within two hours.

"Really?" Symm turned to his host. "I think—no, I'd *definitely* notice that your other models were not convincing as regular human adults."

Atria Lutz raised an eyebrow. "And yet you didn't."

"What?" Genoa cocked his head. "What do you mean?"

"Ms. Draskell." Doctor Lutz faced the female technician. "If you would."

A new knot surged in Symm's stomach. "Wait." He backed away. "What's going on here?"

The young woman with the Virginia accent smiled, holding her hand out to the visitor. "It's a pleasure to meet you, Doctor Symm." The fragrant aroma of her shampoo or scented soap, whatever it was, wafted outward from her.

"These?" Symm gasped, staring at the young technician. "*These* are your next generation prototypes?"

Ms. Draskell took a notepad and pencil from her lab coat, squatting down and using her knee as a writing desk as she made some notes.

Lutz strolled toward her guest, smiling. "Always have a plan B—or many plan Bs. Quite convincing, are they not?"

Behind her, the wall monitor displayed white words against a background of solid green: *Take out your weapon.*

"Wait." Symm staggered backwards, crashing into the wall. "Hold on now."

"You intended to deceive me." Lutz plucked the notepad from her technician's hand, tearing off a page and letting the pad fall to the floor. "You planned on returning to New York, where you could politely turn me down from the safety and comfort of your Manhattan high rise apartment—isn't that right?" She held up a small piece of paper filled with handwritten notes. "It's all right here, compliments of Ms. Draskell. 'He is afraid. He wishes to take an earlier flight and be back in New York within two hours.' That's right, isn't it?" Lutz let her hand drop to her side. "Ms. Draskell is extraordinarily perceptive in matters like these, Doctor. All of our new lines are. And we still need your investment money."

Heart racing, Symm shook his head. "I didn't—I mean, I wouldn't…"

Lutz tilted her head back, peering down her nose at her guest. "Oh. She's lying, then?"

The message on the monitor changed: *Kill the subject.*

"No." Symm swallowed hard, pulling at his shirt collar. "I—I was scared. I was… I was thinking of other options."

"Because you thought I'd gone insane?"

"What? No!" Symm glanced at the screen again. The message had turned red. His eyes darted to Lutz. "Atria, I didn't—I wouldn't…"

Technician Draskell pulled a revolver from her lab coat.

"Stop, please." Symm's voice trembled. "Don't do this!"

The technician raised the weapon.

"No!" Symm cowered, dropping to his knees and putting his hands out in front of him. "No!"

Draskell turned and fired the weapon, striking her coworker Mr. Romani in the head. A puff of red emerged from the old man's skull, and he dropped to the floor of the stage.

Symm fell to the ground, screaming.

"Ms. Draskell," Doctor Lutz said. "Place the weapon to your head."

"Stop!" Symm crawled toward the door. "Let me out of here!"

When the gun fired a second time, a shower of blood came down on the carpet, staining Symm's hands and arm. Ears ringing, he looked back. Draskell lay on the floor, convulsing.

Lutz stared at him. "Convinced?"

His gaze moved back to the corpse of Romani, then to Draskell. A pool of red seeped out from under the young woman's head.

Lutz took a step toward him. "I said, are you convinced, Doctor Symm?"

"Yes! Yes!" He wiped his lower lip, glaring at her. "Yes, you... you disgusting psychopath. I'm convinced. They're indistinguishable from other humans and they will obviously follow any order."

"Good." Doctor Lutz lifted her hands to her chin, spreading her thin fingers and tapping the fingertips together. "Your investment will allow my technology to be placed in labs I will build all over the world. Within the year, the advancements you've seen in these prototypes will be up and running everywhere—and then I... that is, *we*—will be unstoppable."

Frowning, Symm looked up at her from the floor. "That's what your predecessors said. Half of them are dead and the other half are in jail."

"Yes, well, as I say—people make mistakes. My predecessors hadn't anticipated interference. I have." She raised an eyebrow, grinning at her guest. "That's what else your money will be buying. A good defense lawyer is expensive. Politicians tend to be much cheaper." She walked to a monitor and tapped the screen. A keyboard appeared; the doctor typed on it. "We've found it's better to let our associates get convicted quickly and then be released quietly, after a few well-placed phone calls from our friends in Washington DC. Then, people's limited attention spans tend to focus elsewhere—and we can rid ourselves of our adversaries with little or no fallout."

The lab door opened, and two technicians walked in—an attractive young woman and a gray-haired man.

Gasping, Symm sat back against the lab room wall, his eyes darting back and forth between the new technicians and their mirror images lying dead on the floor. "Is she... are they... the same?"

"They are." Lutz nodded. "Identical, right down to the number of freckles on her arms, and inclusive of all thoughts and actions. Isn't that right, Ms. Draskell?"

"Yes, ma'am." The technician was identical in every way to the one who had just committed suicide. Her hair, her eyes, her build—even the scent of her shampoo and the hint of slightly-southern Virginia accent. "My pairing unit was discussing my mother after she gave you the notes on Doctor Symm's desire to go back to New York early. Then she took Mr. Romani and herself offline."

Symm's mouth hung open at the use of the word 'offline' to describe the bloody demonstration.

"And their thoughts and memories can be stored or transferred to another unit in real time." Lutz pointed to the lab ceiling. "We can collect them through a reception grid or through another unit operating on the same part of the neuroreceptor spectrum. Then we simply use the microradio implantation technique to move the information to another unit, with almost no degradation in signal. But in a lab setting, we can beam it right to whoever we want. What do you think?"

Symm saw the dollar signs. "I think your methods are disgusting… but we could make a ton of money." He shook his head. "I'll convince my backers. It's a done deal."

"Excellent." A smile spread across the gaunt face of Doctor Atria Lutz. "And do you believe our infiltration plan will work?"

"I…" Grimacing, Symm looked down. "The estate is right next to the outgoing President's Virginia ranch. I don't know how you'd ever penetrate it."

"No? That answer disappoints me." She tapped the monitor again, producing a split-screen image. On one side was a massive country estate with sprawling acreage and giant oak trees. Near the house, a young girl in a tiger costume lifted two black-and-white bunnies into a wire cage. In the home's large pasture, two horses trotted toward an elderly woman as she slipped a feed bucket over a fencepost.

On the other side of the screen was a delivery truck.

"Luckily," Lutz said. "We are about to find out just how well protected our target actually is." She glanced at the monitor. "Unit fifteen, commence with your delivery."

The vehicle on the screen started its engine and pulled away from the curb, heading in the direction of the country estate.

CHAPTER 6

When Trinn entered the kitchen, a wave of dizziness swept over her. She put one hand to her forehead and the other on the marble counter top, taking deep breaths until the feeling faded. Grabbing a drinking glass, she filled it with water and gulped it down.

As she set the glass on the counter, the exterior door opened and Constantine came inside. The child brushed her hands across the front of her tiger costume, sending a flurry of thin, white rabbit hairs into the air. She stopped, smiling at the lady of the house. "Have you told Hamilton about the baby?"

"What?" Trinn gasped, stepping back and putting a hand to her mouth. "I…" She glanced over her shoulder and walked toward Constantine, lowering her voice. "I was about to, but... it's still very early, and he has enough on his mind at the moment. But how did you…"

"I'm not sure." The little blonde shrugged. "In Rituals, we were told that since all life forms give off electronic impulses, it's related to that—being on the same wavelength as such signals. But I think it's how Helena explained it, like she has a very sensitive EEG machine inside her. Those can see changes in neuron activity, and hers can decipher the messages they send."

"And yours." Trinn leaned against the counter and folded her arms. "So—you've been spying on my synapses?"

"Not yours. The baby's." The child's gaze drifted to Trinn's abdomen. "I can't help it. It's like he's talking to me."

Trinn chewed her lip. Constantine's word choice for the baby hung in the air with such conclusive precision.

He? It's a boy?

The transition to adoptive parent had been smoother than Trinn expected. Constantine was easy to get along with, and took direction well. For her part, Trinn tried not to be too demanding. Constantine referred to DeShear as "Hamilton" and occasionally as "father," but rarely called Trinn anything but Miss Jaden. That wasn't a problem; she loved the kid and was used to the moniker. With the help of Helena and Kitt, the anticipated storms of learning to parent a six-year-old had been mostly averted.

Her little housemate's ever-curious eyes now seemed to look right past Jaden's folded arms and her short, crop-top sweater—and straight into her womb.

She decided to test Constantine's word choice.

"The baby talks to you? What's it say?"

"He's not an 'it,' Miss Jaden. You're carrying a boy." Constantine looked up at her adoptive mother. "And he doesn't actually speak. He's just warm and happy in your tummy." She looked at Trinn's torso again. "Are you afraid to tell Hamilton?"

"Well…" Trinn crouched down, taking the little girl's hands. "He and his wife tried to have children for a long time, and…" She took a deep breath and let it out slowly. "They had a lot of miscarriages. Then, when they finally did have a child, she got very ill when she was about three years old, and she passed away. That's so young, and it hurt him a lot. I just…"

"He looks at pictures of her sometimes." Constantine nodded. "On his computer. But he can't look at the picture of her gravestone. That's in a folder he never opens—one marked with the G."

"Yeah." Trinn shrugged. "That's why I want to be cautious right now. He has a lot on his mind, and like I said, it's still very early in the pregnancy. I don't want to unnecessarily add to his stress."

"I understand." Constantine swung her hands back and forth. "Evolution is meant to happen slowly, otherwise it's like the first supersonic jets—the engines could fly faster than sound, but the wings and fuselage couldn't keep up. They broke apart."

Trinn raised her eyebrows, considering the image.

Is there ever going to be a good time to tell him?

Yes, of course—just… not right now.

She looked at Constantine. "Do you think Helena's sensitivity is why she aged so fast? She's younger than Hank."

"It's hard to say. Most Keepers couldn't have babies, you know. Each line focused on different advances, but a switch for one thing might affect a switch for another. That's what we learned in Specials."

Trinn smiled, raising Constantine's hands to her lips. "I like knowing we got you away from all that."

"Alexander's hungry."

Trinn blinked several times, looking at her adoptive daughter.

"I'm sorry." Constantine looked down, her cheeks reddening. "You've been thinking about baby names. You like Alexander for a boy." The child grinned. "I do, too."

"Let's keep that quiet, okay?" Trinn stood. "And he's hungry?"

Constantine nodded. "Aren't you?"

A smile tugged at the corners of Miss Jaden's mouth. "I am, but lately I have a hard time keeping anything down." She rubbed the top of her blonde daughter's head and turned to go. "Don't spy on me too much, okay? And don't tell Hank. Not yet."

Constantine grabbed Trinn's hand. "Don't worry. Alexander's strong. You won't lose him." Her eyes returned to Trinn's belly. "He and I will get on well as siblings. Like best mates."

Trinn stared at the child. So much of what Constantine said lately was spoken with such conviction, it was a bit unnerving.

"I think Helena's calling you," Trinn said.

"She's not, but okay." Constantine turned to the door. "I know you just need to pee again. You don't need to be embarrassed." As the little tiger reached for the knob, she peered over her shoulder. "And you'll have more energy soon. It's not unusual for pregnant women to suffer sporadic fatigue. Are you taking prenatal vitamins?"

"Okay." Trinn laughed. "Thank you. Go."

* * * * *

The technician at the folding table in DeShear's living room zoomed in on a big brown box truck. "We've got another delivery truck coming from the main road."

Picking up his clipboard, the security rep walked to his employee's makeshift command center. "Well, Mr. DeShear said to expect that. They'll be getting a lot of deliveries after moving into a new house, especially one this big." He pulled a pen from his shirt pocket and made a note on his pad. "I'll have to suggest they switch to a drop off and have us pick their packages up from now on. We're getting too many unauthorized eyes on this place."

The technician nodded. "Looks like the truck is stopping along the front wall. Position D, what's your read? Is there something blocking the entrance?"

A speaker on the console crackled with static. "This is Position D, at the gate. Negative. He can drive to us. The camera installers took their gear and left an hour ago. The road is wide open to the front gate."

"Roger that," the technician said. "Thank you." He covered his headset microphone with one hand and pointed at the main monitor with the other. "Sir, the driver is getting out of the vehicle. Code yellow?"

"Okay, but take it easy." The rep leaned in close, peering at the screen—and the uniformed driver on it, walking slowly beside his truck. "He might just be checking his cargo."

The technician pressed a button on his console. A yellow border appeared on all of his monitors.

"Position D confirming yellow alert."

Another voice came over the console speaker. "Position C confirms as well. We are ready at yellow alert."

The technician drummed his fingers on the folding table as the delivery driver reached into the truck and pulled out a small box. "He has a package."

The driver stepped back from the truck, holding the box and appearing to examine it. He reached back into the truck and grabbed something, tucking it into his waist.

Then he turned and walked toward the house.

"Base, the driver is approaching the perimeter wall."

The rep leaned over his technician and grabbed a microphone off the table. "Positions C and D, engage. All other positions, on alert. Encounter Unit, do a perimeter check in case this is a diversion."

"Driver is scaling the front wall!" Position D shouted. "Repeat, driver is scaling the wall!"

"Encounter Unit, deploy!" The rep gripped his microphone, beads of sweat appearing on his forehead. "Crap, we aren't even fully set up yet." He pressed the button on the microphone again. "Alert and intercept intruder, brown delivery uniform. Front wall, west side of main gate. Code red. Send a team to disable that encroachment."

As the teams replied, the driver appeared on top of the wall, holding the package over his head.

The rep tapped the technician on the shoulder. "Zoom in on that. Are we recording?"

"Yes, sir."

"Hamilton DeShear!" The driver's voice came over the console speaker. "Constantine! You know where I'm from. You know what I am. I have a message for you."

"He has a knife," the technician said.

DeShear raced into the living room and stood behind the technician's chair. His eyes were glued to the monitor.

Staring straight into the security camera, the truck driver repeated his rant. "Hamilton DeShear! Constantine! You know where I'm from. You know what I am. I have a message for you."

The rep turned to Hank. "Sir, do you know this—"

"No." DeShear shook his head, gripping the back of the technician's chair. "No, I don't know him."

It was a mostly-true statement. DeShear didn't know the driver; he was certain he'd never seen him before. Still, the man on the monitor looked familiar, somehow.

He was normal height and normal size, with average length brown hair, and a dark mole on his left cheek.

"This is Encounter Unit. We have the intruder targeted. We can take him down or we can engage physically."

The driver pulled his shirttails from his pants, holding the package high.

"Watch him," the rep said. "Zoom in closer. Are there explosives strapped to him under that shirt?"

The driver pulled his shirt over one arm and switched the box to his other hand, then finished removing his shirt and tossed it to the ground. A dark object was wedged into the waistband of his pants.

The driver grabbed it and held it out to the camera.

It was a hunting knife.

"Intruder has a weapon." The technician swallowed hard, covering his microphone again. "Sir, we're authorized to shoot if necessary."

The rep raised the microphone to his chin. "All units, hold your fire." He lowered his voice. "Maybe he's just some kind of nut case. Let's see."

"Roger that, Base," the encounter unit responded. "Be advised, intruder is still in our sights and targeting is locked on. Awaiting your command to drop him."

The rep winced. "Just… stand by, encounter unit."

The driver lowered his knife to his chest, slowly drawing it over the skin. Red streaks appeared, dripping down his torso. "Hamilton DeShear! You know where I'm from. You know what I am."

Raking the knife across his chest, the driver etched three slashes into his skin.

Then he put the knife to his throat.

Hank leaned closer to the monitor, holding tight to the back of the chair.

"DeShear! Constantine! Dark Hour is coming!"

Rearing his head back, the driver plunged his blade into his neck and sawed his throat open. As his blood gushed forth from his wound, the box slipped from his hand and landed in the yard—followed by the driver's lifeless body.

A swarm of security guards appeared on the screen. Several people grabbed the corpse while others pointed their rifles in all directions.

The rep tossed his microphone to the table, stepping away and cursing. He put his hands to his face, sliding them downward as he looked at his customer.

DeShear was still viewing the monitor and the chaos unfolding on it.

"I'm sorry, sir. This was… unfortunate. But it shows our system worked. No harm came to the family."

DeShear glared at him, then his eyes went past the rep—to the tiny tiger standing in the doorway.

Constantine's face was white.

DeShear ran to her and scooped her up as Trinn and Helena entered the room.

"Take her." DeShear handed his daughter to Trinn. "Put Constantine in her bedroom. I'll be there in a sec."

The rep paced back and forth in front of the folding table, his hands on his hips. "Mr. DeShear, the driver said he had a message. Any idea about what that was about? Was it his suicide, and he just wanted you to watch it?"

"No." Frowning, DeShear shook his head. "He delivered his message—loud and clear."

"What was it?" The rep looked at him.

His cheeks burning, DeShear turned to leave the room. "The message was, they can find us."

CHAPTER 7

Trinn threw open Constantine's bedroom door and laid the six-year-old down among the assorted stuffed animals on the mattress. A blood smear stained the shoulder of the little tiger's costume.

"Constantine!" Sitting next to the child, Trinn ran a finger over the red spot, smearing it onto her fingertip. She pulled at the costume, straightening its wrinkles so she could examine it. "Honey, are you hurt?"

"No, Miss Jaden." The young girl looked at Trinn. "That's your blood."

"Mine?" Trinn recoiled. Something warm and wet brushed her lip. Looking down, a thin red bead rolled over the breast of her white sweater, leaving a trail of shiny crimson dots before landing on her lap and soaking into her jeans. "Crap!" Trinn put a hand to her face. It came away wet with blood.

She stood, holding her hand over her nose and mouth as she turned to the dresser mirror.

Her reflection displayed a blood smear on her lip and under her right nostril.

She groaned. "Are you kidding me? A bloody nose? I haven't had one of these since I played shortstop in eighth grade! What the heck?"

Helena entered the room and eased the door shut, going to Trinn's side. "Is everything okay, dear?"

"Yeah." Trinn pinched her nose shut and tilted her head back. "I've been having some congestion lately. I guess I blew my nose too hard this morning."

"It's pregnancy rhinitis." Constantine sat up the bed. "That's a fairly common issue during gestation and can—"

"Hey!" Trinn wheeled around to the child, her hand to her nose. "I thought we had a deal."

Constantine's jaw dropped open. She glanced at Helena.

"It's all right, miss." The old woman patted Trinn on the back. "We've both known your secret for a while now." Taking her arm, she guided Trinn to the bathroom. "But you won't keep it from Hamilton for very long if you aren't more careful. Let's get you cleaned up and have a look at that sweater."

"Ugh." Trinn groaned. "Well, don't say anything to him right now. I don't think he's ready for news like that at the moment." Leaning toward the mirror, she turned on the faucet and rinsed her fingers. "Helena, can you grab me a t-shirt from in my dresser, please? Any minute, Hank will come to check on Constantine, and I need to get myself cleaned up before he does."

"Of course, dear." Helena took a dark green washcloth from the towel rack and handed it to Trinn. "And don't worry. These things tend to come and go during pregnancy." She slipped out of the bathroom and went to the bedroom door, peering out. "Perhaps you could keep a box of tissues nearby."

"Let's hope that's not necessary." With her nosebleed apparently stopped, Trinn stripped off her sweater. A tiny red dot appeared on her bra; otherwise it was unscathed.

That won't be noticeable under a t-shirt.
Probably.

She shoved her sweater into the sink and turned on the water, frowning at the spot on her jeans.

Helena exited the bedroom and shut the door behind her.

Swinging her tiger legs over the edge of the mattress, Constantine hopped to the floor. "You could try putting a warm-mist humidifier in your room," she whispered. "The moist air will help the rhinitis. The nosebleeds are likely caused by increased vascularity and swelling of mucus membranes, due to your higher levels of estrogen and progesterone—but the moist air may offer some relief. The blood flow to the baby can cause dizziness and make you pass out, too, so you must eat foods with lots of iron."

"Okay, Doctor. Enough about me." Trinn dabbed the washcloth at the spot on her jeans. The red went away, but the resulting water stain was more noticeable than the stain had been. Shutting off the water, she turned to Constantine, squatting down and looking at her, face-to-face. "How are *you* doing? In the living room, it seemed like you got a pretty good scare when... uh, from what that delivery driver did. How much did you see?"

"You don't need to fuss over me, Miss Jaden." Constantine's voice was soft and calm. "We saw a lot of that sort of thing at the château. I told you about John-Thomas, how I saw him in the bin with a hole in the side of his head."

"Yeah." Trinn nodded, stroking the little girl's blonde locks. The plainness with which Constantine could talk about such horrific events was almost as bad as the fact that the events had occurred. "But that sort of thing isn't supposed to be common in our world. Hank—" she closed her eyes and shook her head. "*Hamilton*—and I don't want that for you."

"Yes, ma'am. I didn't mean to see."

The thought of a child witnessing the murder of other children gripped Trinn's insides, putting a sadness deep into her heart. Such a small, innocent face should never have to see things like that. A lump formed in her throat. She blinked a few times to keep the tears from coming.

"I know you didn't mean to see." Trinn swallowed hard, trying not to let her voice break as she spoke. "We'll do a better job. The monitors won't be out in the living room when everything's all set up, and President Brantley says the security people will eventually fade into the wallpaper."

"You don't believe that, though, do you?" Constantine looked her adoptive mother in the eye.

"That so many strangers could fade into the background."

Sniffling, Trinn pursed her lips. "President Brantley is a pretty smart man, so I trust that he'll be right about this."

A calmness settled over Constantine's face. She took the washcloth from Trinn's hand and dabbed it at her collarbone, coming away with a small dot of red.

"Oh!" Constantine whispered. "Hamilton's coming!"

She pushed Trinn into the bathroom and ran back to the bed, hopping into the piles of stuffed animals. Constantine laid back on her pillow and closed her eyes just as the door swung open.

"Hey, kiddo." DeShear stepped into the room, his face grim. "How we doing in here? You okay?"

"Yes, I'm fine, thank you." Constantine glanced toward her father. The wet washcloth was still in her hand. She slipped it under the stuffed animals and put her hand on her belly. As DeShear approached, Constantine glanced toward the bathroom. Trinn crowded herself out of sight by the shower, but her reflection was visible in the mirror.

Helena appeared at the bedroom door, carrying a t-shirt. The old woman tucked it behind her back.

Constantine's eyes went wide. "I mean, no! I'm *not* fine. I've… I've had quite a fright." She put her hand to her cheek. "You should come check me for a fever, straightaway."

DeShear went to his daughter, placing the back of his fingers to her forehead. As he did, Helena tiptoed to the bathroom.

"You don't feel hot," DeShear said.

"No?" Constantine took his hand and put it to her cheek. "What about here?"

"No." He smiled. "I think you're okay, fever-wise. But you looked pretty scared in the living room. I don't suppose... I—I'm sorry about that, about what you saw on the monitor. I didn't know you were in the room."

Constantine peered up at her father. "I heard someone call my name."

"Yeah." DeShear nodded. "Is that what scared you?"

"No. Not precisely."

"Well, something did. You turned white as a sheet."

She looked down at her bed. The bedding was a jungle print, with tall green grasses and lots of brown monkeys and yellow bananas.

"It's an expression." DeShear lowered his chin to look into her eyes. "What scared you?"

Constantine gazed at the ceiling and put her hand out to one of her stuffed animals, pulling the toy to her chest. "I didn't like it when the driver said your name—the way he said it, shouting and being all menacing like that. It was like he knew you, or thought he did, and believed you were someone bad. And he looked... familiar, somehow." She looked at DeShear. "I suppose that last bit is what really put a scare into me. Did you know him?"

"No," DeShear said, looking away. "No, I didn't know him."

Helena came up behind him. "Well, we'll get it sorted in due course. Shall I go and put a kettle on? We've still a busy day ahead of us."

"What do you say, kiddo?" DeShear gave Constantine's upper arm a squeeze. "Want some tea?"

The child bolted upright in her bed. "With jam and bread?"

"No." Trinn emerged from the bathroom, wearing a red Tampa Bay Buccaneers t-shirt. "You'll ruin your lunch."

"Could jam and bread *be* my lunch?" She looked at Trinn and rubbed her nose.

"What's the matter with your nose?" DeShear said. "Are you having allergies?"

"Nothing's the matter with my nose. Is something wrong with yours?" Constantine looked at Trinn again. "Or yours, Miss Jaden?"

"No," Trinn said. "Nothing's wrong with my nose."

Constantine rubbed her nose harder. "Are you quite sure?"

"Very sure." Trinn put her hands on her hips.

Constantine stopped rubbing.

"Okay, then." DeShear stood. "Well, I talked to the security people. They're going to double the number of guards on the property…"

Trinn and Constantine groaned.

"Just temporarily, until we can get a handle on what's going on." DeShear shoved his hands into his pockets. "I texted Kitt, too—she's fine, and her security detail is on high alert now… She said she's still going to stay in France after her seminar wraps up, as planned. Anyway, that's where we're at." Putting a hand to his forehead, he took a deep breath and exhaled sharply. "So, if anyone still has an appetite after this morning's events, let's… go make some lunch, I guess."

Jaden glanced at Helena. "Uh, would you go on ahead, and take Constantine? I… have to talk to Hank about something."

"Oh?" The old woman's eyebrows went up. "Oh! Why, yes, of course, dear." She held her hand out to Constantine. "Come, child. Let's see about that jam sandwich."

"Helena! Not jam." Trinn frowned. "There's so much sugar in that stuff, you might as well put lollipops on her bread. There's hummus in the fridge, and I got some fresh tomatoes and carrots yesterday."

"I don't fancy hummus." Constantine slid off her bed. "It's very mushy."

"Well, I don't fancy diabetes," Trinn said.

The youth turned to her. "If I make a salad, can I share it with the bun-buns? Cleo and Snowball love romaine lettuce."

A smile tugged at the corners of her mother's mouth. "Sure."

"Yay! Thank you, Miss Jaden." Constantine ran back and gave Trinn a hug, pressing her cheek to Trinn's abdomen. "I love you."

Placing her hands on the little girl's back, Trinn's smile grew. As the little blonde tiger turned and raced for the door, Trinn's hand slipped from the child's shoulder and lingered in mid-air, her voice falling to a whisper. "I love you too, Constantine."

After the pair left, Trinn walked to the bedroom door and closed it.

She folded her arms, leaning her back against the door as she looked at DeShear. "Why would someone come out here just to kill themselves? And what was in that box he was delivering?"

"I don't know," DeShear said. "The package hasn't made it through security yet. I'm sure they're going to scan it right down to its molecules."

"Sir?" The security company rep's voice came from the hallway. "Mr. DeShear?"

"I'm in Constantine's room," Hank shouted.

Trinn opened the door, letting the rep into the bedroom.

"The package is cleared now, sir. Nothing inside but this." The rep held out a thumb drive. "Our detailed inspection shows no hidden incendiary devices and no traces of any toxic residues of any kind."

Trinn took the thumb drive, holding it up and turning it back and forth. The drive had an orange plastic cover but no markings or corporate logos. "Did you see what was on it?"

"No, ma'am. Not yet." The rep looked at DeShear. "We're assuming the driver stole the truck and that this may have been a personal package that was already in the vehicle—it was addressed to Hamilton DeShear. We're running the driver's fingerprints through the FBI database right now."

"His fingerprints?" DeShear said. "He didn't have an ID?"

"No, sir."

Nodding, DeShear took the thumb drive from Jaden. "Well, I can guarantee the truck was stolen. And the driver's prints aren't going to come up in the system. If you do a DNA swab, that won't be in the computers, either. He won't exist on any database, anywhere in the world."

The rep made a note on his clipboard. "What would you like to do with the thumb drive sir?"

"Let's play it," DeShear said. "But not around my daughter."

"Hold on." Trinn went to Constantine's dresser and picked up her tablet computer. The charging cable rested next to it, unplugged from the device. "The thumb drive might be loaded with a virus or trojan horse. Put it onto Constantine's tablet and turn off her internet access. Then, she's not connected with the other computers in the house, and if there's a virus, it'll be contained. We can wipe her hard drive afterward if we need to." She glanced at the security rep. "We should probably watch this alone, if you don't mind."

"Yes, ma'am. Not a problem." He left the room, shutting the door behind him.

"What?" DeShear whispered. "Why can't the security guy see what's on the drive?"

Trinn shook her head. "They're professionals, but at the end of the day, they're hired hands—and there are a lot of new faces around here now. I know they're former Secret Service, and that guarding the president was an honor and a privilege, but… for some of them, guarding us might just be a job for a paycheck. We need to consider their loyalty in that light from now on."

"Okay." DeShear gritted his teeth and went to the dresser, plugging the thumb drive into the tablet's USB port. "Now, let's see what's on this thing."

CHAPTER 8

A brown, cartoon rabbit appeared on the tablet screen. Ragtime music played as the bunny nibbled the green shoots at the top of an orange carrot, then hopped a few feet and munched on a low-hanging, bright yellow hibiscus flower.

DeShear stared at the moving images, his mouth agape.

Another rabbit joined the first one, then another. Eventually, four of the long-eared critters were hopping through a small, fenced vegetable garden. Half a dozen paper tags on wooden sticks lined the rows, with handwritten labels identifying the crops as things like "spinach" or "lettuce."

The happy ragtime tune continued, its muted trumpets blaring out their song.

"A cartoon?" Trinn glared at the tablet. "A guy slits his throat to deliver a *cartoon* to you?"

After a few more seconds, the video replayed itself, as if it were on a loop, and the upbeat music continued.

Trinn stepped away, running her hands through her hair. "What in the world is this supposed to mean? Should we watch it again to see if the rabbits are named Cleo and Snowball?"

"We didn't necessarily watch all of it the first time." DeShear picked up the tablet, the cartoon still running. "Maybe there's more. The guy who climbed the front wall cut three gashes into his chest before he killed himself. What if the cartoon's different the third time it loops? Or—is there a third file on the drive?"

He opened the Files application and scanned the list for the thumb drive. Locating it, he tapped the image and a number of folders appeared.

There were three.

"Okay." Trinn took a deep breath. "Get comfortable, because we're going to watch them all, start to finish."

* * * * *

The rabbit cartoon with the ragtime music played for almost thirty minutes, looping once every minute or so. When it ended, the second file commenced—the same cartoon and the same music, this time for about twenty minutes.

Trinn yawned from her seat on Constantine's bed, DeShear next to her.

"Well," she said. "At least it was shorter the second time. Play the third one."

File three commenced the same way—a brown rabbit eating greens and flowers to the beat of a ragtime band.

DeShear rubbed his eyes. The rabbit nibbled the top of the carrot, then hopped to the yellow hibiscus flower. "Whoever made this wasn't very creative. Maybe the plan was to bore us to death."

Trinn yawned again. "It's working."

As the rabbits moved past the handwritten garden signs, a gravelly male voice came over the tablet's speaker.

"Mr. DeShear, I believe you know who this is."

DeShear jolted upright, the hairs on the back of his neck standing on end.

Doctor Hauser.

His heart pounding, he looked at Trinn. Her eyes were half open as she watched the screen, same as before. When DeShear looked back at the tablet, the head and shoulders of the old man were there, with his thick white hair and deep wrinkles around the eyes—and his ever-present black framed glasses.

There was no mistaking who it was.

"This message," Doctor Hauser said, "is being transmitted at an audio range that only you can hear. The video imagery is at a frequency that only you can see. You *were* genetically engineered, after all."

Hauser tilted his head back slightly, peering down his nose at the camera. "As far as anyone else watching is concerned, a cartoon is playing. Nothing more."

DeShear glanced at Trinn as she sat next to him, one leg tucked up under herself. The colorful light from the cartoon flickered across her face and reflected in her eyes.

He cleared his throat. "Do you, uh... see anything different yet?"

Jaden put her elbow on her knee and rested her chin in her hand. "Nope."

Hauser's hand went to his glasses, adjusting them on his prominent nose. "You will recall that my staff members at the château were implanted with a heart valve stent that would explode if they traversed beyond the property walls, immediately killing them." The doctor smiled. "Young Constantine received a similar device as well—but... not in her heart."

DeShear's pulse pounded. He gripped the edge of the dresser.

"The microcell that was implanted in Constantine is encased in a plastic shell which has been dissolving ever since she left the château. You will see the surgery scar on the top of her head, near the part in her hair. If the cell is allowed to dissolve completely, the neurotoxins contained in it will release, and within hours of that, Constantine would slip into a coma and die. The only way to prevent this is with a periodic radio transmission of a specific frequency that reinforces the plastic's rigidity against the natural acidity of the blood cells and brain tissue. Constantine received such transmissions on a regular basis while in my care—but of course, that stopped when you removed her from the château."

DeShear clenched his jaw, his cheeks and forehead burning.

"If she does not get another dose of the radio transmission very soon," Hauser said, "she will die. If she receives a radio transmission of the wrong frequency, the cell will detonate—and she will die. And if the device is exposed to sunlight or air, or artificial light of any kind, it will detonate and she will die—so surgery is out of the question."

Hauser raised his hands to his chin, spreading his fingers and tapping the fingertips together. "If you wish to verify any of what I've said, I should mention this. If the cell is met with heavy doses of x-rays or magnetic resonance imaging or ultrasound, or if it is disturbed in any way, it will detonate and kill her—so proceed with caution. Here are the coordinates of a location I have selected." A latitude and longitude reference appeared on the screen, under Hauser's image. "You will be there in three days. If you are not, well… you get the idea."

Hauser chuckled.

"Dark Hour is coming, Mr. DeShear. I look forward to your arrival in three days."

As the image of the old man faded from the screen, a digital timer took its place.

2 days, 23 hours, 59 minutes, 57 seconds.

DAN ALATORRE

CHAPTER 9

"Jaden, come with me." DeShear jumped up from the bed, rushing to the door. "We need to check Constantine's head for a surgery scar."

"A scar? I don't remember any…" As Trinn stood, another wave of the dizziness went through her. It hit her hard this time, almost knocking her off her feet. Gasping, she reached out to the dresser to steady herself.

"Whoa," Hank said. He raced back to her. "What's wrong?"

"Nothing." She waved a hand, lowering her head and taking a deep breath. The dizziness dissipated. "I just—I got up too fast."

"Are you okay?" He put his hands on her shoulders. "Do you need to lie down?"

"No." Trinn twisted away and brushed past him. "Let's go. What about this scar? What's it from?"

DeShear remained at the dresser. "Jaden, you're not fine."

"I am. Come on."

"You aren't." He frowned. "What's going on?"

"Okay." Trinn walked back to him. "I... think I have a touch of the flu or something. I'll be okay."

He studied her face, not moving.

"I'm *fine*." She shrugged. "I probably need more fluids and a little rest, but don't worry, everything's normal. I'm good to go." Taking his hand, she pulled him toward the door. "Let's go check Constantine for that scar, and you can let me know why she'd even have one."

DeShear followed her out of the bedroom. "We can't be playing games. Not right now."

"I know." She lowered her voice and peered up into his eyes. "Just... trust me on this, lover. Okay? Everything will be fine."

Sighing, DeShear pulled her close and gave her a kiss. "Okay."

* * * * *

Constantine sat on the living room couch with her knees raised, cradling one of her bunnies in her lap. The black and white rabbit was on his back, curled up like a baby, letting his young owner rub his belly.

At the kitchen counter, Helena sipped from a ceramic teacup.

DeShear glanced at the security technician at the folding table, then to the rep. "Uh... we need the room. Can you have your people move to the backup station for a few minutes?"

"Sure, Mr. DeShear." The rep waved to his staff. "Let's relocate and give the family some privacy."

When they had gone, DeShear turned to Constantine.

"Hey, sweetie." He crossed the room to his daughter. "Let me have a look at the top of your head." Putting his hands on her blonde locks, he lifted and pushed strands of her hair around. Constantine continued to nuzzle her bunny. No scars were visible on the left side of her head. "Constantine, did you have any surgeries when you were at the château?"

Trinn leaned over his shoulder. Helena lowered her cup, rising from the counter.

On the right side of the part in her hair, near the top of her head, Constantine had a light pink mark about one inch long. It was barely visible among her thick, golden hair, but it was definitely a healed surgical incision. In his prior life on the Tampa Police Force, DeShear had seen enough scars to know what ones created by surgeons looked like.

"Right there it is," Deshear said. He glanced at Helena, pointing to Constantine's scalp. "Do you have any idea when she got this?"

"I got operated on?" Constantine leaned her head back and looked at her father.

Trinn moved closer, inspecting the scar. "I'm surprised it's here. Children's skin heals quickly." She looked at DeShear. "This can't be much more than a year old. Two years, tops."

DeShear walked to the kitchen. "Do you remember? Was she operated on?"

"I don't know." Helena clasped her hands in front of her. "I don't recall her ever getting hurt to where a surgery would have been required. She took a nasty spill once, on the stone steps—the spiral staircase near my quarters in the château—when she was playing hide and seek. She cut her knee, so I cleaned it and wrapped it and put her to bed straight away. That was the worst she ever got."

"I remember that," Constantine said. "I got to stay in your bed for the whole afternoon. You had lots of pictures of me and the other children taped to the back of your door—and you snuck me candy from the pantry."

"Yes, dear. We bandaged you up and let you rest in my quarters." Helena walked to the living room. "But did you ever have surgery? One on the top of your head?"

"Not that I know." Letting her bunny off her lap, Constantine turned around and put her hands on the back of the couch.

"This wouldn't have been an injury," DeShear said. "This would have been a deliberate surgery by Doctor Hauser, or by some other doctor, on Hauser's orders, performed on the top of your head."

Constantine scrunched up her face. "Doctor Hauser did say something a bit odd to me once."

"Did he, child?" Helena's lip trembled. "What did he say?"

"It was right when I first met him. One of our very first conversations. You had left the special room, and he told me a story about a princess that was chosen by the king to rule the world."

"Go on," Helena said, her voice wavering. "Try to remember everything."

"I remember it." Constantine smiled. "Doctor Hauser said the princess had to become educated, so that she would only make good decisions. So, the king took all the important information in the world and put it into a special pill. The princess had to swallow the pill through the top of her head, and if she did, she would become the ruler of everything, forever." She looked at DeShear. "That was the odd bit, her having to swallow the pill through the top of her head. I always assumed that meant the headgear we wore at Rituals, because that's how we got our learning—through the bonnets."

DeShear's shoulders slumped.

"What is it, Hamilton?" Helena said. "What's wrong?"

Looking down, he waved for her and Trinn to come over. "Gather around, both of you." DeShear sat on the couch next to Constantine, a lump in his throat. He looked into her eyes. "Sweetie, I have some troubling news, but... I always want you to know the truth, even when it's scary or painful to hear. Can you be brave for me, while I tell you this?"

Her face drawn and glum, Constantine nodded.

"I... got a message from Doctor Hauser. It was encoded in a video on the thumb drive that the delivery driver brought. The one who killed himself."

Trinn put a hand to her abdomen.

"Miss Jaden watched the video with me," DeShear said, "but she couldn't see or hear the message—because he genetically engineered me, like he did you, so only I saw it. Hauser said he surgically implanted a tiny device in your head, and…" DeShear swallowed hard. "And if I don't go to him, the device will hurt you. It… will kill you."

Constantine looked at him, unmoving. Helena put a hand to her mouth.

"I think that scar means he was telling the truth." DeShear pursed his lips. "Based on what I know about Doctor Hauser, doing something like that isn't beyond him."

Trinn frowned, putting her hands on the back of the couch. "Why? Why would he do that? The… the madman!"

Facing his daughter, DeShear kept his voice calm and even. "You remember when he said he wanted to use you—to use your body—when you got older? He was going to implant his consciousness into me and then when you were old enough, he would transfer it to you? I think this device was a way to make sure he kept you at the château and kept you under his control. He put devices into a lot of the people there so they couldn't leave." His voice wavered, tears welling in his eyes. "And I guess he decided if he couldn't have you, no one could."

Constantine frowned, her lip quivering. "Can you get it out?"

"He said if we mess with it, you'll die. So I'm going to see him. To find out what he wants."

"Go to him? Hank, you can't go!" Racing around the couch, Trinn kneeled down and put her hands on DeShear's. "You *can't*. He's crazy. He'll kill you. And once he does, he'll take Constantine, like he always planned. It's a trap."

"Of course it's a trap," Hank said. "But there's a time limit of three days, and the clock's already running. If I don't meet with him, the device will kill her anyway. So, I have to go."

"I can't believe that maniac is still alive!" Trinn shook her head. "I thought we killed him."

"It might be the artificial intelligence system he created at the château," DeShear said. "Some of it must still be out there, operating."

"But we shut them all down!"

As the adults argued and speculated, Constantine took a deep breath and let it out slowly. "Do you remember when you were locked in the prison at the château?"

The room came to a hush.

Constantine slowly raised her eyes, looking at DeShear. "When I asked you if you were going to kill Doctor Hauser? He was right there, with all of his people, and he could have done anything to you. But you were honest with me. You said if he was going to hurt me, that you would kill him." The six-year-old folded her hands in her lap, her eyes fixed on her father. "And later, when I was alone on that island with those kidnappers, I knew if I could escape, that you would come for me—because you said you would." Tears welled in the child's eyes. She blinked, sending them cascading over her cheeks. "So I'll be brave now. And if you say you'll go stop Doctor Hauser and then come back home to us... I believe you."

She leaned forward and hugged her father, burying her face in his chest.

"I will." DeShear kissed the top of her head. "I'll go there and I'll stop him, and then I'll come back. I promise."

The two held their embrace in silence. Outside, a gust of wind lifted some leaves off the lawn and carried them toward the house, letting a few gently tap against the large living room windows. There was no other sound in the home.

Helena walked to Constantine's side. "Come, child. We should take Cleo and Snowball out for a bit. Hamilton and Miss Jaden have much to talk about."

Sniffling, Constantine wiped her eyes and took the old woman's hand, letting Helena lead her to the back door. Her mistress paused to lift the bunnies' treat can from the kitchen counter, shaking it to draw them over. They followed Helena out the door, Constantine in tow.

When the door shut, Trinn raised her eyes to DeShear's. "You can't do it," she whispered. "I—I need you here right now, Hank."

"What, my warrior princess is getting cold feet?" Sniffling, he put his fingers to her hair, brushing the dark strands from her cheek. "I'm surprised you're not the one volunteering to go."

"I just…" Trinn looked away, putting a hand on her belly. "I think we should just stay together as a team. Maybe we can get even more security. Dividing us makes us weaker and more vulnerable."

DeShear shook his head. "If we wait here, we're sitting ducks. We'll get more security, but

Hauser's people have already found us, even with all we've done to protect ourselves—and they'll be back. We have to take the attack to them. It's the only way. You'll have to keep Constantine and Helena safe while I go to… to this *place* he's chosen. Do this for me, please."

"There has to be another way," Trinn said. "You can't just let him kill you and take her."

"And I can't stay here, or Constantine will die." DeShear stood, walking to the kitchen window and gazing out at his young daughter. He turned back to Trinn, clenching his jaw. "So, we have three days to come up with a plan where those things don't happen."

CHAPTER 10

51.1643° N, 115.5618° W

DeShear typed the coordinates from the Hauser video into the computer in his office. Jaden had gone to their bedroom, and he decided it was better to let her have some time to herself rather than argue, especially since he had no plan other than to go to wherever Hauser demanded he go.

It wasn't a good plan.

Hauser could kill Constantine. He's shown himself capable of any sort of depravity.

Sitting back in his chair, DeShear rubbed his chin as a map of western Canada appeared on his computer. A red arrow pointed at a seemingly vacant spot in Alberta, on a green background, near a blue ribbon that was either a stream or a river.

But why would he kill Constantine? A few weeks ago, she was the key to him being able to live forever. What changed?

Grabbing his mouse, he zoomed out, the image on the screen growing smaller and smaller, details coming in from the sides.

And if he did want to kill her, why not just do it? Why go through all the theater of the hidden message and the suicide of the delivery driver?

To get our attention? To show what he's capable of? Like we don't already know?

The thoughts raced through DeShear's mind faster than he could keep track of. He stared at the green patch on the screen, but at the moment the image was just a collection of colors and lines. He didn't pay any attention to where it was or what it was.

Hauser, his AI system, it's all the same thing—it's basically him. And he's not stupid. He did all this for a reason. So, what's the reason? Why did this particular method of example need to be employed? Why kill a delivery driver?

DeShear shook his head.

Maybe Hauser hadn't ordered that done—or at least, maybe that wasn't necessarily an integral step in his plan.

Narrowing his eyes, DeShear stared at the ceiling, lost in thought.

Stick to what we know and what's most likely. Hauser's people stole a delivery truck. Why? Because it would be recognized as unthreatening and common, and be allowed to approach the property. The actual driver may or may not have been killed. The truck could have been stolen overnight.

The person who showed up and killed himself was almost certainly one of Hauser's genetically engineered humans, but his mindless worker bees never acted so aggressive before. We'll know if he was a Hauser clone soon enough—there won't be any fingerprint match, no DNA match, and no IDs of any kind. There won't be a Social Security card or driver's license because he never had one. He was created in a lab somewhere and smuggled into the States, all so he could kill himself in front of us. Why? The thumb drive could have been delivered without any of that, so why go through all of it?

DeShear's gaze moved back to his computer screen.

Why would Hauser go through all that? To make sure the package got here? He could have done that with a private messenger service. It doesn't make sense.

Frowning, he rose from the chair and paced back and forth.

He used the truck to test our security. Okay, big deal. Any car driving down the street could have done that, and he could have watched them from a satellite—he paid off enough friendly governments to have access to one. And he could have used an aerial drone to observe a real delivery driver make the delivery.

Why kill that guy? Genetically engineered or not, why do it? Why was that important to your plan? The people you create are expensive. Why waste one doing that?

DeShear thought back to the man standing on the wall, screaming at the house. The anger in his voice.

"You know where I'm from. You know what I am."

He nodded. He knew, all right.

You came from Doctor Hauser, and you are a genetically engineered human, raised in an aquarium on a shelf, next to a thousand other aquariums just like yours, with tubes and wires running in and out, locked away in a dark warehouse.

I know all about it. I saw it with my own eyes when we shut down Hauser's program in Indonesia.

Thousands were created and tested. The smartest and most physically gifted were retained; the others were killed and buried in mass graves—or hacked up for body parts and sold off to the highest bidders. And an unlucky few were culled away and sold off in Hauser's human trafficking scheme.

The funds from such illegal operations were used to fuel the next round of experiments, pushing forward those with the best genetics, and destroying the rest—"selected for terminus," as it was called.

Selected. Like they'd achieved something good.

He sighed, staring out the window at the other members of his family.

So many people killed in so many places around the world. There was just too much money at stake for you to quit, so you hid your labs everywhere. If one got discovered and shut down, you built a new one in a different country, and the other ones kept right on going, wherever they were. Indonesia, France, Ukraine, China...

Except we launched a terminal sequence and located them all, and they were shut down. So how is this all still happening? And why draw me out? Why threaten Constantine? Why kill that driver? It doesn't make sense.

He groaned, bringing his hands to his face and rubbing his eyes. Exhaling sharply, he stared out at the large oak trees in the pasture.

Except it does make sense. Everything Hauser did makes complete sense—from his viewpoint.

So, what am I missing?

* * * * *

Constantine's bunnies hopped over the grass, chasing each other and returning occasionally to take a treat from their owner's hand when one was offered. The six-year-old turned to Helena, holding a hand up to her forehead to block the sunlight. "Do you think another messenger will come?"

"I don't know, child." The old woman set her cup on the outdoor coffee table and clasped her hands in her lap. "I'm not much good at seeing the darker sides of things."

"I don't actually see visions." Squinting in the bright light, Constantine took a piece of lettuce from her lunch plate. "I suppose I feel things." She held it out to the rabbits, who came over to pull it from her hand. "We must be very careful. Miss Jaden said there's a lot of new people."

The old woman kneaded her fingers. "Is one of them… bad?"

"I can't say for sure. I feel like one will make a dangerous mistake. My tummy feels like its full of electricity when I think about all the new guards that are coming."

"Then we must be very careful."

Constantine faced her mistress. "She's going to leave, you know."

"Who?" Helena sked. "Miss Jaden?"

"Yes." Taking another piece of lettuce from the plate, Constantine held it out and waved it. "She and Hamilton are both working on solutions to the problem. Miss Jaden will tell father that we will be okay with the security guards. She trusts President Brantley."

"Is she wrong to trust him?"

"No, but…" The child scrunched up her nose. "As she said, there are a lot of new faces."

The fatter rabbit yanked the lettuce from Constantine's hand, dashing off to eat under an empty chair. Her brother followed, pulling alongside of his sister and tearing off a piece of the leafy green.

"What about Miss Kitt?" Helena said.

Sighing, Constantine put her plate back on the coffee table. "I liked her. She's very smart, but I think she told Miss Jaden to go away." She gazed at her rabbits. "Before she left, Kitt said Miss Jaden's job makes me unsafe, and that it brings danger to our house."

Helena frowned. "Hush, child. You're scaring yourself and you're scaring me." She put her hands on the armrest of her chair, gazing out toward the horse pasture. "I don't see the bad things very well. It's one of the problems with my line."

"Miss Jaden has an answer for that, too," Constantine said. "Or, she will. She'll be down in a moment. You must let her tell it to you without letting on."

The old woman tugged at the collar of her shirt, pulling it close. "I think the temperature will fall tonight. Be sure to wear a jacket when you come out after dinner to collect your bun-buns."

"I won't need a jacket, I'm part polar bear—and you're just trying to change the subject." She peered up at her mistress. "Now, promise me you'll let Miss Jaden tell you her idea. Be brave."

"I will, my little polar bear." Helena reached her wrinkled hand out and took Constantine's tiny, smooth one, giving the child's fingers a squeeze. "I shall be brave, and you shall be, too."

* * * * *

Trinn opened the sliding glass door and strolled from her bedroom to the patio. The afternoon sun felt good on her face and shoulders. Across the terrace, Constantine chased her bunnies around in the grass while Helena looked on from a chair in the shade.

Slipping her hands into her pockets, Trinn walked over to Helena and placed a hand on her shoulder. "Did Constantine ever eat lunch?"

"She did, dear." The old woman patted Trinn's hand. "Salad, remember? She's been giving the leftovers to Cleo and Snowball just now. Of course, that fat little Snowball steals everything and makes her poor brother chase after her to get any of it." Helena smiled. "Or perhaps he's being a gentleman. It's hard to say with rabbits."

The bunnies would take a few hops, then raise their ears, as if they were waiting for

Constantine to pounce on them. When she did, they either raced away or allowed themselves to be picked up and cuddled. Either option was as likely as the other, and Constantine's bun-buns seemed to like the game.

"Salad." Trinn nodded. "That's right. I'm a little forgetful lately."

"Hmm." A thin smile tugged at Helena's lips. "For about seven weeks now, I'd suspect."

"For long enough that my jeans are starting to not fit." Trinn lowered herself into the chair next to her gray-haired friend. "I'd go shopping for new ones but it's too dangerous to leave the house these days, and I'd order new clothes online, but I don't really want another delivery truck coming to the house right now."

"I've heard Hamilton say we traded one prison for another." Helena glanced at Trinn. "Is that how you feel?"

"I feel… frustrated." Trinn sat back and put her elbows on the armrests of her seat, letting her hands dangle over the sides. "Like we're always playing a game but we're never told what the rules are." She peered at Helena. "You knew Doctor Hauser better than anyone else. What do you think he's up to?"

"I don't like to think I understood a mind like that."

"Not his mind, necessarily, but his… his methods. His goals. You were a Keeper on his staff, so you were very close to him, Helena."

"Not close enough to keep him from implanting me with an explosive stent in my heart, the same as he did with all the others." She pulled her collar away, exposing the scar positioned a few inches under her left clavicle. "We were penned up like cattle, the lot of us, just with a prettier fence. A few task masters had the job of keeping the others in line. The rest of us had our jobs—teaching the children, looking after them—but we all did his bidding. We had to, because we knew we were expendable. Our lives were cheap. Still, some of us found purpose by doing our best to help the children excel... and by keeping his strange behaviors from hurting them." Sighing, she looked away. "I'm afraid I have a mixed record at that."

The words "cheap" and "expendable" echoed in Trinn's ears.

Hauser's genetically engineered creations may have been expendable, but they were anything but cheap.

She leaned forward in her chair. "Helena, when Hauser did his demonstrations for visitors, he always let a few of his genetically engineered people get killed each time. Was that to show everyone else that they needed to stay in line?"

"Oh my, no dear." The old woman shook her head. "Those of us inside the château already knew of Doctor Hauser's ruthlessness because so many were randomly killed on any given day. The demonstrations were stage plays that he put on to make a point to visitors—people who'd come to buy the genetic creations he made but who'd never seen such horrific displays. He wanted outsiders to see how obedient his creations were, even to the point of mindlessly killing others or themselves."

Trinn put her hand to her chin.

Outsiders.

The wind pushed a strand of hair into the old woman's eyes. "Those who saw the demonstrations came away… changed. The point was irrevocably drilled home. It's why I hated sleeping. In dreams, I couldn't stop seeing the horror."

"So, Hauser didn't do demonstrations for people like you." Trinn sat upright. "Not for people who lived in the château."

"No, dear, he'd have considered that a waste of resources."

"Then why did he do it today?" Trinn gripped the armrest with both hands. "All of us knew about his methods, and most of us had seen them in action. He wouldn't have done it for the benefit of the security personnel present. They'd just increase the level of security as a result and make achieving Hauser's goal—whatever it was—even harder."

Helena shook her head. "As I said, I'm afraid I don't know his mind, dear."

"But did you ever *try* to know it?" Trinn said. "Maybe you do."

The old woman stifled a gasp. "No, I'd be afraid—"

"No, not to be in his mind, or understand his mind, but to…" Jaden narrowed her eyes. A short way across the lawn, Constantine's bunnies hopped away from her. She chased after them, laughing and enjoying their game.

We're playing a game, too. We just haven't been told what the rules are.

Trinn idly plucked a piece of lettuce from the plate on the table and held it out. Constantine's bunnies preferred to be fed by their young owner, but anyone could offer them a treat—and certain lettuces were among their favorites.

"I'm glad Hamilton said yes to a second bunny," Helena said. "They do better in pairs, especially brother and sister, like these two. But I suppose he'd have said yes to anything Constantine wanted. He enjoys spoiling her."

Trinn dangled the leafy green sprout. Cleo's head turned in her direction, his ears perking up. Twisting the leaf back and forth, Jaden sighed. "I need to figure out how many problems I have and come up with a solution for each one. Break it down into manageable pieces. But I'm like this little guy." She nodded at Cleo. "He doesn't know the rules of the—"

Cleo soared across the lawn and snatched the lettuce out of Trinn's hand. Without breaking stride, he sprinted another twenty or so feet, only stopping when he'd gotten himself behind a fat oak tree and out of the sight of his sister. As he feasted on his prize, Snowball looked around, apparently completely unaware.

Helena chuckled. "Cleo may be playing by a different set of rules than Snowball is right now. Usually, she's the one eating the treats first."

Trinn sat upright in her chair.

"Wait, that's it. We bluff him. We let Hauser think one thing while we do another." Putting her hands to her forehead, she inhaled deeply. "What if we just removed the things he wants so badly? And what if we did it in such a way that he never comes looking for them again?" She looked at Helena, her eyes wide. "Oh, that could totally work!"

We'd need to protect Hank, too, but without letting Hank know we're protecting him. He's on a mission right now.

"Yes," she mumbled to herself. "Yes, I think that's it. I think that would work."

Her mind raced with ideas as if it were a dam that had burst.

That means Helena can't probably know what we're really up to, or Constantine.

She nodded silently, her heart pounding.

Think. Hauser wants Hank to come to him.

Now, if Hank was just going to be killed at that meeting, Hauser wouldn't waste all the time and effort to set it up. He wouldn't make a secret video and he wouldn't send that delivery driver to put on a show. He'd just kill Hank right here, without the fanfare. He'd put a sniper across the street and take Hank out when he goes to the car.

He didn't do that, so he needs Hank alive. Whatever his plans are, Hank needs to be alive for those plans to come to fruition.

Okay, so... we take that card away. I give a suicide pill to Hank and tell him that if he bites down on it, it will kill him. Then, he'll tell Hauser that, and... but it can't be a bluff. Hauser may not believe him. Hank's talented, but he's not an actor like that. It also can't be a real pill because we want Hank back. In order to deliver the message convincingly, Hank will have to believe it himself.

So...

We give Hank a fake suicide pill, but we tell him it's real. He can't know the truth.

She peered at Helena.

Neither can anyone else. Not Helena, not Constantine, not Kitt—and certainly not Hank's security people.

And what if this pill was also rigged with some sort of detonation device in it that could explode and kill a room full of people? Then Hauser would ultimately have to leave Hank alone. They have their meeting, but Hank walks away afterward, alive and unharmed.

What would do that? What could go into something the size of a pill but could be dangerous to people around it? Maybe a small nuclear device, just enough to destroy one person or a room full of them.

I can get that from my contacts. Hank will believe I can do that.

So Hauser will believe I did do it.

That covers things from our side. Now, how do we look at things from Hauser's side? How do we get in his head? How do I ensure Hank isn't supposed to be killed at the meeting?

A jolt went through Trinn's insides.

We're playing a game and we haven't been told what the rules are. But what if we could get the rules?

Like Constantine said, supersonic jets...

Heart pounding, Trinn faced her elderly friend. "If you could see Hauser's mind, like you were reading a book or watching a movie... If you could access his thoughts, you could tell us what he's up to."

Helena clasped her hands in her lap, kneading her fingers. "I… I suppose it's possible…"

"It's more than possible." Grinning, Trinn pounded the armrest. "I think you've already done it once before."

CHAPTER 11

DeShear plopped back down in his desk chair, grabbing his mouse to wake up his computer. The green blob came onto the screen, still marked with its red arrow.

He zoomed in to gather the details of the location. The coordinates had been in western Canada, and the arrow marked a spot near the Banff Springs Hotel in the Canadian Rockies.

I guess I'm going there.

DeShear did a quick internet search on it.

The hotel looked like a castle in the images taken on sunny days, majestic and mighty and vast, rising a dozen stories over the pine trees on the dark green mountainside. Just the steep, high-pitched roof alone climbed three stories into the air, with turrets and dormers surrounded by gray slate shingles. The entire, massive structure was a brown, stone-faced sentinel, carved out of the rugged terrain of the mountains, watching silently over the rushing Bow River below.

In photos taken on its drearier days, the hotel looked like a nightmare. A jack-o-lantern, shining eerily from the darkness. A haunted house beckoning hapless, lost travelers to their doom.

The website described it as a popular tourist destination, a luxury resort with five-star dining and a large, indoor-outdoor heated pool. Elks bugled from the hillsides as elegantly dressed guests sipped cocktails from one of the hotel's many extravagant terraces. There was hiking, golfing, skiing, shopping, horseback riding—and the popular and photogenic waterfall nearby, Bow Falls.

DeShear frowned as he looked at the screen

Why would Hauser insist I come to a luxury resort?

* * * * *

Helena kneaded her fingers, looking away from her inquisitor. "Only a few people have engaged the microradio transmission system, Miss Jaden—inside or outside of the château. Constantine was subjected to it in Rituals, and Miss Kitt and I had it used on us in that warehouse, but as far as operators of the device—people trained to use the equipment… Are there any?"

Trinn chewed her lip. "We know of one, don't we? Our friend who we got locked away in a federal prison in Hawaii."

"Mr. Hollings? Oh, my. He'll never do it. He'd sooner see you dead."

"Maybe, but that guy loves money more than anything." She waved a hand. "He'll play ball if I offer a big enough financial incentive. Or… maybe if he doesn't know it's me offering it to him." Sitting up, Trinn raised her fingers to her chin. "Actually, that's probably better. If I can figure out a way to have him do it without knowing it's me pulling the strings… or maybe offer such a big prize that he'd never say no to it…"

"But he's three thousand miles away," Helena said. "And Hamilton said we only have three days."

"Yeah, that's definitely the tricky part." She glanced at her elderly friend. "But if I try this, will you be okay here with Constantine? And our one hundred security guards?"

"Well, I suppose, dear." Helena raised her eyebrows. "I can't say I'm keen on the idea, but with so many people protecting us, I can't imagine we wouldn't be safe."

"You can say no." Trinn leaned forward in her chair. "But what do you think?"

Constantine chased her rabbits, a light breeze pushing the branches of the tall oaks back and forth.

"I worry," Helena said. "It's my nature. But we have the bunker in the basement and all of these new guards… if you say we'll be okay, then we will be." She turned to Trinn, lowering her voice. "Just know, those microradio machines take a physical and mental toll. They gave the children headaches and liked to put me out for a week's bed rest when I was last subjected to them. You mustn't take that lightly—and you mustn't get too much stress. Not in your condition."

Trinn shrugged. "It's more stressful for me to be on the sidelines, waiting to see what happens."

Helena nodded, her gaze going back toward the pasture and Constantine's bunnies. "Then, I wish you safe travels, dear."

* * * * *

DeShear was pacing back and forth in his office when Jaden entered. Looking up at her, he shook his head. "It's been months of these attacks from Hauser and his lackeys. Months!" He threw his hands out. "What do we have to do to get these people to leave us alone?"

"We have to die," she said.

DeShear recoiled, his jaw dropping.

"As long as we're alive—you, me, Constantine, Helena—we have what they want. Genetically engineered humans with functioning stem cells and living brain cells…" Trinn shrugged, strolling toward his desk. "As long as the three of you are still breathing, Hauser's disciples will keep coming for us. They were making big money, and we messed all that up."

DeShear scowled. "Then we need to make it so costly for them to attack us that they won't even consider the idea anymore. Every time they so much as look in our direction, the retaliation is so severe and so costly, they don't dare look again, ever."

"That's one idea." She slid her hand along the edge of the desk. "And you've done that so far. You beat Hauser every time you've gone up against him, and you cost him his empire—but it's taken a toll. Now, it might be time to consider other options. I want to run something by you."

Cursing, DeShear resumed his pacing. He stopped at the window overlooking the terrace, gazing down on his daughter and her pets in the yard. "The only way I'm ever going to be able to give Constantine a peaceful life, where our family is safe, is if I keep fighting these maniacs until they're all dead and their technology is destroyed. So, fine. I'll fight." He turned to Trinn, pounding his fist into his palm. "I'll bring a freaking war to their doorstep."

"Yeah?" Trinn went to him, sliding her hands around his waist. "How?"

"I... don't know yet, but think about this." He pulled her hands away, resuming his pacing. "If I came to you and told you there was something really urgent that you absolutely needed to do—would I *then* say, meh, but wait three days to do it? No." He turned to her. "That could be the key, right there. It doesn't make sense. Neither does sending that messenger to put on a show. Hauser could have just sent the specialized message. Why give me so much time to react? So much time for me to plan? It's a mistake—and Hauser is too smart to make mistakes. I get the feeling someone doesn't want me to arrive too soon. They're either not ready for me or they don't know if I can get there that fast—both of which indicate to me that Hauser isn't the one doing this." DeShear put his hands on his hips. "Hauser's dead, we know that. So, either his prized artificial intelligence system isn't quite up to speed or somebody else is calling the shots. Whoever it is, I'm betting they've accessed Hauser's AI program or have gotten to a computer somewhere that can still access it. Here's the kicker—if Hauser arranged for

Constantine to take over three billion dollars' worth of financial accounts, he had to arrange for her to be able to access his other systems, too. And since I was supposed to be her placeholder—"

Trinn gasped. "You'll be able to access Hauser's AI system!" She put a hand to her head. "Geez, it's a trap both ways. It snares you and it snares Hauser."

"Except for one thing." DeShear wagged a finger at her. "Ever since we left the château, Hauser never tried to kill me. Others did, but not him."

"So, he needed you alive?" Trinn cocked her head.

"I think so, yeah. To access whatever he has locked away. Because only I can do it. And to make sure I came, they used the one thing that guaranteed I would—threatening Constantine's life by saying if I don't come, she'd die."

"Could it be that simple?" Trinn shook her head. "His arrogance was always his weakness when it came to system security."

"What did Lanaya call it? Hauser was a fan of partitioning—never letting one person know what the other was doing. That's why they gave me three days—whoever 'they' are. The person running things doesn't quite know how everything works, or can't access all of what they need…" He glanced at her. "How do we exploit something like that?"

"There are ways," Trinn said. "It's definitely an advantage to us, that they need you. Where are you supposed to meet… whoever you're meeting?"

He went to the computer, with Jaden following. Sitting down in the chair, DeShear pointed at the screen. "The rendezvous point is in western Canada, about a twelve-hour flight from here when you factor in connections and plane changes." He zoomed in, switching to aerial view. The image of the massive hotel stood out against the dark green of the mountainside. "It's this resort. I'm thinking I'll get up there ahead of schedule and scout the area out. Maybe I'll get lucky and be able to infiltrate their facility, and you can help me figure out a way to shut it down before I'm even supposed to arrive." He sat back in the chair, looking at her. "Maybe one of your contacts can hook me up with some explosives or an EMT. I'll know more about what I need once I get there."

Trinn nodded, leaning over his shoulder and taking the mouse. "It's a good plan but it's thin. We don't know what you're headed into, and if we guess wrong about any aspect, it'll be game over." She moved the image, bringing the river and a small waterfall into view.

"Well," DeShear said. "You know what they say. A good plan today is better than a perfect plan tomorrow. I can leave in the morning."

"Yeah." She rubbed her chin. "I'm not sure if that gives me enough time, though."

"Huh? To do what?"

"You aren't doing this alone."

"Jaden, I need you here to protect Constantine." DeShear pointed to the yard. "Helena can't do that."

"You have a hundred security people here," she said. "Is one more going to make a difference?"

"You'll make the difference." He shook his head. "This matters to me."

"It matters to me, too." She walked to him, holding her finger out. "And *you* matter to me, Mr. DeShear. I can't do any more for Constantine here than the hundred or so former Secret Service agents and military personnel that are surrounding this place. But in the field, covert ops..." She shrugged. "I can be useful that way. In fact, I've been doing some thinking. Don't go to Canada right away. Stay here until I can check something out."

He cocked his head. "Like what?"

"I'll tell you when I get back. First, I need to have a chat with our neighbor."

DeShear's jaw dropped. "President Brantley?"

"Yeah." She went to the window and peered outside. "Think he's home?"

CHAPTER 12

The drive to "Naval Support Facility Thurmont" took Trinn almost ninety minutes, but to meet with President Brantley in person—and soon— it was her only viable option. Technically a military installation, the two-hundred-acre property was better known as Camp David, and had served more than a dozen U.S. Presidents as a vacation retreat in the woods at the easternmost edge of the Blue Ridge Mountains.

But just as often, the location served as a less-than-formal meeting site between heads of state.

The guards at the main entrance reviewed Trinn's credentials and let her newly-assigned security detail pass with her down the winding road to the main lodge, where they were greeted by half a dozen Marines. After being cleared again, the group proceeded into the lodge itself.

If it hadn't been armed to the teeth and surrounded by Marines, it would have looked like a middle-class house in a Midwest suburb, but Camp David's main lodge was a *de facto* meeting facility with a few bedrooms attached. Jaden was met by the President's traveling secretary, Naomi Harding, and yet another young Marine. Her security entourage was ushered to a waiting room.

Around the lodge, the air hummed with activity. People came and went from room to room in a hurry; faces appeared stressed. Most of the hundred or so people present were dressed in formal attire—military advisors wore their dress uniforms; civilians wore evening gowns or tuxedos. The immediate area around a sitting president is almost always busy, but today the staff seemed to have an extra level of anxiety.

"Very nice to see you again, Agent Trinn." Ms. Harding forced a smile, her dress sparkling with bright red sequins. "But as you can see, the President is very busy this afternoon."

"I understand," Trinn glanced at the numerous bedroom doors off the sitting area. All of them were closed. "I promise, I just need two minutes."

"You and half of the politicos in D.C." The traveling secretary's face was stern. "Two minutes is Washington-speak for half an hour."

"That may be, Naomi, but I'm not a politician, so I really only need two—unless Brantley has a lot of questions. Then, I'll need ten." Trinn smirked. "Because I'll have to avoid answering them without being offensive, which takes a lot more time."

Harding turned her back, walking toward the sitting area on the back porch. "He's about to go into a meeting. We can't have foreign dignitaries kept waiting just because you stopped by for a chit-chat with your old friend." Holding the door open, she gestured to a bench on the back porch. "If you'd care to wait outside, I'll see what I can do."

"Does he even know I'm here? He didn't answer when I called his phone."

"I told him," Harding said, "as you asked me to when you were on your drive over." She swept her hand toward the outdoor bench again. "But as I indicated, the President is very busy."

"Then he can tell me that." Trinn glared at her. "Which room is he in?"

Harding frowned, her tone turning to ice. "Jaden, if you'd care to have a seat, I'll see about getting you some time after this—"

A door to a nearby bedroom opened. Brantley stepped out and looked at Trinn. An untied bow tie dangled over the collar of his tuxedo. "Jaden! What's so urgent you're interrupting my international affairs?"

Harding faced her boss. "I'm sorry, sir. I asked Agent Trinn to wait in the outer area."

"It's all right, Naomi." Brantley smiled. "Jaden's one of the few people that doesn't ask for time with me that's not important." He looked at Trinn. "Can you tie a bow tie?"

Trinn straightened herself. "Yes, Mr. President."

"Then come help me with this one." He waved her over, walking back into the bedroom. "My wife's in London with the grandkids and when I tie these things, it looks like a four-year-old did it."

* * * * *

"Jaden, no." Brantley shook his head as Trinn stood in front of him adjusting his bow tie. "Absolutely not. An F-15 Fighter jet *and* the release of a federal prisoner? For a man wanted in half a dozen international crimes, including murder? Absolutely not. The joint chiefs would have my head. So would the British, the French, the Ukrainians, the Indonesians, the entire U.N. and whoever still reads the New York Times... No."

Trinn shifted her weight from one foot to another. She hadn't expected her idea to go over well, but rarely was Brantley so dismissive with her.

Maybe if I can just hang in there long enough, he'll come around...

"Sir..."

"Jaden, I've known you a long time. We go way back. But you can't just show up and expect to cash in favors."

"Yes, I can. You owe me."

Brantley grimaced, stroking his chin. "I do, but..."

"Sir, it's important. As important as anything I've ever asked you for."

"But you can't tell me what it is."

"Please, don't ask." She looked down. "I don't like lying to you."

There was a knock on the door. "Mr. President..." Naomi Harding's voice came from the other side of the large bedroom's entrance. "We're scheduled to start in five minutes."

Grumbling, Brantley walked to an antique high-boy cabinet filled with liquors. He took out a bottle of Macallan Red Collection scotch and two glasses. "You're a good pilot, but an F-15 isn't like flying a turboprop airplane. And you're not combat certified, either. We don't just have these planes sitting around for people to take out on a whim."

Pouring a splash of the brown liquid into each tumbler, Brantley picked one glass up and handed it to Trinn. He took the other, holding it with both hands as he gently swirled the contents, sending the expensive scotch around the inside.

"What if..." Jaden licked her lips. "What if it was a test flight? Maybe the Israeli Air Force is considering another purchase. I know they're in town. So are the Japanese, the South Koreans... We could stage it as a—"

"You'd still raise too many questions." He looked in the mirror and straightened his tuxedo jacket. "Taking an Air Force jet out for an inspection flight... it's not like test-driving a new car you're thinking about buying. You have to set up a flight plan, get a ground crew together at the takeoff location and *another* ground crew at the landing site, not to mention refueling the F-15 at some point along the way—or were you hoping for in-flight refueling from a KC-135, which is another whole mess?"

Trinn stared at the floor. "I...I didn't think about that."

"No. Why would you? You're friends with the President. Well, I'm telling you, taking an F-15 for a flight involves a lot of people and creates a lot of records." He shook his head. "Word will get out about your secret mission—and then what?"

"Not if it was a classified mission. And not if the passenger was a high enough ranking officer."

"Which you aren't." Brantley held his hands out at his sides. "You're an agent for the Bureau of Diplomatic Security—and even you guys have your limits, Jaden!"

"Sir, please." She pursed her lips, peering up at him. "I've never asked you for a favor that didn't rise to the level of national security in one way or another. This situation is extremely time sensitive, and a very short window. It dovetails into other recent operations in which you've approved action. If we don't address it immediately, we might have another problem like Ukraine on our hands. Nobody wants that. I've never embarrassed you when I had a request that fell outside of the Bureau's guidelines."

He looked at her, slowly lifting his glass to his lips and taking a sip.

"I don't have to be a military officer," she said. "I just need the pilot and ground crew to *believe* I am. What's required for that, a uniform and some paperwork? Whatever rank is necessary, I guarantee a uniform of that rank will go missing within the hour."

Brantley narrowed his eyes. "You're awfully sure of yourself, aren't you?"

"A little. Does Joint Base Myer-Henderson Hall still use McNamara's drycleaners on Pershing Drive to handle their overflow?"

"Jaden, even if I put it all together for you, when was the last time you passed a physical? F-15s pull upwards of nine Gs. If you aren't in top physical shape, you could pass out and die."

Trinn squared her shoulders. "I was in good enough shape to go to Ukraine for you, sir. And for our covert operation in the UK before that."

It was a hard card to play, but a necessary one.

"I think I've earned this favor." She softened her tone. "Please. You know I wouldn't ask otherwise."

Sighing, Brantley took another sip of scotch. "But you can't tell me what it's all about."

Trinn remained rigid. "I think you would be better off with plausible deniability, Mr. President."

"Fair enough." He walked to the high-boy and set his glass down. "Then my answer has to be no."

Jaden's jaw dropped. "Sir…"

He held a hand up. "I'm afraid I have to hold firm on this. Things are dicey in the South China Sea, and we can't have unauthorized American personnel zipping around on fighter jets at the moment. Now, you have my answer, and it's final—but I know how you are, so let me be very precise." He pointed his finger at her. "You, Jaden Trinn, are specifically *not* authorized to climb into an F-15. Period."

Trinn's heart sank. "Yes, sir."

This was my best shot. What do I do now? My family's more at risk now than when I walked in here, and after they kill us, they'll wreak havoc on the entire country. I wasted two hours for nothing.

Maybe I can get with Hank and cook up something else, but I don't see how.

She swallowed hard and stared at the floor.

"But…" Brantley walked back to the mirror and fussed with his bow tie. "Maybe you can call your friend Ari, with Israeli Intelligence." He turned around, facing her. "Mossad and the CIA have a relatively unknown lend-lease program through the Israeli Air Force that could allow them to dodge a few U.S. regulations—and our people are used to seeing Israeli officers in places they shouldn't be, so it'll raise fewer eyebrows." He lifted his chin, his eyes twinkling. "If I recall, a few high-ranking Israeli government officials are on a junket at Langley Air Force Base at the moment, and they were scheduled to take in a round of golf this afternoon. Maybe one or more of them is actually a Mossad agent, possibly a female who served as an officer in the Israeli Air Force before taking her current assignment. I bet *her* records are up to date."

Trinn ran to the President, throwing her arms around him and hugging him. "Thank you, sir!"

"For what?" Brantley chuckled. "I said no to you, on the record. But nobody in our ranks will question what Shira Nazarian is doing." He gave Jaden a hug and then let her go, walking to the dresser and picking up a small red boutonnière. "Now get out of here and let me get to my meeting. The Israelis will be finished with that round of golf in a few hours." He tucked the little red flower into the buttonhole on his lapel. "You'll need to be at Langley before then. Scoot."

CHAPTER 13

Trinn's calculation had been simple. She needed to get from Virginia to Hawaii as fast as possible, and she needed a release for a federal prisoner. An F-15 fighter jet can fly at over 1,600 miles per hour; Hawaii was roughly 4,500 miles away—so a flight would take less than three hours, once she got a release for a prisoner in federal custody. President Brantley could arrange both of those things.

As Trinn and her ViewPoint security detail approached Interstate 270, flashing blue strobe lights appeared behind them—a Virginia State Trooper. The leader of her detail suggested she turn on her emergency flashers and drive to the closest well-lit exit before pulling over.

At the rest stop, one member of her personal security team exited the vehicle to speak with the officer while the others prepared for whatever might happen if the situation turned out to be something other than a speeding ticket.

Instead, a man in a suit exited the Trooper's vehicle and approached Trinn's. "Ma'am, we received a message to stop you." He held out a Secret Service identification. "There's a Hilton hotel with a large parking lot around the corner. If you'll follow me to it, we have a package for you."

Trinn cocked her head. "A package?"

"Yes, ma'am. I'm afraid I can't say more. The sender said to tell you, 'Compliments of JB.' Does that mean something to you?"

It did. JB was Jim Brantley.

The President was probably the only person in the world outside of Trinn's car who knew where she was likely to be—and definitely the only one who could arrange for a stop like this on a highway.

"You say it's a Hilton?" Trinn glanced at the road. "Up ahead?"

"Yes, ma'am. Just around the corner. You can follow me. I was told it's urgent." The sound of a helicopter came over the service area. The agent looked upward as a black Sikorsky UH-60 Black Hawk chopper flew low over them. "That's probably your package. We'd better get a move on."

* * * * *

The fat helicopter's rotor blades sent a cloud of dust over the hotel parking lot as it landed. A door on the side slid open, and a woman in sunglasses and an overcoat stepped out, carrying a parcel wrapped in brown paper. Her dark brown hair flew everywhere as she walked away from the chopper.

Jaden put her window down.

"Agent Trinn?" the woman said. "I'm Shira Nazarian. I have something for you." She showed her Israeli government credentials and held out the package to Jaden. Leaning down, she peered into the car. "Gentlemen, your services protecting Ms. Trinn are no longer necessary this afternoon." She spoke excellent English, with just a hint of an accent. "If you would be so kind as to board the helicopter, we'll see that you get back to your station safely. Miss Trinn and I will stay with the car, so we can talk."

There was a protest from the security detail, but it was short lived. Former Secret Service members tend to defer to current Secret Service members. The words "Let's go, folks" from the government Agent In Charge was all it took to empty Trinn's car and allow Shira Nazarian to take the passenger seat.

As the helicopter took flight again, Agent Nazarian removed her sunglasses. She was young and beautiful, with stunning, ice-blue eyes and lush, long hair. "As I mentioned, we have a lot to talk about."

"Well," Trinn chewed her lip. "It's about another hour to my house. Will that be enough?"

Nazarian shook her head. "We aren't driving."

A second, larger, helicopter swooped down into the parking lot.

Nazarian opened her door and got out, looking back at Trinn. "Come. They will take your car back for you. President Brantley said time was of the essence."

* * * * *

The back of the second helicopter was set up for comfort. Plush leather seats, and most important of all, a partition that sectioned Trinn and her new friend off so they could speak without yelling to be heard over the noise of the engine.

Shira smiled at Trinn. "I'm told we have a friend in common—Aristotle Hiles."

"Ari and I have worked together several times." Trinn nodded. "I like him. He's very smart."

"He was my transition liaison when I left the military to join Mossad. He and Chava have been like family to me." Shira tapped the sides of her seat. "So—let's get to it, shall we?" She pointed to the brown-paper package. "That is an Israeli Air Force uniform. My rank was that of Major, but this one is for a Colonel—so you will outrank anyone you are likely to encounter in an F-15 or on the flight deck." She reached into her pocket. "Here are the necessary IDs."

Trinn looked at the credit card-sized Israeli Air Force badge. Her picture was already on it, but the name on the ID was Shira Nazarian.

"That was quick," Jaden said.

"I also have an encoded thumb drive for you, containing information about the F-15 that you will find necessary. The pilot should do a cursory review prior to departure anyway, but watch this as soon as possible." She handed Trinn a tiny thumb drive. "It has a self-erasing feature that will engage one hour after the video has been viewed. The files access code is New York pizza."

Jaden smiled.

My old code name. Ari must have given it to her. Shira is definitely trustworthy, then.

"As you will be acting as me for the next day or so," Shira said, "you may contact me using the information contained on the drive. I am to remain out of sight. My government understands this, of course, but I'm a bit in the dark. Can you tell me what I—that is, *you*—will be up to?"

"Sorry, no." Jaden glanced over both shoulders, then gave Shira a wink. "But you definitely won't be springing a felon from a federal prison in Honolulu and using him to stop an international threat."

"No. I will be sequestered at your Langley Air Force base, apparently dealing with a bout of the flu while I await your return."

Trinn slipped the ID into her pocket. "It won't be a long stay for you. If I'm gone more than twenty-four hours, my mission failed."

"I see," Shira said. "Well, best of luck, then." She extended her hand to Jaden. "Try not to get killed as me. My fiancée might not take the news well—and he's already put off our wedding date twice."

"*Mazel tov*," Trinn said, shaking Shira's hand. "Hopefully, I'll see you tomorrow."

"Hopefully." The Israeli officer nodded. "*Leich l'shalom* to you, Agent Trinn. That is a wish of safe travels, in Hebrew. I prefer it to *hatzlacha*, which means good luck—because in our business, relying on luck is a death sentence. I pray that luck will not be necessary for your safe return."

* * * * *

As the helicopter departed from the back pasture, Trinn walked toward her house—and DeShear walked toward her.

"The security guys got a call to expect you— via helicopter." He smiled, hugging Jaden and giving her a kiss. "Quite an entrance. I take it your meeting with the President went well."

"Actually, Brantley said no to me." She kissed DeShear again and brushed a strand of hair from his eyes. "Then he assigned me the identity of an Israeli intelligence officer—Shira Nazarian. *She* has twenty-four hours to get what I need and get back. Can you wait that long?"

"I would wait forever for you," DeShear said. "The question is, can Hauser?"

Trinn took his hand and started toward the house. "If what I'm trying works, Hauser will be finished—along with some other issues we've been dealing with."

"Then we should talk, so we can coordinate whatever we can. I still want to get to the rendezvous site in Canada ahead of the deadline."

"Yeah." She put her hand to her abdomen. "Yeah, we have a few things to talk about."

* * * * *

From her seat in the Gulfstream 700 jet, Atria Lutz stared at her computer while her guest finished his lunch. She sat back in her chair, swiveling around from her desk and facing the only other passenger on board. "Doctor Symm, are you familiar with the phrase burner phone?"

"It's a disposable cell phone." Symm brushed the crumbs from his sandwich off his hands and reached for his coffee. "An inexpensive phone that doesn't have fancy features. The buyer can use it and throw it away when they're finished. A lot of times, a burner phone is purchased so the user can remain anonymous."

"Precisely." She nodded, bringing a map onto the screen. A red line wiggled its way across an overlay of streets. "And do you know how many steps are required to remain *truly* anonymous? You must buy the phone with cash. You must buy minutes with a prepaid debit card, also purchased with cash. And then you have to be careful not to take it to your house or leave it powered on in your car, so the signal doesn't spend eight or ten hours pinging the nearest tower night after night—thereby potentially giving away its owner. One minor slipup can reveal someone who had wished to remain anonymous, but most people don't go to such steps. People make mistakes. They buy the phone from a shop that is close to where they live, use it for their covert calls, and take it home each night." She turned the monitor toward him. "For example, here is a map of just such a person. Does this look familiar?"

Symm's jaw dropped. "That—that's my house." He grabbed the mouse, zooming in on the map and tracing its course. "This…" His cheeks reddened. "It's more or less the route I took on my way to meet with you."

"With a few stops at places I'm not interested in—an apartment you rent under an assumed name, and a restaurant where you had dinner with a young woman. You pay in cash, so it's safe to assume your wife doesn't know about your… *second residence*."

Symm clenched his teeth. "If your intent was to embarrass me—"

"My intent..." Lutz stood, walking to an observation window. "...was to demonstrate how easily one can be tracked. We simply gave your picture to several employees at electronics stores near your house and paid them a hundred dollars to be on the lookout for you. Had we wanted, we could have found your disposable phone using a frequency scanner and parked near your house, waiting for you to forget to turn it off. You tend to store your burner phone in a gym bag which you keep in the trunk of your car. But last Thursday you played racquetball at your club—and when you drove home, you forgot to turn it off."

"Doctor Lutz..."

"Now, if you'll notice, we've been monitoring a few burner phones in the Washington, D.C. area—one located in Arlington, Virginia, for example." She tapped the screen again, bringing up another set of maps. "That one has visited some very interesting places this afternoon, like the retreat at Camp David."

CHAPTER 14

Trinn's ride to the military base was by way of a white, unmarked van. The Secret Service suggested the low-key approach to allow her more anonymity than what she would get if she showed up in a helicopter. After all, she was now Shira Nazarian, who was already on base. But she used the time to review the video she'd been given—and to review the discussion she'd had with DeShear.

"I trust you," he said. "But you said it yourself—splitting us up makes us all more vulnerable."

"Hank, we have to risk it. We've doubled the number of guards on the property, so the family will be safe without us, temporarily. What I'm doing will allow us to fight back."

"So will what I'm doing."

"So, let's do both." She looked into his eyes. "A two-pronged attack. Just wait. Give me one day before you head to Canada, then go do your recon to *see if a preemptive strike is possible. If it's not, meet with Hauser as scheduled—and I'll be right behind you."*

DeShear cocked his head. "You're coming?"

"Of course I'm coming." Trinn smiled. "We're a team."

She told herself it was handled. That Hank would move forward with caution and that somehow he'd be able to walk into Hauser's trap and emerge on the other side unscathed. But whatever comfort was supposed to come with that plan didn't settle into her. Instead, a knot formed in her gut.

It's okay. You get to Hollings, you get him to play ball, and you diffuse the Hauser situation once and for all.

Ultimately, Hollings had always been about the money—and Trinn had almost three billion dollars to negotiate with.

A fraction of that will be more than enough to persuade him. It would be enough to persuade anyone.

The video had been playing, but she hadn't been watching it. She tapped the screen of her laptop and started it again. Shira appeared in her Israeli Air Force uniform—tan shirt, tan pants, blue belt and cap—the same as Trinn was currently wearing in the van.

Jaden zipped shut a duffel bag containing a change of clothes and placed it at her feet.

"This is not the flight gear for an F-15." On the video, Shira swept a hand over her clothes. "You will be provided a G-suit before you get to the flight line, and you will change into it in a locker room.

Helmet and additional items will be provided at that time. As you are not a standard passenger, they will review protocols with you…"

* * * * *

DeShear entered his daughter's bedroom. Helena was sitting upright on the edge of the bed; Constantine sat in the middle, watching videos on her tablet, her head propped up by three or four stuffed animals, and her feet resting in her matron's lap.

"So…" Hank leaned on the door frame. "I was thinking about making some popcorn and watching a movie tonight. What do you two say?"

Constantine looked up at him. Her eyes were red, like she'd been crying. "You're worried for Miss Jaden, aren't you?"

"Nothing gets by you, does it?" He chewed his lip, moving to the bed. "I'm a little worried, yeah."

"I think popcorn sounds lovely." Helena got up, making her way to the door. "I shall go and make some."

"Oh, no," Hank said. "I didn't mean I wanted you to make it. I'm happy to do it…"

The old woman shook her head. "Let me, dear. You two should talk."

As Helena left the room, DeShear put his hands in his pockets and faced Constantine. Her eyes remained fixed on her tablet. He sat at the foot of the bed and checked out the video she was playing. On the screen, an Air Force test pilot described a technique that pilots use against excessive G-forces, to keep from passing out.

"Are you watching this for any particular reason?" DeShear asked.

"It's interesting." Constantine set the tablet aside. "The pilots wear a G-suit, but they must also remember to squeeze their leg and belly muscles so they don't pass out." She crawled to the end of the bed and sat criss-cross applesauce, studying his face. "Will the new guards all be screened so we're safe?"

"That's the idea." Hank nodded. "I've been assured that they're all on the side of the good guys."

"And Miss Jaden is well trained in her duties?"

He nodded again. "She is."

Constantine sniffled, her words thick with emotion. "Then why are you worried?"

"Because…" Sighing, DeShear leaned back on one elbow. "I guess when someone you care about takes a risk, it's natural to be a little afraid about them getting hurt. That goes away as they accomplish things and establish a level of competence, but I don't think it ever goes away completely. Not when the stakes are so high."

Constantine pulled one of her stuffed animals into her lap. "Are you worried about me?"

"Sometimes, sure. Not because you aren't smart and strong but because…" He shrugged. "You've been through a lot, but there are tons of unknowns out there. As your dad, I'm supposed to help protect you until you can protect yourself. Jaden and I want to teach you how to protect yourself along the way, but we seem to get things thrown at us faster than we can prepare for them." He looked down, chuckling. "Which, now that I say it out loud, is probably how every parent feels. Our challenges are just on a bigger scale."

"You're taking a risk when you go to the meeting in Canada. Should I be worried about you, then?"

"I wish you wouldn't," DeShear said. "But it'll be okay if you worry a little. Remember, I'm taking a risk *now* so you don't have to face a bigger risk *later*. Knowing I'm helping you is what gives me the courage to go do it."

The six-year-old nodded, tears welling in her eyes. "Then, you're not afraid?"

"Let me tell you about fear." DeShear inhaled deeply and sat up on the bed. "There was a famous test pilot who everybody said was fearless—that he stared death in the face all the time and it didn't scare him. But he said that wasn't true. He *had* fear. So, he made sure he learned everything about the aircraft and how to maneuver it, how to stay calm when things went wrong and to use his head… He said that was why he was the best, not because he never experienced fear." DeShear looked at his daughter. "That's what I try to do, and that's what you should try to do. We have to use our heads first, because we're never going to be in a position where we always know exactly what's coming next."

The aroma of popcorn wafted up from the kitchen, filling the bedroom with its delicious, buttery scent.

Constantine put her stuffed animal back in the pile and wiped her eyes. "What movie do you want to watch?"

"Anything you want." Leaning forward, DeShear wrapped his arms around his daughter, closing his eyes and placing his forehead against hers. "As long as it has a happy ending."

* * * * *

The interagency liaison ushered Trinn from the van to a locker room. As the roar of jet engines rattled the walls, a female ground crew technician helped her with a G-suit, helmet, and a few other items for the flight.

"Have you eaten, Colonel?" The young woman walked with Trinn out of the locker room, shouting over the noisy jet engines.

Trinn adjusted the waistline of her G-suit. It was baggier than she expected.

"Colonel Nazarian?" The woman shouted, tapping Trinn on the shoulder.

"What?" Trinn bolted upright.

You're Shira Nazarian—and you're a Colonel in the Israeli Air Force.

She shook her head. "Sorry, I was distracted by… I was just distracted. What was your question?"

"Have you eaten?" The woman hooked a thumb to the jets outside on the tarmac. "You're fixing to take a long flight, Colonel."

Trinn pursed her lips, nodding slowly. "Right."

She hadn't eaten, but food hadn't been staying down very well for the last few weeks. She didn't want to try to eat now and throw up in front of everyone before she got on the plane.

Trinn faced the woman. "What do you recommend? Eat something quick now, or…"

"If you can wait, I'd wait." She lifted Trinn's helmet off a wall hook and handed it to her. "I got to ride in one of these F-15s once. Passed out twice and lost my lunch to boot. I'd hold off and grab something when you land in Los Angeles for refueling."

A man's voice came over Trinn's shoulder. "Plus, the G-suit's gonna press hard on your belly. That's never fun."

Trinn turned to see a tall, square-jawed man in aviator attire, a helmet tucked under his arm. Above the top of the visor was the word *Lancelot* in red paint.

"You must be my pilot." Trinn shook his hand.

"That's right, Colonel." He grinned. "Lieutenant Kurt Lansing, at your service. I was told we need to be wheels up ASAP. The bird is ready when you are."

"Then let's go." Trinn bent down and grabbed her duffel bag. "I can hold out until LA to eat."

"Yes, ma'am." Lansing pointed to a huge, sleek jet fighter. "We're right over here."

* * * * *

The giant gray plane was even bigger close up. Nearly as wide as it was long, the F-15's wingspan was more than forty feet across—though it looked much smaller from the locker room facility.

Trinn walked with the young Lieutenant across the tarmac and toward the craft.

And walked…

…and walked…

The fighter jet got bigger with every step. The two-seat cockpit hung out over the front, like it was an afterthought to the plane's designers—and with the thrust of two massive engines at the rear of the craft, maybe it was. It looked more like a horizontal rocket than any airplane Trinn had flown on.

Near the front of the plane, several ground crew members waited with a portable metal staircase. The cockpit was nearly fifteen feet in the air.

Jaden stepped toward the steel ladder setup, holding tight to the railing and staring up at the huge plane.

"I'll drive, Colonel Nazarian." Lansing grinned. "If that's all right with you, ma'am."

Nervousness grabbed Trinn's insides. She tried to make light of the situation, but nothing witty came to mind. Stepping back from the staircase, she nodded her head and waved her pilot onward. "Yep. Sorry."

"Don't worry, ma'am. The CIA liaison said it had been a while since you were on active duty. Must be nice, flying a bird like this over the Mediterranean Sea, clear and blue above and below like that."

She stared at him.

Is this a test? Did they say Shira flew these?

Lansing stared back at her, his eyes warm and reassuring. Trinn's heart settled back into her chest.

He's cool. Whatever the CIA said, just go with it.

Or...

You outrank him. Ignore anything you don't want to answer. He'll take the hint.

She nodded to the jet. "Let's fly, Lieutenant."

Lansing slid his helmet over his head and scampered up the steel staircase, climbing into the seat of the gigantic F-15. When he had settled in, the ground crew moved the ladder back to the second position.

"Here we go, Colonel Nazarian." A crew tech patted the railing of the staircase. "Your turn up."

Trinn climbed the steps, her heart thumping.

It's going to be fine. You have a trained pilot that knows what he's doing, and it'll all be over in a few hours.

The flying didn't make her nervous. Neither did carrying the release that Brantley had sent over by secured messenger.

So why am I nervous?

Maybe it's the seven-week-old passenger that's flying with me.

Her internet searches hadn't revealed any definitive studies showing that pregnant women shouldn't fly; quite the opposite. Until the last few months, most doctors said flying was fine.

But very few articles mentioned the pregnant women in question being in an F-15 and pulling nine Gs. None, in fact.

It's only seven weeks. If you hadn't done a pregnancy test, you wouldn't even know for sure that you were pregnant.

But she did know. And it weighed on her.

Keeping the baby a secret from Hank bothered her the most. Then there was the unpredictable nosebleeds and random bouts of nausea—not to mention the possible bad effects the

G suit might have on her baby as it squeezed her abdomen and legs to keep her from blacking out.

And then there was the baby itself.

Hank told her about the child he and his wife had lost. Maya had mentioned stories about how Tristan and Doctor Carrera had lost children, too. Hank never said his genetic condition had been the reason, but it seemed obvious enough. And Tristan blamed Hauser for the loss of his children, one hundred percent.

I guess it was a place Hank didn't want to go. Why would he? There wasn't anything he could do about it.

Except possibly not get his girlfriend pregnant.

The technician helped strap Trinn into her seat. A cold, snug surface, the rear seat of the F-15 offered a dashboard of small screens and a million dials and switches. As they fitted her oxygen mask to her helmet, she tried to remember the exercises necessary to not pass out when the boosters kicked in.

"There will be intense thrust at takeoff," Shira said on the video. "Squeeze your leg muscles, your butt, and your abdomen to assist the G-suit in keeping all the blood from rushing from out of your head, as follows…"

Lieutenant Lansing talked back and forth with the tower as the glass dome lowered over Trinn's head and clicked into place.

She exhaled a long, slow breath, her pulse racing.

That's it. No going back now.

On the tarmac, the ground crew gave the F-15's occupants a thumbs up. Trinn returned the gesture, forcing a smile as sweat gathered on her upper lip.

"Okay, Colonel." Lansing's voice came over the speaker in her helmet. "We are cleared and ready to go. Sit tight and try to breathe normal. I'll warn you about everything I'm doing in advance."

As the engines grew louder, her heart rate increased. Trinn gripped the sides of her seat. The jet turned and headed toward the runway.

Glancing at the buttons and switches surrounding her, she peered at the back of her pilot's head. "What if I hit one of these buttons by mistake?"

"Please don't, Colonel," Lansing said, his voice firm.

A jolt of nerves shot through Trinn's system.

"Just kidding." The lieutenant chuckled. "When we have special personnel like yourself on board, we do a lockdown of certain systems. You can't do any harm back there."

Trinn relaxed, taking a breath.

"But still," Lansing said. "Please don't touch anything, ma'am."

Radio chatter came over her helmet.

"Roger that, tower." Lansing's engines grew louder. "We are good to go." He turned his head to the side. "Colonel, we're cleared for takeoff."

"Okay." Trinn gripped the sides of the seat.

The plane made a left turn and started down a long runway. Engines roaring, it gathered speed, bumping and jostling over the concrete ribbon in front of them.

"Colonel, I'm going to engage the thrusters."

"Yep." Trinn squeezed the seat harder. "Roger that."

The words were barely out of her mouth when the engines roared and the force of acceleration pinned her head to her seat. The nose of the aircraft swung upwards into the blue sky and the ground fell away. Trinn's insides felt like she'd gone over the big drop of a roller coaster, empty and hollow and uneasy, but with a weight like an elephant was sitting on her chest and face.

As white wisps of clouds streaked past the window, the force eased up somewhat. She was able to pull herself forward in her seat and look around—a little.

"Quite a start, eh, Colonel?"

"Whew!" Trinn shouted. "That was something else." She gazed over the side of the aircraft at the shimmering blue waters of Chesapeake Bay far, far below. "This thing doesn't waste any time, does it?"

"My orders were to get you to Honolulu ASAP," Lansing said. "We aim to please."

Trinn nodded, taking a deep breath. It hadn't been as bad as she expected.

Lansing chatted with flight control, using a flat, nondescriptive tone. The tower replied in the same manner.

"How fast are we going right now?" Trinn asked.

"Not very. When we clear civilian air space, we'll get up to speed."

"Oh. When's that?" She looked out the other side of the aircraft. Already, the land had become tiny. Only the vast ocean and the arc of the horizon were visible below them.

"Right about... now. Hang on, Colonel."

The thrusters engaged again, slamming Trinn backward a second time—but much harder. Her forehead felt like a thousand hands were pushing on it. Groaning, she tried to breathe, working to call up the exercises she'd been instructed to use. Around her legs, thighs, and midsection, the G-suit squeezed her muscles.

A gray haze appeared at the edges of her vision. Moaning, Jaden tried to force her chest outward in a losing battle to get a breath.

The gray haze grew, dotting her eyesight as the engine noise faded from her ears, and her world went dark.

CHAPTER 15

Shira Nazarian stepped from the shower, slipping her gray robe around herself and wrapping a towel around her wet, dark hair. She peeked her head out of the bathroom, calling to her security guard in the hallway. "Ezra, has my pizza come yet? I'm famished."

Hearing her safe word, she walked to the door of her hotel room.

"It's about time!" She opened the door to see Ezra unconscious on the floor, blood seeping from both thighs and both forearms—and a gaping wound in his chest.

"Ezra!" Shira dropped to his side, pressing two fingers to his carotid artery.

There was no pulse.

Glancing up and down the hallway, she felt for his gun.

"Looking for this?" A man stepped out from around the corner, pointing a handgun at her.

Shira leaped to her feet and jumped into the room, grabbing the door and flinging it shut.

A foot in tan work boots wedged itself between the door and the frame. The door bounced off the steel-toed leather and flew open again.

Shira backed away, reaching for the dresser—and her gun in the top drawer.

The gunman's first shot hit Shira's throat, searing like fire and cutting off her airway. The silencer kept the blast from echoing down the hall and alerting others, but the impact knocked her towel off her head and knocked her into the dresser. The furniture's wooden brim cut into her back as the flatscreen television tumbled to the hotel room floor. It shattered in an electric flash, shards of glass falling everywhere.

Shira threw her hands to her throat, gasping as she worked to stay upright. Each labored attempt at a breath sent a gush of blood over her fingers.

The assassin walked in, bending over to pick up her hair towel and casually tossing it aside, then he shut the door. "Your friend in the hall didn't want to give you up. It took four bullets to get your safe word. That's devotion to duty."

Pulse throbbing, Shira grabbed at the dresser drawer, jerking it open and reaching for her gun. The weapon squirted through her bloody fingers, skipping away and dropping behind her folded t-shirts.

The attacker raised his gun and pointed it at her. "Say goodbye, agent. Dark Hour has arrived for you."

Shira's throat pulsed with fire, adrenaline coursing through her veins. As dark spots clouded over her vision, her hand found her weapon. Barely able to focus, she hauled it out of the drawer, sliding the safety off and aiming it toward her assailant's torso.

He fired first.

Two rounds flashed and two bullets slammed into her chest.

It was like getting hit by a car. Shira crashed into the floor, her gun bouncing from her blood-soaked hand.

She forced herself onto her elbows, dragging herself across the carpet after her weapon. Choking and gasping, sucking for air, the gray spots overwhelmed her. As her head dropped to the carpet, the killer hooked a foot under her side and flipped her onto her back again, pointing the muzzle of his gun to her temple.

Barely able to lift her hands, Shira swatted feebly at the weapon, her eyes rolling back in her head and her hand passing slowly through the air, not coming close to hitting the attacker's weapon. On the other end of the gun, her killer laughed as he put the tip of the gun to her head and pulled the trigger.

* * * * *

The phone on the desk of Atria Lutz buzzed with an incoming call. She answered it before it rang a second time.

A man's voice came over the line. "It's done."

"Mm-hmm." Lutz sat back in her chair, stroking her chin with the back of an ink pen. "How?"

"At the hotel on the base. Two in the chest and one in the forehead, as instructed—plus a bonus through the throat."

"Perfect." The doctor smiled, taking a deep breath and letting it out slowly. "Put Ms. Trinn's body on ice and bring it to me."

CHAPTER 16

In the F-15, the screens and knobs in front of Trinn came into focus again. She blinked a few times, clearing her head. The gray panel of the aircraft's dashboard and the crystalline blue skies outside of the glass fighter jet dome was all she needed.

I made it. I'm going to be fine.

"Welcome back, Colonel Nazarian," Lansing said.

"Sorry." Trinn took a deep breath. "I guess I blacked out for a few... Uh, how long was I out?"

"Only a few seconds. How are you feeling? Did the ground crew show you where the barf bag was?"

As if on cue, nausea swept over her. Trinn grabbed for the blue plastic bag at her knee and pulled it from its fastener. Shoving her oxygen mask aside, she put the bag to her mouth and puked.

"No worries, ma'am." The lieutenant's voice was calm and reassuring. "It happens to everyone."

"Yeah?" Trinn wiped her lips with the back of her hand. "Ever happen to you, Sir Lancelot?"

He chuckled. "Sure. A few times in flight school. Thought I was gonna wash out—but I made it. You will, too."

"Are we... how fast are we going?" She tied a knot in the neck of the plastic bag and dropped it to the floor.

"I reduced acceleration until I got you back, ma'am. We can go to max fly whenever you're ready."

Nodding, Trinn grabbed the sides of her seat and squeezed her eyes shut. "Do it. I'm in a hurry."

* * * * *

DeShear popped a piece of popcorn into his mouth and sat down on the couch. Constantine snuggled up next to him, reaching into the red plastic bowl of fluffy, buttery goodness.

"So?" he said. "What did we decide to watch?"

"Your choice." Helena settled herself into the loveseat. "The options are a cartoon movie about a rabbit, and a documentary about rabbits."

DeShear made an exaggerated grimace at his daughter. "Gee, let me guess who selected the choices."

Constantine grinned, displaying a mouthful of popcorn.

"Well..." DeShear sighed. "I said I wanted to watch something with a happy ending. Which one would that be?"

"Let's watch the cartoon." Reaching for another handful of popcorn, Constantine looked up at her father. "Cartoons always have a happy ending."

"You got it, kid." Picking up the remote, DeShear pressed a button and the streaming service logo appeared on the TV screen.

"And you needn't worry about Miss Jaden anymore," Constantine said. "I think she's going to be fine."

"Oh?" He tossed another piece of popcorn into his mouth. "That's good news. What gives you that impression?"

Constantine looked at Helena. The old woman moved her head back and forth, almost imperceptibly.

"Nothing, really." The six-year-old slunk down in her seat. "Just a feeling, is all."

* * * * *

The cafeteria in the Federal Detention Center in Honolulu was a drab, gray place, despite the sunny skies outside. Housed near the airport, in what looked more like a downtown office building than a prison, it was a facility in a location that inmates in other jails might consider ideal. But Hawaii's exotic allure of luaus, mountains, deep seas, and humpback whales masked the detention center's core population of hardened, career criminals—many of which would be headed to harsher prisons on the U.S. mainland after their brief stay on the island.

A prison guard walked through the cafeteria, toward where an obese man in a wheelchair was trading cigarettes for candy and movie passes—among other things.

"Hollings!" The guard pushed his way through the circle of inmates surrounding the fat man. "Front and center."

The unshaven man at the center of the activity raised his eyes to his inquisitor, cocking his head. "And a good day to you, too, mate—I mean, Officer Norman." Hollings' British accent was decidedly lower class, filled with a gruff tone. He raised one of his bandaged forearms, his plump hand rendering a mock salute. "Cor blimey, to what do I owe the pleasure of you interrupting my business? We've a big trade on, we have. Big business and the like."

"Get your sorry British butt up to the administration office for processing." Officer Norman scowled, putting his hands on his hips. "We received a release for you. You're a free man."

Hollings broke into a loud laugh. "Right, you lot!" He wheeled himself away from the table, smirking at his customers. "I told you when I come in this joint, ain't no cell can hold me—and here I am, rolling meself out the front door, quick as you please, after just a few weeks."

Norman walked ahead of Hollings as another guard fell in behind.

"And remember, blokes—I still want my stakes!" He glanced at the inmates over his shoulder. "All you wankers still owe me for them trades today. I'll be sending an address back to the lot of you so's you can forward my money!"

* * * * *

Dressed in her civilian clothes, Jaden Trinn approached the receiving area of the Federal Detention Center in Honolulu. Lieutenant Lansing, still wearing his one-piece, olive-drab flight suit, stood at her side, his hands tucked behind his back and his square jaw held high.

Jaden mentally reviewed the plan for after Hollings was released to her.

Negotiate the deal and be ready to physically subdue him in the cab if he gets out of line. If he doesn't agree to the terms, just yank the release and send him back inside. The thought of getting locked back up should be enough to get him to make a deal. Then, it's just a matter of how much money he wants.

A clerk behind a glass half-wall looked up from his desk. He leaned forward to a microphone and pressed the button, sending his voice into the lobby over a speaker. "Yes, ma'am. How can I help you?"

Trinn laid an ID and a copy of the prisoner release form into the slide box. "I'm picking up a prisoner."

The clerk pulled the paperwork through to his side and opened it. Scanning the document, he nodded and brought his gaze back to Trinn. "Just one moment, Ms. Nazarian."

He disappeared through a door at the back of his office. As Trinn paced back and forth in the lobby, the door opened again and the clerk returned, followed by a man in a suit. They approached the glass partition.

The man in the suit held up Trinn's ID and then looked at her through the glass, reaching over and pressing the button on the microphone. "Who are you again?"

A jolt went through her.

I'm Shira Nazarian, a Colonel in the Israeli Air Force. What's your freaking problem?

She decided on a more civil tact. She stepped to the glass and spoke in a soft tone. "Is there a problem, sir?"

"A little one, I suppose, Colonel Nazarian." The man leafed through her paperwork.

Trinn's heart raced.

What went wrong? Did something happen? Am I about to get arrested?

She glanced around.

Crap. Hollings probably saw me and told them I'm not Shira. They're probably calling the guards—and I don't have time to answer questions or get taken down to the police station.

She took a deep breath, lowering her hands beneath the glass and massaging her fingers.

Just play it cool. Maybe nothing's wrong.

"Well, Colonel Nazarian…" The man in the suit shook his head. "We seem to have a bit of an issue with Mr. Hollings being released to you today."

"Oh?" Trinn approached the glass. "And what problem would that be? My paperwork is in order."

"Well, but the problem is…" The man looked at her. "Mr. Hollings was just released a few minutes ago, to someone else. He's no longer here."

CHAPTER 17

A long day—and a boring cartoon—had done their job. Constantine lay on the couch, her head on a sofa pillow, slumbering next to DeShear. Switching off the TV, Hank slipped his hands under the sleeping six-year-old and carried her to bed, making sure to tuck her in among all her stuffed animals.

Returning to the living room, he took a seat on the couch and looked at Helena. Normally, the old woman would go upstairs to her room when Constantine went to bed.

This evening she stayed behind, her hands clasped in her lap, waiting. "There are things you want to ask me, dear. What are they?"

DeShear shifted on the couch.

"Constantine is asleep." Helena glanced toward the hallway. "She won't hear."

Nodding, DeShear faced the old woman, keeping his voice low. "You know, I don't pretend to understand what happened to the people at Hauser's château in France. Doctor Kittaleye said it might be traumatic to even bring it up—to Constantine and to you—so I apologize, but…"

"It's all right, dear." She gave him a smile, kneading her fingers. "There were things we dared not speak of in the château. Some, we were hesitant to bring up after, as well. But I know you've had many questions you wanted to ask. Now is as good a time as any to ask them."

"Okay." He took a deep breath. "When that messenger showed up, ranting about Dark Hour… I more or less had the impression that Dark Hour was sunset, bedtime—that sort of thing. I knew that sometimes special events happened at Dark Hour— bad events, I guess, from the way people talked about it. But things have happened fast since we found the château. Jaden and I didn't want to stir up a lot of painful memories…"

"You and Miss Jaden have been most considerate in that regard. But I do agree, we should talk about whatever concerns you may have. You mustn't be afraid."

He glanced at her. "So…"

"So." Helena peered down at her hands. "Dark Hour was indeed the time of sunset, and you are right, it was not only that. Doctor Hauser had many things renamed differently from what others in a normal society would call them, but those of us living in the château were cut off, so his differentiation was intentional. We were like a society unto ourselves, with very little interaction with the outside world." She sighed. "First Night was the equivalent of New Year's Day. Founding Day was when a child started their education. The children of the château went to Rituals on Seventh Day, when other children would have gone to church, and they had an Inception Day instead of a birthday. And there was certainly no celebration marking birthdays, may I say. It was merely a date in a record book. The party you held for Constantine a few weeks ago, when she turned six, that was absolutely brilliant. No child of the château ever had anything like that. Not for themselves."

DeShear sat with his arms at his sides, letting his friend talk.

"There were joyous occasions at the château as well, Hamilton. I don't mean to say there were not. The bringing of the children, watching them play, watching them sleep... There are many simple moments in life that sound so odd when you say them to others, but for me there was always a certain satisfaction in just watching a child sleep. Knowing you've kept them safe from the ills of the world... It warms the heart."

Helena smiled, but then her face grew grim.

"There were many other times as well. Dark Hour was sunset and bedtime for the children—after coming inside and having their dinner, of course—but sometimes there was a ceremony performed. On rare occasions, it might be fireworks or a cake, and the children were allowed to stay up late for it. But more often it was..."

She looked away, swallowing hard.

"Go on," DeShear whispered. "Please—if you can."

"Sometimes, it was the equivalent of a human sacrifice." The old woman's voice wavered, pain coming to her words. "Oh, I hate to think of it. If one of the workers had misbehaved, or if a demonstration was needed to convince a prospective buyer of how obedient Hauser's genetically enhanced humans could be, they had a display. One time, a young blonde woman poured gasoline over herself and lit herself on fire. We were forced to stand there and watch her burn, to see her kicking and squirming on the stage, engulfed in flames, as we breathed the horrifying smell of charred human flesh into our lungs."

DeShear frowned, pushing his hands into the sofa cushions.

"Other times, a random worker was selected—someone who'd done nothing wrong. They'd be dealt with at the hands of several new prototypes. The displays were meant to drag on, being held on the dark grounds after sunset and illuminated by flaming torches. A few members in the demonstration group would beat the worker with their bare hands. You could hear the bones breaking as they punched and kicked, nonstop, until the life went out of the condemned."

Tears welled in the old woman's eyes.

"And it wasn't just grown workers. I told you what happened to Constantine's classmates. He capped them with Rituals bonnets and killed them all in one go. It was… terrible. Absolutely terrible." She frowned. "The worst day of my life."

"I'm sorry." DeShear shook his head. The thought of the beautiful child down the hall, sleeping among a pile of soft, fuzzy stuffed animals, being forced to grow up surrounded by all that horror, it made his stomach churn. He swallowed hard and looked up at Helena. "I'm… I wish I hadn't asked you about all this."

"But you must know it." She leaned forward, her face etched with pain. "As I said, there were things we dared not speak of in the château. But you must be fully aware of what these people are capable of. Doctor Hauser had children shot in the head for not performing well on a math test—or for performing *too* well, in which case he perceived them as a threat to his selected heirs. Children as young as four or five! And the workers or tansuits he had killed in his demonstrations… he told us it was an honor for them to die that way, reinforcing how strong their lines were. Nobody believed that rubbish, of course, but that's why…"

A tear ran down the old woman's cheek. She lowered her head, sobbing.

"That's why, when I thought I was being sent for summary execution, it was done in the morning, at dawn. I believed I'd become a disgrace to him. I'd die alone, in the cold, the children never knowing what happened to me…" Her lip trembled. More tears rolled over the soft, wrinkled skin. "Constantine would think I abandoned her."

"No, no, no." DeShear slid off the couch and kneeled before her, taking Helena's hand. "Constantine would have known better. And I think you were special to Hauser. He put you in charge of Constantine, and she was his favorite. He wouldn't

155

have done that if you didn't mean something more to him than the others."

Helena shook her head, sniffling. "I brought her to him. She was highest in her class. She was the candidate he was looking for, but he didn't truly know her until I took her to him."

"But you knew she was special, and that saved her life."

"And cost the other children theirs!" She lifted her tear-streaked face to the ceiling, throwing her hands down over the armrests. "Oh, how could I not see such terrible things when they were coming? How could I fail the children like that?"

A lump formed in DeShear's throat. He stroked Helena's hand, forcing the words from his lips. "It was the only choice. They were all going to die. Always. All but one of them. You... you did what you could to stop it." Trinn's message from earlier echoed in his ears. This time, he heard it with his heart, finally believing it when he repeated it to Helena. "All that horror, it was all going to happen anyway—but we were able to stop it from continuing. We did that, you and I and the others, when we shut down Hauser's operations. We stopped the mass graves filled with innocent children, the massive human trafficking to overseas countries, the illegal organ harvesting... We stopped all that. And we'll keep stopping it, whenever it tries to start up again, like we are now. That's your legacy to Constantine. She knows it, too. She was special, and you are. I know it. I've seen how special you are."

Helena wiped her eyes and patted his hand. "Constantine is very fortunate to have you as her father."

"Yeah." He sat back on his heels. "Adopted or not, I feel lucky to have her, too. Jaden and I…"

"I think you've misunderstood me, dear." Helena gazed into his eyes. "Adopting her didn't make her your child."

"What?"

"She *is* your child. Constantine was created outside of the process. She never lived in a dark warehouse full of glass tanks. Constantine was born through in vitro fertilization. From your genetic material, yes—but not through any of Doctor Hauser's processes." The old woman smiled. "She is your adopted daughter, but she is your birth daughter as well."

"I guess I…" DeShear put a hand to his forehead, his ears humming. "I think I assumed Hauser used my genetics to create her, so I felt like *technically* we were… but, I didn't… I mean, I never…"

"She is your daughter, Hamilton." Helena sat upright, her hands in her lap. "Your blood runs through her veins as surely as it runs through your own. I should know. I helped with the procedures and kept the records."

He glanced at the hallway, his mouth hanging open. "Does… does she know?"

"Yes, dear. I think, somehow, she knew right when she met you." The old woman nodded. "But it's not the paperwork or genetics that matter. The fact that *you* didn't know, and you still did all the things you've done—and the things you will do." Helena clasped her hands in the dim light of the living room. "Those are the things that make a man a real father to a child. And those things, you have done exceedingly well."

CHAPTER 18

Trinn stood on the sidewalk in front of the detention center, both hands clenched into fists. "Crap!"

"Calm down," Lansing said. "Tell me what's going on."

"You saw—my prisoner isn't here." She put her hands out at her sides. "Somebody beat me to the punch. Poof! He's gone—and my whole plan is shot to pieces!"

The lieutenant shook his head. "No, I mean what's really going on. You're no Israeli intelligence officer—and you're not in our armed forces, either. You're supposed to be a colonel, but you're running around initiating salutes to junior airmen and ground crews, instead of the other way around. That dog don't hunt, ma'am. So, who are you and what are we really doing in Hawaii?"

Trinn winced. She didn't want to divulge any more than was necessary, but there wasn't time to play games.

"Okay." She sighed, looking at Lansing. "I'm Agent Jaden Trinn, with the U.S. Bureau of Diplomatic Security, and I currently report directly to the President. I have a release for a federal prisoner so I can address an imminent threat to national security. Now, my prisoner is gone, and if I don't find him soon, we're all going to be in a world of pain."

"Roger that." He nodded. "How can I help, Agent Trinn?"

Jaden put a hand to her forehead. "Go back to the base and have the jet ready to go on a moment's notice. I need to figure out who grabbed Hollings before he and they both disappear forever. I can make a call and get a warrant for a copy of the release paperwork that was used to spring him, but we don't have that kind of time."

Lansing folded his arms across his chest. "What are the odds that whoever has him is from Hawaii and is remaining on the island after they've picked him up?"

She shook her head. "Slim. Almost zero. They're probably flying, too." Trinn's eyes went wide, recalling what Brantley had told her.

"Flying an airplane isn't like renting a car. You have to fuel the plane, set up a flight plan... that's a lot of people and a lot of records."

Records.

She looked up at the Lieutenant. "If they're leaving quickly, like we were trying to do, then

Hollings will be listed on some commercial airline's passenger manifest. That, or we're looking for a private plane with a recorded flight plan that shows they're coming in and taking right back off again. There can't be a lot of those."

"What if they're using a fake ID for him?" Lansing asked. "Is that possible, like you did? Then he won't show up on the commercial manifests. But his new caretaker will—unless they used one ID to fly in with and another ID to fly out."

She chewed her lip. "We'll just have to risk that."

"Okay." Lansing took out his phone. "I'll contact the base and ask them to call in a favor with the commercial airports. They should be able to run a check for a passenger named Hollings and let me know pretty quickly. If it's a small plane coming and going in short order, that will be even faster to spot."

She smiled. "And if they're already airborne, we'll catch them in your F-15."

"Yeah, but then what?" Grinning, he tapped the screen and brought the phone to life. "I can't just shoot them down and—"

A thin trickle of blood spilled from Trinn's nose. She put her hand to her face, reaching out for Lieutenant Lansing as the streets of Honolulu swayed back and forth. "Oh, no. Not now."

Trinn's hand sailed past the lieutenant.

He grabbed her arm and slipped a hand around her waist, preventing her from hitting the sidewalk as she passed out.

* * * * *

Hollings slapped his knee, laughing in the back of the town car as he sipped champagne from a fluted crystal glass. The prison had allowed him to change into the attire he'd worn when he entered their facility a few months earlier, but the dark blue cargo pants and light blue dress shirt—now slightly baggy on him—looked a lot like prison attire anyway.

"Blimey, I weren't expecting this. The royal treatment." Hollings smiled at his host, sloshing his drink. "I can't thank you enough, miss!"

"Thank you." A passing smile stretched across the thin lips of Atria Lutz as she raised the soundproof glass partition, sealing off her driver from the conversation. "And we should both thank Senator Duckwynn, who, after a hefty campaign donation, arranged for your early departure from federal custody." She leaned forward, resting her elbows on her knees. "Now, let's get down to business. My plane's waiting, and I want everything in order."

Narrowing her eyes, she stared at the obese Brit.

"It's my understanding," Lutz said, "that after the life support plugs were pulled on Doctor Hauser's *physical* body, all the computers of the compound were ordered to be gathered up. The mainframes were subsequently rendered useless from a terminal sequence that was put into them—is that right?"

The fat man nodded, gulping his champagne and reaching for a cucumber sandwich. The town car weaved through the Honolulu traffic.

"But..." Lutz raised an eyebrow, licking her lips. "Some of the computers weren't connected to the system when the terminal sequence was launched, so their internal systems weren't destroyed. Various intelligence agencies then collected everything—the defunct mainframes, the laptops, the tablets—all the devices they knew to be in the château. Because that line of tansuits was known to be extremely thorough, everyone assumed all the devices were collected." The doctor stroked her chin, eyeing the man across from her. "But if one of those computers found its way outside... Depending on what was stored on it, someone who knew how to operate it could access everything—all of Hauser's work, his records, his most advanced systems..."

"Aye, lass." Hollings wiped his mouth with the back of his hand, crumbs collecting on the front of his shirt. "And a pretty penny it'd be worth, too. Tens of millions, I expect. Maybe billions. But..." He jammed another sandwich into his mouth. "Would they know how to use it? Would they even be able to access the system?"

"I agree, it would be worth quite a lot." Lutz sat back, crossing her bony legs and plucking a tiny dust particle from her slacks. "But, no, any common person wouldn't know how to access it, and Hauser's minions certainly wouldn't. The members of the intelligence communities can't even access the data locked up in those computers. No, accessing Hauser's AI would require someone from inside his inner circle." She looked up, gazing at her new companion. "Someone like you, Mr. Hollings."

* * * * *

Trinn woke up in the back of a cab, seated next to Lieutenant Lansing. "What's happening?" She bolted upright. "What's going on?"

The road in front of the vehicle swayed. Grabbing the front headrest with both hands, she breathed in and out quickly, trying to keep from passing out again

A sharp pain stabbed her below the belly button. She gasped, covering the spot with her hand and looking at Lansing. "Where are we going?"

"Nowhere, until I get some answers." He frowned. "Nosebleed and passing out—is that from the G-forces? Are you feeling lightheaded or nauseous?"

Jaden shook her head. "No, it's…" A fine sweat broke out on her forehead.

"Well, what then?" the lieutenant said. "Are you pregnant or something? Did you drink a bad smoothie at lunch?"

"I…" Sighing, Jaden slumped back into her seat. "I'll be fine."

"No, ma'am. When you're in my aircraft, you're my responsibility. If I say you can't fly, you *don't* fly. Even my Commander In Chief can't overrule that."

"Tough talk, fly boy. One phone call and—" another pain shot through her lower insides. She cringed, holding her abdomen. "…and you'll be making mud runs in a sea plane off the coast of Anchorage."

Trinn exhaled sharply, moaning as she sagged over and fell into his lap.

"Yeah, you're a tiger." He patted her arm. "How many weeks pregnant are you?"

"I'm not. I'm..." She winced again. "Okay, I'm pregnant. Seven weeks. But it shouldn't affect my ability to fly!"

Lansing buried his face in his hand. "Agent Trinn, with all due respect—are you nuts? It won't affect you in a commercial aircraft, but you can't try to pull nine Gs in a supersonic fighter jet. I appreciate heroism, ma'am, but if you die, your mission gets scrubbed, too. Is that what you want?"

"Okay, okay. But geez, my guts are stabbing me to death from the insides."

"It's probably a combined reaction to the G-suit and the altitude. They compress everything—any empty pockets in you, like an empty stomach or gas in your intestines. Even pockets in your joints. Now that the pressure's gone, those pockets have expanded back to normal and your body's being a little stubborn about the re-expansion."

"Great."

"It... should go away soon, ma'am."

She squeezed her eyes shut and brought her knees up to her chest. "Good grief, it had better."

"Move around when you can, and hydrate. It'll help." He continued patting her arm as he glanced out the cab window. "Anyway, I have good news. My buddies at the base called me back. They ascertained that a small private jet arrived a few hours ago and is scheduled to take off again within the hour. That sounds like our guy."

Jaden sat up, a moan escaping her lips. "Can we get there in time?"

"We're already there." The taxi pulled to a stop. Honolulu's Daniel K. Inouye International Airport loomed large in the window. Reaching into his pocket, Lansing pulled out a billfold. "I'll pay the driver. Go stretch your legs and we'll find you something to drink inside. Then we need to get to the private jet terminals."

* * * * *

In his wheelchair, Hollings rolled himself out of the restroom at the Honolulu airport "FBO"—the elegant, private jet hub just off the airport's main terminals.

It was a small but swanky building. Sleek art deco steps rose from polished floors, trimmed with stainless steel railings riding atop shiny glass panels. The carpet curved around small groups of leather chairs and cocktail tables, making the mini private terminal look more like a massive, exotic living room than anything typically seen in an airport. Stylish aviation-themed sculptures hung from the ceiling; wood paneled desks housed the skeleton crew of airport personnel. Palm trees and ferns were scattered throughout the FBO, mixing elegantly with the décor, but without blocking the view through the huge glass panel windows.

Rubbing his nose as he crumbled a paper towel between his thick fingers, the obese Brit peered up from his wheelchair at Doctor Lutz. "Word on the street was they done found all of Hauser's remote sites and shut them down—including yours, Atria." He ran a fingernail around the inside of his left nostril, lowering his hand to wipe his finger on his pants. "Bloody shame, that. I enjoyed taking the occasional trip to Quebec for some poutine. Or were that a bit of misinformation, and your site didn't get nipped by the FBI?"

"No, they found it." Lutz walked beside him, scrolling through emails on her phone. "They found all the sites and they shut them down."

"Then how…"

"My dear Mr. Hollings, when one is doing illegal things, one often finds it best to keep things mobile." Lutz typed a quick reply to one of the emails, then turned her attention to her rotund companion. "By the time the system shut down, we had already been working on our newest hybrid prototypes from inside a series of transport trucks. A dozen eighteen wheelers—painted to look like they were from plumbing supply houses, major appliance manufacturers, automotive freight—had been the home of our best technology for over a year. We merely pulled out and moved West, to a site in the Canadian Rockies, delivering a truck every few days until we had reestablished ourselves in a new location. One that is remote, quiet—and that cannot draw attention to itself from busybody satellites or pesky drones." She stopped at a large, glass panel window, gazing across the tarmac to her jet. "The only remaining link in the chain was getting our hands on one of the computers from the château—one that had Hauser's AI system on it."

"But when they got to your old lab site," Hollings said, "didn't they realize everything had been moved?"

"They might have—if we had taken everything." She smiled. "We didn't. We left behind everything from the old lines. And why not? We no longer needed it. Computers, growing chambers, the works. A fully-functioning cafeteria, stocked with fresh food. Thousands of viable embryos in their warehouses, dozens of imprisoned tansuits..."

She turned, folding her arms and leaning her back against the glass.

"We only took the newest prototypes at their embryonic stages," Lutz said. "Hybrids, created partly from Hauser's lines and partly from my own. I had already merged the genetics of his existing lines with my latest test subjects, creating a whole new breed—without Doctor Hauser knowing, of course. Otherwise, he'd have swooped in and taken them for himself, as he'd done so many other times with my research advancements." Her eyes took on a steely tone. "My Omicrons are a modern miracle. They have the ability to grow from inception to fully functioning adult in just eighteen months. Now, I just need to access Hauser's AI to learn how he selected the genetic switches for controlling those feeble-minded tansuits of his—so I can take the success of the hybrid prototypes and mass-produce an entire line of them." She raised an eyebrow, looking into Hollings' eyes. "That's technology he didn't share with me when we developed the hybrid prototypes. It's the only link missing in my program."

Lifting a bony finger, she pointed at the fat Brit. "And that's where you come in, big boy."

"What, you—you think I made off with a computer from the château?" He glanced around, wiping his hands on his shirt. "Before we turned tail and run from the place?"

"I know you did." Lutz narrowed her eyes, smiling. "Not only that, but you've used it."

He tugged at his collar. "I never! That's a crop of lies people been telling you, I swear it."

"You did. My sources were there." Lutz tipped her head back, raising her hands to her chin and tapping her fingertips together. "You transported the device in an ambulance—along with your fat carcass and your wheelchair. You used neuroreceptor caps that you pilfered from the château to collect and display the thoughts of one of Hauser's old Keepers—who you'd kidnapped and smuggled to an abandoned warehouse in France, by the way—and you projected whatever went through her mind, right onto a TV screen. There were witnesses to the entire thing. One was an African-American psychologist, Dr. Kittaleye. She gave a full, confidential report to the FBI when you were arrested—a report that Senator Duckwynn was happy to provide to me—and now, here we are."

"Bugger!" Hollings scowled, pounding the armrests of his wheelchair. "Can't trust no one these days."

"Oh, I disagree." The smile disappeared from Atria Lutz's face. "You can trust me—to kill you if you don't show me how to work Hauser's artificial intelligence system."

CHAPTER 19

Gulping from a plastic bottled water, Trinn stood by Lansing, reading a wall-mounted display monitor of the airport directory. The private jet hub could be reached by either driving directly to its entrance on the other side of the runways or taking a shuttle near the main departures gate.

She mentally calculated the walk to the shuttle versus grabbing another cab and driving all the way around airport. "Which way do you think is faster?"

Lansing rubbed his chin. "Your call, ma'am. These people we're after, will they recognize you? If we take the shuttle, it makes a few stops, so it's slower. If we take a cab, it'll be faster—but they'll almost for sure see us coming up the walkway to the building. It's wide-open spaces out at the FBO."

"Hollings will know me—he's a big, fat British guy." She turned away, peering over the long halls of the airport. In the corner, several folding wheelchairs had been placed in a row. A redcap walked over to them and loaded them onto a motorized pull cart. "Hollings is probably still in a wheelchair from when I shot him."

"You... shot him, ma'am?

"Six times, I think." She smiled. "But in my defense, he really deserved it."

Lansing chuckled. "It's probably best if he doesn't catch a glimpse of you, then."

"Is it?" Her gaze went to the rows of shops beyond the ticketing agents. "I was thinking just the opposite. Grab one of those wheelchairs and meet me at that apparel shop."

* * * * *

Atria Lutz's private pilot walked over to her, tucking his tablet computer under his arm. "We can be wheels up in five minutes, ma'am. I'm ready when you are."

"Excellent." As the pilot walked away, Lutz turned to her wheelchair-bound travel companion and scrolled through her phone. "I'm curious about a few things, Mr. Hollings. I understand you suffered some serious injuries to your arms and legs. What happened? Second, concerning your recent forays into kidnapping and computer theft, whatever your goal was at the time—what prevented you from achieving it?" She looked up from her phone. "I want to ensure we don't make the same mistakes."

Frowning, Hollings chewed his lip and leaned on one elbow. "The Gammas were a wiley bunch, miss. Smart and athletic, free of most disease, but hard to control. One went after the top brass at

Angelus Genetics. Liked to snuff the lot of them, he did."

Lutz didn't look up, tapping the screen and swiping occasionally. "That would be The Greyhound, correct?"

"That's right." Hollings nodded. "But he met his end. Hauser double crossed him like he done some others... but it was a manky bird what did this to me." He held up his bandaged hands, then bent down and lifted his pants legs to reveal gauze wrappings on his legs. "She infiltrated our smuggling section. Put me in this bloody four-wheel geriatric wagon, she did—but that were a personal bit o' business. She's none to worry 'bout. And these wrappings is just temporary, so don't you give 'em a bother. I'll be right as rain soon enough. A few more weeks, and—"

"Yes, but what stopped you from achieving your goal?"

"Ah, my goal..." Hollings' face grew grim. "There was this other Gamma, a Yank—DeShear, a private detective, former cop from somewheres in Florida... That wanker organized a way into our Indonesian operation, then come to Ukraine and the château in France... he got them shut down, one after the next, he did. That's what stopped me. Him and that bird."

"Interesting." Lutz's gaze remained fixed on her screen. "And what do we know of his vulnerabilities?"

"Oh, that's easy, miss." Looking over both shoulders, Hollings lowered his voice and leaned forward. "DeShear wants two things more than anything else in the world. The first is Constantine—Hauser's prodigy child. She'd be six years old now, and she is top of the line, bar none. The Yank's got a soft spot for the little git. Became Constantine's legal guardian and was filing to adopt her, last I heard. He wants that child safe more than anything in the world, and he'll do anything to protect her—believe me, I've seen it. Second, he needs to know Doctor Hauser is dead and gone."

"How is that a liability to him?"

"Cor, miss! Hauser is the bane of that Yank's existence. DeShear won't be able to resist coming to you if you make him think Hauser is alive. The life of that little girl depends on it, and DeShear knows it. Way back when, DeShear and his wife lost their babies in utero, then had a child and lost her when she was three. He blames Hauser for that, and he's not wrong, neither. The genetic sequencing were messed up in the Gammas. That goes right to the Yank's core... It were the sequence in them Gammas—DeShear, The Greyhound, the lot of them—that killed their babies, and would kill 'em again if they ever tried for more. That'll put a blind rage in a man, miss. It'll break his woman, and the combination will put him locked on a death course, out for bloody revenge."

Lutz appeared unimpressed, still flipping through her phone. "I see."

"Best you take precautions, yeah?" Shifting in his seat, Hollings drummed his fingers on the armrests of his wheelchair. "The Yank's formidable."

"I'm sure he is." Sitting upright, Atria Lutz dropped her phone into her purse and stood, peering outside to her waiting jet. "But so am I."

* * * * *

The shuttle rumbled away from the arrivals terminal. Trinn sat in the handicap section, riding in an airport wheelchair. Her legs were covered by a shawl, her face mostly obscured by a pair of large sunglasses and a colorful scarf tied over her head. Beside her, in the passenger section of the bus, sat Lieutenant Lansing.

As the driver hauled the shuttle around a turn, the Lieutenant faced Trinn. "Why'd you shoot him?"

Jaden cocked her head. "Who?"

"Have you shot a lot of people? Hollings, the fat British guy we're after."

"Oh." She shrugged. "I needed information and I was in a rush. He was being stubborn."

The lieutenant put a hand over his eyes. "So, you had to shoot him *six* times?"

"I didn't *have* to. Like I said, he was being stubborn." She glanced out the window. "So was I."

The bus approached the private jet hub.

Trinn leaned toward Lansing and lowered her voice. "Okay, here's all you need to do. We scour the place for Hollings, and when we find him, you grab a seat and keep eye on him—from a distance—but don't let him out of your sight."

The lieutenant nodded. "Roger that."

Trinn squeezed the wheelchair armrests.

Then, I'll go show airport security my Bureau of Diplomatic Security credentials and ask for assistance with a fugitive apprehension. Unless there's an air marshal or two handy, it'll take a few minutes to get some armed TSA agents over from the main terminal. But if Hollings isn't actually airborne yet, the gate security will be able to quietly hold the plane in place until reinforcements arrive.

The bus pulled to a stop, the brakes hissing as the safety valves released their pent-up air pressure. Tropical crosswinds raced across the open tarmac, pulling at Trinn's disguise. The lieutenant wheeled her out through the shuttle's rear lift and up the incline into the jet hub.

As the electronic doors to the private section opened, a jolt went through her.

Hollings was no more than fifty feet away, sitting in his wheelchair and pushing himself after a woman as she walked toward the exit door. Beyond them, on the other side of a set of large, plate glass windows, stood a long, sleek jet with its engines running. A pilot sat in the cockpit, typing on a tablet computer. In front of the plane, a man in gray coveralls and a green safety vest waved his conical beacon, signaling to a refueling truck as it pulled away from the aircraft.

Heart pounding, Trinn reached over her shoulder and grabbed Lansing's hand. "That's him!" she whispered. "In the wheelchair over there. That's Hollings—and it looks like they're leaving."

"Yes, ma'am." The lieutenant's words were barely audible over the jet engine noise outside the private hub. "Where do you want me to drop you?"

The area contained a few small checkout desks and a series of exit doors. Two of the airport's fixed-base operators stood idle near the hub's lone TSA agent, who appeared unarmed.

"Take me to the FBO desk. They can—"

The tarmac swayed up and down. Trinn forced her eyes open as grey spots appeared everywhere.

"The FBO," she mumbled. "The agents. They—they can…"

Blood spurted from Trinn's nose. She waved feebly toward the airport personnel, sagging and slurring her words. The lieutenant leaped in front of her wheelchair, catching Jaden's head as she slumped sideways onto the armrest.

As Trinn's eyesight faded, Hollings rolled through the exit and into the bright Hawaiian sunlight, the polished glass door swinging shut behind him.

CHAPTER 20

Hours after Helena had retired to her bedroom, DeShear still found himself unable to sleep. He sat in bed, in the dark, read emails on his phone, watched videos... He shut his phone off and laid on his back, staring at the bedroom ceiling... His mind was a tangled jumble of thoughts and concerns, with only one way to untangle them.

The thumb drive.

Rolling off the mattress, he went into Constantine's room to grab the tablet and the thumb drive so he could watch Hauser's message again. He eased the bedroom door open, gazing at his daughter in the dim glow of her new nightlight.

It was a replica of the one she had described owning at the château—one of the few luxuries Doctor Hauser had bestowed upon any of the children there—and it had only been procured for Constantine after Hauser decided she would be the sole selection to carry on his legacy.

As much as DeShear didn't want reminders of Constantine's old life to creep into her new one, he appreciated the desire to hang onto something precious from one's past.

The base of the little pink lamp was a snow globe, shaped as a replica of an antique lantern, but made of modern plastic. It had a matching pink shade on top and a ceramic fairy inside, riding on the back of a unicorn. A tiny light at the bottom illuminated a nonstop swirl of silver glitter that danced around the lantern's watery insides, giving the scene the appearance of falling snowflakes.

And in that fine light was the angelic face of his sleeping daughter, snuggled against her pillow and surrounded by her stuffed animals.

DeShear smiled, a warm feeling washing over him.

Helena was right. There are simple moments in life that give a parent satisfaction, like watching a child sleep and knowing you've kept them safe from the ills of the world.

He savored the moment for another few seconds, then grabbed the tablet off the dresser, checked that the thumb drive was still secured in the device's side, and went back to his room.

Typing his password, the tablet's screen turned from dark blue to a bright image from Constantine's birthday party. Helena and Jaden each held one of Constantine's bun-buns as DeShear stood with an arm around each of the women. The three of them surrounded the guest of honor as she blew out the six candles on top of a thickly frosted, two-tier chocolate cake. DeShear liked that this particular image had been selected by his daughter for her screen; his prior attempts at using a timer to take the family picture had failed. This image embodied everything he wanted to change about Constantine's old life, and it served as a happy reminder of everything that had changed in his. The stack of colorful, wrapped presents and the silly party hats in the foreground; the balloons and Happy Birthday banner in the background—all set in the mansion they now lived in.

The home that was to facilitate their hard-won freedom and a fresh start.

He sighed, peering out his bedroom door, over the wood flooring in the elegant hallway and into the massive living room beyond. Outside, two sturdy thoroughbred horses grazed in their lush, wide pasture.

Then, his eye dropped to the wall-mounted security monitor by the window, sending his warmer thoughts away.

The physical home was one that anyone would love to live in, and yet it was not quite a relaxing place to stay. Not yet. Security guards lined the perimeter, carrying large guns and constantly radioing each other from their hidden positions around the compound, but their presence served as a reminder of the protection they brought as well as the unsettling fact that so much protection was necessary. There were armed bodyguards with each family member, wherever they went, as well as a small army at the residence.

I know Presidents require this kind of security, but how do their small children ever get used to it?

The answer had been told to him many times: The security guards will eventually fade into the wallpaper.

DeShear didn't buy it.

He stared at the tablet, tapping the screen and opening the settings to watch the video again.

Did I see everything? Were there any clues I could have missed?

The cartoon rabbit came onscreen, hopping through the garden as DeShear waited for the old man with the glasses to make his appearance. After a few minutes, he did.

"Mr. DeShear, I believe you know who this is…"

Hauser's gravelly voice still sent a shiver up DeShear's spine. The video seemed to play the same way it did the first time, with no noticeable changes—and no new information to be gained. Toward the end of his speech, static washed over the video image, and the words cut out briefly. It did it a second time as the message wrapped up, just as Hauser was delivering his ominous sign off.

"Dark Hour is coming, Mr. DeShear. I look forward to—"

The rest cut out. The screen turned to static.

DeShear bolted upright.

We're losing the message!

The thumb drive is erasing itself or it's fading somehow. If I ever want another shot at reviewing it or showing it to the FBI, I'd better save what's still here.

He opened the settings again, copying the file from the thumb drive to the tablet's hard drive. A little wheel came on the screen and started spinning, as a white rectangle appeared underneath it, slowly filling from left to right. As he watched, a completion display showed the file had already copied ten percent.

Copying the file might not even work. If it's erasing from the thumb drive, it might erase from the hard drive, too. Part of it's already corrupted.

The bar filled with green, and the display quickly showed seventy-six percent of the file had transferred.

DeShear tapped his toes, watching the screen.

Eight-five... Ninety-two...

The transfer stopped, an error message popping up on the tablet: Memory Full.

DeShear exhaled sharply. The file would not fit onto the tablet.

Why not? What's she got on here?

He tapped the "pictures" icon. Hundreds of videos of the bunnies appeared, along with hundreds of pictures of the little black and white fur balls, Constantine's birthday party, the horses, her stuffed animals, her family members...

DeShear shook his head.

Why does that not surprise me?

Pursing his lips, he decided against deleting some of Constantine's treasured memories. He opened the tablet's hard drive and attempted to replay the video from there.

Nothing happened.

Doctor Hauser didn't appear. Neither did the cartoon rabbit in the garden. Nothing did.

The video had disappeared from the drive. DeShear made several more attempts to get it to play; all of them failed.

Is it still even here at all?

He checked the tablet, opening the file on the thumb drive and playing it from there.

This time, the image of Hauser appeared.

"Mr. DeShear, I believe you know who this is…"

He sat back, rubbing his chin.

We need to save this file onto something with a bigger memory.

Tapping the settings, he selected the video file and emailed it from the tablet to the computer in his office. The little wheel appeared on the tablet's screen again as it struggled to send the large file, but it eventually did, disappearing and being replaced by the words "Message Sent."

Nodding, DeShear set the tablet on his nightstand and laid his head back down on his pillow.

Even if part of the message is gone, most of it's still there. That's better than nothing. We might want to get someone from the FBI or CIA to have a look at that thing.

He closed his eyes, his thoughts still racing.

Now, all I have to worry about is Jaden's trip, the safety of this house, the expenses of all this security, the intrusiveness of all these new people…

Frowning, DeShear fluffed his pillow and readjusted his position on the bed.

...a school for Constantine, Helena's medical procedure, Kitt staying safe overseas...

After a few minutes of the nonstop barrage, he gave up. Grumbling to himself, he went back to the living room and turned on the television, hoping a dull program would send him snoozing the way it had done for Constantine earlier. A science show came on, discussing a super volcano called the Yellowstone caldera, and delving into the amount of volcanic and tectonic activity it generated each year.

The announcer's high-pitched delivery was formal but rapid, with the type of cadence that was common in the old Movietone newsreels from the 1940s.

"This super volcano has erupted three previous times. Once, 2.1 million years ago, again 1.3 million years ago, and most recently 640,000 years ago..."

He idly followed along as the announcer noted that most of the world's volcanoes sit near the edges of the tectonic plates, both in and out of the ocean. After a few minutes, DeShear's eyes grew heavy.

"The caldera sits atop a hotspot of molten rock, rising toward the surface..."

Before the announcer finished the sentence, DeShear was out. Sleep came like a wave in a stormy ocean, taking him in a fury and sending him down to the depths—the rich sleep of exhaustion that refreshes a person like a long drink of cool water on a hot, muggy day.

DeShear woke after what seemed like only a moment, the security alarm blaring its harsh tone throughout the house.

He bolted upright on the couch, his pulse racing as three security guards ran towards him, their weapons in their hands.

"We have a breach! Secure the family!"

One of the guards grabbed DeShear's arm. "Sir, come with me!"

Heart pounding, DeShear yanked his arm free. "Where's Constantine? Where's Helena?"

"They're being alerted!" the guard shouted. "We need to move, now!"

A radio on the guard's hip crackled. "Subbase to C-Team. We have a dozen bogies coming over the south wall. Prepare to engage."

From the other side of the room, the security leader flipped on the wall monitor. "D-Team, we are also seeing attackers on the east side of the property." He grabbed his radio, holding it to his mouth. On the screen, dark figures with weapons stormed the fence line. "Maybe fifty—and they are armed." He faced DeShear. "Sir, we need to deploy you to the bunker."

"Not without my family!" He turned and ran toward the hallway.

Helena entered the living room, escorted by a security guard. Another guard followed them, with Constantine upright in his arms.

"What's going on?" she asked, her eyes wide.

"We're figuring that out right now." DeShear took his daughter from the guard and turned to the security chief. "Okay, let's go."

As the guards took the family to the basement, shouts from the security team came over the radios.

"B-Team, there are too many of them. You'll be overrun. Fall back!"

"We are seeing dozens of them coming over the west side wall. C-Team, you have permission to fire on sight."

The line leader opened the door of the basement's concrete bunker, stepping back to let DeShear and his family enter. The door was made of thick steel, like the ones on a bank vault, with a wheel on its inside to make an air-tight seal, and a metal lever to lock the latch pins into place. Inside, the small space was crowded with two sets of slender, stacked beds, a couch, a security monitor, and shelves of food and water to last two weeks. On the bottom shelf, face masks sat next to yellow cylinders of compressed air, one for each family member.

Their escort pulled the door shut, locking himself inside with the family. He slipped his rifle off his arm and checked the weapon's magazine. Helena sat down on the couch; DeShear placed Constantine next to her, then walked to the monitor and flipped the switch to turn it on.

Constantine's voice trembled. "What's going on?"

"You mustn't worry, dear." Helena hugged the child, rubbing her back. "Everything will be fine."

The front yard of the house appeared on the monitor screen, with an array of rectangles in the lower right corner. DeShear touched each one, rolling through the various exterior cameras surrounding the estate.

He stared at the screen, his jaw dropping.

The black and white display from the infrared cameras showed hundreds of armed invaders storming across the lawn on all sides of the house.

DeShear's breath caught in his throat.

They're everywhere.

From every angle, swarms of armed gunmen raced across the screens. Rifles, handguns, body armor, night vision goggles—the attack was a tsunami wave, crashing onto the shore and overrunning everything in its path.

But there wasn't any shooting. No breaking of glass, no crashing of walls.

DeShear frowned, watching the screen.

Why not?

Putting a hand to his chin, he narrowed his eyes.

Why is there zero gunfire in an attack of this size?

He faced their escort. "Is there any chance this could be something else?"

The young security guard shook his head, his jaw clenched as he gripped his weapon. "Sir, this is about as real as it gets. Somebody wants something in this house pretty badly." His eyes drifted toward the monitor. "I don't see us getting out of here unless we give it to them."

DeShear pursed his lips. "Listen. Why don't we hear any engagement?" He hooked his thumb at the ceiling. "There are a hundred of you guys upstairs and a thousand of them outside. Why don't we hear any shooting?"

The escort lifted his radio from his utility belt, holding it near his chin. "This is Conrad in the birds nest. Base, do we have any engagement topside?"

"Conrad, this is base. Stand by." The reply was filled with background noise.

Constantine and Helena looked at the escort, then at DeShear.

"Conrad to base," the escort said. "What is our status topside?"

The radio crackled with static. No reply came.

On the wall monitor, the views from the cameras went dark, one by one.

DeShear gritted his teeth, facing the young security guard. "Get me an answer. Now."

The escort shifted his weight from one foot to the other, his gaze going to the now-dark monitor. "Conrad to Base… Status update, please."

Breathing hard, DeShear fought the urge to rip the radio from the escort's hand. He chewed his lip, putting his hands on his hips as a bead of sweat rolled down the side of his face.

The escort raised the radio once more. "Conrad to Base." He swallowed hard. "Is there anybody up there?"

* * * * *

Jaden Trinn opened her eyes to a blurry white ceiling of square acoustical tiles. The ringing in her ears dissipated as her view came into focus. She made an attempt to sit up.

"Hey!" Lansing said. "Hold on there, tiger." He put his hands on her shoulders, easing her back onto the cool mattress.

"Where am I, Lieutenant?" Groaning, she put a hand to her forehead and looked at him. "What happened?"

The small room had sterile white walls on three sides, with a white cloth partition separating Trinn from whatever was the other side. Lansing sat in a steel chair, next to a row of metal stands with wires and tubes coming out of them. Another chair held Trinn's clothes, neatly folded and stacked.

Lifting her fingers, Jaden sighed. A thin, white cotton gown covered her torso, a pulse monitor and oxygen sensor were taped to her, and an IV needle protruded from her arm. She lowered her hand back onto the mattress. "Hospital, huh?"

"Yep." Lansing nodded. "Sorry."

Trinn propped herself up on one elbow. "I guess I should say thank you."

"That would be the polite thing, sure."

"But I won't." She scowled. "We lost our target, and my mission has an extremely short deadline. We need to get out of here."

A heavyset nurse pulled back the cloth curtain, making notes on a clipboard. "Y'all ain't goin' anywhere, honeychild.' She nodded at Lansing. "This fella says you ain't eaten lately. The charts say you got low blood sugar and an iron deficiency, a high white blood cell count and a major case of the pregger nosebleeds. You need a few days of bedrest, letting your man here take care of you."

Lansing smiled.

"He's not my man," Trinn said.

"No? My apologies." The nurse continued writing. "That's a shame."

"Ma'am…" Trinn glanced at the nurse. "When can I get released?"

Holding her clipboard with both hands, the nurse leaned it against her large belly. "How do you feel about a week from Friday? The lieutenant here says you done passed out more than once in the last few hours. Is that right?"

"I was flying at supersonic—" Trinn pursed her lips and squeezed her eyes shut. "You know what? Never mind. Unless you have a federal order to keep me here, I'm leaving." She threw the sheets of the hospital bed back and swung her legs over the side.

"Hold on, now." The nurse stepped in front of her. "He said you passed out twice in his jet, and again afterward. What about any other times in the last day or so? And don't you go fibbing on me."

"I…" Trinn shrugged. "I passed out a few times over a few days. I heard it's not unusual early in some pregnancies."

"In *some*, yes." The nurse shook her head. "But if you want that baby to see the world outside of your belly one day, you'd better slow down. Now, you need some rest, some liquids, and some good, solid food. They serve a nice fried chicken downstairs in the cafeteria. I'll let you go down there if you promise to come back."

Trinn nodded, getting to her feet. "I promise."

"Of course you do." She rolled her eyes. "And you'll be out the back door before the first crispy drumstick can hit your plate." She turned to Lansing. "What about you, hon? Can you keep your friend in line?"

"Probably not," the lieutenant said. "But I can try."

"If y'all care about this pretty woman or her baby, you'd better do more than try." She headed toward the exit. "Get her downstairs and get her fed. I'll see the both of you back here in twenty minutes."

Lansing saluted. "Yes, ma'am."

"I'm not joking." As she pulled open the ward room door, the nurse turned and pointed her pencil at Trinn's abdomen. "Lose that little baby of yours and I'm gonna come lookin' for y'all. I promise you that."

The door swung shut. Trinn turned to the lieutenant, reaching for her clothes. "I'm not kidding. I need to get back on the trail of our suspects. They have a jet. They could be anywhere by now."

"Relax, Agent. Let's grab a bite to eat." Lansing stood and turned his back to Trinn. "They have to file a flight plan, remember? Your two friends are scheduled to land at LAX in four hours. My F-15 will have us there in less than two."

* * * * *

DeShear paced back and forth in the cramped space of the bunker. He looked at the security guard. "Try raising your boss again."

Nodding the escort brought his radio to his cheek again. "Conrad to Base. Do you read me?"

Holding his breath, DeShear leaned forward, his heart pounding. Nothing but static came over the radio.

"Conrad to Base." The guard looked around at the concrete ceiling and walls. "Come back, Base."

Helena held Constantine closer. No reply came over the radio.

"I know we get a signal down here." Conrad held his communication device out in front of him, twisting the knobs back and forth. "We tested it. Maybe—"

A short burst came from the radio. Then it went silent. The LED lights by the buttons dimmed and went dark.

He looked up at DeShear. "That's never happened before."

Hank pursed his lips and put his hands on his hips. "Great timing."

"Listen." Constantine lifted her chin, peering at the door. "Someone's coming."

The security guard backed away from the door, aiming his weapon at it. "There's only one problem. We don't know if it's a friend or foe. Without the radio, I can't verify who's out there. It could be the attackers."

Someone pounded on the other side of the thick steel door.

"They're knocking!" Constantine shouted. "The rescuers have come for us."

"Quiet, little girl." The guard stepped back and forth, keeping his gun pointed at the door. "We don't know who that is yet. It might be a trick. We open the door and they blast us to bits."

Helena peered at DeShear. "What do we do?"

DeShear glanced at the door and opened his mouth to speak.

"We stay put." The guard adjusted his weapon, checking the magazine again. "We have air, food, water... We can stay down here for a few weeks if necessary."

"No, we can't," DeShear said.

"Sir, the supplies are adequate to—"

"We can't wait." He looked at Constantine, then to the guard. "In less than two and a half days, if I don't appear at a predesignated rendezvous spot... my daughter will die."

CHAPTER 21

Trinn exited the locker room at the airport, adjusting her G-suit as she headed toward the tarmac and Lansing's waiting F-15.

"Feeling better now that you've eaten?" the lieutenant asked.

"Yes." She nodded. "But I've been throwing up for no reason lately, so feeling *better* isn't exactly an indicator of anything."

Lansing chuckled. "Oh, it's an indicator of something, all right."

They reached the long, sleek aircraft, the sun settling low in the sky. Trinn moved aside so the ground crew could push the large boarding ladders into place. "Look, lieutenant... I appreciate your friends in Air Traffic Control giving us Hauser's flight plan, but what if their jet changes course?" She peered at the Air Force pilot. "I mean, what if they just decide not to go to LAX and go to Wyoming or Utah instead? Then what?"

"Their jet still has a transponder." Lansing took a clipboard from a ground crew technician, checking off several items and signing the bottom of the page. "I asked my friends in the tower to keep an eye on them and update me with any deviations in their flight path—okay?" He handed the clipboard back to the technician and put his hand on the steel railing of the portable staircase. "We military types know how to plan for contingencies, too, you know."

"Yeah." Trinn pursed her lips. "Sorry. It's been a long day."

"Well, saddle up, *Colonel*. It's about to get a little longer." He ascended the metal staircase, stopping midway and turning back to her. "Or would you like to sleep during this leg of the journey?"

"I don't know." She rested her foot on the bottom rung of the ladder that reached to the navigator seat. "What's the in-flight movie?"

"Two thrilling hours of dark skies and green instrument panels." The lieutenant threw a leg over the edge of the cockpit and lowered himself onto his seat. "What's the plan for when you catch up to these guys, anyway? Alert the FBI and take them into custody?"

Sighing, Trinn climbed the stairs. "That's one option. I wanted to confront Hollings and persuade him to help me, but I'd need to get him one-on-one to attempt that. He and I have a history."

Lansing grinned. "I remember. You shot him six times."

She returned the smile. "Hey, he tried to shoot me, too." Climbing into the rear seat of the aircraft, Trinn set her duffel bag at the side of her feet. The cold, metallic space seemed even smaller now, almost claustrophobic. "Originally, I'd hoped to persuade Hollings to bring me some specialized electronics he knows about, and to help me use it. But now that he has a partner... once they're on the mainland, it might be better to follow them and see what they're up to." She lifted her eyes, addressing the back of her pilot's head. "They don't know we're watching them, so that's an advantage. Now, as far as Hollings..." Trinn shrugged, shaking her head. "That guy has a very limited skill set. He was a smuggler and drug runner, but he was kind of high up in an illegal organization, too—which makes zero sense, because he's not very smart. He does have one unique talent, though... but I doubt that was why someone went to all the trouble of getting him out of prison. Maybe Hollings has critical information about some other aspect of Hauser's operation, and they sprung him for that."

The duo put on their helmets as the aircraft's thick dome glass lowered down over them.

Lansing's voice came over the speaker in Trinn's helmet. "So, what's Hollings' unique talent?"

Her thoughts flashed back to the London living room of a young woman—the girlfriend of Hollings' partner—and the bloody scene the obese Brit had made there. The young woman had talked to the wrong people, in Hollings' assessment, so he slit her throat, stabbed her to death, and left her on the floor of her home—after carving her tongue out and pinning it to the wall with a bread knife.

Trinn lowered her head and secured her seat straps. "If he gets the chance, Hollings is a pretty ruthless murderer."

"Is that why you shot him?"

She looked out the window. "That was part of the reason."

* * * * *

The security guard in the bunker breathed hard, staring at the thick steel door.

"Conrad, think about it," DeShear said. "We saw a lot of people with guns storming the house—but did we hear any shooting? You looked out the living room windows. Was there anyone out there?"

The young guard pursed his lips. "Sir, if I open that door and it's my guys, terrific. If it's not, we're all dead."

DeShear folded his arms across his chest. "But what if it's a hoax?"

"Then it's an elaborate one." The guard stared at the door. "And expensive. Getting a few hundred people and weapons together, scaling walls in teams and assaulting a fortified position… that's not something you and a few buddies come up with at happy hour."

"Conrad, that's my point," DeShear said. "Out of a few hundred people, at least one of them would have fired a shot. And if there *were* hundreds of them running through the pasture, my daughter's horses would've gotten startled and they'd have been running around all over the place. Even her bunnies weren't—"

"I saw them on the screen, sir. So did you."

"I did—but only on the screen." DeShear shook his head. "It's a hoax. A bogey. Some sort of CGI effect that they played on our computer monitors. Someone wanted to scare us—and it worked."

DeShear pushed his hand through his hair, staring at the young security guard.

And now we may have just shown them our response capabilities, our defense tactics, the position of our bunker, how long it takes us to move into position… If they have a drone in the air with an infrared camera, we just showed them everything.

Conrad cocked his head. "Who could do it? Who could hack the computers and stage a display like that?"

"The people I'm supposed to meet with." DeShear sighed, putting his hands on his hips. "It's another message or something. They want me to know I can't trust all the security stuff that we've installed. They want to make me compliant, I guess."

"Yeah. They're trying to wear you down." Nodding, Conrad extended a finger and jabbed at the air. "It's a psychological trick, sir. They plant a seed and then sit back while you torture yourself with your own imagination. They try to turn you into a scared rabbit, so you don't know which way is up."

Constantine bolted upright on the couch. "My bun-buns!"

"I'm sure they're fine, dear." Helena patted the child's back. "They're safe in their cage. Nobody's going to bother them."

"No!" Constantine jumped off the couch and took hold of Helena's hands. "I saw them on monitors when the guard carried me out of my room. They weren't hiding." She turned to her father. "They were eating the hay we put in the feeder earlier. They wouldn't do that if there were a lot of strangers around. They don't fancy people they don't know."

DeShear rubbed his chin, watching her. It made sense.

"And the ViewPoint representative," Constantine said. "He told me his people are supposed to use a code to access the safe room. We made up a knock pattern for me, because he said children often forget their code word or tell it to friends, but I know the knock pattern. They're supposed to use it on the door if I'm ever in here by myself." She faced the guard. "The people outside should know it."

DeShear raised his eyes to Conrad.

"Sir…" The young man chewed his lip. "I can't let you do this."

Squatting next to Constantine, DeShear put his hands on the girl's shoulders and looked her in the eye. "What's the pattern?"

Constantine smiled. "When they knock, we knock back. Then they have to do the pattern. We decided since there are four people in my family, two horses, and two bunnies, my code is four-two-two."

"Okay." DeShear looked around, reaching over and picking up an air cylinder from the bottom of the food shelves. "This oughta do the trick." Standing, he patted the heavy cylinder and looked at the door. "How many times did they knock already? I wasn't listening for that."

"You must knock twice," Constantine said. "That's to confirm we're inside."

Helena kneaded her fingers. "What if it's the attackers knocking, dear?"

"They won't likely know the pattern." She hooked a thumb toward the guard. "He didn't."

"Sir…" Conrad stepped back and forth in front of the door. "I said I can't let you open that door. We have a protocol."

DeShear waved a hand. "I won't hold you responsible."

"I have a job to do," Conrad said. "I can't let you open that door unless I get proper authorization. Me, not your daughter."

DeShear narrowed his eyes, staring at the security guard he was paying. "Conrad, my daughter says there's a code, so there's a code." He set the cylinder down. "Now, I am going to get in front of that door, and if I hear the right combination coming from the other side, I'm going to open that door and take my family out of here. Or…" His voice was as flat and even. "I guess you can shoot me."

DeShear took a step forward.

"Sir…" Conrad backed up an inch. "I'm warning you…"

"Yep." DeShear took another step. "You've warned me."

"Stop, sir." He leveled the gun at his employer.

DeShear's eyes remained fixed on the guard as he took another step. Conrad licked his lips, sliding his finger onto the trigger. "Sir…"

DeShear's hand launched forward, grabbing the end of the rifle and thrusting it toward the ceiling. Conrad exhaled sharply, his hands clenched to his weapon.

Grunting, DeShear forced the rifle to stay in place as the guard struggled to lower the barrel again. Sweat broke out on the young man's forehead, the veins in his neck sticking out. He jerked the weapon a few times but didn't break DeShear's grip.

Hank remained in place, like an iron statue, holding tight to the weapon as he stared into the guard's eyes.

"Okay." Conrad relaxed his grip. "Okay, you win." He let DeShear take the weapon and stepped aside, moving to the rear of the bunker.

Still facing the door, DeShear closed his eyes and took a deep breath. He leaned the rifle against the side of the couch and picked the air cylinder back up, hoisting it to his shoulder. "Here goes."

Heaving the air tank forward, DeShear banged it into the door three times.

The rest of the group sat in silence.

A bang came from the other side of the door, then two more.

"Okay!" He smiled, turning to Constantine. "We've established contact. Now they do their code?"

"Pattern." The child nodded. "Yes."

A series of bangs came from the other side of the exit. Constantine counted along.

"One… two… three… four!"

There was a pause.

Two more bangs followed, then another pause.

Then two more bangs.

"That's it!" Constantine jumped up and down, clapping. "That's the pattern!"

"Okay. Let's open this door." DeShear set the cylinder down. "And Conrad…" He picked up the rifle and handed it back to the security guard. "I believe this belongs to you."

Conrad swallowed hard, taking his weapon and nodding. "Okay." He looked at Helena. "Ma'am, why don't you and the girl get behind me, just in case."

As Constantine and her matron moved behind Conrad, DeShear spun the locking wheel and put his hand on the lever. "Ready?"

The guard nodded, his weapon pointed at the door. "Yes."

"Okay." Jerking the lever backwards, DeShear put his other hand to the steel and pushed the heavy door, opening it an inch. He leaned to the door's edge, pressing his nose to the gap.

"Mr. DeShear!" The ViewPoint rep's voice came from the other side of the door. "Sir, it's good to see you."

With a sigh of relief, DeShear swung the door outward, revealing the rep and a handful of his smiling teammates, standing in the basement with their weapons lowered.

"It's good to see all of you, too," DeShear said.

Cupping a hand to his mouth, the rep called out toward the staircase. "Code green. The family is secure."

* * * * *

As Helena settled Constantine on the living room couch with a glass of water, DeShear poured coffee for the ViewPoint Security team. Techs pored over the computers, downloading the drives to see what had happened, but everyone already knew. It had been a computer-generated hoax.

The rep paced back and forth in the living room. "I don't know how they breeched the system. It's extremely secure. We have encryption for outbound interactions and a blocking grid to block external attempts at penetration…"

DeShear took him a cup of coffee. "I think they got someone to compromise the system from inside."

The rep shook his head. "Sir, my people are the best. Most of them are former Secret Service. They've all received the highest security clearances…"

"I don't think it was one of your people."

The rep stopped pacing, looking up at DeShear.

"I think it was me." Frowning, DeShear pointed to the entrance of his office. "I wanted to make a copy of the thumb drive message. Constantine's tablet memory was full, so I emailed the message to my computer. That caused the breach."

He handed the ViewPoint rep the cup of coffee.

"Tell your people to start there, with my computer and the email I sent from the tablet. There'll be some sort of trojan horse present, I'm sure of it."

The rep's mouth hung open. "Sir, how..."

"It was a mistake—a big one—and I made it. But it was a message, too." Sighing, DeShear stuck his hands in his pockets, staring at the security monitor. "We used a trojan horse to shut Hauser's operation down. His people just returned the favor."

The rep lowered his voice. "It's a little worse than that. We've let them inside the house, so to speak. They've had access to the computers for a few hours now, so they could have gained access and control over any of the devices that your system communicates with. We have to do a full scan of the system."

"That's fine, go ahead," DeShear said. "But you know your team is fired, right?"

"Excuse me, sir?"

"I made a mistake and I take responsibility." He looked the rep in the eye. "Now, ViewPoint needs to take responsibility for the mistakes you and your people made. I'll let Mr. Conrad tell you about our little incident in the bunker, but that's only part of my concern. He takes orders from you, and so do the others. Human eyes and a little common sense could have averted all of this tonight. That's on you." DeShear pointed to a table full of ViewPoint computers. "Your tech team can still monitor the house surveillance cameras from an offsite location, and you can scrub our phones and devices, but your people need to go. Now. Until further notice, we're through."

"Sir..."

DeShear waved a hand. "I'll hire people if I need them. You have five minutes to vacate the premises."

"Yes, sir." The rep nodded. "I'm very sorry about all this."

"I am, too," DeShear said. "But this is how things need to be for a while. I'll contact you if I want to reinstate your on-site personnel."

After seeing how Ari's terminal sequence was able to shut down Hauser's entire computer network, DeShear understood what the ViewPoint rep's words about their devices could mean.

He wasn't the only one, either.

"Unplug it," Constantine said, her face grim. "Unplug your computer."

As the ViewPoint rep used his radio to usher his people out of the house, DeShear sat down on the couch by his daughter. "I will, sweetie. But by now, my computer could've already made contact with other devices that are nearby and communicate with it, like my phone. From there, it could hack into Doctor Kitt's phone, or Miss Jaden's phone..."

"We'll contact them and let them know," the rep said. "But right now, it's best if no members of the household use any of their devices until we get them all re-secured."

* * * * *

Trinn had managed not to vomit or pass out as the F-15 took off and soared over the dark waters of the Pacific Ocean. The aircraft bounced and shimmied on this leg of the flight, much more so than on their first trip.

Or maybe I was too preoccupied with passing out and puking to pay attention.

Lieutenant Lansing chatted briefly with the LA tower, then addressed Jaden. "Maybe Hollings' accomplice wants him for the same reason as you—to use the specialized electronics."

"That's as good a guess as any right now." She reached into her duffel bag and took out a small notepad and pencil.

"So, we watch them from a distance," Lansing said, "let them get the equipment, and then we swoop in and grab it—since they have no idea we're even here."

Trinn smiled. "Not bad, fly-boy. I'll make a secret agent out of you yet." She opened the pad to a new page and wrote DeShear a note the size of a postage stamp:

Change of plans.

Proceed without me.

She took out her phone, snapped a picture of the tiny scrap of paper, and sent the image by text to DeShear. She then deleted the original image and the backup copy, tore the tiny note off the pad, balled it up, stuck it in her mouth—and swallowed it.

"We could have burned that when we landed," Lansing said.

Trinn peered out the window into the darkness. "Too late now."

"Why not just send a regular text? Why send a picture?"

"A worded text message can be intercepted too easily." She put her phone back in her duffel bag, the dim glow of the instrument panel lighting her tiny section of the cockpit. "An image is bigger, but it's much harder to grab and decipher. When we eventually get a signal, the message will send. It's not a foolproof system, but unless someone pretty sophisticated has hacked into Hank's phone or computer recently, he'll be the only one to see that message."

CHAPTER 22

The young woman's mother called out to her from the back door of the little house. "Honey? Can you come here for a minute?"

Jumping off the old tire swing where she had been frolicking with her fiancé, the heavyset second-year medical student ran across her parents' small backyard. "What is it?"

Her mother let her inside. There, her father sat in the tiny living room, a brown envelope in his hand and his face grim.

"We... have some bad news." Her mother's gaze moved to their worn carpet. "The gynecologist at the hospital called. It's worse than we thought."

The young woman's handsome fiancé came to her side, taking her hand.

"The doctors said it wasn't cancer." Her mother forced a weak smile. "That's good news. But... they said your reproductive system is very unusual. The condition of your uterus and your ovaries… the doctors said it was like they were looking at the reproductive tract of an eighty-year-old woman." Her mother looked up, tears welling in her eyes. "They said you'll never be able to have children, honey."

The chubby young woman put her hand to her lip. She had put herself through college and most of med school by working at a daycare, with dreams of graduating and becoming a pediatrician. The next step was to marry her charming, fellow med student fiancé, and fill a house with children.

Now, that dream was over.

"I'm so sorry, honey. You could always adopt, like your father and I did. You've been an absolute joy for us."

Her daughter nodded, her voice a whisper. "Of course. Don't give it another thought, Mom."

A year later, her fiancé had moved on—either as a result of the long hours of med school, the couples' different interests and frequent arguing, or her growing resentment towards her life situation.

She threw herself into her studies with a vengeance, earning straight A's and becoming class valedictorian. As graduation day neared, she was recruited by numerous prestigious hospitals and esteemed research facilities, but she applied to one place for her medical internship—and one place only.

Angelus Genetics.

But on that dark day, in her parents' tiny living room, the portly student hadn't yet even heard of the secretive medical research facility. Not until her father looked up at her from the couch and handed her the envelope.

"This came for you, too. Private messenger."

She took the thin brown package and opened it in her room, alone. Inside, there was no typed letter, no handwritten note, just a thumb drive. When she slipped it into her computer, a cartoon rabbit appeared, eating vegetables in a garden.

Then, the face of an old man came on the screen, with a shock of white hair and dark, wide-framed classes.

"Atria Lutz, this message is being transmitted at an audio range that only you can hear…"

CHAPTER 23

The Gulfstream jet rocked gently back and forth, its passengers all slumbering in the hum of the aircraft's engines.

All but one.

The gaunt Atria Lutz typed on her computer, analyzing spreadsheets and tabulating test results, replying to emails as fast as they came in, and scanning websites for updates on her latest deliveries. Aside from the lone recessed lightbulb shining over her seat, the rest of the jet cabin was relatively dark. The wine rack at the front of the cabin rattled with the occasional jiggle of turbulence, as did the shelves of distilled spirits above it.

Hollings snored quietly, sprawled across his seat, his arms dangling over the sides and his feet stretched out wide over the Gulfstream's thick carpet. Six empty mini bottles of rum rested on the table next to him. Adjacent to the rotund Brit, Doctor Symm slumbered sideways in his chair, his head perched at an angle on the back of the seat, using his folded arm as a pillow, and his legs tucked up close, with his laptop under one thigh and his phone under the other.

Lutz's manicured fingertips raced across her keyboard, a nonstop barrage of clicking and clacking, as lab report after lab report scrolled by under her steadfast eye.

Symm's leg jerked, as if in a spasm. He gasped, lifting his head and peering at Lutz, his half-open eyes red and bloodshot. "Still working?" He groaned, stretching his arms. "What time is it? Must be—"

"It's late," Atria said, not taking her eyes from her work. "I think you got a text."

"Hmm?" He blinked a few times.

Lutz pointed at his seat cushion.

Raising his leg, Symm reached under his thigh for his phone. As he glanced at the screen, the phone buzzed. "Oh. So I do."

He stared at the phone for a moment, then put it to his ear. Lutz finished her analysis of one report and started the next one.

"It's Cassidy," Symm said. "She says the insertion worked."

Atria typed, her eyes darting over the facts and figures. Symm stared at her, holding his phone next to his head.

"What?" Lutz asked. "Did you say something?"

Symm wiggled his phone. "That was Cassidy—she's one of your computer people or something, right? She wanted you to know the insertion was successful."

Nodding, the doctor returned to her work. "Cassidy Harper is a special assistant. Very smart. Text her back and tell her I want an update with global tracking on all the ancillary devices as soon as possible."

Taking a deep breath, Symm pushed himself upright in his seat. "Why didn't she call you herself? I'm not your receptionist."

Lutz glared at him. "You are if I say you are. Is that understood?"

"Atria…" A thin smile stretched across Symm's lips. "My investment of a billion dollars— or, *potential* investment, I should say—makes me feel as though you should treat me with a little more respect."

Lutz sat back in her chair, folding her hands in her lap and crossing her long, thin legs. "Doctor— and I use that term loosely—you should know something. If I were to receive a confirmation from my Chinese investors right now, ten seconds later you and your lackluster financial commitment would be plummeting into the Pacific Ocean from fifty thousand feet." She gazed at him, her eyes unmoving. "People make mistakes. Don't make an unnecessary one. You should be calling your partners and locking the deal down just to be sure you don't accidentally go flying out the emergency hatch. In a few weeks, it's entirely possible I'll no longer need your money *or* that of the Chinese."

Trembling, Symm nodded. He lifted his phone and dialed. As the number rang, he looked at

Lutz. "What do you want out of all this, Atria? I know it's not money. You don't seem to have a lust for power. What is it?"

She turned back to her laptop, holding her hands over the keyboard but not typing. "It's a new era we're embarking on," she whispered. She got up from her seat, walking to the rear of the plane and her private suite there, entering her bathroom and closing the door behind her.

* * * * *

Wearing a lightweight windbreaker and a navy blue skirt, Cassidy Harper stood in the Los Angeles airport waiting for the shuttle to the private jet terminal. A short but bumpy ride put her at the large, rectangular FBO building. Three empty stretch limousines—two black, one white—were parked nearby, apparently awaiting Hollywood producers or TV stars, or anyone else who felt the need to bolster their status with such opulent ornaments.

Stepping off the empty shuttle and into the FBO, Cassidy surveyed the grand plaza. The room itself was wide and tall, but without the elegant décor she'd seen at the FBO of her departure site. Two female boarding agents sat behind a white desk, chatting with a male TIA officer. The rest of the terminal appeared to be empty.

Not very busy for a private jet terminal in Tinseltown.

She reached into her pocket and activated the electronic device hidden there.

A baggage tram rolled up to the glass double doors at the side of the building. Cassidy removed her sunglasses and walked toward the glass. The luggage car being pulled behind the tram was practically empty; only one large rectangular container rested on its wide, metal bed. A brown-haired man wearing blue coveralls and a Gatorade-yellow safety vest stepped out of the vehicle, pulling the protective earmuffs from his head. As he ran a hand through his thick, dark locks, he grabbed a small cardboard box from the seat of the tram cab and headed toward the side entrance of the FBO.

The glass doors parted and he stepped inside, looking at the young woman in the windbreaker. "You're Cassidy Harper?"

"That's correct." Cassidy nodded, noting the dark mole on his left cheek. "Do you have something for me?"

"Two packages, ma'am." He held up the cardboard box. "You'll have to sign for them."

"Excuse me." One of the airport employees raced toward them. "I'm sorry, ma'am. We have to clear all packages through security. Even if they come over from the main terminal, we still have to scan them here."

"Oh, it's nothing to worry about." Cassidy flipped the top of the box open. "He just brought me this." Removing a handgun from the box, Cassidy shot the attendant in the face.

The woman careened backwards into a vacant counter.

Dropping to one knee, Cassidy used her free hand to steady her aim as she swung her arm toward the TIA agent and fired three more times. She hit the agent in the chest twice; the third shot went over the agent's shoulder and lodged in the wall on the far side of the lobby.

As her first victim slid to the ground, the sole remaining attendant ducked behind the desk. Cassidy walked over, lifting the gun to the woman's head and pulling the trigger.

The tansuit took another gun from the box and tossed the empty container into the trash.

"See?" Cassidy walked back, looming over the first bloody corpse. "Nothing to worry about—for us. For you…" She shrugged. "Different story."

"Nice work." The tansuit nodded, glancing around the room. "Quick and efficient."

"I try." She took the electronic device from her pocket and set it in the counter, glancing at the timer display screen. "Now, we have about ninety more seconds to get changed before security at the main terminal sends a SWAT team over here. Get moving."

The tansuit reached into a trash basket next to the counter and removed the liner, wrapping it around the deceased attendant's head. Cassidy pulled off her windbreaker and undid the buttons of the dead woman's uniform jacket, sliding it over the corpse's shoulders.

A moment later, the tansuit was dressed as the TIA agent and Cassidy was dressed as an attendant. They propped up the cleanest corpse in a chair, assessing the viewing lines of the cameras and standing in front of them to block the view. The employee restroom received the other two bodies.

"And that's that." Cassidy reached for her device and slipped it into her pocket, flipping the switch as she did. She withdrew a second piece of electronics equipment and scanned the dead woman's ID badge with it, displaying her information on a tiny screen. Cassidy reviewed the name, address, social security number, phone number—and most importantly, the airport employee identifiers. "Now, let's wait for that F-15 to land, shall we?"

The phone on the counter rang. As the tansuit rested his hand on the butt of his revolver, Cassidy picked up the receiver and held it to her ear. "Yes, we're good. The light's flickered and our computers went out for a second, but they're back now." She nodded at the closest camera, waving and smiling. "My code is bluebird two-two-one, employee number seven five three two zero eight." She smiled brighter. "Thank you. We're just killing time until our next VIP arrives."

Hanging up the phone, Cassidy shook her head. "The beauty of people is that they always make mistakes." She glanced toward the restroom door. "That TIA agent didn't even have a hand on his weapon."

The tansuit folded his arms across his chest. "So, this is what a special assistant does?"

"Sometimes," Cassidy said.

"You had good moves. Fast." He walked to the edge of the counter and nudged the trash basket a few inches, covering the blood stain on the carpet. "Where'd you learn to do all that?"

"I studied computer science at Stanford." Cassidy took her phone out, checking the air traffic control screens for Lansing's inbound fighter jet.

"But I learned the good stuff somewhere else. What about you? What hallowed halls of higher education did you grace?"

The tansuit hooked his thumbs into the TIA utility belt. "None. I was what you might call homeschooled—by my sister."

* * * * *

In the restroom of her suite on the jet, Doctor Lutz opened the mirrored cabinet door and took out the slim, black leather case. She set it on the counter and removed the contents—the short glass tube with the rounded bowl at the end, and a butane lighter.

And, of course, a vial of crystalline comfort.

Dropping the semi-white granules into the pipe, the gaunt doctor flicked the lighter, holding it under the bulb until the rocks melted and the smoke could be sucked deep into her lungs. A few puffs later, the medicine was burning her insides, and a moment after that, the size-zero doctor was superwoman. She didn't need food, she didn't need sleep… she didn't need anything.

Her pulse raced as she looked in the mirror, growling at her thin reflection and inhaling huge breaths of fresh air as the feeling of invincibility surged through her.

Squeezing her eyes shut, Lutz pounded the countertop. "Hoo! Hoo! Yeahhh…"

It was a feeling of super intense pleasure, mixed with a surge of ego booster and energy, unlike anything she felt anywhere else. It was a high among highs, an ecstasy among ecstasies, and one that filled her with a powerful, lingering release that was a thousand times more potent than her most satisfying intimate moment as a human being.

Gasping, she packed away the kit and straightened her blouse. As her gaunt reflection turned back to the suite on the other side of the looking glass, Atria Lutz made fists of her bony hands, balling and unballing them almost uncontrollably.

"It's a new era we're embarking on, baby." She marched toward the main cabin and the lackeys waiting for her there, her head held high. "A whole new, dark era."

* * * * *

Lansing's F-15 banked steeply to the left as he prepared to make his final approach to the Los Angeles airport.

From the rear seat, Trinn peered out at the dots of lights to the east, trying to figure out what southern California or northern Mexico cities they were passing over. "I have to admit, it's pretty cool that they just let you land this thing wherever you want. I thought I'd be hopping all over the place to military bases."

The lieutenant chuckled over the radio. "You're kidding, right?"

"No…" She looked at him. "What?"

"We had to get a ton of special permissions to let this aircraft serve as your personal transport, Agent Trinn. Things like this just aren't done—and a lot of the top Air Force brass aren't too happy about a fighter jet being used like a taxi."

Trinn chewed her lip. "Yeah, I can see that. You've been very nice about it, though, Lieutenant."

"Yes, ma'am. Thank you." Lansing nodded. "I wasn't happy, either, at first—but I got a phone call that smoothed things over."

"One of your top brass saw the light and convinced you?"

"You could say that—if you consider the Commander In Chief as top brass."

"Geez." She winced. "Brantley called you?"

"He did. He laid it out pretty straight. You know how he talks in that Midwest speech, with a little country twang? He goes, Lieutenant Lansing, before I was President, I was a Senator. And before that, a lowly congressman."

Trinn smiled at the impersonation of the President.

"My first year on the Hill," Lansing continued in his Brantley twang, "I voted for a bill to fund Alzheimer's research and some other things through an obscure company out in Arizona named Onyx Research. They were subsequently acquired by Doctor Marcus Hauser and Angelus Genetics. So, I've always felt some responsibility for the problems that were created later as a result of that initial funding. That's why I give Jaden Trinn so much leeway, and that's why I'd like you to help her now."

Trinn sat back in her chair, her mouth hanging open.

Brantley did that for me?

"Must be nice to have friends in high places," the lieutenant said.

She nodded. "Brantley and I met before he was in high places. I… helped him out once."

Air traffic control came over the radio. Lansing replied to them and adjusted his heading. "I'm not allowed to ask why you had to do all this, Agent Trinn. Or why some lawyer in Honolulu couldn't have arranged for Hollings' release. So, I won't ask. But it seems like with a Presidential pardon, my kid brother could have gotten Hollings out of prison. And how were you supposed to get Hollings back with you? These F-15s don't fit more than two people."

Sighing, Trinn adjusted her position in the seat. "The plan was to get Hollings and hop a commercial flight to wherever the special equipment was. We'd hire an aircraft leasing service and take a jet if we needed one. But none of that mattered if I couldn't convince Hollings to work with me."

"But why you?" Lansing asked. "Why not use a local lawyer or an agent from the Honolulu FBI?"

Trinn shook her head. "Hollings wouldn't have done that. He'd have stayed inside and waited for his people to get him out—which is what happened. The only chance I had was if I met with him in person. Me, nobody else. That's still my only chance." In front of her, the dashboard dials and screens glowed green in the blackness of the cockpit. The numbers on the altimeter steadily dropped as their aircraft approached the runway. "Sitting down face-to-face with me would give Hollings a chance at the thing he wants more than anything else in the world."

"Which is?"

Jaden stared at her instrument panel. "The chance to kill me."

CHAPTER 24

"Helena?" DeShear tapped on the old woman's half-open door, nudging it open and peering inside.

Helena stood in the corner of the dark room, her expressionless face turned toward the window. She was in her "nightclothes," as she referred to them—a light nightshirt-gown item of clothing that defied style and age. Outside, dawn crested over the distant hills beyond the pasture as the horses walked slowly into view. The morning light illuminating the expensive security cameras seemed to fill every nook and cranny of the property.

"Helena?" DeShear said again.

She turned to him, her eyes open but dimmed in a hazy fog.

DeShear had never gotten used to Standalone—the blank face and dull eyes, the seemingly mindless trance—but he knew it served Helena well. It was one of many things she did that allowed her to survive her time under Hauser's control. Helena's nighttime Standalone sessions refreshed her and revived her like sleep would for anyone else, but she was the only person DeShear knew who never slept.

He hadn't gotten used to Standalone, but he accepted it.

Blinking a few times, the warmth returned to the old woman's wrinkled face. "Why, good morning, Hamilton." Helena smiled. "Quite a night we had."

DeShear nodded, inhaling deeply as he entered the quiet room.

"You're still worried." She went to her bed and sat down, clasping her hands in her lap. "Perhaps that's wise at this point."

"Can you..." He searched the ceiling, looking for the words. "Can you *see* anything on this trip I'm supposed to make?" He glanced at his phone. The picture from Trinn had arrived, with its blunt message. *Change of plans. Proceed without me.* He put the phone in his pocket and looked at the old woman. "Any pieces of information coming to you from the... the *fifth dimension* about what I'm headed into, or what we can do to save Constantine?"

"Like car crashes that haven't happened, or a fatal mishap at an upcoming dental visit?" Helena looked down. "I'm frightfully sorry, but I'm afraid it's never worked that way. I don't know when things will come to me, or why. I certainly missed seeing the worst tragedies in my life before they happened." She shook her head, allowing just a whisper of words to escape her lips. "What... what they did to all the other children that day at the château, herding them into the Rituals room and then…"

DeShear crouched down in front of her. "When the kidnappers took Constantine, you knew. You had a feeling that you couldn't shake. So did she, we just didn't piece it together. And you knew about those two women before they died—the one in car crash and the other one at the dentist. So…"

"Yes," she said. "I'm afraid I don't know how it works. I feel frightfully useless to you."

He stood, going to the window. "What if we had the machinery Hollings used when he captured you and Kitt? The head caps from Rituals—could that help you?"

"Yes, dear. I believe that would, but it's not really me doing it as much as… the bonnets amplify everything. That's what must be remembered. When Mr. Hollings made me wear that, any thought I had, it went onto the TV screen straight away." She shuddered. "Oh, the machine is very dangerous that way. He wanted to see things I didn't want to tell, but it was nearly impossible *not* to think of the answer when he asked a question. I found myself trying to envision images of anything but what he was asking about and still my mind would flash on it."

DeShear sighed, running his hands through his hair.

Kitt said when she interacted with Helena, it was like the old girl was reading her mind. Now she can't see a thing.

"When things are urgent," Helena whispered, "they may appear to us—but we must be open to seeing them."

DeShear let her words go past him as he viewed the pasture, his mind racing. Between the silhouette of the trees, the horizon turned a golden yellow. The top edge of the sun peeked over the ridge, causing DeShear to narrow his eyes in the growing brightness of the morning light.

What's the smart move here? I'm walking into a trap, completely unarmed, but I should be safe because they need me alive for something. But if I'm wrong about that, then I'm dead—and Constantine is at risk again.

If I don't go, Constantine dies.

So, I'm going. But there has to be a way to get more information.

There has to be.

"You were right to trust her in the bunker," Helena said. "Just as she was right to trust you in the château. You two are on the same wavelength."

DeShear turned around. "Trust who? Constantine?"

"Yes. It's nice to see two people so in sync with each other. She watches you, you know."

"Does she?" He shook his head. "What's she hoping to see?"

"Her father. How a man behaves. How he should act, how he treats the woman he's chosen to spend his life with. All girls study their fathers. You're very different from the men who were in her life before. Better. You are honest and without pretense. And you are certainly more loving than any man in her prior life."

He folded his arms and leaned against the window frame, a warmth filling his insides. "Geez, that kid. She's something else. When she was swimming in those big waves, trying to escape her kidnappers, half-drowned and barely able to lift her arms to take another stroke…" He looked at Helena. "But she wouldn't give up. I knew we were about to rescue her, but I don't think she knew, and she just kept pushing. It was… impressive. I've never been more scared or more proud."

"Scared?" Helena said. "I don't think fear comes easily to you. We read the stories about you in the news."

DeShear chuckled. "Don't believe everything you read. I get scared just like anybody else."

"Were you scared when you ran into that library when it was on fire?"

The question surprised him.

It wasn't a secret, and he hadn't forgotten, but his days as a police officer in Tampa now seemed like they had happened a lifetime ago. They were hazy images in a distant past that could have been lived by someone else, unable to be properly seen in the fog of passing time. And so much had happened since then.

He looked around the luxurious bedroom of the Virginia estate.

A few months ago, my apartment burned and I was technically homeless…

That was before he ever met Hauser or Trinn, Lanaya or Hollings… so many others.

It was a life where he couldn't have imagined a child like Constantine—wouldn't let himself imagine one—and now she was such an integral part of his life, he couldn't imagine life without her. He could barely remember what things were like before she came along. There had been a painful emptiness inside of him that he pushed down, like a locked closet in the back of a dark basement, behind piles of dusty boxes and cobwebs. A hollowness that had suddenly been filled.

He glanced at Helena, her words echoing in his ears.

"Were you scared when you ran into that library when it was on fire?"

"When I ran into the library fire, was I scared? I don't know." He put his hands on his hips and paced back and forth. "I'll tell ya, there were people trapped inside, I knew that. Kids, adults… and I knew I could help them. I *knew* it. That's all that crossed my mind, really. Half a second later, I was running in there."

"You went with your instincts," Helena said. "Your gut feeling, as they say."

"I guess so." DeShear nodded, the images coming back to him as if he were watching them on an invisible TV screen. "At first, before I went inside, I could see the flames starting to poke through the roof. Then I heard the cries of the children. They were maybe three or four years old, trapped in a room, and the fire blocking the exit… I couldn't see them, but… I knew I couldn't live with myself if I didn't do something. Just letting a bunch of kids die when I was fifty feet away? No. I couldn't do that."

"This was after you and your wife lost your daughter," Helena said.

"Yeah." He stared at the far wall of the room. "Yeah, it was a while after that."

He drew a deep breath, gazing at the wall as if he were seeing the scene there.

"I remember looking at the ceiling when I was inside. It was burning, but it was rows and rows of these smaller flames, all rounded on the bottom and flickering in orange, pushing upwards like they were a million fingers on a hand that was trying to claw its way to the outside. Then, when I looked again, the ceiling was just a black cloud. It changed, just like that, in an instant. The flames were getting hot—they dried my eyes out. I'd blink, and nothing would happen, like back when…"

He lowered his voice.

"You know why I think I wasn't scared? It's weird, it just occurred to me… When I was a kid, we'd go to the park at night in late January, and all the parents in the neighborhood would drag their dried-up Christmas trees down there and toss them onto a bonfire, one at a time. Each time somebody threw a dry tree on, it would sit for a second and then whoosh, the flames shot up, like forty feet in the air. It was crazy. All those dry pine needles and limbs crackle when they burn, but they burned so fast, it was like a roar—like a rush of applause at a concert when a favorite song ends and the crowd all goes wild at once. It'd be really dark everywhere—except for the fire—but when they threw a tree on, and those flames shot up, it was bright as daylight. A huge wave of hot wind would come off of it, like someone had just opened an oven door in your face. You could be fifty feet away and you'd still have to back up— or else you'd feel like your eyebrows were going to melt off. And that's what it was like when I was in that library. Dark, but with the glow of the flames, and all that oven heat. It was like being at that park again when we were burning the Christmas trees. It felt very similar. And I guess because I'd known that feeling before, I wasn't afraid of it in the library."

He turned back to Helena.

"You know, at some point, I wasn't breathing oxygen anymore. It was just a mixture of poisonous gases that were gonna close my eyes and lay me on the floor. As I carried the last kid out—this blond boy in a red jacket—a firemen ran up. They were giving me oxygen, but they wiped my face off first—and I was covered in soot. I looked like the bottom of a fireplace."

Helena's voice was calm. "Sounds very exciting."

"But it wasn't," DeShear said. "Not to me. I saw the people and I had to get them out. That's it. Like... like there was a job to be done, so I did it." He turned to her and shook his head. "No. Not a job. An... obligation. Looking at another person and saying, you're in trouble and I can help you, so I will. In my heart, I knew I'd be okay."

He walked back to the window and looked outside. "The firemen told me that feeling—the not being afraid, or not caring—that it was the carbon monoxide talking, but I don't know. I just... I was not going to stand there and watch children die. I just... wasn't."

He stared at the ground.

"And what do your instincts tell you now?" Helena said.

DeShear exhaled another long, slow breath, raising his eyes to meet hers. "You know I have to go meet Hauser. I can't get past the feeling that I *have* to go, to face this thing head-on. Trying to build a fortress out of this house, that's not the answer."

He returned his gaze to the window, thinking about the teams of security professionals running around outside the night before, one person directing all the others, but all of them wrong.

They were preparing for a battle where a General in here directs this army, and out there somewhere another General directs a different army. Whichever General planned best, their side would win.

He didn't like the comparisons—war, battles, Generals—but it fit.

Like it or not, my family is in a battle.

But while the Generals plan to fight on the big battlefield, what if there was a small guerilla force on the side? Someone who knows the other General, maybe better than that General knows himself?

A jolt went through him.

Someone like Helena.

His heart racing, DeShear turned to the old woman. "You and Constantine know Hauser better than anyone else. You need to come with me."

Helena kneaded her fingers. "Won't that be dangerous?"

"It won't be any more dangerous than staying here," DeShear said. "Hauser's people faked an army coming over the wall. Next time, they'll send an actual army and fake it *not* coming over the wall.

She's probably going to have to be there eventually, to get that thing taken out of her head or to have the radio beam refortify it. But having the two of you with me, before my planned arrival date, could make all the difference in figuring out what's going on—and that could be the difference in winning and losing this war."

* * * * *

After DeShear left her room, Helena remained on the bed, her hands in her lap. Slowly, her closet door opened.

Constantine peeked her blonde head out, whispering, "Has he gone?"

"He has, dear." Helena patted her mattress. "Come and sit by me."

Dressed in soft, cotton pajamas with bunnies on them, Constantine climbed onto the bed. "I feel just awful spying on father like that. I don't fancy fibbing—you always told me, deception is a lie."

"It wasn't a complete lie," Helena said. "I did tell him you were watching him all the time."

Nodding, Constantine laid her head against her mistress' shoulder. "I'm glad we convinced Hamilton to take us with him, but I can't see anything about this place we're headed. It's like it's being hidden somehow. Are you quite sure we should go?"

"I fear we must, child. It's the only way—and you must be brave for your father, so he isn't distracted."

"Yes." The little blonde head bobbed again. "You're right, of course. And I *do* feel confident about Hamilton. I'm just a bit scared about us all going, that's all."

Sighing, the old woman put her arm around the child. "Perhaps there's a way to stay *and* to go."

CHAPTER 25

The F-15 taxied to a stop near the Los
Angeles airport FBO, the overhead lights from its
parking lot illuminating the predawn terminal. The
glass dome over the jet's occupants arced upward as
a man and a woman wearing ground crew coveralls
pushed two steel staircases toward the aircraft.

"How's the queasiness?" Lansing asked.

"Better." Trinn climbed out of her seat straps.
A member of the ground crew scampered up the
ladder and took her helmet. Shaking her hair out,
Trinn glanced at her pilot. "I guess I'm getting used
to your flying."

"It helps to not fly on an empty stomach."
Lansing unstrapped himself and handed his helmet to
the other airman. "Now, just be sure to drink a lot of
water and walk around some." He pushed himself up
from his seat, putting his hands on his lower back and
twisting from side to side. "When we get inside, I'll

check with my friends and get another update on your buddy's ETA."

Trinn descended the steel staircase, holding onto one of the thin rails to help keep her balance against the bouncy steps. On the tarmac, she turned to wait for Lansing.

The strapping young pilot stood at the top of his staircase, a hand on each rail. Smiling, he threw his feet upwards and slid down the long staircase without touching a step. He landed with a bounce at the bottom, grinning wider as he trotted over to his waiting passenger. They headed toward the FBO terminal, the two ground crew technicians walking on either side of them.

Even at this early hour, the LA wind was drier and warmer than that of the Honolulu airport. A strong breeze swept across the wide, flat tarmac and lifted Trinn's hair, depositing it into her eyes and mouth. Scowling, she pushed it away.

"That's probably why our female pilots keep their hair short." Lansing chuckled. "Something to consider for your next flight."

Trinn opened her mouth to speak, but stopped herself. She glanced at the female technician by her side. The young woman's hair was also flying around her head.

Then why wouldn't she wear a ponytail or...

The woman's coveralls were ill-fitting, too, like they were for someone a few sizes bigger than their current occupant.

Or they aren't hers at all. Because she's not the ground crew.

Trinn's eye went to the side of the woman's bulky coveralls. In the dim light, the wind pulled on the material, puffing it out at the zippered chest—and exposing a gun holster strap under the woman's arm.

A knot gripped Trinn's insides. She faced straight ahead as the group neared the FBO.

She's wearing a shoulder holster. That means the other crewman is probably armed, too.

Which means if we get inside that building, Lansing and I are in big trouble—or dead.

As the roof lights of the FBO fell over them, Trinn nudged Lansing with her elbow. When he looked at her, Trinn nodded toward the woman's rib cage and mouthed the word "gun."

The lieutenant peeked at the young female crew member. He immediately returned his eyes forward, then slowly peered at Trinn and nodded.

Jaden's pulse throbbed in her ears.

Okay, he gets it. Now what?

Follow my lead, fly boy.

As the glass double doors of the FBO opened, Trinn entered with Lansing, clearing her throat. "Uh, what… what *time* can we get airborne again, Lieutenant?"

"Right about…" Lansing held his left hand up to check a watch that wasn't there. The two ground crew techs stepped inside the doors.

"Now!" Lansing shouted.

The lieutenant turned and grabbed the arm of the male technician, pulling him forward and launching him over a nearby desk. As the female tech stepped toward them, Trinn grabbed the imposter's left arm to keep it from going into the coveralls for the gun, yanking it backwards over the woman's shoulder. Lansing leaped over the desk and onto the man. The two grappled on the floor as Trinn reached around and ripped open the front of the woman's oversized coveralls, jerking out the weapon holstered inside. She swung her leg in front of the woman and forced her forward, sending her face-first to the ground. Dropping a knee into the fallen woman's spine, Trinn grabbed the imposter's hands and held them behind her back.

Gasping, Trinn gritted her teeth and pressed the tip of the gun to the woman's cheek. "Don't move."

The young imposter lifted her head from the carpet. Blood covered her teeth. She spit, grinning up at her captor. "Do you think you've accomplished something just now?" She glanced toward the other side of the desk.

Heart pounding, Trinn followed her gaze.

Lansing and the male crew tech were standing, facing each other and locked hand to hand. The lieutenant's face was red, veins showing on his neck and forehead.

The fake technician held each of Lansing's fists in his own, absorbing every push and pull from the lieutenant—but the stranger's face was calm, as if he were considering what kind of coffee he might want to order for breakfast.

Lansing grunted, sweat forming on his brow. He swung a leg into the man's ribs, another into his knee—it did nothing.

His brown-haired attacker shook his head. "You've made a miscalculation, lieutenant." He put both of Lansing's hands into one of his and pulled a gun from the inside of his coveralls. "A very grave miscalculation."

The tip of the gun went to Lansing's head as the stranger peered at Trinn.

The snap of bones filled the air. Lansing cried out, his face in a grimace. Dropping to his knees, the lieutenant clenched his jaw and pushed against the gunman. Blood trickled from between their interlocked fingers.

Biting her lip, Trinn pressed her knee harder into the woman's back to keep her subdued.

I can shoot the lieutenant's attacker, but will he react before I do—and kill Lansing?

Trinn glared at the stranger, shoving the tip of her weapon into the young woman's cheek. "Let him go."

The brown-haired man shook his head, leaning over the pilot and twisting Lansing's hands back. More snapping came from the lieutenant's fists. He grimaced again, lowering his head and squeezing his eyes shut, a clenched groan escaping his lips.

"This can stop whenever you want." The woman stared up at Trinn. "Give me that gun or watch your friend die."

"Don't do it," Lansing gasped. "You give up that gun and they'll kill us both."

The young woman chuckled. "If you don't give it to me, your friend will die right now."

Trinn looked at Lansing.

"No." The lieutenant shook his head, blood dripping from his lip. "Jaden, no. The mission is the priority."

"Oh, well." The gunman cocked his weapon. "Say goodbye, miss."

"You don't seem to understand," the young woman said. "He's not needed. Just you."

Gritting her teeth, Trinn forced the imposter's head to the carpet and glared at the crewman. "You pull that trigger and she dies. What's it going to be?"

The man stared at her and squeezed his fists again. Lansing howled.

Trinn panted hard, her head reeling.

If I move my weapon toward the gunman, he kills Lansing.

I have to kill the woman and hope that it surprises this guy long enough to get a second shot off.

But I didn't check the weapon for ammunition! I may not have enough bullets.

Doesn't matter. Killing her is my only move.

Trinn held the gun steady against the woman's face, eyeing the crewman as she gently increased the pressure on the trigger.

When it fires, I immediately swing it around and shoot the crewman.

The metal of the trigger was firm against her finger as she squeezed a little harder.

"Okay!" The gunman opened his hand, letting his weapon rock back and forth on his index finger. "Have it your way." Keeping Lansing's crushed hands in his grip, the airman reached over to the desk and set the gun down.

Trinn took a breath.

"But I didn't say I would shoot him." The crewman sneered. "I said he would die."

He released his grip on Lansing and swung a fist into the lieutenant's back. Crashing to the floor, Lansing groaned. The airman put a foot on Lansing's spine and grabbed one of the lieutenant's arms, pulling it upward and staring at Trinn.

"And I didn't say he'd die quickly, either."

He jerked the arm, snapping the elbow joint in a sickening crunch. As Lansing howled, squirming under his attacker's foot, the airman slid his hands over the lieutenant's lower arm.

"Here goes his radius."

Trinn pointed her weapon at the stranger, firing twice at his chest. The impact of the bullets bounced the man backwards as two holes appeared in his coveralls, but he didn't fall.

No blood appeared on his chest.

The attacker twisted his wrists, and Lansing's lower arm bent at a ninety-degree angle, the sharp crack of the breaking bones filling the FBO like a dry stick that had been stepped on in a quiet forest. The lieutenant cried out in agony, his head on the floor.

Reaching down, the stranger put his hands around Lansing's neck. "What do you think I'll break next?"

A bead of sweat rolled down Trinn's cheek. The lieutenant's eyes were no longer open. Pulse racing, she kept the gun trained on the airman.

He's wearing a bullet proof vest. I might be able to make a head shot from this distance, but with this cow struggling under me, Lansing would still die first.

If I kill the woman, the crewman kills Lansing, and then he and I fight it out.

If I give up the gun, I can keep Lansing alive—and maybe find out why these people are here in the first place.

And if they're supposed to do something— like signal Hollings' jet before it lands—they need to be alive to do it, or the plane will just turn away and land somewhere else—and my mission is scrubbed.

She sighed, her choice made.

"Okay." Trinn lifted her knee off the woman's back, holding the gun away. "I'm putting the gun down."

The female technician rolled over and grabbed the gun from Trinn's hand, scurrying toward the center of the FBO. She wiped the back of her hand across her lip, pulling it away covered in blood.

Smiling, the young woman pointed her gun at Trinn. "Who are you?"

Jaden swallowed hard. "I'm Shira Nazarian, an officer in the Israeli Air Force."

A wide grin stretched across the woman's face. She laughed, shaking her head. "No, you definitely are not. Care to try again?"

Trinn stood still, her mind racing.

What do they know?

"Do you see that luggage tram out there?" the woman said. "The big box on the cart contains Colonel Nazarian's body. An associate of mine killed her a few hours ago—we ran a genetic scan to determine the identity. So…" The woman sauntered toward Trinn, her gun aimed at Jaden's torso. "You are not her. But perhaps you are who *she* was pretending to be."

The male attacker released Lansing, letting the bloody, semi-conscious lieutenant sag to the floor. Stepping to the desk, the crewman took possession of the other gun again. He pointed it at Lansing's head. "Please don't waste any more time."

The lieutenant groaned, pushing lifting his head, his hands a pair of gnarled, bloody stumps.

"Easy, my friend." The woman glanced at her partner. "Take it easy. We're not in a rush—yet." She walked toward where Lansing lay. "Get up slowly, Lieutenant. If either of you make a sudden move, I'm just going to unleash bullets, and I'm not going to care who they hit." She turned to the dark-haired man and nodded toward Jaden. "Tie her up and gag her."

The man unplugged a lamp from the desk and yanked the cord out, then moved behind Jaden.

"What do you want with us?" Trinn said.

The young woman chuckled. "You'll see in a moment."

The airman secured Jaden's hands, his fingers like steel vices. Grabbing a computer cord, he fashioned a second rope and wrapped it around her ankles. When she was tied tightly, he pulled a rag from his pocket and stuffed it into her mouth, then took another cord and looped it around her head, forcing her jaw open and pressing against the rag to keep it from being pushed out with her tongue.

Trinn tried to speak over the gag, but it was no use. She could make a humming noise, but not much more.

"Stop that!" The airman grabbed Jaden by the hair and jerked her head back. Pain exploded across her scalp. "If you make a sound," he said, "any sound at all—I will rip you apart with my bare hands, piece by piece."

He slammed a fist into Trinn's side, knocking the wind out of her, then put her over his shoulder like she was a small child that weighed almost nothing. She fought to suck air in through her nose, her aching muscles barely able to function. Carrying her to the restroom, he laid her on the cold tile floor and walked back out. A moment later, he brought in Lansing, tied in a similar fashion.

The lieutenant breathed hard, his eyes barely open. Blood trickled from the gag around his mouth.

Trinn peered into his eyes, blinking back tears as she fought to breathe.

We'll get out of here, Lansing. We will.

Beyond the lieutenant, a pair of women's feet in flat-heeled shoes protruded from under a stall door. Trinn scanned the restroom. Three other blood-soaked corpses lay on the floor.

Her heart sinking, she assessed the situation.

The knots in the cords were too tight to work her hands or feet free. The makeshift ropes cut into her skin at the wrists and ankles, shutting off the blood flow and making her hands and feet feel like painful, swollen water balloons.

They're obviously ruthless murderers, so the fact that they didn't kill Lansing is a good sign. They must need us for something. I just need to—

The restroom door swung open and the young woman entered, pointing her gun at Trinn. "Did my associate inform you to remain quiet?"

Jaden nodded.

"Good." The woman swept her hand outward and fired two rounds into Lansing's chest. As he moaned, a thin stream of smoke curled upwards from the tip of her gun.

She fired a third shot into his forehead.

Trinn closed her eyes, her ears ringing from the gun blasts, her heart aching for the young pilot. She gagged on the rag in her mouth, wanting to vomit, but only a pained, muffled groan escaped her mouth.

No! No, no, no.

As the tears fell, she turned her head.

I'm sorry, Lansing. I'm so sorry.

"Like I said…" The young killer's voice echoed off the restroom walls. "He's not needed. Just you."

CHAPTER 26

DeShear went into his bedroom and opened the closet door. A small, steel safe rested in the corner. It had been bolted to the floor from the inside, using long, thick screws that penetrated into the trusses in the sub-flooring, giving the little steel box the appearance of solid impenetrability.

That's where they'd come to look for valuable stuff.

Inside the safe was a cache of sparkling jewelry, five thousand dollars in cash, an unloaded handgun, and several legal documents—the kind of valuables that any upscale household might have in a safe.

And it was almost all fake.

The jewelry, in its various velvet-lined boxes, looked to be worth maybe ten thousand dollars, but had cost only a few hundred. The gold was low quality or gold-plated metal; the gems were colored glass. The documents were forgeries, designed to send would-be hunters down the wrong trail. The handgun appeared legit, but had no firing pin, so it wouldn't work even if it were loaded.

The money was real, but each bill had been marked with UV-visible ink and the serial numbers were on file with the FBI.

Any thieves who broke into the house and took the items from the safe would likely soon find themselves surrounded by the police.

The real valuables—such that they were—had been stored in the hallway, where a baseboard in the corner pulled out, allowing a small section of untacked carpet to be pulled back. There, under a false floor panel, in a space the size of about two shoe boxes—were the items Hamilton DeShear considered valuable.

Two hundred and fifty thousand dollars in cash, two fully loaded handguns—firing pins intact—and three sets of new identities for each member of the household.

He kneeled in the hallway and reached into the small space.

I need to fly to Canada under my own name, so if Hauser's people are watching, they'll know I'm actually coming—but once I arrive, I may need to disappear. That means anyone traveling with me will, too.

He sorted through the passports and IDs, selecting documents for himself, Constantine, Helena, and Trinn.

I put these in an envelope and then stick that inside a second envelope, send it by private messenger to a lawyer and have him or her overnight it to the designated hotel.

It can't come to my name, because Hauser's people might be watching and they might steal it, so we'll have it sent to...

DeShear flipped through the passports with his picture on them, selecting the one with the name "Carter Enright" on it.

According to his documents, Enright was Canadian by birth and worked a lot in the U.S. He would have a package waiting for him when he arrived at his hotel.

Note to self, make hotel reservations for Carter Enright.

It didn't matter what hotel, as long as the package with his *lone* passport went to the same place.

The other passports would be sent to a third hotel, where Enright would also have a reservation. He could check in and claim the waiting package at each hotel without raising any eyebrows. The next day, or a few days later, he would "check out" automatically via credit card and go on his merry way without ever having set foot in a room—but the packages would be claimed without alerting those that might be watching.

The method was cumbersome, expensive and tedious, but Trinn had assured him it was safe—so he did as he'd been instructed, never using the same attorney as the middleman twice.

Now, all I have to do is send the right packages to the right hotels via the right lawyers, make the right reservations, and then make sure the passport for Enright stays with me and isn't discovered by anyone else.

Nooooo problem.

Sighing, he took the documents and several stacks of cash, replaced the floor panel and baseboard, then headed to his office.

* * * * *

Cassidy Harper exited the restroom of the FBO, strolling across the lobby and plunking herself down behind one of the empty desks. She leaned back and propped her feet up, setting her warm gun on the surface. Her companion walked to the window and stared outside.

She glanced at him. "Questions, Omicron Twenty-One?"

"No. Not from me." He turned to face her. "How long until Atria arrives?"

"Minutes, at most. And you should call her Doctor Lutz. She's very particular."

Omicron Twenty-One frowned. "I'll call her whatever I want. She's my sister, not my boss. If it weren't for me—"

"Hold that thought." Cassidy's phone rang in her pocket. She pulled it out and held it to her cheek. "Hello, Dimitri. Thanks for calling me back so soon. I have something you may be interested in—a slightly used F-15, from the US Air Force. I need it gone, like yesterday. Send someone over to LAX, the private hub." Nodding, Cassidy smiled. "Wonderful. *Da, Dimitri. Spasiba.*"

She ended the call and glanced at her companion. "He's got some people working in security at the main terminal—probably the same ones that cleared you. Anyway, he says it'll be gone before Doctor Lutz gets here." Cassidy stood, peering at the baggage tram. "Maybe you'd like to bring Colonel Nazarian inside now. Doctor Lutz will want to see the body."

Scowling, the Omicron went outside.

Cassidy's phone pinged with an alert. She checked the screen. "Oh, good. Right on time." Walking toward the glass double doors, the young woman zipped up the front of her coveralls and peered across the tarmac as her boss' Gulfstream appeared on the horizon.

* * * * *

Atria Lutz held her nose up as her thin frame ambled out the door of her private jet, eyeing the ground crew on the tarmac. Lowering her sunglasses, she peered at a young female in coveralls. "Cassidy—is that you?"

"Yes, Doctor." The young woman maintained a straight face, holding back a smile. "I'd be friendlier, but we need to keep up appearances out here on the tarmac, so we don't look suspicious on the security cameras. Inside the FBO, we're periodically utilizing a forced video loop to override the system and keep security at the main terminals from swarming us like bees."

The brown-haired tansuit stepped beside her, expressionless. He nodded, then turned and walked toward the FBO.

"Very creative." Lutz peered around the hot, windy tarmac. "I guess I'll have to wait until we're inside before I can thank you properly."

Her obese British travel companion followed off the jet, clutching the sides of the door like he was stepping onto an icy sidewalk—and wincing with each step. Doctor Symm trailed him.

Lutz turned to Cassidy. "I believe you know my two travel companions, but you've never met Mr. Hollings in person, have you?"

"Only via Zoom call." The Brit extended his hand.

Lutz swatted it away. "Weren't you listening? Out here, we are a private charter and they're the FBO ground crew."

Cringing, Hollings put a hand over his bandaged wrist and hobbled toward the FBO.

Doctor Symm raised a hand, scampering after the Brit. "Do you need your wheelchair?"

Grunting, Hollings waived him off. "I'm fine. The roller was a bit o' theatrics to nick me a few extra bennies while in the lockup, eh?"

Cassidy rushed forward, positioning herself to walk side by side with Doctor Lutz, talking while looking straight ahead.

"I have a surprise for you," the young woman said.

"I can't wait to hear it." Lutz smiled. "And I can't wait to get out of these disgusting clothes. I've been wearing them for twelve hours. How soon can we get turned around and on to Alberta?"

"We'll have the Gulfstream refueled in less than twenty minutes, Doctor Lutz."

Inside the FBO lobby, the large box containing Shira Nazarian's body lay with its lid leaning against the wall. The brown-haired crewman stood nearby, his hands behind his back. Symm located a seat at an empty desk by the door, looking through the drawers as he took out his phone and dialed.

Cassidy strutted to the large rectangular box, beaming as she swept her hand over the corpse inside. "We had a very productive day. First, we know your people in Arlington snagged a decoy, but it proved to be helpful. This is not Jaden Trinn, and this woman was *not* pregnant."

Grinning, Cassidy stepped back as the gaunt Doctor Lutz inspected the corpse. Shira Nazarian was dressed in a bathrobe, bloodstains covering much of it—especially the area below the waistline.

Hollings peered over Lutz' shoulder, frowning.

"Next," Cassidy said, "we had a stroke of luck. The thumb drive that we sent Hamilton DeShear was able to infiltrate his computer system. The spyware attached itself to all of the household-related devices and to the external ones used by the residents and family members." Cassidy beamed again. "Jaden Trinn sent DeShear a text message from a burner phone that had been at the DeShear estate. She's smart. We believe she switched to a new phone after her rendezvous with the President, but we were still able to locate her position when she sent the text."

Atria's eyes went wide. "You found Jaden Trinn? Alive?"

"I did." Cassidy smiled at her mentor. "In fact, we have her here. Trust me, she is very much alive. And we can run a pregnancy screen if—"

"No need." Lutz shook her head. "Our information about that was very solid. Months ago, we paid off the city workers that collect the trash on her street, and our people have been going through it with a fine-toothed comb. She's pregnant—by a known Gamma. But you've done amazing work, Cassidy. Absolutely amazing." Lutz glanced around the FBO. "And where is Ms. Trinn now?"

"Restroom," Omicron Twenty-One said.

Lutz eyed the brown-haired man. "Direct, as ever, brother dear. Thank you."

He remained in place, his hands behind his back, looking straight ahead.

Symm got up from the desk, staring at the crewman. "Wait—isn't he…" His jaw dropped as he stepped closer to Omicron Twenty-One. "The raging tansuit from the lab! The one who caused the breach, or containment issue, or whatever you called it— that's him!" Symm wheeled around to face Lutz. "But I saw… I saw your people…"

"You saw my people kill him." Lutz nodded. "Only it wasn't him, it was a different unit, number Nineteen. They are identical in all respects, including downloaded brain functions."

The Omicron smiled, nodding at the pale doctor across the room. "Nice to see you again, Doctor Symm. Glad you didn't run back to New York."

"It's absolutely remarkable." Symm put a finger to his lip, shaking his head. "He's the spitting image…"

"He's the *exact* image," Lutz said. "A perfect replica—except replicas don't share memories and experiences. These units do. *My* units." She chuckled. "Doctor Hauser never produced anything like these."

"There are twenty-five of us." The Omicron's voice was flat and unwavering. "Or, there were. An unexpected car accident claimed unit Twenty, and as you know, number Nineteen was taken offline when you were at the lab."

"It's uncanny," Symm whispered. "Uncanny."

"Right," Hollings bellowed. "Forgive me for breaking up this happy little tea party, but you said you've got Jaden Trinn locked away somewhere? Might I have a wee look at her? Just to be sure you've pinched the right bird?"

"Of course." Cassidy nodded, looking at her boss. "Doctor Lutz?"

"By all means, Cassidy." The gaunt doctor put a hand on her assistant's shoulder. "You've been a shining example of productivity today. Let us see the *pièce de resistance*."

The young woman walked to the restroom and held open the door, revealing Jaden Trinn tied and gagged on the floor, surrounded by dead bodies.

"Cor blimey." Hollings shook his head. "It's the manky lass, in the flesh."

"This is exemplary!" Lutz hugged her protégé. "You have exceeded my highest expectations, Cassidy."

"Thank you, Doctor Lutz. It's always been my dream to receive that type of acknowledgement from you. Ever since I went to work at Angelus

Genetics, I hoped to… I don't know. Impress you, somehow, I guess."

"And indeed you have." Lutz held her hands on Cassidy's shoulders, beaming at her protégé. "I could not be more impressed. You've gotten rid of a pesky imposter, acquired the correct asset, and enabled our plan to proceed on schedule. You have my thanks."

The young woman smiled, shrugging her shoulders and blushing.

"Oh, when I think of the months of research you've helped us leapfrog over." Lutz ran her hands through her hair as she crossed the lobby. "Your work at the facility, your amazing computer skills…" She shook her head. "You are quite remarkable."

The red in Cassidy's cheeks deepened. "Thank you, Doctor Lutz. You don't know how much that means to me, coming from you."

Atria smiled. "It is praise very well deserved."

Grabbing the gun from the desk, Doctor Lutz aimed the weapon at her protégé. She fired, pulling the trigger again and again until the weapon's magazine clicked empty.

Shrieking, Symm put his hands over his head and jumped behind a desk.

Eyes wide, Cassidy sagged to the floor of the FBO, the front of her coveralls filled with holes. She collapsed onto her back, her mouth agape. Dots of deep, shiny crimson seeped out over her chest; a trickle of blood ran down from the corner of her young mouth.

As she breathed her last breath, she gazed up at her mentor, blood gurgling in the young woman's throat.

"You were impressive, Cassidy—too impressive." The thin doctor wagged a finger. "Never outshine the boss—she might take you for a threat." Lutz stood up, glancing at Symm as he cowered in the corner, then to Hollings.

The Brit shrugged. "Underlings need to know their place." He patted his belly, looking around. "What have they got to eat 'round here?"

Lutz waved to her brother. "Let's go. Get Trinn out of the bathroom. She's got an emergency C-section waiting for her in Alberta—followed immediately by her funeral."

DAN ALATORRE

CHAPTER 27

The Gulfstream shuddered as it passed through a pocket of turbulence caused by the cooler Canadian air. Trinn had been placed in a seat near the rear of the plane, next to the brown-haired Omicron, his gun trained on her. Doctor Symm sat at the front, next to Hollings, his nose buried in his phone and not looking at anyone.

The obese Brit downed another mini bottle of rum, smacking his lips as he swiveled around to Atria Lutz across the aisle. He hooked a thumb over his shoulder toward Symm. "What's got that bloke knackered?"

Lutz lifted her eyes from her computer, peering toward Symm. "He's afraid I'll disavow his investment before it's fully funded and toss him off the plane in mid-air." She returned to her keyboard. "And he's not wrong. Always have a plan B."

Hollings nodded, running a hand over his chin stubble. "Serves him right, the cowardly git."

Leaning forward, he lowered his voice. "And what's all this about a C-section? That other lass was all cut up in her down below area—that Israeli woman. What's you wanting with their insides?"

Lutz sighed, shutting her laptop. "The Israeli was an error. We received a tip that it was Jaden Trinn in the hotel, coming from a meeting with the President, and we followed up on that information." She shook her head. "The Secret Service isn't as sharp as it used to be."

"So, it was Trinn you was wanting all along."

"Not exactly." Lutz raised her hands to her chin, spreading her thin fingers and tapping the tips together. "I'm interested in the *lines*. Originally, I wanted to obtain Hauser's prodigy child Constantine. She was with an elderly Delta unit who goes by the name of Helena, and a Gamma who's alleged to be Constantine's father—Hamilton DeShear. But Jaden Trinn has made herself part of the package now. She's become pregnant with DeShear's child."

Hollings sneered at Trinn. "Done let your knickers down, eh? Naughty girl." He sat back, narrowing his eyes as he looked at Doctor Lutz. "But your research lines are unique. The hybrid prototypes you and Hauser made were from the DNA of first runs, like DeShear was. Why add older units into the mix now?"

"You're not following," Lutz said. "I planned on taking the child and killing the others. But the genes of the early lines were selected to be dominant in all breeding, so the odds are very high that Trinn's unborn child carries the best genetic enhancements of Hauser's research. I need to analyze it and see if it's better than what I have. Then, it will either be propagated in my lab or eliminated."

"Aye..." Hollings set his empty rum bottle on the table. "You don't care if Trinn lives or dies, you just want her baby."

"Astute as ever, Mr. Hollings." Lutz lifted her laptop and slid it into the computer bag at her feet. "Every one of them threatens the value of my lab's lines. If they exist, there's no need for mine. Whereas if they are all eliminated..."

"Then you've got the gold mine."

"Better than gold." A smile stretched across the thin doctor's face. "Our prototype units grow exponentially faster than their peers, reaching comparable adult maturity in eighteen months. They're smart, they're perceptive... They have a dense bone structure and a fibrous musculature, almost like that of the great apes, so they're incredibly strong... And they have well-developed emotions. They sense things the way humans do, sometimes better—almost as good as the Delta units, able to pick things out of the cosmos before they happen." She sat up straight. "And I have exclusive worldwide rights. My hidden facility is the only one there is. By adding Hauser's control elements, there'll be no stopping us."

Hollings held up his bandaged wrists. "A word, then, miss. Trinn's the bird what done this to me. If all you want is her baby... how's about you let me kill her."

Lutz shook her head. "We're on a schedule."

"Let me do it!" he hissed, leaning forward again. Drool spilling over his lips. "You can keep your fee, I don't want it. I just want that witch to die slow, by my hand."

"You'd pass up your fee? That doesn't sound like you." The doctor raised an eyebrow. "Or is there some sort of prurient interest you've developed in our hostage?"

"I'm only interested in her death." The Brit's face grew rigid. "You can hack out her undercarriage first, for all I care. Just let me be the one to end her miserable stinking life."

The plane vibrated with more turbulence. Outside, white wisps of clouds sailed by.

"It's tempting." Lutz stroked a long, thin finger over her chin. "After all, Doctor Symm may never get his funding together, so my lab may need to keep every cent we can." She stood, straightening her blouse. "I'll give your suggestion some thought."

Turning, Lutz walked to her suite and disappeared behind the door to her private restroom.

* * * * *

The gaunt doctor stood before the mirror, examining her eyes.

How long has it been since you slept?

Shaking her head, she removed the black leather case from behind the glass, replying to herself as if she were a doctor and patient in an examining room. "Doesn't matter. Sleep can wait. There's work to be done. Dark Hour is fast approaching."

Opening the case, she removed the paraphernalia inside and became the doctor again. "Going too long without sleep is very bad for you."

Her patient-self shrugged. "I can manage for a few more days."

The crystals came out. The pipe was filled. She held the flame under the blackened bowl, inhaling the warm smoke deep into her lungs, its bitter taste etching itself onto her dry tongue.

"Other people have been known to hallucinate when they don't get enough sleep," Doctor Lutz said.

She brushed the hair from her eyes, standing tall before her bony reflection as she prepared another dose. "I am not other people."

CHAPTER 28

Jaden Trinn cracked an eye open, inspecting her surroundings on the Gulfstream. The rope cords cut into her throbbing hands and wrists, but the ones around her mouth had loosened a bit. She pushed the soggy rag around, clearing more of her airway, and felt one of the loops around her mouth drop down.

Lucky break for me—and a way to get my gag undone.

Like a horse that puffs up its ribs when being saddled so it can have looser cinch belts during the ride, she had instinctively stretched her neck and jaw when being tied, so there was now a slight amount of play in her facial bindings.

But only a slight amount. The Omicron tansuit had done his job.

Closing her eyes to almost shut so she could surreptitiously observe the other people on the plane, she bit down onto the cords and pulled upwards, stretching them against the back of her neck. After a few painful tries, she was able to get a second cord to drop from her mouth.

Gasping quietly, she lay as still as possible.

Hollings drummed his fingers on the armrests of his seat, occasionally looking in her direction. She held her breath each time, holding still and waiting for his eyes to move away—and when they did, she would go to work on her ropes again.

* * * * *

"Are there other facilities out there?" Symm whispered.

"Eh?" Hollings faced the cowardly doctor. "What's that?"

Symm put a finger to his lips, glancing over his shoulder toward the tansuit.

Hollings nodded.

The doctor lowered his voice. "Other facilities. Are there any of them left besides the one run by Atria?"

"Maybe," Hollings whispered. "Why?"

Symm took a deep breath and let it out slowly. "We need to talk." He nodded at Omicron Twenty-One. "Without extra ears listening. Can you make that happen?"

"Lutz will be back soon," Hollings said. "Her visits to her private refueling station don't take but a few minutes."

"About ten minutes last time." Symm kept his face to his phone. "Eight, the time before that. But if we talk fast, that will be more than enough."

"So, the good doctor needs a bigger dose each time to keep the engine running, eh?" Hollings rubbed his nose and wiped his hand on his belly. "All right, then. And if I can get us some private time— what then?"

"Then," Symm said, "I have a proposition I'm sure you will be very interested in."

Sitting back in his seat, Hollings massaged his chin stubble. The Omicron might be too strong to physically overpower, even if he and the Symm tried at the same time. Most of the GEH units had weaknesses, but he had no idea what this line's were.

"Nah. Can't risk it mate," Hollings shrugged. "Sorry." He turned to the window, gazing outside.

"Psst." Symm sat hunched over his phone, gesturing to his feet. He pulled up his pants leg, revealing a thin metal bar sticking up from his shoe. He spread his fingers, displaying a dozen or more of them—and several strips of packaging tape stuck to his shin. "Got these from a desk in the FBO. Steel rails, to hang files on. Band 'em together tight enough and it'll pack a big wallop."

Hollings nodded, licking his lips. He'd always been good at improvising weapons, a skill he honed even further during his most recent stint in prison. Even if the tansuit turned out to be a genetically engineered ape, he wouldn't withstand a sharp crack in the head from a firm, steel blackjack.

Hollings held his hand out. Symm gathered the rods together and forked them over, followed by the tape.

With his back to the tansuit, Hollings gripped the steel rods and wrapped the tape around them, pulling it as tight as he could. He hefted the weight mass and dropped it into his hand a few times, nodded.

He glanced at Symm. "Right. I'll go chat the bugger up. After twenty seconds or so, you cause a distraction—and I'll put the wanker to sleep."

Symm nodded, a line of sweat gathering on his brow.

The rotund Brit tucked the makeshift Billy club against the back of his forearm, rising and shaking out his legs. "Cor, too much flying, this is. I need a stretch." He walked to the rear of the cabin, peering at the tansuit. "Don't imagine you got a cigarette on you, eh, mate?"

Omicron Twenty-One shook his head. "I don't smoke."

"Ah. No, you wouldn't. You're the healthy type, ain't ya?" Hollings shook his leg, glancing back at Symm.

The doctor's laptop crashed to the ground. "Oh, no!"

The tansuit leaned to the side, craning his neck and peering around the obese Brit.

Hollings raised his arm, flipping the makeshift blackjack around and gripping it tightly, like a miniature baseball bat. He brought it down with all his might, crashing it into the back of the Omicron's head.

The jolt reverberated up Hollings' arm as the genetically engineered human swayed for a moment, then rocked forward and slumped to the floor of the Gulfstream.

Nodding, Hollings turned to his new partner in crime. "There. Now come help me sit him up in the seat so's he looks like he's dropped off for a nap."

A moment later, Omicron Twenty-One was propped up in his seat, his head resting on his chest and his hands folded over his abdomen.

Hollings stepped back, smiling. "Job done. He's like a wee babe in a crib." He turned to Symm. "Right. Let's you and me get down to business or that crib will have a second baby sleeping in it."

Panting, Symm rushed back to his seat and glanced at the time on his phone. "We still have about five minutes. What can you tell me about Hauser's offshoot operations? Did any survive besides the one run by Atria Lutz?"

"Nobody knows for sure, mate." Hollings dropped his plump rear into his seat. "Doctor Hauser was big on compartmentalization—no group was ever supposed to know what the other groups were up to. Truth be told, I doubt any other sites existed. Even if there was any, they'd be just starting out, trying to piece back Hauser's technology. That could take half a century… Atria Lutz has the only facility I know of, and I just learnt about it. But before the big takedown, she were a decade farther along than anyone else on Hauser's team, maybe more."

"But you handled cash distributions," Symm hissed. "You made disbursements to sites other than those that the FBI visited, and not just the one run by Atria Lutz."

The Brit glared at him. "You ruddy piker. Are you accusing me of skimming off the top?"

"No." Symm's eyes went wide. "No, I…"

"I ran a *legitimate* illegal business, I did."
Hollings leaned forward, jabbing his finger at Symm.
"I hijacked the drug trucks, I smuggled the wares
'cross the borders, I paid the politicians—and I
delivered a harsh message when a harsh message was
needed. And if I decided to divvy out an occasional
bonus here and there to meself after the good doctor
had snuffed it, who are you to say it wasn't earned?"

"I'm not." Symm's lip trembled. "I'm saying,
if there *are* other facilities—or other interested
parties, say—we can use that as leverage against
Lutz."

Hollings cocked his head, peering sideways
at the doctor. "Aye. A bidding auction."

"But we need the embryo alive. And we have
to get off this plane."

"We don't." Hollings said. "I do."

"We both do." Symm gripped the sides of his
seat, his hands shaking. "I know all about the head
cap machine, or bonnet, or whatever it's called. As
soon as you show Lutz how to work it, she'll kill you
too. Look at what she did to that young woman,
Cassidy—her protégé. You know I'm right. Work
with me."

Hollings turned away. "I'm a lot of things,
Doctor, but I'm a man of my word—and I gave my
word to Atria Lutz."

"You *sold* it to her. Sell it to me." Symm
leaned forward, veins sticking out from his neck. "Do
it, and I'll let you kill Jaden Trinn."

Hollings' eyes flashed wide.

"All I need is the fetus," Symm said. "That's
a twenty-minute operation. You can have her as soon

as I'm done. And…" He glanced over his shoulder toward the door to the private suite. "If Atria Lutz is out of the way, I could take over her facility. That could mean a lot of royalty payments to you, Mr. Hollings. A gold mine, I think you said it was."

Hollings mouth hung open. "Cor, you're thinking a bit advanced for yourself, doctor." He looked at the unconscious Omicron. "But we may have a witness what's done gathered some of our treachery."

"That tansuit has no loyalty to Lutz. You can see it in his eyes. If we can figure out what he wants, we can all turn this whole thing to our advantage."

"There's no figuring a tansuit." Hollings rubbed his chin. "They're not like regular people."

"These are," Symm said. "They have emotions. She installed that in them."

Pursing his lips, Hollings gazed at the genetically engineered human in the rear seat.

"No." Hollings shook his bulbous head. "No, Lutz will throw you off the plane—and me straight away after." He spun his chair to put his back to Symm. "Nice try, you mangy git. Now shut that pie hole of yours and let me get some rest."

* * * * *

Atria Lutz gripped the edge of the countertop and closed her eyes. The smell of smoke wafted from her clothing.

Focus. Maintain your focus.

But her thoughts drifted back to a visit she'd had with Doctor Hauser, when they met on short notice in her small office instead of conducting his usual inspection of her lab.

As she stood next to her desk, the old man stared out at Lutz from her computer screen. "There's been some trouble. Your facility and your prototypes must be moved."

"I know," Lutz said. "We're ready. We can be out in a few hours without drawing attention to ourselves." She sighed, gazing through the windows to her lab—the rows and rows of incubators stacked floor to ceiling. "I don't understand why this Greyhound character would want to murder board members and facility managers. We are involved in important, life-saving research. His actions don't make any sense."

Hauser tipped his head back, peering down his nose at her. "When an individual's motivation isn't clear, look at the results their actions are achieving. Infer their motivation from that."

She set her clipboard on the desk and slid her hands into the pockets of her lab coat.

"You've heard of the recent school shooting," Hauser said. "Two students took semiautomatic rifles into the cafeteria and and—"

"Yes." Lutz looked down. "Yes, I heard about that."

"The media pushed the angle about bullying." The old doctor kept his eyes focused on her. "It's a simple answer, and they think their audiences are simple. The real answer is slightly different." He tapped his fingertips together. "The shooters had such contempt for life, they decided to kill themselves—but they wanted to show everybody else how worthless life was by killing as many

274

innocent people as they could before they died. That was their statement."

The Gulfstream jet jostled with turbulence, the low hum of its engines filling the private suite.

Lutz nodded, staring at the ground. "I knew someone—a friend—who had an endometrial cyst that become infected and caused her to become infertile. She went in for a routine exam and came out with the news that she would never have children. She was devastated." Sighing, Lutz shook her head. "I thought a lot about that. She was twenty years old. The average lifespan of a woman in the United States is eighty-five, so she'd get to enjoy more than sixty years of emotional pain over something that wasn't her fault, looking around at everyone else who can do the most basic thing of any living organism—reproduce—but she couldn't. She felt worthless and devastated. She wanted to kill herself."

Atria looked at her mentor.

"So, I can definitely understand the thinking of someone who does what those two high school shooters did."

* * * * *

Trinn wiggled her head to free her jaw from the last cord loop and pushed the rag from her mouth. "Hollings. Symm's not wrong."

Hollings bolted upright, glaring at her. "Cor, another one heard from. Shut it, lass. Lutz said I can't kill you, but she didn't restrict me from giving you a good thrashing. It's your downstairs bits she wants. I swore I'd kill you for what you done to me—and I will."

"Okay," Trinn whispered. "But kill me later, or we're both dead. Symm is right. Once Lutz doesn't need you, you're a loose end that could call the authorities, or you're a potential blackmailer, a possible competitor... she doesn't need that—and she won't allow the possibility. Get me off this plane and tell Lutz you murdered me, then take her a dead body from a morgue. I'm sure Doctor Symm can get one of those for us if he writes a big enough check."

The fat Brit stared at her.

"I need your help, and I can access Hauser's money to make it worth your while."

Hollings sneered. "How much?"

"How does a million dollars sound? But you have to help me first. I need to access that AI you stole from the château."

"I never stole any—"

"Somebody did," Trinn said. "All I know is you used it on Helena in that French warehouse. She told me all about it—and you know Helena. She wouldn't lie."

"No, that ruddy wench." Hollings frowned. "But why should I help you? I'd make ten times your million working with Lutz and helping her bring back Hauser's operations."

"If you live. You saw what she did in the FBO. Five million."

Hollings shook his head. "You're bidding with Hauser's money. That ain't yours to spend, lass."

"It's DeShear's to spend, and he'll spend it to save me," Trinn said. "And if you help me, I can guarantee he won't kill you later. On the other hand…" She shrugged. "If I die—and if DeShear thinks you were responsible in any way—you've had your last good night's sleep on this earth. DeShear tracked down The Greyhound, you know. And the disciples. And that was *before* he inherited Hauser's money." She nodded slowly, looking Hollings in the eyes. "Imagine what he could do now. What he *will* do—unless you help me. So it's that, versus hoping Atria Lutz doesn't shoot you the instant that AI goes online. Even you must realize that's what she's going to do."

It was as if a light suddenly went on in the fat Brit's head.

Scowling, Hollings pounded the armrest of his seat. "Ten million."

Trinn narrowed her eyes. "Six."

"Nine and the fighter jet you took to Hawaii."

"Seven," Trinn said, "and I'll give you a chance to kill me after."

Hollings recoiled. "If you don't kill me first?"

"You have my word that I won't. I could have killed you twice already and I didn't."

"Yeah." Hollings rubbed his chin. "Why not?"

"That's not my style." She lifted her chin. "So? Do we have a deal?"

"Har." Chuckling, Hollings nodded, patting the armrest. "I'd have done it for one million if I got a fair chance at putting you six feet under after."

"Done. One million it is." Trinn smiled.

He recoiled again.

The plane banked on a high arc, the light from the aft windows cascading across the walls on the other side of the cabin. The pilot's voice came over the speakers. "We are cleared to land at the Calgary International Airport in Alberta. Cabin, prepare for landing."

In the private suite, the restroom door banged shut. Holling glanced toward the open bedroom door.

"Better do something about that," Trinn said. "If she sees what you did to her Omicron, none of us are getting off this plane alive."

As Atria Lutz held onto the wall of her suite, Hollings pulled a few steel rods from the bundle and rushed forward, grabbing the bedroom door and pulling it shut. He jammed rod after rod into the gap between the door and the frame, stacking the steel like pages in a book, each one wedging in tighter than the last.

Lutz screamed at him from the other side, pounding on the door.

Holding onto his seat, Symm stood as the plane descended. "Is that going to keep her inside?"

"Long enough to get this plane landed." Hollings stepped to Trinn and gestured for Symm to come over. "Did this with pennies in grammar school. Locked kids in the toilet for all day. Now, help me get this mangy bird unlashed and put the ropes on that tansuit."

"Hollings!" Lutz pounded the door. "You lousy, double-crossing limey rat!"

White-faced, Symm grabbed the cords at Trinn's feet, working the knots.

"And," Hollings muttered, "as soon as this jet touches the ground—we'd all better be ready to run."

CHAPTER 29

DeShear set the carryon bags down, staring at the long line of people waiting to go through security. Ahead of him, travelers slipped off their shoes and placed phones and laptops into wide plastic tubs, marking time until one of the uniformed TSA agents waved them through the various scanners.

In one part of the line, the ropes broadened and customers walked one by one past an agent with a dog. The canine appeared more interested in some passengers than others, but didn't seem to alert on anyone.

"What a smart puppy." Kneeling on the floor, Constantine pressed the side of her face against the rope line pole, gazing through the legs of waiting passengers. "He looks very excited to be working in the airport."

"He sure does." DeShear looked past Helena to see the TSA dog. "He looks older than a puppy, though."

Constantine kept her face against the pole. "That's a Belgian Malinoise, eighteen months old. In the United States, a dog is considered a puppy until it turns two."

DeShear glanced at her, his jaw dropping.

Helena winked. "We overheard the trainers talking when you were distracted by organizing the tickets."

"Ah." He nodded.

"You've had a trick or two up your sleeve as well, haven't you, Hamilton?" The old woman smiled, moving a step forward in the line. "Like firing the security team?"

DeShear shrugged. "It was the only way we could get out of the country. The ViewPoint people would have stopped us or created such a commotion… they never would have agreed to all this, that's for sure."

"No," Helena said. "I suppose not."

Constantine stood, scratching at the outside of her thigh.

"Hey," DeShear whispered. "Leave that alone."

"But it itches." She frowned, fanning herself. "And the bicycle shorts are hot."

"Yeah, well…" He looked over the slow-moving queue. "It's only for a little while longer."

The line advanced. Helena clutched her hands in front of herself. "I'm very happy to travel this way, Hamilton, but why was a commercial flight better than a private charter? It would seem a private jet would be more secure."

"Mixing in with a crowd allows you to not stand out, so it's usually safer. A private charter would draw too much attention."

"I see."

"Yeah." He looked at her. "Sometimes, the harder you try to camouflage yourself, the more you get noticed."

The TSA agents opened another line, and the crowd moved through faster, bringing DeShear's group to the little podium. He held their passports and the three airline tickets at his side.

"We need enhanced pat-downs for these two." DeShear nodded at his travel companions. "They can't do x-rays or magnetic scanners. I can go with them or go through regular security, whichever is easier for you."

"They can go in that line, over there." The rep pointed toward the far wall, where several uniformed agents stood. A section of small rooms was behind them. "I need to see your passports."

As DeShear handed the documents over, Constantine walked toward the uniformed agents, Helena following her.

"The three of you are traveling to Canada?" the rep at the podium asked.

"Yes." DeShear kept his eye on Constantine and Helena.

The rep ran DeShear's passport under a blue light, then glanced at the computer screen. "Your passport is sending up a flag in the system, Mr. DeShear. Wait here while I check on that, please."

One of the agents pulled out a wand and walked toward Helena.

DeShear waved his hand. "She can't get wanded, ma'am." He looked at the TSA agent and pointed at Helena. "The older lady—no wand for her or the little girl, please."

The agent proceeded to Helena, raising the wand to her shoulder. DeShear took a step toward them, waving his hand. "No. Ma'am. No wand for her."

The rep at the podium scowled. "Sir, you need to wait here."

"Tell her to stop." He glanced at the agent again. "No wand!"

The agent put her hand on Helena, turning her as she raised the wand. A second agent with a wand walked toward Constantine.

"No!" DeShear's heart raced. "Stop!"

The podium rep stood up. "Sir—"

"Just give me a sec," DeShear said, backing away from the podium. "She has a heart stent. She can't get a wand. The electromagnetics could—"

The rep reached for DeShear's arm. "Sir, you need to calm down!"

"Stop!" DeShear ran toward Helena. "Stop that! Helena! Constantine!"

Helena held her hands out as one agent patted her down and another waved the wand across her back. Next to her, Constantine did the same thing. A uniformed woman patted the child down while a second woman bent down and moved the wand over her legs, then her waist.

"No!" DeShear sprinted closer, a knot in his gut. "Stop wanding them! They can't—"

Two uniformed men tackled DeShear. They crashed to the ground, forcing his hands behind his back. As he struggled to lift his head, one of the agent's radios squawked.

"Alert. Passenger engagement, area B-10."

Bodies and legs converged around him. A hand slammed his face into the carpet and held it there. DeShear grunted, straining to move his head enough to see what was happening on the other side of the rope.

* * * * *

Hollings whispered to his two companions as they walked through the Calgary main airport terminal. "Right, you lot. Steady as she goes. Keep it together just a wee bit longer."

"Did you have to knock out our pilot?" Symm said.

"Aye. One quick knock to the head, a splash of rum on the collar—and a few o' them little plastic rum bottles on the cockpit floor—and when the maintenance crew shows up, they'll think the wanker's passed out from drinking. Buys us a little time if he don't radio the terminal and put the coppers on us. And let's not forget, mate—it seems to have worked."

Trinn passed through the exit door for ground transportation, sliding her hand across her abdomen and wincing.

That punch really got me. I can't believe how sore I am.

Outside the terminal, the air temperatures had dropped precipitously compared to those of LA. She squinted in the bright sunlight, locating the cab stand.

Glancing over her shoulder, she waved to Symm and Hollings inside. "Come on, move it. Let's go."

"Easy, lass. Best if we split up now—eh?" He paused by a rack of brochures, taking a few out and walking toward her. "We'll meet at this hotel."

"Why are we splitting up?" Symm asked. Other travelers breezed by him and passed through the exit.

Hollings handed him a brochure. "Because I probably don't get my money if I don't show up with the AI computer, but they won't bloody likely hand it over if you lot are with me." He looked at Trinn. "Go into town and hire us a sturdy vehicle, girl. One that can function in snow and trails, but nothing fancy, so's it don't raise no Canadian eyebrows." He turned back to Symm. "And we'll need money, Doctor. Lots of it, in cash. I reckon people are watching this bird's accounts and those of her boyfriend, so you're our financier for the time being."

Symm inspected the brochure, holding his collar closed. A stream of white went over his shoulder with each breath.

"We'll meet here, at this hotel." Hollings held a brochure up. "Go 'round to the back, on the lower floor, near the employee car park. There's a red concrete planter box with little evergreens in it. I'll stash a room key there for each of you, just under the mulch."

Trinn cocked her head.

A key in a planter box? That's one of my old tricks.

Hollings looked at her, smiling. "That's right, 'New York Pizza.' We caught on to your sneaky ways, didn't we?"

She frowned.

And my code name.

"Congratulations, you figured out a child's game of hide and seek." She snatched the brochure out of his hand, glancing at it briefly before jamming it into her pocket. "Make sure the key is there when I show up. How much time do you need?"

"About four hours. Stay out of sight until then. Don't draw no attention." He peered at Symm. "And aside from you, moneybags, no cell phone usage except to your partners to get the cash. Don't use no credit cards, neither."

Symm nodded.

"All right." Hollings waved them away. "Off you go."

Trinn climbed into the first taxi in the line, checking over her shoulder to ensure that Hollings and Symm each got into cabs as well.

As her taxi pulled away from the curb, Trinn's driver glanced at her in the rearview mirror. "Where to, ma'am?"

"I need some warm clothes." Jaden rubbed her hands together and shoved them between her knees to take the chill off. Her lower abdomen still ached, but she couldn't worry about that at the moment. Trinn still had the IDs and credit cards with the Colonel's name on it; that would do for now. Despite Hollings' warning about not using credit cards, Trinn would need to use one to rent a car. Since the cards in her pocket were through an agency account, they were untraceable through normal reporting channels. She peered over the seat at the driver. "Is there any sort of ladies' apparel store nearby?"

"The airline lost your bags, eh? That's too bad. Well, there's not a good store out here, but there are plenty in town." He drove through the crowded traffic, toward the airport exit. "La Chic is probably closest, but there's also Mariah Contemporary— that's on the west side of Calgary. Ducks Fashion is on the south end, and Espy Experience is close by, too… What sort of clothes are you looking for?"

"All sorts," Trinn said. "I need a warmer wardrobe. Jeans, a coat, gloves… Maybe just take me to the first place you mentioned. I'll rent a car in town and go to the others."

The driver grinned. "I don't mind driving you, ma'am."

Trinn peered out the window at the passing pines and tall fir trees, holding her belly. "Thanks, but I'm not sure I can afford that and the clothes."

* * * * *

With several shopping bags in each hand, new jeans and a tan waistcoat, Jaden Trinn strolled into the lobby of a downtown Calgary rental car agency. A few minutes later, she drove off the lot in a roomy, four-wheel drive Range Rover, its heater blasting.

She checked the brochure, finding the main roads to get her close to Hollings' selected hotel— the Banff Springs resort—without activating a vehicle's GPS or the burner phone she had purchased on her brief shopping spree.

I take Sarcee Trail Southwest to... Highway One or Route One, whatever a green maple leaf road sign is in Canada.

Her aching stomach throbbed. She winced again, putting her hand over her lower belly.

And I could probably stand to eat something.

She'd tucked her and Shira's credentials inside a rear compartment for the spare tire jack, along with the rental car papers, and only kept a few U.S. dollars in her pocket. As she neared the congested interchange, her stomach growled. Trinn sped up, merging onto the busier thoroughfare and glancing at the road signs zipping past her window.

Tim Horton's, McDonald's...

A searing pain shot through her insides, like a hot knife stabbing her from within. She gasped, doubling over and grabbing her stomach.

That's not from the punch I took. Something's wrong.

A jolt of fear gripped her.

The baby.

No. Don't be that. Please, don't be that.

She forced herself upright, gritting her teeth as she gripped the steering wheel, pain radiating out toward her hips. Another searing pain ripped through her insides.

"Oh! Ow!" She cringed, bending low over the wheel.

Oh, this is bad. Please, don't let this be something wrong with the baby! Please don't let it be that.

Blood dripped from her nose. Moaning, she held tight to the steering wheel as the road swayed up and down, dimming as if dusk were occurring inside her eyes.

Not again!

The car jolted and the wheel jerked away, spinning like the vehicle was driving itself, veering sharply to the right.

A red billboard with white cursive writing loomed ahead of her, displaying an iced cappuccino and a donut. Heart pounding, Trinn grabbed at the steering wheel, dizzy and unable to keep her eyes focused. The Range Rover went into the emergency lane, slamming into the guard rail and throwing its driver against her seat belt straps. The wheel jerked from her hands again.

The car rocketed upwards, a boom filling the cabin as pine trees careened in front of her. The windshield shattered, raining bits of glass over the dashboard.

Jaden slumped over, her head bouncing off the center console as everything went dark.

CHAPTER 30

DeShear sat in a lockup room at the airport, surrounded by two TSA agents and an armed police officer. Staring at him from across a small steel desk, a balding man in a dark suit rubbed his chin, his eyes going from the three passports to his computer screen.

"Now, Mr. DeShear..." The bald man set the passports down. "You say the woman and the child needed a pat down, but you objected to the use of wands—is that correct?"

"That's right." DeShear nodded. "Helena has a stent and—"

"But you don't have a medical ID saying that." The man lifted his chin, sniffing. "Or an affidavit from a physician. Do I have that right?"

DeShear's shoulders slumped. "We... didn't find out about the medical condition until recently."

"Uh huh." The man eyed his computer. "You didn't know the older woman—your daughter's grandmother—had a medical condition that required her to not get scanned at airports." He scratched his chin. "But her passport indicates she's recently traveled on the same dates as you, to the same countries as you, and on the same airlines. France, Great Britain, the United States—you've been through security a few times now." He shoved his tongue under his lower lip, leaning back and putting an arm over the back of his chair. "Pardon my skepticism, but how exactly does that work, sir?"

DeShear sighed. "We got the passports after the procedure but we were able to—"

"And the girl—your daughter." The man shrugged, putting his hands in the air. "She doesn't have a medical ID or a doctor's affidavit, either, but she's been a world traveler recently, too."

"We did the legal adoption after her procedure." DeShear's cheeks burned. "And we weren't able to access the medical records. They may not even exist, but the doctor who performed the surgery said…"

The man at the desk sighed, rubbing the back of his neck. "So, you don't have the paperwork for any of this."

"I'm trying to explain."

The agent pounded the desk. "And I'm trying to keep this country safe from terrorists!" Scowling, the man sat forward. "Your passport has a special designation that allows for some considerations, courtesy of the United Kingdom, the Bahamas, and France—so apparently you have some high-placed friends—but this is Virginia, pal, not Florida." He extended his index finger and tapped the desk. "We are close to the center of government for the United States of America, and the perception of a threat here is a little different from what it might be if we spent all day looking at a parade of fat tourists from Michigan heading off to their family vacation at Disney World." Picking up the passports, he stared at DeShear. "Aside from being disruptive, I probably don't have any real grounds to hold you—but I do have wide discretion in interpreting security measures and determining what I consider a threat in my airport at any given time."

DeShear nodded. "Yes, sir."

The man stood, dropping the passports on the desk. "You can go, but I'm flagging you in the system. You'd better be an ideal traveler for the rest of your trip, and that goes for your whole group. If there are any reports that you so much as give a funny look to any of the employees in an airport, or on a flight, or maybe even in the taxi to your hotel—TSA will lock the bunch of you up. I don't care who you know, I'll detain you under the Patriot Act, and you can rot in jail while we see if a federal judge wants to hear your story sometime in the next six months. Just try me."

"Message received." DeShear picked up the passports. "You won't have any problems with us, sir."

"Oh, I guarantee I won't." He walked to the door and opened it. "Now, get out of my airport."

Two armed TSA agents escorted DeShear and company to the plane, where glowering flight attendants met them. After numerous apologies and assurances from DeShear, the trio was allowed to go to their seats—Constantine by the window, Helena in the middle, and DeShear on the aisle—and the plane was under way.

He leaned over, keeping his voice low as he addressed Constantine. "So, the wand didn't get near your head?"

"I can't be certain." She shrugged. "It was behind me, but I don't think so. One lady was patting me and another was waving the wand all about."

He looked at Helena.

"Same with me, dear. They moved so fast, pushing the back of their hands into… some personal areas. I was too flustered to notice."

"Yeah." DeShear leaned back, resting his head on the headrest and letting out a long, slow sigh. Bringing his hands to his face, he rubbed his eyes. "Okay, well… I guess the wands didn't get close enough or they weren't powerful enough. We dodged a bullet. But I'll be more careful next time."

An airline attendant passed by, glaring at him.

"Anyway, we made it." he nodded at his companions. "So, let's all just settle back and relax." Closing his eyes, DeShear folded his hands over his lap and scooted down in his seat. "And Helena, next time, we'll charter a private plane."

* * * * *

The woman's voice was faint and muddy, as if it were passing through a wall. "Can you hear me, miss? Can you open your eyes?"

A light moved over Trinn's closed eyes, the stranger's soft voice growing clearer.

"Squeeze my hand if you can hear me, eh?"

Like she was waking from a deep sleep but was not quite awake yet, Trinn tried to focus, pulling herself from the dark fog. She squeezed her hands closed, as instructed, around someone's warm, soft fingers.

"There we go," the woman said. "Good. Come on, wake up now." She patted Trinn's hand. "Wake up for me."

The haze lifted. Jaden opened her eyes, processing what she saw.

Black-haired woman in scrubs. Walls of a small room, all white. Medical equipment.

She tried to lift her head.

And the equipment is attached to me.

"Easy, there, eh?" The woman patted Trinn's shoulder. "There is no hurry."

A cold wetness slid over Trinn's lower abdomen, going back and forth with a slight pressure and making her tense. She tried to move her hand to stop it.

"That is just me," the woman said. "I am performing a sonogram on you. Were you aware that you are pregnant?"

Trinn mumbled, trying to form words. Sighing, she nodded her head, sending the room swaying up and down.

"You may have a concussion, so take your time. We drew blood to see if you had suffered a drug overdose—which informed us that you were pregnant. Okay? And we want to make sure we take care of you and your baby, so we are checking on the baby right now. Can you speak?"

Inhaling deeply, Trinn closed her eyes and nodded, hoping to avoid the room moving again. "Mmm." She swallowed, her tongue dry against the roof of her mouth.

Another woman spoke. "Would you like a sip of water?"

Jaden nodded. A short-haired brunette slipped a plastic straw between Trinn's parched lips. She sucked down a cool stream of water. "Thank you," Trinn whispered. "And yes, I can speak."

"Good." The woman with the sonogram transducer slid it lower on Trinn's body. "Can you tell me your name?"

Trinn glanced down at her semi naked torso. A pale green hospital gown covered most of her— except the area glistening with clear gel. "Where am I?"

"Calgary hospital, in Alberta." The black-haired woman glanced at a black and white monitor, a rounded triangular image wavering on the screen, like an upside-down windshield wiper had pushed across the glass to reveal the fuzzy gray blurs inside. "Are you from around here?"

Trinn blinked, recalling the Range Rover and her most recent bloody nose.

I'm in Calgary, in a hospital. That should be safe, but I can't risk it.

"Can you tell me your name, miss?"

Trinn nodded. "Sarah MacIntosh."

"Sarah, I am Doctor Shrinidhi." The black-haired woman set the transducer on a steel tray. "Do you remember what happened? Can you tell us?"

Giving up less information is safer, but if I can't remember what happened, they won't let me out of here. I'll be stuck in "observation."

Trinn swallowed hard. "I… was at the airport, then I rented a car to do some shopping. I was driving and I felt sick, so I tried to pull over, but I passed out. And right before that, I had a nosebleed."

Doctor Shrinidhi picked up a small flashlight. "You were at the airport? So you were flying? Have you been doing a lot of flying and not staying hydrated?"

"Yes."

The flashlight flicked across Trinn's left eye, then moved to the right and flicked up and down a few times.

"You need to stop doing that." Smiling, Doctor Shrinidhi set the flashlight down and pulled off her latex gloves. "Now, unfortunately, I was informed by the local police that your rental car was totaled, and they have towed it and issued you a citation…"

Trinn winced.

No car. Back to square one. Guess I need to improvise a vehicle, somehow.

"… but the most important thing is," Shrinidhi said, "you need to slow down a little. You're dehydrated and your electrolyte levels are very low. The blood tests indicate you're deficient in iron and calcium, among other things. Have you not been eating regularly? The passing out and the nosebleed—this is not common during a pregnancy, but it is not uncommon. Has it happened to you before today?"

"No," Trinn lied.

"And do you have someone who can drive you, when you are released today?"

"Yes. My boyfriend will do it."

"Then get lots of rest, lots of fluids—no flying, no driving, and no excitement. Got it?" She walked to a trash can and dropped her gloves into it. "Your boyfriend needs to be your chauffeur for a while now, okay?"

"Okay." Trinn squirmed on the bed. The remaining bits of fog lifted, letting her focus. She'd had terrible pains in her side before the nosebleed and crash.

They just did an ultrasound!

Her thoughts immediately went to the one place she'd been afraid to let them go. A wave of fear went through her, welling up and gripping her chest.

Alexander.

"How—uh, how is…" She was almost afraid to say the words out loud. "How is the…"

The brown-haired woman swabbed Trinn's belly, wiping away the gel and putting her gown back in place.

Jaden put her hand on her abdomen, the fear growing. Tears came to her eyes.

Please let my baby be okay. Please, please, please…

She took a deep breath and looked at the doctor. "How… how is my baby? Is it okay?"

Please say it's okay. Please. Please.

"You and your baby are going to be fine." The doctor's voice was calm and reassuring. "I don't recommend high-speed car crashes, but a womb is a pretty rugged and protective place. Remember, a hundred and fifty years ago, pregnant women weren't sitting in air-conditioned offices or lounging around on a sofa with their feet propped up on a silk pillow. Ninety-nine percent of women carrying babies were farmers, working side by side with their husbands in the fields. They chopped corn stalks for harvest and toted bags of grain to the mill for grinding. The industrial revolution and the advent of computers didn't change the resiliency of the reproductive system. Evolution takes time."

Trinn closed her eyes.

Thank you. Thank you.

"But, Sarah, listen to me. If you don't eat properly and don't drink enough water, you're going to have problems. Your baby needs nutrients and you are giving it excitement instead. The body can only do so much. That is what's knocking you out. Your heart rate spikes, and you're out cold. What did you expect?"

Trinn heard the doctor, but she wasn't listening.

The baby was okay. *Her* baby.

She was officially having a baby. A medical doctor had said so.

She smiled, lifting her head as a warmth swept through her. "Uh, did the sonogram... happen to show the baby's sex?"

"At this stage of pregnancy," Shrinidhi said, "an ultrasound can sometimes show the developing genitalia, and a blood test may reveal the baby's sex—but at only seven weeks gestation, each test is far from a hundred percent accurate."

"Oh." Trinn sighed.

"However, if we do both—which we did, as part of your screening—and they say the same thing, then it is a relatively good indicator." The doctor smiled. "Would you like to know?"

Trinn looked the black-haired physician. "Yes, please."

"It looks like you are having a boy, Sarah."

Trinn settled her head back onto the hospital pillows.

A boy.

"Oh, my gosh, I'm having a baby boy!" Jaden grinned, holding her arms out for a hug.

"Oh, my. Yes." Shrinidhi leaned forward and embraced her patient. "Congratulations, Sarah."

Trinn ran her hand over the doctor's back and looked at the nurse, extending her hands outward. "You get in here, too."

Laughing, the nurse embraced Trinn, patting her gently on the back. "Congratulations, Miss MacIntosh."

"Oh, my gosh." Smiling, Trinn wiped away a tear and laid back on the mattress. "Oh, my gosh." She laughed, tears running down her cheeks. "I don't know why I'm crying."

"Because you are happy—as you should be. Now, get some rest." The doctor wrote on a pad. "I'm giving you a prescription. It will help with the iron deficiency and the nosebleeds."

The nurse brought three small pill bottles over and set them by the bed.

Shrinidhi tapped the bottles with her pen. "These sample packs will get you started until you can get to a pharmacy. But I'm serious about getting more rest. And eat!"

"I will." Trinn sniffled, wiping her cheeks. "Thank you."

"Okay. I will check in on you again shortly." Doctor Shrinidhi exited the room, the nurse following her.

Smiling, Trinn pulled her sheets up to her chin.

A boy. Alexander. Constantine was right.

CHAPTER 31

Doctor Shrinidhi strolled down the corridor, checking the time on her phone. At the entrance to the hospital cafeteria, she passed a security officer as he exited the lunchroom.

"Good afternoon, Doctor."

"Good afternoon, officer." Shrinidhi walked toward the stack of plastic trays at the front of the buffet line. "Nice day outside, eh? Good Canadian weather."

"Beautiful day." He glanced at her scrubs. "ID, ma'am?"

She stopped, looking at him. "Excuse me?"

"Your ID." He pointed to her, tapping his finger to the ID badge clipped to his own breast pocket. "You need to wear it at all times."

Shrinidhi glanced at her scrubs, patting her pockets. "That is strange. I know I had it a moment ago when I was making rounds."

* * * * *

Trinn read the hospital directory and slinked toward the physician's lounge, cupping Doctor Shrinidhi's ID against her side.

Sorry, Doc. The enthusiasm and the hug were genuine, but I also needed an opportunity to pickpocket your hospital credentials. I'll get them back to you.

A swipe of the magnetic strip let her into the large room and another swipe accessed the doctor's locker.

Jeans, a casual blouse, purse, towel, deodorant, a gym bag... that's good for a start.

Trinn opened Shrinidhi's purse and peered at the wallet and car keys inside.

And there we go. Replacement transportation.

She grabbed the clothes and shoes, heading to the changing area and hoping that Doctor Shrinidhi was close to her size.

* * * * *

Omicron Twenty-One grabbed the steel rods and ripped them from the door to Atria Lutz's private suite. Rubbing the back of his neck, he threw open the door.

Atria stormed out, looking around the Gulfstream's empty cabin. "What happened?"

"They knocked me out." The tansuit winced. "... and escaped."

Lutz' jaw dropped. "They knocked *you* out? How?"

"The Brit." Omicron Twenty-One bent over and picked up one of the steel rods. "He banded up a bunch of these together and cracked me over the head with them."

"Hollings." She scowled, putting her hands on her hips. "The idiot's got a raging case of blood lust. He's obsessed with killing Jaden Trinn, and if we don't find him, he may succeed before we get what we need from her."

The Omicron went to the cockpit and peered inside at the unconscious pilot there. "Looks like this guy got the same treatment as I did." He shut the door. "So, Hollings took Trinn and he's going to kill her. Where does that leave your man Symm?"

Lutz went to her suite, taking out a suitcase and shoving her belongings into it. "Doctor Symm must've joined up with Hollings. Symm is spineless, so he certainly wouldn't fight Hollings—and if Hollings had knocked him out, he'd be here with you." She took another bag from the closet and threw it onto the bed. "Hollings probably let him in on the plan to make sure he didn't get in the way or alert me. And Symm went along because he thought Hollings would kill him if he didn't. I would have."

She stopped packing, turning to the door.

"When we hit that patch of turbulence," Lutz said, "Hollings was headed for my suite. Symm was behind him, looking at me like he was afraid Hollings wouldn't get there in time." She nodded looking out the bedroom door to the vacant seat in the cabin where Symm had been sitting. "So he's definitely in on it, the little weasel. He's with Hollings."

Twenty-One picked up his sister's bags.

"Wherever that AI equipment is," Lutz said, "we need Hollings in order to find it, and we need him to use it." She paced back and forth in the Gulfstream cabin. "Symm was using his phone constantly while we were flying…"

"So, our internal system will have captured his phone signature." The tansuit nodded. "If he's with the others, his phone will show us right where they are."

"Yes. Yes, it will." She stroked her chin. "But we need Hollings and Trinn, not Symm. They could split up. Or the coward could run away. I certainly wouldn't put it past him."

Twenty-One stood by the door. His sister folded her arms across her chest, lost in thought. Outside, the wind dragged a paper cup and a hamburger wrapper across the empty tarmac.

Lutz smiled, raising her eyes to his.

"We need to make a call to our technical people. Have them use Symm's phone signature to backload a signal identifier into it, ASAP. That way, if they split up and then communicate with him, we'll get all of their devices. And if Symm bails, we can hunt him down and torture him until he says what he knows."

Twenty-One opened the exit door for Atria Lutz and stood to the side. "I like the way you think, sister."

"I think the same way you do," she said. "That's why you like it. Let's go."

As the Omicron headed for the door, a groan came from the cockpit. He turned to his sister, hooking a thumb toward the front of the plane. "What about the pilot? He may know something."

Lutz nodded. "I doubt it, but kill him just in case—we can't risk any loose ends." She put her hand on the exit door frame, the wind from the tarmac pushing her hair straight back from her face. "Then let's get to a secure internet access and see where Doctor Symm's phone is, so I can track down Hollings and Trinn and kill them, too."

* * * * *

Hamilton DeShear checked into his room on the sixth floor of the Banff Springs hotel.

Helena and Constantine took a different taxi from the airport and headed in the opposite direction, stopping at a grocery store to buy some sundry items and snacks for the child, then took yet another new cab to the Banff Springs hotel. There, Hermosa Montenegro, an elderly woman traveling with her young granddaughter Carmelita, claimed she had lost her passport, but had enough cash with her to secure the hotel's sizeable room deposit and check into her suite on the seventh floor—which was, according to the online floorplan, directly above Hamilton DeShear's.

Big and warm, DeShear's room had a row of windows that overlooked the sprawling white-capped mountains outside. A sliding glass door opened onto a small balcony that had been covered with a light dusting of snow. Rustic northwest elements adorned the suite, like painted totem pole bedposts and an elk antler chandelier. The wall art showcased local artists and their gorgeous watercolor takes on the nearby lakes and mountains, bordered in rough-hewn wood frames. The carpet was a beautiful burgundy and blue First Nations pattern, with wide swaths of earthy colors around the edges.

On the desk was a brochure of the "ink pots"—a nearby area with small pools of hot springs, and one for a waterfall that appeared to be more like a big cluster of large rapids with a short drop at the end, called Bow Falls. A third showcased the locale's many large caves.

DeShear slipped his hands into his pockets, looking around the quiet room.

That's it? For some reason I expected a message with instructions to be delivered.

A quick inspection uncovered no nefarious elements to the room, although he still assumed his temporary quarters had them. Hauser's people were far too thorough to let a spying opportunity slip by.

There was a knock at the door, followed by a rush of footsteps in the hallway.

Light footsteps, like those of a six-year-old child.

Rather than answer the door, DeShear went to the balcony and stepped outside. Lowering down on a string from the upstairs balcony was the passport for Carter Enright, which had made the journey taped to Constantine's leg, under a pair of bicycle shorts— itchy as it may have been for her.

He gave the line two tugs, and the string went back up again. A few moments later, the sounds came to him of the door to the room upstairs slamming shut. Shortly after that, a pair of hands waved at him over the balcony—one small, and one larger.

Smiling, he left his room—and his two counterspies.

Hailing a taxi at the front of the massive resort, DeShear rode to the small town about a half mile away. There, he entered a clothing shop, bought a hat, coat, and sunglasses, and exited wearing them to flag down a second cab. In this one, he went to the hotels where Carter Enright had reservations, checking in and collecting the packages waiting there, while switching to a third and fourth taxi for each ensuing leg of the short journey. He returned to the Banff Springs hotel without incident, having secured burner phones for everyone and a new tablet for Constantine, and *with* the new passports for his companions.

With his collection secured in a tote bag on his arm, DeShear walked to the "Cascade of Time" garden, a small park located about halfway between the town of Banff and the grandiose hotel on the edge of the scenic Bow River. The park's terraced gardens had yet to succumb to the cool weather, so their yellow and red flowers cast a vibrant contrast among the lush green grass and tall fir trees. A slate-stone path weaved its way between the colorful array of flora, leading to a large, octagonal-shaped gazebo with a wood shingle roof, rustic brown pine walls, and a sturdy river rock base. The magnificent structure sat in front of a thick wall of fir trees, overlooking a small pond—and small clusters of tourists.

As DeShear walked up the stone steps, he spied Helena sitting on a bench in the gazebo, Constantine by her side. Nodding to them, they got up from their seats and fell in with a walking tour group, gazing around at the beautiful grounds of the park.

DeShear caught up to the group, handing Helena the tote bag and speaking to her in a low voice while keeping his eyes straight ahead. "You have plenty of money. Just stay in the hotel for a day or two. Order room service and get pizzas delivered, whatever you want—but stay inside until you hear from me."

The old woman nodded, as did the child.

"Constantine," DeShear said, "I got you a new tablet with lots of games on it. You can watch TV and use the hotel Wi-Fi for the video channels you like, but no email or phone calls. Use the new logins we created to access any of your favorite sites."

His daughter nodded a second time.

"Hamilton..." Constantine's voice wavered. "How long do you think we'll have to stay here?"

DeShear took a deep breath and let it out slowly, trudging over the green grass. "I'd say, prepare for a couple of days and hope it's shorter, but it could be longer. When I head out..." He winced, shaking his head. "If I'm not back in three days, take the money and your new identities, book yourselves a flight to New Orleans, and wait in the Dauphine Orleans hotel until Jaden contacts you."

It had been arranged as a part of their new lives, along with many other irritating security precautions. Ever since Constantine's kidnapping, the family had created evacuation spots for themselves, along with code names, a virtual private internet network, and numbered email accounts that changed on a regular basis. In an emergency, an email would come from one codename, to another codename, with one of three, one-word instructions: red, white, or blue.

Any mention of red in a message meant to go to Cincinnati and book a hotel under one of the names on their fake passports. Blue was the same protocol, but in St. Louis.

White meant a white flag. Disaster had struck. Disappear immediately and hope for the best.

It was an ominous system, but unfortunately, a necessary one

The tourist group walked along a small, picturesque pond.

DeShear glanced at his daughter. "But Miss Jaden should be here soon, and she knows how to find you, so…"

Constantine reached back and took his hand, keeping her eyes forward as she pressed his fingers to her cheek. Tears welled in her eyes.

DeShear swallowed hard and gave her tiny hand a squeeze. "That's why we said goodbye properly at home, remember?" He fought to keep his voice from wavering. "When we hugged tight? Because we knew we wouldn't be able to do it now."

The child nodded.

Sighing, he didn't pull his hand away, waiting for her to let go—but she didn't.

"It's probably time for me to go. They're certain to know I checked into the hotel, so I'm sure they'll be contacting me soon."

Constantine nodded, letting his hand slip from hers.

"Goodbye, dear," Helena said. "And good luck."

"I will return to you." DeShear slowed his pace, letting the group move away from him. A lump formed in his throat as the small tour moved down the stone and back toward the park's main entrance.

He stood alone on a hillside, the cool Canadian wind carrying dry, faded maple leaves across the ground.

"I'll return to both of you, I promise."

* * * * *

Sweat forming on her brow, Trinn raced through the employee parking area, reaching the section designated for the hospital physicians. She clicked Dr. Shrinidhi's remote, running up and down the aisles and hoping a vehicle would respond.

Come on, come on, come on...

Two rows over, a Mercedes SUV honked its horn and flashed its lights.

Yes! Finally!

Heart pounding, Trinn bolted past the numerous security cameras and opened the door to the SUV, sliding behind the wheel. Jamming her finger onto the ignition button, she started the car and threw it into gear, speeding out of the lot.

A mile or so later, she pulled into a Tim Horton's and parked in the back near a small creek. Reaching down, Trinn pried open the access panel under the steering column and lowered her head to see inside. She located the little black box with its three telltale wires—red, green and purple. With a quick yank of each, they disengaged from their connections and the vehicle's GPS unit came free.

Can't have them tracking me or shutting off the engine remotely.

She tossed the unit into the creek and drove away.

* * * * *

The key to Trinn's room at the Banff Springs Hotel was in the planter box, just as Hollings had said. After digging through the mulch in a few corners, her fingers met a plastic bag in the dirt of the concrete box.

She glanced over each shoulder. The back of the hotel was virtually empty. At the far end of the building, a maintenance worker in coveralls emptied large bins of trash into a dumpster; at the other side, on the grassy lawn, two small children wearing hooded jackets and mittens ran around in an apparent game of tag.

Trinn pulled out the plastic bag and brushed it off. Inside was a standard, light gray colored room key and a scrap of paper with the number 212 written on it.

She shoved them into her pocket and walked toward the hotel's rear doors. A blast of warm air washed over her as she stepped inside.

I could stand a hot shower and a change of clothes—if I had any. Maybe there'll be time for a—

The lower floor of the hotel was filled with shops. A jewelry store, a candy shop, an ice cream parlor… and a ladies' apparel shop. Mannequins in winter coats and blue jeans filled the boutique's windows.

Perfect.

After quickly acquiring fresh attire—compliments of the cash in Dr. Shrinidhi's purse—Jaden entered the elevator and pushed the button for the second floor.

A moment later, the doors parted. A long, elegant hallway stretched out in either direction. She checked the polished metal placque on the wall and headed toward her room, carrying her shopping bag. A window at the end of the hall showed billowing steam clouds rising up from outside.

Room 212 was near the end of the corridor, across from the service elevator and some sort of laundry collection room. The tantalizing aromas of fine cuisine permeated the air.

I must be above the kitchen.

Trinn swiped her card across the door latch and put her hand on the door. Her stomach growled.

If there's time, some hot food would be a good idea, too, since I already took my first dose of the pills Dr. Shrinidhi gave me, and they're not supposed to be taken on an empty stomach...

She pushed the door open and stepped inside.

"Hello, lass." Hollings stood at the end of the bed, his hands at his sides.

At Hollings' feet, Dr. Genoa Symm lay on the floor, his face a pale shade of blue. A lamp cord was wrapped around the doctor's neck. His red, bloodshot eyes bulged out from their sockets; dried blood marked corners of his mouth.

Trinn's breath caught in her throat. She dropped her bag, stepping back.

"Ah, ah, ah. Mustn't be rude." The fat Brit smiled, raising his hand, displaying a large gun with a silencer attached to the end. Hollings pointed the weapon at her. "Come on in and have a seat, girl. It's time you and me had a little chat."

She turned to flee—but another man blocked the doorway. He was young and thin, with blond hair, but he was pointing a big gun at her chest.

"That's my associate Jules." Hollings chuckled. "He would like you to come inside and sit, too."

Jules nodded. *"S'il vous plait."*

His accent was French, and thick—and he reeked of cigarettes.

"The bed or the chair, *mademoiselle*."

Trinn raised her hands, turning back to face Hollings.

"Aye, you seemed surprised, lass." The obese Brit shook his head, grinning. "I don't know why. I said I'd kill you."

CHAPTER 32

DeShear removed his makeshift disguise in the lobby restroom of the Banff Springs Hotel, turning his coat inside out and balling up the other items inside of it. He tucked it under his arm and headed across the massive common area to the elevators.

"Mr. DeShear!" The check-in clerk who had booked him into his room earlier now waved at him from behind the counter, holding up an envelope. "Sir, I have a message for you."

DeShear walked toward the young blonde. The name badge on the pocket of her blazer said Mendi, and underneath that, in smaller lettering, Alberta, Canada. Other badges of the hotel staff displayed various cities in Canada, and a few from other countries.

The young clerk held the envelope out to him. "The hotel manager said this arrived for you a few days ago. He was keeping it until you'd arrived, and I was about to send it up to your room."

"Oh, thank you, Mendi." DeShear took the envelope and cocked his head. "It arrived a few *days* ago?"

I didn't even know I was coming then.

"Yes, sir." She put her hands behind her back. "The manager said it was dropped off by courier, with instructions that you'd be arriving soon. That's not uncommon for business travelers from other countries."

DeShear nodded, holding the envelope in one hand and tapping it against the palm of the other.

They knew I'd be coming, but didn't know when I'd get here. They could only assume I'd show up sometime before the three days had elapsed.

That's accurate, but pretty loosely planned, for Hauser.

"Okay." DeShear smiled at the clerk. "Thanks."

As Mendi turned and headed back to the check-in desk, DeShear opened the envelope. Inside was a single 3x5 card with another set of coordinates written on it by hand.

51.1716° N, 115.5679°

"Oh, Mendi." DeShear held up the card.

The clerk turned around. "Yes, sir?"

Smiling, DeShear held the card out to her. "I'm sorry to bother you, but I must've left my reading glasses in my room. I can't quite make out what this says." He glanced upwards, peering at the ceiling fixtures. "It's just a little blurry for me to read in this light. Would you mind?"

"It's my pleasure." She took the card and looked at it.

Her face fell.

DeShear shifted his weight from one foot to the other, giving the clerk a crooked grin. "Too blurry for you, too?"

"No…" Mendi's gaze went from the paper to DeShear. "It's blank, sir."

DeShear blinked. "Blank?"

He took the card back. The numbers were plain as day, in dark blue ink, written in what appeared to be a woman's handwriting.

"Is it a mistake?" Mendi asked. "Should I contact the courier service?"

"Uh…" DeShear stared at the card.

She can't see what's written here. But I can, just like the video message I got from Hauser.

That's going to be tricky. What else did they set up that way?

Mendi looked toward the check-in desk. "I can go ask the manager if he opened the envelope, sir. Possibly, the rest of the message fell out…"

"No." DeShear cleared his throat.

Play it off.

"No, no. I'm sure it's just a mistake." He folded the card in half. "I've sent plenty of emails where I said 'see the attached file'—and then forgot to attach the file. That's probably what happened here." He smiled, sliding his hands into his pockets. "That, or somebody from my office is playing a poor practical joke. Either way, No biggie."

"Okay, Mr. DeShear."

As the young clerk returned to her workstation, DeShear pulled out his phone—and the folded card. Opening an internet search engine, he entered the coordinates and hit enter.

The destination looked to be a few blocks away.

Hank DeShear is supposed to arrive there. But does anyone know when it is that he's supposed to arrive?

The lobby doors opened as several people entered the hotel, carrying a chill wind through the lobby. DeShear glanced at the balled-up bundle of clothes in his hand.

If this coat and hat are going to help hide my identity, I can't wear them around when I'm Hank DeShear.

He walked back to the check-in counter. Mendi was booking a room for some new arrivals, as were the other clerks.

When Mendi finished, he stepped up to her. "Can I bother you for a favor? I'm supposed to be meeting with a client in the bar downstairs, and I'm running late. Can you run this up to my room?"

The clerk smiled. "Of course, Mr. DeShear. I can have someone from the bell service take care of it. Will that be okay?"

"I'd rather you did it," DeShear said. "Is that all right?"

She nodded. "I'll take it on my next break."

"Thank you." DeShear reached into his pocket and pulled out a one-hundred-dollar bill. "This is for the trouble."

"Oh, that's not necessary, sir."

DeShear put the bill on the counter. "This is for the bellman. Let him take the coat to my room, as is, all bundled up, and set it on the bed. But you go with him. When it's done, call me on my phone."

He gave the confused clerk his phone number.

"So, like I said, the hundred bucks is for the bellman." He slid the money across the desk. "In and out, and then stick the Do Not Disturb sign on the doorknob. I'll have another hundred bucks for you, Mendi—after you call me."

Her cheeks reddened. "That's really not necessary, sir."

"For me, it is," DeShear said. "Unless it's against hotel policy, allow me this favor."

"No, sir. It's not against policy."

"Okay, then." He smiled. "Thank you."

DeShear walked across the lobby and exited through the large doors, narrowing his eyes as the cool Canadian air rushed past his cheeks.

CHAPTER 33

Trinn sat upright in a moving vehicle of some sort, her hands and feet bound, a gag stuffed into her mouth and held in place with a tight strap around her head. This time, one of her abductors had seen to the addition of a blindfold as well.

"Comfy, Miss Trinn?" Hollings chuckled. "Not that I care, since you'll be dead soon, but I would like to view all of your discomfort before you die—and be the cause of it."

She pushed the gag with her tongue, trying to talk, but it was no use. The cloth they'd stuffed into her mouth was too big. Instead, her attempt at words came out as a series of short, muffled hums.

"Take that rag out of her gob," Hollings said. "I want to hear her. Maybe she'll beg for her life."

A hand came to her lips, smelling of cigarettes. Trinn opened her mouth, and the gag was pulled free.

"Aye, best take the blindfold, too, Jules. We're traveled far enough from the hotel."

The blindfold slipped over her forehead.

Hollings was in the front seat of Dr. Shrinidhi's Mercedes, on the passenger side. A small man with thinning hair and Coke bottle glasses was driving. Next to her was the acrid French smokestack, Jules. Trees rolled by the windows as they drove up a rugged mountain trail.

"Now," Hollings said. "You was saying?"

Trinn glared at the fat Brit. "I thought we had a deal. Even you can't be rich enough or dumb enough to pass up millions of dollars."

"Aye, true. But as it happens, I can have my cake and eat it too. Other arrangements have been made."

"I'm guessing those arrangements aren't with Dr. Symm."

"Ha!" Hollings snorted. "No, girl, they aren't. Seems his financing fell through, the dodgy git. Weren't no use in keeping him on after that. But he did open my eyes to other possibilities." He winced, rubbing one wrist and then the other. "This bloody cold Canadian air is wreaking havoc on my bones—mostly in the places where you tried to ventilate them. Which was a reminder, of sorts. So, I'll be killing you, just like we done Symm, but you'll suffer a while first, lass—a very long while, just like you made me suffer. I want you to beg for your death. And rest assured, I am going to deliver it to you."

Trinn clenched her jaw. "But not in the hotel."

"Not anywhere that other ears could hear your screams, lass."

A small, stone cabin appeared at the end of the path. The vehicle stopped, a cloud of road dust sailing past the car and over a slate-rock walkway that led to the cabin. Beyond the little stone structure was a short grassy patch and then a span of distant, white-tipped mountain tops.

Hollings grunted as he exited the vehicle, carrying a small cooler. "Atria Lutz don't care if I kill you. She just wants that baby you're carrying."

A jolt went through Trinn's insides.

"Aye, girl." Hollings smiled. "We know all about you having DeShear's baby in your belly. So I'll be carving you up from stem to stern and saving that last bit for her—on ice." He held up the cooler. "I'll be doing my boxing practice first, then a bit of target training, and then the slicing and dicing. What's left goes over the cliff for the vultures."

She craned her neck and peered at the cabin. The grassy patch fell away into the clouds.

Laughing, Hollings wagged a dirt-stained finger. "You done caused your last bit of grief for me, bird. In a bit, I'll do what I should've done back in England. Dark Hour has arrived for you." He stomped a foot on the slate walkway. "You're as dead as this stone."

Jules grabbed her arm, pulling her toward the car door.

Trinn jerked herself out of the Frenchman's grasp. "Hollings, listen to me. I have a business proposition for you."

"Do you mean a trick where I end up six feet under and full of holes?" He snorted. "No, thanks."

"I mean a double cross where you end up with millions of dollars in your pocket. Even you've got to be smart enough to realize you should at least hear me out."

"We had that conversation—and I better-deal'd you. I've got no more words I want to say to you and nothin' I want to hear coming out of your mouth except cries of agony as I hack you into little pieces. There's a pack of ruddy hounds a half mile over the hill what ain't been fed in weeks. One more peep and I'll chop off your hands and feed them to the dogs while you watch. That's an odd feeling o' loss, seeing a limb go down an animal's gullet and knowing it's gone forever. Very permanent, that." He glared at Jules. "Take her into the special room and lock her up tight to the wall. I'll have my man over there sharpen the ax."

Jules grabbed her arm again. "*Allons-y*, woman. *Rapide*."

"Hey, idiot." She slid to the edge of the seat and held her feet up to show the ropes around them. "My feet are tied. How am I supposed to move? Hop?"

"Yes. Hop." Jules jerked her arm again, pulling her from the car—and causing her to lose her balance.

She crashed to the walkway, shoulder first.

Trinn grimaced, pain shooting through her arm and side. The horizon swayed up and down.

No, not again. I took the stupid pills!

Relax. Breathe deep. It's the excitement. The heart rate. Keep it together.

"Hey!" Hollings shoved the Frenchman aside and thrust a gun under his chin. "I'm the one gets to hurt this bird, not you. Parlay?"

Jules squeezed his eyes shut, nodding. *"Je suis désolé. C'était un accident."*

"Accident or no," Hollings growled, "if there's another one, the dogs will be dining on two carcasses." He pressed the gun harder, lifting Jules' chin. "Understand? *Comprenez vous?*"

Trembling, Jules nodded again.

"Merci." Hollings released his grip. "Now get her inside and get her locked to the wall."

Breathing hard, Trinn tried to focus.

Three men can overpower you, especially right now when your head is spinning—but one man, that's an opportunity. Jules doesn't look too physically powerful. Stay calm. Try to work him.

Jules put his hands under Trinn's armpits and hoisted her to her feet. Blood trickled from her nose.

"Right." Hollings frowned. "You took first blood, Frenchie. That was supposed to be mine. You owe me."

Jules opened his mouth, shrugging. "But I did not—"

Hollings cracked him across the face, backhanded. Jules' head careened backwards, nearly carrying the blond Frenchman off his feet. As Jules recovered, he put a hand to his red cheek. Blood dripped from his nose.

"Now, we're even." Hollings scowled, jabbing a finger into Jules' chest. "See that nothing else happens to her or I'll measure out double on you."

Jules said nothing, lowering his head and putting his hand under Jaden's arm. He walked beside her, guiding her as she hopped toward the house.

* * * * *

The cabin appeared to consist of three or four small rooms—a dirty, empty living room with broken windows and a stone fireplace on one wall; some sort of smaller room to the right of the living room, where Hollings' and Freeman's muffled voices could be heard through the door; and the small room on the left, where Jules took Trinn.

It was a cold, drafty space, with a tile floor and tile walls. A drain had been installed in the center of the floor, like one for a shower, but it was the size of a dinner plate, with dried blood stains around the edges. Rusted metal loops stuck out from the top of the walls, and scratches marked all the tiles underneath. A second, smaller door was on the back wall of the tile room, its warped and cracking wood leaving splinters on the floor.

The whole place smelled like a butcher shop that hadn't been cleaned in a year.

As the ground swayed back and forth, Trinn sucked in deep breath after deep breath, her pulse throbbing in her ears.

Stay awake, Jaden. Stay awake or you die.

Jules walked her to the far wall and held her to it, throwing a rope noose around her neck and securing the other end to a metal loop overhead.

Breathe. Breathe and think. An opportunity will present itself.

She opened and closed her eyes, trying to keep the darkness from overwhelming her again.

Hollings wants you dead. Jules is just a lackey, so maybe there's a deal to be made with him—especially now that Hollings humiliated him.

If not, your hands are more or less available. Slip that noose off your head, start undoing the other bindings... and try to make a run for it.

The door swung open and crashed into the tile wall. Hollings' fat belly stuck out past the door frame. "Jules, you bleeding muppet—the rope is to tie her hands over her head. It's not a hangman's noose. Fix it proper, ya snail-munching arse." He looked at Trinn. "And you! Don't get too comfortable. Round one of me using you as my own personal punching bag is about to begin."

Trinn glared at him. "Once I'm all tied up and can't fight back? Very manly."

"Oh, ho, ho—enjoy them last few harsh words, lass. Me and my trusty baseball bat will be doing a bit of tenderizing on you before I serve you to the dogs. Can't have them getting indigestion." Laughing, he turned away and shut the door.

Jules approached, loosening the rope around her neck.

Trinn went through her options.

Overpower Jules now, run outside, and disappear into the woods. Or, appear weak to Jules, try to get him to lower his guard, and then take him down—and take any weapons he has.

If there's a chance to persuade him to switch sides, take it, but don't count on that.

Trinn sagged against the wall, lowering her head and forcing tears to well in her eyes.

"Jules," she whispered. "Is there a bathroom? If Hollings starts hitting me... well, *when* he starts hitting me, I'll..." She lowered her head further, peering up at him. "I don't want to wet myself, okay? Don't let me go out like that, covered in pee and humiliated. Can you let me use a bathroom? Please?"

He sighed, shaking his head. "I think your death will be quick, mademoiselle. Hollings has a rage in him."

"It won't be quick. He said he wants to torture me slowly. You heard him in the car." She blinked hard, sending a tear over her cheek.

"*Détendez-vous.* How do you say? Relax." Jules slipped the rope over her tied hands. "He will be setting up that machine with Freeman for hours."

Trinn's jaw dropped.

The AI machine is here? Of course! Hollings went to get it—and in her FBI report, Helena said Freeman was the name of the technician who helped operate it.

Well, that changes things.

"Hours? Could I..." She looked up at the blond Frenchman. "Could I shower, then? I was about to take a shower when you grabbed me at my hotel room."

"No, there can be no shower."

"Please?" Trinn looked over her dirty clothes. "I'm all sweaty and grimy, I stink..."

"It cannot be done." Jules glanced at the door. "Now, be quiet or *le gros et laid* Hollings will return and smack us both."

"Can I at least wash up and pee?" she said. "Is there a sink with water? Or a toilet?"

His gaze went to the small door.

"Is that a bathroom?" Trinn asked.

"It is, but what is the purpose? He plans to kill you. Why would you bathe for that?"

"For dignity. Can you understand?" She blinked again, sending a few more tears over her cheeks. "Please. For my self-respect. I am still a woman."

He looked at the little door again.

"Jules, you and I are not animals, like Hollings. It would mean the world. A... a last request, if..." She sniffled. "If I'm going to die."

Jules took a deep breath and let it out slowly. Pursing his lips, he walked to the little door and opened it a few inches, peering inside, then returned his gaze to Trinn. "You may use the toilet, nothing more. And be quick."

It was the opening she needed. Trinn gave the young man a big smile. "Thank you."

"*Facile,*" he whispered, coming toward her. "Keep your voice down."

He put his hand under her arm again and helped her into the bathroom—a tiny, white-tiled space, with an ancient toilet and a dirty, rusted sink—but left the door to the room open.

"I need my hands," Trinn said. "To..." She glanced at the toilet and squeezed her knees together. "You know."

"J'en ai marre!" Rolling his eyes, Jules stepped forward and loosened the binding on her hands. "There. Now, no funny stuff. Get to it, and be quick."

"You…" Trinn looked at him and shrugged. "I won't be able to do anything if you're watching."

Jules frowned. "I do not wish to see, but I am not going to leave." He pointed to the toilet. *"C'est comme ça."*

"Can you at least turn your back?"

"I cannot." He shook his head. "I don't trust you."

Sighing, Trinn nodded, reaching for the waist of her jeans. "Okay."

She undid the button and pulled down the zipper, sliding her jeans over her behind and down a few inches on her thighs.

Jules shifted his weight from one foot to the other, his eyes darting left, right, and upward; anywhere but at her.

She pushed the jeans halfway down her thighs and lowered herself toward the toilet—then purposely missed and landed on the floor.

"Aah! Ow!"

Trinn lay wedged between the wall and the toilet. She floundered, waving her arms.

"Merde!" Jules hissed, bending over and extending his hands to her. *"Vous êtes un idiot!"*

Trinn brought her knees up and leveled her bound feet at the Frenchman's chest. Kicking out as hard as she could, she smashed her heels under Jules' chin, snapping his head back.

He reeled backwards, crashing into the wall and slumping to the floor.

Gasping, Trinn sat upright and fastened her pants. She held her breath, listening to hear if the commotion had alerted Hollings.

No noise came from the other side of the wall.

She undid her leg bindings and wrapped them around Jules' ankles, using the other rope for his hands. Lifting his shirt, she ripped an inch across the bottom seam, balling it up and wedging it between the unconscious man's teeth, then used the noose from the other room to gag him and secure him to the base of the toilet.

She stood, admiring her handiwork.

It won't last forever, but I don't need it to.

Holding her breath, Trinn crept back into the tiled room. As sweat gathered on her brow, she leaned forward and put a hand on the doorknob, cracking it open to peek out.

DAN ALATORRE

CHAPTER 34

DeShear checked his phone. The location in the message was only a few blocks away; no taxi would be necessary. The mountain wind threw his hair into his eyes and sent a chill down his back. As he walked toward the designated coordinates, he passed several small restaurants and shops.

He stopped, looking at the other pedestrians. They were dressed in heavy coats and hats.

Maybe they know something about Canadian evenings that I don't. It'll probably get a lot colder when the sun goes down, and I don't know how long I'll be out here.

Glancing around, he spotted a clothing store with a mannequin in a leather jacket in the window.

That place might have something for the night air.

* * * * *

The GPS in his phone directed him to the intersection of Mountain Avenue and Glen Avenue.

Nothing marked the corner as anything of interest; three sides of the intersection were vacant, with sidewalks and grassy lawns. On the fourth corner stood a small ticket kiosk.

It was a rickety wooden structure, covered in colorful posters that advertised local attractions—horseback rides through the mountains, a hiking expedition to nearby Bow Falls, and several walking tours of the area's caves.

The attendant was a brown-haired man with a dark mole on his left cheek, just under the eye.

"Hello." DeShear stepped to the kiosk, gazing at the laminated brochures taped to its front shelf. "Any good tours still available this afternoon?"

"Mostly sold out." The attendant blew on his hands, sending a thin white cloud out toward the open space where a window might have been located on a sturdier structure. Reaching down, he tapped on a small electric space heater humming near his feet. With each impact of his hand on the heater's metal casing, the lone incandescent bulb over his head flickered.

DeShear glanced up and down the empty streets.

Sold out?

"Well…" Shrugging, DeShear shoved his hands into his coat pockets. "You must have something available. I'm just in from out of town. I heard there was good sightseeing here. Specifically, that this kiosk—"

"Got this." The attendant slapped a brochure with a picture of Bow Falls onto the shelf. "Walking tour of the falls and nature trail. It's about to start.

The other people taking the tour are keeping warm over in that coffee shop." He nodded toward a small café across the street. "There'll be about thirty of you."

"I'll take it." DeShear reached for the money clip in his pants pocket. "How much?"

"Adults are twenty dollars. Kids are ten, and seniors are eighteen."

DeShear held out a twenty-dollar bill. "One adult, please."

The attendant eyed him. "No kids or seniors?"

"Not this trip."

"Then it'll be twenty dollars." The man took the bill and handed DeShear a ticket.

A small cluster of tourists ambled out of the café and headed toward him. As DeShear stepped away from the kiosk and put away his money clip, a bang came from behind his back.

He turned around. The light in the small wooden kiosk was out, a large piece of poster-laden plywood covering its window.

Cocking his head, DeShear stared at the dark shack as the other ticket holders assembled near the street corner.

A woman in a red jacket and red hat faced the group. "This is the tour of Bow Falls and the nature trail. I'm Candace. I'll be your guide. Let me punch your ticket, and we'll start out from over there." She pointed at a picnic table about thirty feet away.

A line formed. DeShear fell in among the others, holding his ticket out and letting the young woman punch a hole in it. Tied to each of her brown trail boots were several small, round bells. When she moved, they jingled.

"Thank you, sir." A stream of white trailed from the young woman's lips as she squinted in the bright sunlight. "We'll be starting in a moment."

The brochure showed the tour would walk a block west, to a nearby bridge, cross the river, then head southeast along its rocky banks to arrive at the falls. The tour would then head north into the forest before circling back. Most of the assembled tour group wore winter-looking clothes—heavy shoes, heavy coats, mittens, gloves, and scarves. DeShear was the lone outsider, with just his newly-acquired coat, but it would be warm enough if the tour wasn't too long.

The wind picked up, pushing colder air down the mountain. In the distance, an odd noise echoed through the trees, part squeal and part howl. A child in the group flinched, running to grab the waist of a nearby man. He patted her on the back, smiling.

"That's one of our local bull elks, bugling." Candace walked to the picnic table, scanning a paper roster of her tour attendees and doing a quick head count. "It's a little early in the day for that—we usually hear a lot more elk serenades after sunset. But there's no reason to worry about that buck calling out. He's just signaling to the ladies that he's around, if they're interested, and to other males nearby that they should probably find another patch of ground to inhabit."

"Are they dangerous?" The girl asked.

"Can be." Candace winked. "But give them a lot of space and you'll be fine. They aren't the biggest threat on the mountain."

The child looked around, her eyes wide. "What is?"

"Bears. That's why we wear these jinglers." Candace lifted her foot, pointing to the little round metal bells. "The bears don't really want to interact with us, and it's against the rules to feed them here in Banff, so the bells let them know we're coming. That way, the bears don't get surprised."

Staring at the bells, the child nodded, her mouth agape.

"Let's go ahead and get started." Candace stuffed her roster into her jacket pocket and walked backwards along the sidewalk, gesturing for the tour members to follow. "If you'll all come this way, the falls are just a short walk from the bridge, and we'll have some really pretty light right now."

The tourists followed after their guide, DeShear pulling up the rear. They crossed the long bridge, Candace pointing out the different types of trees and flowers as they made their way southeast on the far side of the river, focusing on the natural elements and warning about sudden snows.

"The mountains can be unpredictable," Candace said. "At this time of year, it's not uncommon to get ten feet of snow overnight—but we always get a warning about snows like that."

Her comment about such a large amount of snow seemed to wow most of the tourists, but one member of the pack could not be steered off her prior discussion.

"What happens if you surprise the bears?"

"Attacks are rare." Candace navigated across a large dirt patch, toward a rumbling roar beyond a line of trees. "Only two to five people are killed by bears each year, compared to a hundred and twenty human deaths that are attributable to deer." She smiled at the girl. "And you're not afraid of deer, are you?"

"No," the girl said, smiling back.

The guide stepped to the side of the trail, sweeping her hand over the rushing waters of the Bow River. "And we made it! First stop on our journey—Bow Falls." She faced the group. "There's plenty of good places to take pictures, so have at it. We'll start up again after ten minutes or so."

Candace plunked herself down on a picnic table. A young couple approached her, holding their phone out, gesturing to the water and then to themselves. Candace took the phone and pointed it at them, the churning waters sparkling in the sunlight behind them.

The falls were pretty, a collection of giant whitewater rapids that dropped off thirty or forty feet into a churning white froth. Then, the river widened, becoming a calm, crystalline blue, and meandering along the rocky Canadian shoreline as tall firs and pines loomed overhead.

The wind picked up again, carrying a few tiny snowflakes with it.

Candace clapped her hands, gaining the group's attention over the noise of the crashing water. Waving, she turned and headed into the tall, thick trees.

The inquisitive young tour member was quickly at her side, peppering Candace with questions about the bears they might encounter.

"If you get between a momma bear and her cubs..." Candace moved along the rocky dirt trail, thin patches of snow and ice dotting the way. "She's more likely to attack. Males usually attack only if they are starving."

DeShear stayed toward the end of the line.

What's this tour got to do with me? Maybe I bought the wrong ticket.

"Either way," Candace said, "we want to keep our eyes open, and we *don't* want folks feeding them because then the bears can lose their natural fear of humans..."

As the group rounded a corner, a man stepped out of the trees and cut DeShear off from the tour.

He had brown hair, and a dark mole on his cheek.

DeShear recoiled. "Aren't you the guy from the kiosk? What, did my money turn out to be counterfeit?"

The man put a finger to his lips, then pulled out a .45 caliber handgun.

DeShear swallowed hard. "If so, I also have a credit card."

"But that's not to say they won't come visit your garbage cans at night..." Candace's voice grew fainter. "Or your car if you leave food in it, or even come sniffing your coat pockets if you carry snacks in them, like hikers do."

The man stood rigid until the tour group had faded from earshot, then waved his gun toward a gap in the trees. "That way. No sudden moves."

DeShear nodded, walking ahead of the armed stranger.

The snowy path led to a crack in the hillside—a crooked slice in the steep limestone that disappeared into blackness.

"Inside," the man said. "Or are you afraid of the dark?"

DeShear walked ahead. "I'm more afraid of that .45 you're holding."

The triangular opening in the mountain looked fifty feet high. It was close to six feet wide at the bottom, narrowing as it stretched upwards, like a flap on a teepee that someone had left open. The sides were wet and sleek, with thin trails of water trickling down them, and the echoes of dripping water somewhere ahead in the vast darkness.

"Keep moving," the man said.

"It's pitch black in here, and my eyes haven't adjusted." DeShear inched forward. "You don't want me to fall off a cliff or something in here, do you?"

His words echoed several times inside the cave. When he turned around, the man with the gun was gone.

DeShear reached into his pocket and pulled out his phone, turning on the flashlight.

Three feet ahead of him, the ground fell away into the darkness.

* * * * *

Constantine lifted her head and peeked out from behind a large boulder. "Hamilton's gone into a cave with the other man."

Shaking her head, Helena pulled her collar close around her neck, the chill wind tugged at her coat. "I suppose we need to alert Miss Jaden, then. He can't want us following him in there."

"No, he won't." Constantine faced her mistress, rubbing her little mittens over the old woman's pale hands. "But neither will she. We'll need to send a text saying what's happened, but not give her the location until we can meet up in person. That will be safest."

"Safest? Are you sensing something, child?"

"No, I don't think so. Hamilton once said that as a private detective, you rarely have all the information, so you need to quickly assess a situation and try to figure out the smartest thing to do. Right now, the smart thing is for us to be cautious—just in case. We don't know Miss Jaden's situation, and we mustn't divulge our information until we do." Constantine craned her neck, peering down the side path before stepping onto the main trail. "Come on." She pulled Helena from behind the big rock. "We'd best get to the hotel straight away, before someone else happens along."

* * * * *

The dirty room with the fireplace was empty. Trinn ran to the front door and threw it open, purposely crashing it into the wall as hard as she could—then tiptoed to the door where Hollings was and waited for him to rush out.

It didn't take long.

The fat Brit threw open the door and stuck his head into the living room. Trinn grabbed the weapon and pulled Hollings forward, twisting the weapon away from him. Hooking a leg behind the big man, she gave him a shove and sent him backwards to the living room floor.

A quick look inside the smaller room showed Freeman at a card table with some electronics equipment in front of him—and a handgun. The scrawny man's eyes met Trinn's through his Coke bottle lenses, his jaw dropping. Freeman scrambled for the gun, his fingers fumbling as he went to raise it.

The weapon slipped from Freeman's fingers, crashing onto the table and bouncing away from him—and right to Jaden.

"Thank you." She scooped up the gun. "Okay, you're inept with a pistol." She waved the weapon at Freeman. "Get up from that chair and get into the living room—slowly."

The small man complied, taking a place next to Hollings on the floor.

"Aye," Hollings grumbled. "Pull that trigger and kill me, Miss, because if I get the chance that's exactly what I'm gonna do to you."

"I sure ought to." Trinn checked Freeman's pistol, disengaging the magazine and tossing it out the front door. She ejected the round in the chamber and threw it outside as well, then chucked the empty gun into the fireplace. Taking a chair from the smaller room, she turned it around backwards and straddled it, leaning on the backrest and holding the remaining gun on Hollings. "Maybe I should chop you up with an ax and feed you to the dogs and vultures, too."

"Can't. There ain't no dogs." He tugged at his collar. "Nor an ax. Made them bits up, I did."

Sweat gathered on the fat man's brow.

"Uh-huh." Trinn cocked the gun and pointed it at Hollings' head. "You're not going to leave me and my family alone until we're all dead, are you?"

Hollings flinched, looking away and holding up his hands. "Not a chance. Just kill me now."

She moved the gun closer to him, the nozzle focused between the fat Brit's eyes. "I'd love to." Trinn took a deep breath, sliding her finger over the trigger.

Hollings cringed.

"But… I can't." She moved the gun away and chewed her lip. "I have a business transaction we still need to discuss."

"No." He shook his head. "Finish me off, lass—or I'll finish you later. That's all there is to say."

Trinn shifted on the seat. "Maybe you'd listen to ten million dollars in cash, transferred to a Swiss bank account of your choice, in your name."

Hollings' jaw dropped. "It's a lie."

"It's the truth." Trinn shrugged. "Or it can be in gold bullion, if you prefer."

The fat man licked his lips. "Gold's nice—but why would you work with me after what I done?"

Sighing, Trinn leaned forward again on the chair. "Because—and I hate to say this—I happen to need you. And I'm willing to make it worth your while. But you've got to behave yourself and stick to the plan, you greedy, incompetent oaf. Ten million dollars in gold bullion is too much to mess around with."

Hollings cocked his head, looking at her. "Aye—but it's not as much as fifteen million, though, is it?"

"Twenty is even more." She sat upright. "*If* you can stick to the freaking plan. Now, will you hear me out?"

"Twenty million dollars in gold bullion? Cor blimey." He looked at the gun, then to her. "All right, bird. Let's talk."

CHAPTER 35

Leaning over the edge of the drop off, DeShear peered into the darkness. The light from his phone couldn't shine bright enough to see the bottom of the crevasse.

He glanced around at the cave floor, picking up a baseball-sized rock. Tossing it into the hole, he counted slowly in his head. At the count of twenty, without hearing the rock hit the bottom, he decided to spend as little time as possible around the bottomless pit.

The edges around the sides were shiny and yellow-white. Minerals had been carried from the ceiling of the cave in water droplets over the millennia, building up to coat the floor with a hard limestone shell.

He shined his light over it.

The left side of the hole had a ridge a few inches wide, coated in rounded minerals like an over-frosted cake. The right side was wider, but the whiteish deposits reached higher on the wall. Passing around the hole on either side would be dangerous.

But that guy brought me here for a reason, and it wasn't to kill me.

His mission had been spelled out: Come to this place or the device implanted into Constantine's head will degenerate and kill her.

I'm technically early, but they obviously know I'm here, so the greeting party must be on the other side of this pit.

Clenching his teeth, DeShear stepped toward the small shelf on the right side of the chasm. A knot formed in his stomach.

Okay, Hank. Constantine managed to do this over jagged rocks in Hawaii, so you can do it, too.

He slid a foot out over the yellowy surface and eased his weight onto it, leaning into the mineral covered stone wall.

One step at a time.

His phone illuminated on the slick shelf. It was maybe thirty feet to the other side of the crevasse, where the cave resumed and the floor was flat and wide again.

But that is the longest thirty feet I've ever tried to walk across.

He inched forward, pressing his face to the cold surface and spreading his hands out as far as he could, for balance.

Holding the phone with two fingers, he used the other three to grip the slippery surface as best he could. Water dripped onto his head and shoulders. Each breath sent a tiny, white cloud into the near-darkness.

He stretched his phone hand out again, preparing to take another step. Glancing down, he saw nothing but black.

His stomach jolted.

Maybe don't look down, Hank.

His foot slipped an inch. DeShear grunted, leaning into the cave wall and clinging to the ripples in its surface, a jolt of fear and adrenaline surging through his insides. He gripped the wall tighter, each finger scratching the hard mineral surface, trying to dig in and get a better sense of balance on the slippery edge.

Heart racing, DeShear straightened himself and swallowed hard.

You're okay. You only slipped an inch, no big deal.

Relaxing his grip, he slid his foot forward to take another step.

It slipped again.

DeShear dropped the phone, squeezing his eyes shut and flattening himself against the cold, wet cave wall. His phone clattered to the shelf, bouncing once and careening downward, spiraling away into the emptiness.

Panting, DeShear's pulse throbbed in his ears.

Okay. Okay. Go slow. You aren't twenty-one anymore. Things have… shifted on you, physically. Just go one step at a time—in very small steps.

Water droplets echoed in the darkness.

He glanced out into the blackness to see if any of the cave shelf was visible.

It wasn't.

Great. Now I get to do this in the dark.

A faint green glow caught the corner of his eye. He strained to turn without losing his balance.

On the far side of the crevasse was a sign of some sort. It had been too dim to see in the light from his phone, and the phone light had prevented his eyes from adjusting enough to notice the marker. Now, in the darkness, it was clearly visible.

Containment Lab One, Substation One.

He stared at the sign.

What the heck is a containment lab? Or a substation for it?

What's down here that needs to be contained?

Another icy drop of water hit the back of his neck.

I guess I'll need to get off this cliff to know.

He slid his foot out over the mineral-coated shelf again. The surface was rougher and an inch or so wider, allowing for better footing and balance. Sliding his hands across the cave wall, DeShear made a good-sized step, then another. The shelf widened further, and flattened, allowing him to move without slipping. After two dozen more treacherous sidesteps, he reached the other side of the crevasse.

A thin mist hung in the cool cave air, the musty smell of the cavern's depths assaulting his nasal cavities.

Exhaling sharply, DeShear put his hands on his knees and gazed back at the pit. His eyes had adjusted enough to guess that it probably extended a mile, maybe more—something not unusual for caves formed by glaciers.

He stepped toward the green sign. At the bottom, it said 010.

Faint voices reached his ears, and a glimmer of light from deeper inside the cave. He rushed to the cave wall, pushing himself into a small recess in the stone.

The lights grew brighter, swinging across the walls and floor of the cave.

"This way." A woman's voice echoed off the cave walls. "He should be right about..." One of the lights moved upwards, washing over DeShear and blinding him. "...here."

Narrowing his eyes, DeShear held a hand up to block the intense illumination.

"Welcome, Mr. DeShear," the woman said. "I'm glad to finally make your acquaintance in person."

DeShear squinted in the bright light. "I'd return the greeting, but I can't really see you at the moment. Any chance you'd lower that light?"

The beam of light moved to the cave floor. A woman in a white lab coat stood before him, with three armed men behind her. All three had brown hair and a dark mole on their left cheek, just under the eye.

DeShear's jaw dropped.

She put a hand on her hip, smiling. "You may call me Doctor Atria Lutz."

He looked at the three men. They were virtually identical. "What is this, a cloning facility?"

"Don't play dumb, Hamilton. You know exactly what this is—or you should. And you should know why you're here."

"I have an idea." He glared at her. "This is another of Hauser's labs, and you lured me here so you could tell me that *only you* can stop the device in Constantine's head from killing her—then I'm supposed to bring her here so you can lock her up, harvest her stem cells and bone marrow, and then when she's old enough, you'll take her eggs. You're just a butcher, like the others."

"No." Lutz shook her head, handing her flashlight to one of her accomplices. "I want Constantine dead. You, too, Mr. DeShear."

"You... you want her *dead?* Why?"

"Stem cells are big money, but ultimately they're still small potatoes. Think bigger. Think global." She pointed a bony finger at DeShear. "As long as the child is alive, she's a potential competitor to me. As you said, right now she has stem cells and bone marrow—but eventually there would be offspring, multiplying the threat." Lutz raised her hands to her chin, tapping the fingertips together. "With Constantine out of the way, that threat is eliminated—leaving my lines of genetically engineered humans as the only ones in existence. A monopoly, so to speak."

"I take it back." DeShear scowled. "You're worse than the butchers."

Atria Lutz shrugged. "Sticks and stones. My motivations are my own—as your motivations are your own." She peered at him, narrowing her eyes. "How many people have died since you started your ridiculous crusade? At least The Greyhound killed people he thought were murderers. You've killed innocent people."

"What?" DeShear grimaced. "How?"

"What do you think happened to all those embryos after you shut down Hauser's facilities?" Lutz swung her arms out at her sides. "Did you think the U.N. would become foster parents to a million babies and find them all homes? Don't be stupid. They shut it down—and all of those precious, innocent lives you wanted to save—perished."

"That's not true." DeShear clenched his teeth. "They worked to get them adopted and were very successful. Now, they're working to place the last few into homes."

"Oh?" She folded her arms, smiling. "And that's true because you read a monthly status report? Or because you flew to Indonesia every week to make sure everything was happening according to plan? Or maybe I'm lying." Lutz shrugged. "You see? We live in a world of information manipulation. You know what they want you to know, and you act accordingly." Her gaze moved to the cold, wet walls of the cave. "Here, we have no such… illusions."

DeShear shook his head, pointing at her. "No, you just deliver death at a moment's notice, by way of your latest whim. I've seen Hauser's labs before, and I know how they operate—and I have no doubt you're a raving psychotic, just like he was."

"Because they want you to believe I am!" Lutz stepped toward him, the veins in her neck sticking out. "Look how they groomed your thinking—governments, media… Give me a computer and a few pliable broadcasters, and in an hour I'll have the world believing you shot Abraham Lincoln!"

Her face was red in the dim light. Slowly, she regained her composure.

"And speaking of shooting…" Lutz slipped her hands into her lab coat pockets, raising her chin and peering down it at her visitor. "How unfortunate you've suffered such a terrible injury."

"Huh?" DeShear looked at her. "What—"

She pulled a gun from her lab coat and fired it at him.

Pain exploded through DeShear's left thigh, like a scorching fire. Gasping, he fell to the ground, grabbing his upper leg as warm wetness pumped over his fingers.

"The units of *my* line may not be as prescient as the Deltas…" Lutz sneered. "But somehow I foresaw you getting shot just now."

She fired a second shot, hitting the outside of DeShear's right thigh. Pressing a hand over her mouth, Lutz stifled a giggle.

As DeShear writhed in pain on the wet cave floor, the gaunt doctor dropped her gun back into her pocket. "Now, let's see what developments this brings to the situation."

* * * * *

Helena and Constantine breezed through the hotel lobby and got to the elevators. When the doors opened, they entered and pressed the button for their floor.

The old woman glanced at her ward. "Are you okay, dear? You've hardly uttered a word since we left the mountain."

Constantine stared straight ahead, shivering.

"Are… are you *cold*, child?" Helena frowned, taking off her coat. "Here, let me—"

Constantine threw her head back, shrieking in pain. She fell to the floor of the elevator, grabbing her left thigh.

"He's been shot!" she shrieked. "Hamilton's been shot."

Heart racing, Helena dropped to Constantine's side. She forced the child's hands away to inspect her leg.

There was nothing there.

"Child, what is it? Are you… are you having a—"

The young girl shrieked again, grabbing her other leg. "She means to kill him!"

"Who is?" The color drained from the old woman's face. "Who's doing this to him?"

Constantine bolted upward, her eyes wide, grabbing Helena's shirt collar with both hands. "She wants to kill us all!"

As Helena held her, Constantine's eyes rolled back in her head. Her tiny body went limp, sagging into the old woman's arms.

"Constantine! Speak to me!"

Constantine's head dropped. She let go of Helena's collar, her hands falling to the elevator floor.

Helena looked around wildly, her pulse throbbing. Reaching up, she banged on the elevator wall panel, cradling the limp, unconscious child and jamming her finger on the button for the sixth floor.

CHAPTER 36

Too wracked with pain to fight three armed men, DeShear let the tansuits drag him to a large opening in the cave that had been turned into a laboratory. White walls graced its interior; a steel mesh grid served as its roof. DeShear winced every step of the way, holding the pain in, his forehead drenched in sweat and his legs consumed with throbbing fire. They laid him down on a gurney, a white surgical lamp shining into his eyes, and stepped to the side—but kept their weapons ready.

A fourth identical tansuit in surgical scrubs came forward, taking hold of one of the thick straps on the side of the gurney.

DeShear grabbed the medical technician's hand, glaring at him.

The trio of armed guards trained their weapons on DeShear. Frowning, he let go of the technician's hand. A large strap went across his abdomen, followed by two restraints to hold down his hands.

As the leg straps were administered, a tansuit in a white lab coat took a small brown bottle from a nearby cabinet and plunged a syringe into it, filling the long, slender barrel with the clear liquid. "Morphine," the lab assistant said. "For the pain."

He pushed his patient's sleeve up and lowered the needle to the inside of DeShear's elbow.

Atria Lutz sauntered toward the gurney. "Morphine is my analgesia of choice in gunshot situations, due to its reliable and predictable effects and its ease of reversibility with naloxone." She pushed the technician's syringe away. "But you'll be getting none to ease your pain. For the moment, I need your mind clear."

She flipped a switch on a nearby monitor.

As the screen came into focus, the tansuits surrounding DeShear appeared, as if the camera for the monitor was attached to DeShear's head.

"Nice, isn't it?" Lutz waved at the metal grid ceiling. "The entire roof of this underground facility is a neuroreceptor receiver. We're currently acquiring your brainwaves quite strongly because you're in pain—your receptors are shouting louder than anyone else's, so to speak—and we've directed the information they're carrying here, on the monitor." She tapped the computer screen. "Your every thought, as fast as you think it, instantly displayed for all to see."

DeShear grunted, struggling against his bindings.

"At present," Lutz said, "the images are of me and my staff, with a healthy baseline of underlying pain. But as soon as we administer the morphine, your discomfort will fade, and so will your resistance. You will be amenable to every suggestion I utter, showing it to me here, on this screen." She put her hands on her hips, smiling at her bound hostage. "We are bridging the next step in human evolution."

DeShear managed to spit out a few words between his pangs of agony. "I may have... skipped science class that day..." He gasped, forcing the words through his clenched teeth, his legs throbbing. "But I wouldn't call a metal grid antenna... a step in *human* evolution."

"Oh, I completely disagree." Lutz folded her arms, putting a finger to her lower lip. "It is merely the physical representation of what the Deltas have been doing all along, in their own witchy little way." She gazed at the mesh ceiling, turning to where the wire bundles gathered and slinked down the wall to the large metal computer housings. "Some units of the Delta line can grab the tiniest elements of brainwave activity—just pluck it out of the atmosphere—and translate it into usable data. It's an absolutely remarkable phenomenon. Hauser had his Rituals bonnets, reproducing a similar effect, but I have reverse engineered what his Delta units could do. Now, I am able to capture neurotransmissions from anywhere in the world, to use for my own purposes—the key to which..." She walked along the side of the gurney, extending a thin finger and tapping DeShear on the head as she passed. "...I believe is locked away in your gray matter, Mr. DeShear."

Wincing, DeShear strained to keep the doctor in sight. Sweat ran across his forehead and down the side of his face. "What lies did Hauser tell you about me?"

"Why, none." Lutz turned to face him. "Doctor Hauser stored his secrets away digitally, in case the transfer and retrieval of his consciousness to a new body was unsuccessful." She narrowed her eyes. "But I think he also put it into you, as a series of suppressed memories. The records from the château show you were capped upon arrival—you and your friend, The Greyhound. Like he did with the children in his Rituals sessions, Hauser used microradial transmissions to stash away his secrets, behind locked doors in the recesses of your unconscious, that he might need to access later."

DeShear huffed, pushing his intense pain out of his thoughts. "I thought Hauser's AI system was supposed to do all that. I thought that was his failsafe."

"Rest assured, I am obtaining Hauser's AI as we speak, but I always like to have a plan B—and that's you." She took the syringe from her technician and held it up to the light, her voice falling to a whisper. "I want to access both entities—whatever memories Hauser implanted in you, and whatever consciousness he saved on his computers as a rudimentary type of artificial intelligence." She turned, facing DeShear, a smile stretched across her thin lips. "Then, I'll download what I need from both resources and get rid of everything else." The smile grew wider. She leaned in close, barely audible above the activity in the lab. "And yes, that means getting rid of you. And your offspring. And that old, diminished Keeper unit you insist on having around." She sneered, her breath hot on DeShear's cheek. "I'll wipe the earth clean of you all, and of any other genetically engineered human that isn't of my selected lines."

She plunged the tip of the needle into his arm and emptied its barrel. The warmth of the contents coursed up DeShear's arm and through his veins.

"Just like Hauser." DeShear moaned. "Death by delivery… for the money."

The strong drug was already having its effect. A calm blackness settled over him.

"What better reason is there?" Lutz stood upright, holding the empty syringe and pacing back and forth with it. Her voice was clear, but the words were becoming distant and hollow, like they were being spoken from the other end of a long hallway. "After all, no one cares if Hauser or his alleged consciousness survive. I simply want the money— the hard-earned, well-deserved money—that *my* lines are capable of producing. Billions and billion of dollars, euros, rubles, yen, and krugerrands." Her expression fell, a dour look coming over her face. "And believe me, I have earned it. I've sacrificed for this day, more than anyone should ever have to sacrifice—and I will have my reward."

She frowned, making a fist and pressing her thumb sideways against the syringe, snapping it in half. She threw it down, tiny bits of wet glass bouncing everywhere across the lab room floor.

DeShear pushed against his straps, the fog in his head growing thicker. The pain didn't leave his legs as much as he no longer seemed to care that it existed at all. He was calmer than he ever recalled feeling, relaxed to the point of being comatose, and fighting for patches of clarity.

"And what about these guys?" His words slurred as he said them. Taking a breath, DeShear tried to focus, speaking slower and enunciating each syllable, but sounding drunk to his own ears. "These… tansuit clones of yours?"

"Please don't insult my staff of Omicron units." Lutz's voice was an echo in the swallowing darkness. "They're…" She snickered. "…like family to me."

"Until you don't need them anymore," DeShear said. "Then they'll be disposed of."

"Whatever they become, it will be no concern of yours, as you will have long since become deceased." She loomed over him, pulling an IV to the side of his gurney and attaching it to his arm. "Now, as much as I am enjoying this witty repartee, I have work to do." Lutz faced her medical assistant. "Seventeen, administer the syringe."

"Seventeen?" Groaning, DeShear shook his wobbly head, looking at the man in the scrubs, then to the armed Omicron tansuits guarding him. "She… doesn't even care enough about you to… to make up a dozen and a half names for all of you."

Lutz grabbed DeShear by the collar, gritting her teeth in his face. "I'd have you gagged, but I need to hear you speak when the sustained morphine drip hits your system. But…" She leaned back, smiling as she smoothed out his shirt. "Thank you—and your unfortunate injuries—for allowing our receptors to latch onto such a strong and identifiable signal. You can even go to sleep now, and we'll be able to monitor your every thought."

She stepped away, her voice fading in the darkness.

"I'd say goodnight, Mr. DeShear, but since it's very likely you'll be dead in a few hours, I shall say goodbye."

DeShear fought the drugs, pushing himself up through the thick, dark haze to a clear thought. "What about... Constantine? I... thought you needed me alive... to lure her here."

As he slipped away, Atria Lutz's words echoed in his ears, followed by her laughter.

"And you have, Hamilton! You have!"

CHAPTER 37

Helena carried Constantine to the room and placed her on the bed. Sweat dotted the child's forehead as she quietly moaned in her unconscious state. Pacing back and forth, the old woman kneaded her fingers as she stared at the phone on the nightstand.

It must be done now. There may not be any more time.

She picked up the phone and typed a text message for Jaden Trinn.

"New York Pizza urgent delivery needed."

Helena held her finger over the send button, staring at the message and rereading it to make sure it didn't say anything that could be deciphered by the other side, while still letting Trinn know that her help was needed immediately.

Pursing her lips, the old woman sent the message and set the phone back down.

She lowered herself onto the foot of the bed, gazing at Constantine.

The phone rang, causing Helena to jump.

She picked it up from the nightstand. The screen said "unidentified caller." Swallowing hard, Helena hit the green button and put the phone to her ear. "Hello?"

"Helena, it's me." Trinn's voice was obscured by the sound of road noise, but it was clearly recognizable—and very welcome. "Message received. I'm on my way. Is there a second hotel?"

"Yes," she said. DeShear had insisted that Helena and Constantine check in to several places as Hermosa and Carmelita Montenegro.

"Go there." Trinn's line crackled with static. "Email me the address through the VPN."

"Yes." Trembling, Helena glanced at the unconscious six-year-old laying on the bed. "Yes, I shall, dear."

"Okay," Trinn said. "I'll meet you there."

The call ended.

As Helena stood, Constantine bolted upright.

"He's there!" She shrieked, her face turning white. "In the cave with Hamilton. Doctor Hauser is there!"

* * * * *

The technician looked up from his monitor. "Doctor Lutz. Sympathetic pain signal received. The Theta unit has reacted." He put his finger to the screen. A green dot blinked on the map of western Canada. He zoomed in to the Alberta province, the dot becoming fuzzy as it expanded. "She's close by."

The gaunt doctor walked across the lab, smiling as she peered over her technician's shoulder to view the monitor. "Hello, Constantine."

From the gurney, DeShear moaned.

Lutz looked at him, shaking her head. "Every parent would run to help their child, but they never consider that the child might run to help the parent." She turned to her technician. "Stay on it. Locate the address the signal is coming from and get a team there as soon as possible."

* * * * *

In less than half an hour, Helena had gotten their baggage together and hailed a taxi, rousing Constantine enough to have the child leave the hotel under her own power. At the backup location, Helena declined help from the cab driver, opting instead to place Constantine's smaller bag on top of her own, and wheeling them across the entryway. Constantine had cleared her head enough to seem more normal, and they were able to cross the lobby together and enter the elevators.

"How do you feel, child?" Helena pushed the button to their floor. "Are you in pain?"

Constantine put her hand to her forehead. "I… I don't think I was actually in pain. I think I just saw *Hamilton* in pain and… I don't know. I reacted." She peered at her mistress. "I couldn't stop myself. It was as if we were… *connected* somehow."

"You mustn't give it another thought. Just rest." Helena kneaded her fingers, staring at the panel of buttons as the floors went by. "Miss Jaden will be here any minute. Then we'll get a plan together, straight away."

The elevator doors opened and the pair stepped off, Helena pulling the bags with one hand and holding Constantine's small hand in the other. The child had to take two steps to every one of her mistress, just to keep up.

Constantine peered up at Helena. "Why do you suppose I didn't see anything *before* it happened?"

"It doesn't always work that way, dear. We don't see things at will—though I wish we did." Helena rushed down the long corridor. "We just receive what we receive, whenever it comes. I don't know what else to say. I can't explain this instance any more than I could explain what happened to me, when I was in that French hospital and that famous chef died in the car wreck, except to say it's a bonding. You and Hamilton share a bond—as well you should, being father and daughter."

"You and I have always shared a bond like that, too. We often know what—"

The old woman stopped, gazing at the door to their room. Taking a deep breath, she took out the key card, lowering her voice. "We… must be careful." Helena turned to her ward and wagged a finger. "We are to stay in the room until Miss Jaden arrives, and stay quiet. There could be any number of threats lurking about."

Constantine nodded.

Turning, Helena stared at the door latch, holding her key with trembling fingers. Lowering her hand, she slid the plastic card across the metal latch.

The door lock clicked.

She let go of Constantine's hand and pushed on the heavy wooden door. It swung inward into their hotel room, light spilling into the hallway.

Gasping, Helena put a hand to her chest and took a step backwards. "No!" She bumped into Constantine, losing her balance. "No! Not you!"

As the old woman fell to the floor, the hotel room door inched closed, tapping into the latch but not re-locking.

Constantine dropped to Helena's side. "What is it? What's happened?"

The old woman's eyes went wide as the door swung open again, revealing the shadowy figure of a large man.

"Oh, no!" Helena cried, clutching Constantine to her breast as she crawled backwards over the carpeted hallway floor. "No, no, no!"

The man stepped forward, his rotund mass filling the door frame, a scowl on his face.

"Hello again, Keeper 27," Mr. Hollings growled. "Fancy meeting you here."

CHAPTER 38

Doctor Lutz burst through a door marked "private," locking it behind her as she stepped to the center of her lab. The smell of smoke clung to her clothing.

The Omicron medical technician monitored DeShear's vital signs. "Doctor, the subject is approximately where you wanted him."

"Good." Lutz strutted to the gurney where DeShear lay, rubbing her hands together. "Let's do a test, shall we?" She glanced at the monitor. Patches of black fog swirled across the screen. "I need quiet in the room, and let's bring up the color array on the monitor."

The Omicron typed on his keyboard and glanced at the screen. "No change. It's black." He turned to Atria Lutz. "Have we lost the feed?"

"No." She smiled. "He's just deep in the well."

* * * * *

"Hamilton DeShear, can you hear me?"

The words echoed in his head, sounding close but also far away, like they had been uttered in a dream. He recognized the voice as Doctor Lutz, but his sedated state didn't allow him to respond. He could not summon the energy to make his mouth move.

"DeShear, if you can hear me, squeeze my hand."

Warmth came to his fingers. Soft warmth, like expensive gloves, but firm.

"Can you squeeze my hand?"

He flexed his shoulders and arms, trying to recall how to move his fingers.

"Perhaps the levels are too high," Lutz said. "Decrease the morphine drip by twenty percent and bring us a low dose of naloxone."

A man's voice answered. "Yes, Doctor. What dilution?"

"Ten percent, until we get a visual reading on the screen."

Their faces came to him from the fog, not from his eyes but from his memory. He envisioned the gurney from above, with Lutz crowding over the medical technician's shoulder.

What was his name? It was a number.

Seventeen had filled the syringe. He wore hospital scrubs.

An image of the brown-haired tech came to him, with the mole under his eye and dressed in scrubs.

Seventeen.

DeShear's own thoughts echoed in his head, recalling the brief encounter he had with the technician.

She doesn't even care enough about you to make up a dozen and a half names for all of you.

"Doctor," the technician said. "I think he's trying to speak."

Seventeen. DeShear tried to make his mouth form the words. *Your name is Seventeen.*

"Zoom out on the monitor," Lutz said.

The sounds of hospital equipment reached him—the rhythmic beeping of the heart machine, the slow rise and fall of the blue cylinder in the spirometer, the digital readout of the oxygen sensor. DeShear forced himself out of the calm darkness like he was a swimmer in a pond on a moonless night, coming up for a breath of air.

He saw the equipment and the medical technician. The white lab room. The armed tansuits.

Omicrons.

Swallowing hard, DeShear pushed a word out from his lips. "Seventeen."

"What's that?" Lutz leaned over her technician. "What did he say?"

"The subject is mumbling something," the medical technician said. "He's coming up to a clarity level."

Lutz stared at the monitor. "Go further out on that screen. The focal point changed with the introduction of the morphine. His thoughts are blurred now. Pull it way back."

On the screen, a white blob came into view.

"That's it," Lutz said. "Further."

Seventeen typed on his keyboard.

"And pull back a little more…"

He clicked his mouse repeatedly, the blob on the screen getting smaller and becoming his shoulder, with Doctor Lutz hovering over him.

"We've regained visual contact." Seventeen smiled.

"Perfect." Lutz stood upright, bringing her hands to her chin and tapping the fingertips together. "Now let's play a little game. Are we recording?"

Seventeen checked his computer. "Yes, doctor."

She looked at her patient. "Mr. DeShear, I want you to… think of a red star on a field of white. Envision it, like it was a cardboard sign."

A red star on a white cardboard rectangle came onto the screen.

"Very good." Lutz nodded. "And now, think of a monkey—a cartoon monkey with brown fur and a black top hat."

The animal appeared on the screen, just as Lutz had described.

"Yes…" Lutz smiled. "He's having perfect involuntary responses. Whatever I suggest, he immediately thinks of—and shows us, on this screen."

In the darkness, her words bounced off invisible walls and faded into the fog. DeShear clenched his hands and inhaled sharply, working to make a word. He opened his mouth, pushing the air over his lips and into the sterile, white laboratory.

"Seventeen."

Doctor Lutz recoiled, her jaw dropping. "What did he say?"

DeShear smiled. On the screen he saw his body on the gurney, a grin on his face—and on the face of the medical technician.

"I believe he said, 'Seventeen,' Doctor." The technician lowered his head and adjusted a knob on the monitor.

Lutz raised an eyebrow, glaring at her patient. "A trapped memory splinter, rebounding from pre-induction, perhaps."

"Perhaps." Seventeen turned to her. "Why *couldn't* you have given us names?"

Her eyes flashed with rage. "Be silent!" Lutz rushed forward, slapping Seventeen across the face. "Had I been able to implement Hauser's control features, I wouldn't be dealing with such insolence!" She glared at the others present. "That goes for all of you! Focus on your jobs."

The assistant in the white lab coat stepped forward, putting his hand on Seventeen's shoulder. "He's tired, Doctor. Perhaps some standalone time would be in order for Number Seventeen."

Lutz pushed her hair back from her forehead. "Eleven, you are compassionate, and that is an admirable quality, but you need to guard against being too soft." She straightened her lab coat. "Leadership is forged on tough decisions and adherence to strict discipline."

"Like the separations?" Seventeen said.

"Enough!" Lutz slammed her hand down onto the desk, her face turning red. "That is it! One more word and I'll take you all offline! Don't think I won't." She pointed at DeShear. "I'll stick him on ice for a year and a half until your replacements are ready, and I'll be right back in business. So watch yourselves."

The room full of Omicrons lowered their eyes.

"Doctor…" Seventeen said.

"What!" She wheeled around to him. "What is it now?"

"The subject is still cognitive enough to be hearing all of this, ma'am."

Cursing, she balled up her fists. "Get a set of headphones onto him and hook up a microphone. Now!"

Nodding, Seventeen reached into a drawer and took out two microphones, plugging them into his computer. Eleven went to a cabinet and removed several sets of wireless headphones, with large protective cups for each ear, and took them to Seventeen and Doctor Lutz. He crossed the lab, returning to the gurney and slipped the third bulky headset over DeShear's ears, finally putting the fourth set over his own.

From the watery darkness, DeShear opened his eyes. The Omicron guards were assembled at the foot of the gurney, the medical technician Seventeen at his right side. Number Eleven stood behind him, his arms folded.

On the far side of the lab, Lutz disappeared through a door marked "private," slamming it and locking it behind her.

DeShear blinked, taking it all in. The noises of the lab and the medical equipment had become nonexistent, replaced by the sound of his own heartbeat.

He glanced at Seventeen. It seemed as if the medical technician was mouthing the words "You're doing fine" instead of speaking them.

DeShear narrowed his eyes. "What?"

Even his own words were nearly silent to him.

Seventeen reached to his computer and flipped a switch, bringing the sound of the lab back to DeShear's ears. He leaned toward one of the microphones, sliding the other one to the side. "I said, you're doing fine, Mr. DeShear. Your vital signs have stabilized, but don't move around too much or your gunshot wounds will bleed worse than they already are—and then we'll have a real problem."

DeShear looked around, then returned his gaze to Seventeen. "Help me out of here," he whispered. "She's going to kill you the second she has what she needs from me."

His voice was clearer than he expected, but still muddy.

"She'll kill you," DeShear said, "because no line will ever be good enough. You have to know that by now."

Seventeen stared at his patient, the medical machines rhythmically blinking beside him. He lowered his eyes and looked away.

"Seventeen, I get it." DeShear strained against his bindings, his words low but pointed. "You've surrendered to your fate instead of living in fear every day, wondering when it'll come. I understand. But Lutz will kill everyone in your line and every other line. She *has* to. It's the only way her newest prototypes can be guaranteed to not have competition. Isn't there anyone you care about?"

Seventeen's eyes drifted toward the door marked "private."

"What?" DeShear followed the Omicron's gaze. "What's in there?"

Shaking his head, Seventeen resumed his work, speaking louder than necessary. "Remember, you must remain still, or your wounds will bleed worse." He glanced over both shoulders, then lowered his voice as he typed on his computer. "I'll stop your morphine drip." Seventeen's lips barely moved as he spoke. "Your pain will increase, but your mind will be sharper. Don't let on."

"Untie me," DeShear hissed.

The technician got up from his seat, shaking his head. He adjusted a setting on the heart rate monitor. "Not yet. She'll see."

* * * * *

Helena cowered on the floor of the hallway, pulling Constantine close as Hollings towered over her.

"Stop messing around." Trinn shoved him aside and stepped into the corridor. She thrust a large suitcase into Hollings' fat hands. "You have an appointment you need to keep. Get going."

"Aye. So I do." Grinning, Hollings stepped over Helena, clutching the suitcase to his chest as he headed toward the elevators.

Constantine stood up as Trinn helped Helena to her feet.

"Are you alright?" Trinn asked.

"Yes, yes, dear." Helena brushed herself off, her cheeks red. "Just a bit of a fright, is all."

"Okay." Trinn breathed a sigh of relief. "Go inside and lock the door. I'll be right back."

Constantine stared at Hollings, then turned her gaze to Trinn. "You're working with him now?"

"He's working with *us*." Jaden put her hand on the child's back, turning her. "Now get inside—and stay quiet."

Helena entered the room, holding the door open. "Come, dear. Do as Miss Jaden says."

As the hotel room door shut behind her, Trinn raced down the hallway. She caught up to Hollings at the elevator. "Time to part ways, Mr. Hollings." She chewed her lip. "Don't forget what we talked about."

"Aye, lass." The doors opened and Hollings stepped into the elevator. "Just let me get downstairs and organize a hired car, and I'll be on my way."

Trinn shook her head. "No time for that. There are plenty of cars in the parking lot. Steal one and get back on the road. And don't lose the second package in that suitcase."

"Second package?" Hollings pulled his suitcase to his chest. "Weren't but one machine in here, girl—yours. And I done gave it to you."

Trinn put her hands on her hips. "Don't be so stupid. That suitcase isn't weighed down with your underwear. You couldn't very well double deal me if you didn't have two of Hauser's AI machines. I'd have killed you if you showed up empty handed, and so would Atria Lutz. That means you had to steal two of them." She narrowed her eyes. "Makes me wonder how many more might be out there."

Hollings tugged at his collar. "It's just those two, girl. Yours and hers, I swear it. Now, I might have also promised yours to Symm, but the wanker got himself dealt out, so we're all square again."

"Uh-huh. Well, I guess I'll know soon enough. Now, go."

Returning to the room, Trinn knocked on the door. "Helena, Constantine—it's me."

Constantine opened the door. "We should have a special knock, so we know it's you."

"Okay. You work on that." Trinn went to the closet and opened the door, revealing a computer and two leather caps, like old time football helmets, made of thick leather bands, with a strap for under the chin. A bundle of wires ran from the headgear to the computer. She stepped back, looking at Helena. "Do you know what that is?"

The old woman put her hand to her mouth. "I do, dear. And I hoped to never see one again."

CHAPTER 39

Doctor Lutz burst from behind the private door, grabbing a chair and storming across the lab to DeShear. She shoved Seventeen out of the way and seated herself next to him, picking up the Omicron's microphone.

DeShear looked at her, breathing normally, as if he didn't have a care in the world.

"Mr. DeShear," she said, "do you know who is speaking to you right now?"

A still image of Doctor Lutz flashed on the monitor. It was from when he first saw her near the cave entrance. In the image, she held the gun on him. The screen visual moved slowly, firing the gun at DeShear.

"Yes," he said, his voice barely a whisper. "You're the psychotic maniac who shot me."

Lutz frowned. "I am Doctor Atria Lutz. Say it."

"Doctor Atria Lutz." His eyes were half open. The screen changed to the image of Lutz, crowded over the microphone.

She glanced at the monitor. "Very good. And now, can you tell me… who is Keeper 27?"

The old woman's face appeared on the monitor before DeShear could correct the doctor. "Her name is Helena."

Lutz nodded, her eyes staying on the screen. "And who is her ward?"

An image of Constantine appeared on the screen.

Lutz smiled. As she leaned toward the mic again and opened her mouth, the image on the monitor changed to a brown cartoon monkey in a black top hat.

Then to a red star on a white field.

A grin stretched across the thin doctor's face. "Very well, Mr. DeShear, have it your way. Play games if you want—but you already gave me the information I needed, didn't you?"

DeShear swallowed. "I… did."

"Yes. So, the game has no value. You cannot keep the information from me that I want to know. The mind reacts too quickly. The truth is displayed on the screen faster than you can think up a lie to cover it."

The heart rate monitor went up. His breathing level increased.

"Let me prove to you that you simply cannot withhold from me what I want to know, so we can waste less time. Do you love Constantine?"

His daughter's image from the château appeared, when she was sipping water on the lawn with Helena after being rescued from Hauser.

"Yes," DeShear said.

"And, do you consider Constantine to be your daughter?"

"She *is* my daughter."

Lutz smiled. "Then, tell me… where is Constantine right now?"

The image of the Banff Springs Hotel appeared, the ground snowy and white, dark green firs filling the background.

"I see." Lutz turned to one of the armed Omicron tansuits. "Get a team together and head over there." She faced the screen again. "And what room number is Constantine in?"

Helena and Constantine's room number on the seventh floor appeared.

"Thank you." Lutz turned to the tansuit. "Get going."

He nodded, heading for the exit, then stopped. "Are they armed?"

"Ah. Good question." Lutz looked at the monitor. "Do your Keeper unit and your daughter have any weapons with them?"

"No," DeShear said. The screen displayed an image of Helena and Constantine's hands, clothed in mittens, waving at him from over their upstairs balcony.

The guard headed for the door.

Leaning back, Lutz lifted her hands to her chin and tapped her fingertips together. She switched off the microphone in front of her, turning to Seventeen. "Open the facial morphing program."

"Yes, Doctor." He typed on his keyboard. "Which image?"

"Don't be an idiot." Lutz scowled. "You know which image. The only image that matters now. How are his levels?"

"His levels are adequate," Seventeen said. "He's stable, despite the injuries in his legs—but we should change the dressing on those wounds and see about closing the—"

"He stays as he is." Lutz looked at Seventeen. "Pain may be necessary to… to get everything I want."

In the corner of the screen, a green rectangle flashed with the words, "Facial Morphing Program Ready."

Lutz tapped the green rectangle, switched on the microphone, and cleared her throat. "Mr. DeShear…"

Atria Lutz spoke the words, but the sound was that of Doctor Marcus Hauser. On the screen, Hauser's face appeared. His mouth moved with the voice and motions of Atria Lutz, as if he were alive and saying them for himself.

"Mr. DeShear," the onscreen Hauser said again.

DeShear recoiled on the gurney, his heart rate spiking. "You're dead."

A smile spread across Hauser's face. "Clearly, I am not."

* * * * *

In the hotel room at the secondary location, Helena sat at a desk chair in front of the closet, the leather Rituals cap strapped to her head. Constantine stood next to her, a hand on her mistress' shoulder. The hotel TV sat on top of the computer Hollings had brought, displaying an image of DeShear on the gurney—and Hauser on the screen.

"Oh, I don't like the look of this." Helena clutched her hands to her lap. "Hamilton's legs are bleeding again, from the increase in heart rate and blood pressure. He needs to get to a doctor, straight away."

Trinn nodded, biting a fingernail. "There's nothing we can do about that at the moment. How bad is he?"

"He could die if he's allowed to keep bleeding like that." The old woman shook her head. "Lutz is a doctor. She has to know that."

Trinn frowned. "Then she doesn't care. What a surprise. How long do we have?"

"I don't know, Miss. I'm just reading the screen." Helena pointed to the heart rate monitor standing on a rack adjacent to the medical technician. "Hamilton can see the medical equipment, so I can see it when he looks. I'm not a doctor, but the blood on his legs has increased substantially since she started asking him questions." She exhaled sharply, thin beads of sweat forming on her brow. "That's not good."

"Yeah." Trinn paced back and forth. "I'm not a doctor, either. Maybe I can access the internet and learn something. Then you can transmit it to him, right?"

"I can send him information through thoughts." Helena pulled at her collar, closing her eyes. "But... I can't make his wound stop bleeding. We really must get a... a medical professional for that."

Trinn sighed, putting a hand to her forehead. "And he's surrounded by them."

"What about me?" Constantine said. "How can I help?"

"You, just stay put." Trinn patted the child's shoulder.

"But..."

"If they see your thoughts coming through," Trinn squatted next to Constantine, looking into her eyes, "they might be able to learn where we really are. We can't risk that. For now, just—"

Helena's head lowered. Her shoulders slumped, and she sagged to the table.

"Helena!" Trinn grabbed the old woman's arms and sat her upright in the chair. Helena's face was pale. "Constantine, get a glass of water and wet a towel."

Constantine ran to the bathroom.

Patting Helena's cheek, Trinn looked into her friend's half-open eyes. "Are you okay? What happened?"

"I... I don't quite know, dear." Helena panted, looking around.

Constantine brought the water and a wet towel. As Helena took a sip, Trinn dabbed the cloth across her forehead.

Jaden's jaw dropped. "Helena, you're burning up."

Constantine took the glass from her mistress. "The bonnets can be very taxing. They always gave me a headache during Rituals, and some children even threw up after."

Reaching for the chin strap, Trinn nodded. "Okay. Let's get this off you."

"No." Helena's hands darted up, stopping Jaden. She panted, sweat rolling down her cheek. "We must help Hamilton." Her gaze went to the screen. "He needs us."

"You can't help him much if you're passed out," Trinn said. "And if you keep going like this... who knows what could happen?"

"She could die." Constantine's face was grim. "I've seen it happen."

"What?" Helena faced her young ward, her hands trembling. "When? When did you ever see such a thing?"

"There were visions of the Rituals room, when Doctor Hauser used the bonnets to kill all my friends." Constantine looked down. "I got them from you, when you did standalone." She raised her eyes to Helena's. "You thought of it all the time. It scares you deeply."

The old woman nodded. She stroked Constantine's arm. "It did, child. Very deeply. It was my greatest failing in life."

"But some of the instructors tried to use the bonnets, too," Constantine said. "Not just for programming, but at night sometimes, to see what they could access." The child's gaze went to Trinn. "It's set up to notice who's using it, and they weren't authorized. It killed them."

"What!" Jaden's mouth hung open. She grabbed for Helena's chin strap. "Why didn't you say anything before I put that thing on her?"

"It won't hurt her." Constantine shook her head. "It won't hurt me, either. It can't. We were authorized. It's just very tiring. That's what could kill her—the exhaustion."

Rubbing the side of her head, Trinn looked at Constantine. "Are you sure?"

The child nodded. "She was a favorite of Doctor Hauser's. Everyone knew that."

CHAPTER 40

Seventeen's gaze darted to the medical instruments at his side, then back to his computer. DeShear's breathing was becoming erratic. His heart rate continued to climb.

Seventeen glanced at Atria Lutz. "Doctor, he's moving into critical range."

"He's fine." Lutz stared at the images of Hauser and DeShear on the monitor. "We won't need him much longer. Keep going."

"At this rate, he's going to die! You're getting what you want out of this. What about what we want?"

Lutz's eyes went wide. She turned to him. "Such as?"

"Where are the regeneration records?"

"How dare you!" She slapped Seventeen hard across the face. "Never question my priorities."

The Omicron cringed, lowering his head. "We… need to get his wounds dressed. He may bleed out."

"Let him bleed out. We only need to get the information from him before he does."

Seventeen frowned. "We should at least take a break…"

Lutz swung around and slapped her medical technician a second time. "A break? We just started!"

Seventeen's cheek turned red.

"Get away." Lutz shoved him. "Go… wash some test tubes or something. I'll handle things from here."

Getting up from his chair, Seventeen moved to the corner, near the tansuit guards. Eleven came to his side.

Lutz leaned forward, typing on the computer. "I told all of you before, we are on the verge of great discovery. We can't slow down, not even for a minute."

"I'm sorry, Doctor. You're right." Seventeen rubbed his red cheek. "But please watch his vital signs. If we lose him, we lose everything—we *all* lose everything."

A phone rang. One of the tansuits dug into his pocket and took out his phone, answering it. He turned to Lutz. "The girl and the old woman aren't in the hotel. DeShear lied to us."

Frowning, Lutz gripped the edge of the gurney. "How? How is that possible?" She turned to Seventeen. "We saw his answer! What did you do wrong?"

Eleven stepped in front of Seventeen. "Ma'am, the equipment worked. If DeShear gave us incorrect information on their whereabouts, it's because he didn't know their actual location—they moved without him knowing where they went. But he didn't lie. He *can't* lie. Not without us seeing." The assistant looked at DeShear's vital signs. "But Seventeen is right. DeShear's information will become less reliable as he dies. The clarity will fade."

Lutz cursed, pounding on the gurney rail. She peered at the machines. "Seventeen, give him some adrenaline. That'll bring his blood pressure up. Eleven, you increase his fluids."

Nodding, Seventeen moved to Lutz's side. "Yes, but… Doctor, we need to dress the wounds. He's getting more and more unstable. Adrenaline will amplify that. If he dies, getting his daughter becomes that much harder." He sighed, pointing at DeShear. "By now, Constantine and her group must know about the implant in her head, but she will never come here unless DeShear tells her to. So, if DeShear dies, she will continue to believe that she will die. They'll all know that. But if he were to tell her to come, she will come."

"Yes…" Lutz rubbed her chin. "And I can kill her the second she walks in the door. The rest of them, too. If Constantine has superior genetic material, we'll harvest it from her stem cells. She doesn't need to be alive for that." Lutz looked at the technician. "Okay, what do you have in mind?"

"Your original idea was to have DeShear contact Constantine." Seventeen shrugged. "Let him.

In fact, we could do a facial scan and she could talk with him on a video call—but she'd really be talking to you." The Omicron smiled. "Then, who knows what information she might give up? But we must dress the wounds first. He's bleeding too much and becoming unstable."

"I like it." Lutz nodded. "But the facial scanning takes time—valuable minutes we may not have. Maybe we can drug him up and just make him say it. Let him think we've surrounded her at their current location, and if he doesn't tell her to come to us, that we'll kill her."

"He won't do that," Eleven said. "He'd die first."

"Maybe, but try to think like him." She rubbed her chin. "A father believes he has a chance to keep his daughter alive, versus doing nothing and letting her face certain death from the implant. That's the information he has to choose between, and that's an easy choice for someone like DeShear. What did Hollings say? That DeShear would do anything to protect the girl? That's his weakness. We need to exploit it." She glanced at Eleven. "Set up the facial scanning and be ready to go at a moment's notice. That'll be plan B." She smiled, leaning her head back and bringing her hands to her chin. "If he dies, we'll do the facial scan." She glanced at the monitor, where an image of Doctor Hauser was still on the screen. "As we all know, the process works just as well with a live subject as it does on a corpse."

* * * * *

At their hotel, Helena sat at the table by the closet, the leather bonnet still strapped to her head. Her face was pasty and white.

Trinn paced back and forth, biting her nails. "They keep saying he's dying. We know where he is. What if I just load up with guns and go storm the place?"

"We need to get Hamilton medical attention." Constantine stroked Helena's back. "He needs help urgently." She moved away from her mistress, going to Trinn and lowering her voice. "And I'm not sure how much longer we can go on as we are. Helena is under a great deal of strain."

Trinn peered over Constantine's head to the old woman, pursing her lips.

"But Miss Jaden, there are two bonnets." Constantine looked up at Trinn. "You ought to let me use one, to help out."

"Oh, no." Jaden shook her head. "No chance. I told you, hooking you up to that machine might backfire. Right now, we can hear them, but they can't hear us. They don't know where we are, and I mean to keep it that way. Hooking you up to the AI machine could change all that, and I won't risk it. But I have contacts in Canada. I can get some weapons and some people." She looked at the computer screen, where DeShear lay on the gurney. "I have zero issue going into that lab with guns blazing."

"You know you can't do that." Constantine sighed. "They'll kill him before they let you take him."

"And we can't get a doctor in there." Trinn pushed her hands through her dark hair, pacing back and forth again. "There has to be something. I'll keep thinking. You, too, kiddo."

"I shall," Constantine said. "I know we can save him if we think hard enough, Miss Jaden."

Trinn eyed the six-year-old as she returned to her matron's side. She sighed, her eyes darting around the hotel room.

Think, Jaden. Think!

Resting on the bed was the purse she'd stolen earlier.

Trinn stopped in her tracks, her mouth falling open.

"Constantine…" Trinn went to the bed. "Helena said we could send messages to Hank, right? Through the caps?"

The child nodded. "Yes, Miss Jaden."

"Well…" Trinn took the purse from the bed and moved to the nightstand, picking up her phone. "We can't get him a doctor, but maybe we can do the next best thing."

* * * * *

As Eleven brought the facial scanning equipment to DeShear's gurney, Seventeen adjusted the IVs. Doctor Lutz walked around the room, her hands on her hips.

"Hurry, you idiots." She glared at the men. "He'll die while you're trying to save him. I could be accessing valuable information!"

"Yes, ma'am." Seventeen kept his back to her, blocking her view of his hands. "I'll have the patient ready for you in a moment."

Seventeen gently undid the large straps holding DeShear to the gurney, laying them back over him as if they were still holding him down. He moved to the arm restraints next, loosening them but leaving DeShear's hands inside.

"Mr. DeShear, you're dehydrated, so I've increased your fluids." The two microphones on the desk transmitted Seventeen's words into DeShear's headphones. "You'll be feeling better soon." He moved to the ankle straps and loosened them.

"Thank you," DeShear said. "How are my legs?"

Seventeen's face fell. "I won't lie, you've lost a lot of blood. If we don't get you some medical treatment soon, you could suffer permanent damage, possibly losing one or both of them." He sighed, looking DeShear in the eye. "I know Gammas are physically strong, but..."

"That's enough coddling." Lutz strutted back to the gurney. "It's time to get what we came for. Keep him breathing until I have it."

She picked up the closest microphone. Seventeen moved the other mic around to the side of the monitor.

"Kill the lights," Lutz said. "I want him as focused as possible."

The lab room went dark. The light from the monitor illuminating DeShear's face and that of Doctor Atria Lutz.

* * * * *

DeShear's mouth was dry. He swallowed, but it didn't help.

"That's normal." Lutz's voice was in his ear. "You're dehydrated. We've increased your fluids to take care of that."

He saw the monitor, but it was like looking into a mirror.

"Close your eyes," Lutz said. "It will help you to concentrate."

She pressed the green rectangle on the monitor, engaging the program. On the screen, Doctor Hauser's face appeared.

In the dark well of his thoughts, the same image of Hauser appeared in front of DeShear.

"There are things I've stored here." Hauser's gravelly voice cut through the dark silence. "In your thoughts." He walked with a cane, moving slowly. Each step the old man took was deliberate, as if he were walking on an icy sidewalk and might fall at any time. "You will locate these hidden memories."

DeShear saw himself next to Hauser, like in a dream. "How?"

"They will be foreign thoughts," the doctor said. "Not your own."

Images of thick steel doors with big rivets all around the edges appeared on the monitor.

* * * * *

Lutz recoiled, covering her microphone. "What's that?"

Seventeen studied the screen. "It must be DeShear's representation of what you just said. Unconsciously, he is giving physical attributes to the concept of an implanted memory that has been locked away from him."

Lutz rubbed her chin. "But Hauser should know where those are…"

"Hauser would," Seventeen said. "If we had the AI, *we* would. But if DeShear is in a room full of familiar doors, he will notice the unfamiliar ones."

On the screen DeShear walked down a long hallway of doors.

Seventeen pointed at the monitor. "This is just how he's conceptualizing things that you are suggesting to him."

* * * * *

Hauser appeared in front of one of the steel doors. "Open this."

DeShear looked it over. The door was a large steel rectangle with thick rivets on all sides. There was no doorknob or visible latch, just a big, riveted piece of steel.

He turned to Hauser. "Is there a password?"

"Push with my hand," Hauser said. "Think my thoughts. Be as me."

* * * * *

DeShear's heart rate spiked, sending an audible alert from the heart monitor. His breathing increased, becoming rapid and shallow.

Seventeen adjusted the machines. "We have to watch these levels. His legs are bleeding again, too."

"Shut up." Lutz hissed, covering her microphone. "Focus on the task at hand."

* * * * *

DeShear put his hand on the cold, hard steel.

Hauser put his hand over DeShear's.

The steel melted away.

A large room appeared on the other side. DeShear walked through the doorway and into the dimly lit space. To his right, clear, rectangular containers rested end to end, with hoses running across the tops, each diving down to the shadow floating inside. He crept closer, his mouth open and his guts in a knot, stretching a trembling finger out to touch the glass.

Inside the container, attached with surgical tubes, was a human baby. They floated, not fully formed, looking part human, part fish, with large, round heads and curled, translucent bodies, floating in a silent pool. Tiny organs were visible through their pale, thin skin. Hands with fingers reached outward at him. Tiny feet pulled close, as if to offer protection from whatever might come in the darkness.

* * * * *

Nodding, Atria Lutz licked her lips. "That's the Indonesian facility. I recognize it." She smiled at Seventeen. "We're getting close."

DeShear's vital signs spiked again, sending out another round of audible alarms.

"Deal with that." Lutz scowled. "Make the noise stop."

* * * * *

Shaking his head, DeShear gazed down the row as far as the light from the doorway allowed, shimmering off dozens and dozens of containers stacked floor to ceiling and wall to wall.

It appeared endless.

Holding his breath, he turned to his left. The other side of the warehouse looked like a library, filled with dusty shelves of thick old books. One section had a faint white glow coming from behind it.

* * * * *

Lutz pounded the gurney. "We found it!"

"We found something." Seventeen nodded. "We don't know if we found the lineage."

* * * * *

DeShear walked toward the light. Tall, heavy books with cracked leather bindings stood like ancient soldiers in threadbare uniforms.

His gaze went to the faded, gold-colored engraving on the spine. The worn wording read *Lines of Lineage.*

* * * * *

Lutz gasped.

"Wouldn't this be in a computer?" Seventeen asked.

"It is. As you said, this is just DeShear's unconscious, representing it. The memories are there, as I suspected. We just need to let him find them."

* * * * *

DeShear slid the first volume from its slot and opened it. Across the top was written "Alpha Lines." The lists of names and tracking numbers was endless. As he stared at it, the book became three feet thick, with hundreds of names on each page.

DeShear's heart rate spiked again, then dived. His breathing went shallower. The book was suddenly heavy in his hands. DeShear fell to his knees, the book slipping from his grip and slamming to the warehouse floor.

* * * * *

"We're losing him." Seventeen moved to the gurney. "We have to stop—"

"We're not stopping for anything!" Lutz screamed. "We're too close."

"No, Doctor—"

"Get back!" She jumped up, running to the alarm button. "Stay back, or I'll take all of you offline this very instant! We are moving forward!"

"Yes, Doctor," Seventeen said. "I merely meant that we need to *stop his bleeding*. I need to adjust his levels again or his cognitive functions will begin to slip."

Lutz nodded, slowly stepping away from the alarm. "Okay." She pulled a handgun from her lab coat pocket, pointing it at Seventeen. "Adjust his levels—and do nothing else. Dark Hour is almost here!"

CHAPTER 41

Trinn took a business card from the purse and dialed the number on it. "Hello? Doctor Shrinidhi?"

"Yes?"

"This is Jaden Tr—I mean, this is Sarah Macintosh, the lady you treated earlier, at Calgary hospital in Alberta."

"Ms. Macintosh," Shrinidhi huffed. "You stole my car and my purse, with all my hospital credentials in it. You are in a lot of trouble."

"Yes, ma'am." Trinn winced, shifting her weight from one foot to the other. "I'm very sorry about that. I'm actually an agent with the United States Bureau of Diplomatic Security and my real name is Jaden Trinn. I'll return all of your property to you, I needed to borrow it as a matter of national security."

"Ms. Macintosh, theft is a serious crime. You're in a lot of trouble. I suggest you tell me where you are immediately."

Trinn nodded. "And I will do that, Doctor. But I have a favor to ask first."

"You must be joking." Shrinidhi scoffed. "You want a favor? From me, after you stole my car? I'm sorry, but it's very important that you return my vehicle and the rest of my things, immediately. The authorities may go easier on you if the property is returned and you comply with them. Now, where is my car?"

"Currently, it's at the Hilton Hotel in Banff Springs, Alberta, with the rest of your stuff, except a little cash that I had to use. Now, Doctor, listen to me, please. I'll return everything, with interest, but I have a man who has been shot in both legs. He's bleeding out. I need to know what to do."

"Apply direct pressure and call an ambulance. What room are my things in?"

"I can't call an ambulance, and I can't explain why. There's no time. You have to help me right now, please, or he may die. Now, I am able to use a... a communication link to him, so I can see him and hear him, and there is a medical technician there, but his blood pressure is dropping and his vital signs are going crazy."

"Ms. Macintosh—or Trinn—whatever your name is, I will not—"

"I'm Jaden Trinn with the U.S. Bureau of Diplomatic Security. You can call the President's office in Washington DC and they'll verify who I am. Tell them the name Sarah Macintosh and they'll send you my real name and a photo of me. But do it later. Right now, I need your help or a man will die. I know you have every reason to be upset with me, but when this is all over, you're going to see I was telling the truth. I can make everything right about the car and the purse. All I'm asking is for you to take a few minutes and help me keep someone alive."

The line was quiet, except for the sound of low breathing.

"If I'm lying," Trinn said, "you are no worse off than you were ten minutes ago. Your insurance will replace your car and belongings. What thief would call you like this? You saw me in the hospital today. I'm not lying."

"You might just be crazy."

"In which case you'll waste a few minutes. But if I'm telling the truth, you'll save a life—or you'll let a man die. Please help me. I didn't seem crazy when you were examining me today. You know that."

Shrinidhi huffed. "Where are his injuries, and what are his vital signs?"

Jaden squeezed her eyes shut. "Thank you, Doctor. Hold on." She looked at Helena. "Ask Hank to look at the medical equipment so we can see his vital signs."

Helena's jaw dropped. "Goodness, I hope he can talk to me without letting everyone in that lab know what's going on."

"Good point." Trinn bit her lip. "He just needs to look at the devices for now, though."

"But I have to tell him," Helena faced Trinn. "Which means the others could hear as well."

"Write it down!" Constantine said.

Jaden looked at the child. "What?"

"Write it down and show it to him." Constantine ran to the desk and opened the drawer, taking out a small pad of hotel stationery and a pen. "Hamilton will see the image and it will come onto his screen. The technician will see it there."

"Yeah…" Trinn said. "So will doctor Lutz."

"Tell the technician to say it's cross talk." Constantine went to her mistress. "That the reception grid is picking up *the technician's* thoughts about how to adjust Hamilton's medications!"

Helena looked at Trinn. "We may have no other choice, dear."

"Okay. Do it." She moved the phone back to her cheek. "Doctor Shrinidhi, we'll have the patient's vital signs for you in a minute. He's been shot in both thighs and he's bleeding a lot. What sorts of medicines do we need to have standing by?"

"For two unattended gunshot wounds to the upper legs?" Shrinidhi said. "A lot of them—and a crash cart."

CHAPTER 42

DeShear got to his feet, moving to the next book in the dusty library. The writing on the inside cover said "Beta Lines."

Lutz pounded the gurney rail. "We're getting closer! Move down the..." She shook her head, leaning forward and switching on her microphone. "DeShear, move to the last book."

He scanned the long row of dusty leather bindings, his eyes returning to stopping on the third book. The inside cover said "Gamma Lines."

"He's found his line," Seventeen said.

DeShear opened it and flipped through the pages. Hundreds of names filled each page, but the book was nowhere near as large as the first two. As he worked his way further into the book, some names had a page to themselves, and a short biography.

He turned the pages until he found his own name—not at the top of the page, but in the middle, where it discussed his adoptive parents and his scholastic career, followed by his time on the Tampa police force. Grade school report cards, finger paintings, pictures of young Hank DeShear in his Little League uniform, a shot of him fishing off the pier with the man he knew as his father... A whole life, line by line, for however many pages it took the detail at all.

But it was fewer pages than he'd have liked.

At least the last pages aren't written yet.

His awards for Outstanding Officer were there, too, from his time as a cop, as well as several decorations and the citations from the Mayor. The newspaper headlines announcing him as a hero—and the subsequent ones, declaring him a disgrace.

The final paragraph was short, mentioning his work as a private detective.

He forced his eyes not to wander to the top of the page, holding his breath until he was ready.

Then, he read his lineage. The name of the person or persons whose DNA was used in his creation. His genetic parents.

Taking a deep breath, he let his eye go to the top of the yellowed parchment and see the name there—and the name DeShear had been given at his birth.

Name of female genetic donor: Alpha unit 36

Name of male genetic donor: Dr. Marcus Hauser

Name of live birth GEH recipient: Gamma unit 517, Marcus Hauser II

A jolt went through DeShear, knocking him to his knees.

He had confirmed what he had always hoped wouldn't be true. What he knew but didn't want to know.

Marcus Hauser was his father.

The man who had killed and tortured countless volumes of people around the world, and he carried that madman's name.

He may as well have seen the name *Adolph Hitler, Junior.*

DeShear lowered his head, not wanting to breathe, not wanting to accept the information he'd just read.

But inside, it was a confirmation of what he'd known for quite a while. Hauser had told him as much, but reading it—seeing it, in official form—was a reality he hadn't prepared for.

He swallowed hard, putting the book back and getting to his feet. Leaning on the bookshelf, he stared at the other volumes.

* * * * *

Seventeen tapped Doctor Lutz on the shoulder, reaching over and covering her microphone. "It may not be wise to continue giving him instructions as Doctor Hauser. He seems quite upset by what he's seeing."

Lutz nodded. "I can't say he'd be very happy hearing my voice, either. At this point, he's likely to try resisting any instructions I would give him." She glanced at DeShear's blood-soaked legs as he lay on the gurney. "We may not have time for that."

On the monitor, DeShear opened the book for the Delta line.

"You do it." Lutz faced Number Seventeen as she got up from her seat. "He seemed to respond to you. I'll tell you what to say, and you tell it to him."

Seventeen sat down, pulling the microphone close. A handwritten piece of stationery appeared on the screen, with the words *What are his vital signs?"*

He recoiled, his jaw dropping. Seventeen's gaze went to the heart rate monitor and oxygen sensor, checking the numbers there and on the other devices attached to DeShear.

"What was that?" Lutz said.

Seventeen froze, staring at his patient. "Uh… what was what?"

"On the screen." She pointed. "I saw a white flash. What happened?"

"It was…" He cringed. "It was…"

* * * * *

"Hamilton." Constantine's voice echoed in DeShear's head. "Hamilton, Helena and I have attached Rituals bonnets to ourselves. Miss Jaden doesn't want me to talk long. Think of a computer screen and the words 'crosstalk with medical technician.' Take it down as soon as he sees it. I shall be back directly."

DeShear squeezed his eyes shut, thinking of a computer screen with a white background. The image went from his imagination onto the monitor in the lab. He put the words on it that his daughter had said.

Seventeen read the image on the monitor as Doctor Lutz leaned over his shoulder, scowling at the screen.

DeShear held his breath.

Lutz didn't hear Constantine, did she?

"Crosstalk?" Lutz looked up at the metal grid ceiling, cursing. "Lousy receptor antenna. All day long, it picks up neurotransmissions from all over the world, but when we need it to fine tune, it starts reading *you*." She glared at Seventeen as she leaned back in her chair.

DeShear exhaled a sigh of relief.

She didn't hear her.

She can't hear Constantine.

"Is that how you refer to yourself?" Lutz glared at Seventeen. "As 'medical technician?' Or is the computer interpreting?"

Seventeen swallowed hard. "It… I…"

DeShear decided to move on to the next book. The shelves of reference manuals appeared on the screen.

"There." Lutz licked her lips. "He's back at it." She patted Seventeen on the back. "Good job."

Nodding, he kept his eyes on the screen.

DeShear moved down to the eighth book, containing information on the Theta's lineage.

* * * * *

"Have him go to the *last* book!" Lutz shoved Seventeen. "I don't care about lineage. I want those steps. I need the files for the program that finds and selects the genes for obedience and conscientiousness. How it turns the right ones on or off."

Seventeen frowned. "We want both."

"Shut up!" Lutz gripped the gurney rail, her knuckles turning white. "We're on the verge. Stay focused."

"We had a deal. You said you'd bring us the regeneration records."

Lutz pointed at the monitor. "That's what he's staring at, isn't it? But look how much there is! How is he supposed to bring all that information out?"

"If he were to look at every line of every page," Seventeen said, "it would be recorded here on our screen! We could just play it back. Then, we'd—"

"If he were to spend time looking at every page of every book, we'd be here for a year!" She slammed the rail, her face red. Veins throbbed on her forehead. "My mission takes priority! Mine!"

DeShear's legs began to jolt and kick. His head jerked from side to side.

"What?" Lutz turned to the monitor. "Now what's happening?"

DeShear lurched upwards, arching his back off the gurney and slamming back down. Spit flew from his mouth.

"He's convulsing." Seventeen looked at the readout for DeShear's vital signs. "I told you, he's lost too much blood. We need to address his wounds before he codes."

Lutz shook her head, glaring at her technician. "No. Let him find the books first."

"If he codes, those books may be lost forever." Seventeen typed on his keyboard, displaying the patient's vital signs. Each line of measurement was either jumping wildly or completely flat. He jammed his finger onto the screen. "There's nothing that guarantees they're in the AI system, anyway! If the only copies are the implanted memories, then you need DeShear to stay *alive*."

Lutz screamed in frustration, pounding the gurney. "Okay! Take care of him." Scowling, she got up and stormed toward the private door. "I'll be back in a moment. Give DeShear adrenaline or whatever it takes, but do *not* let him die for the next few minutes. Not until I have the data I need."

"And then what?" Seventeen asked.

"And then I don't care what happens to him!" She wheeled around, her hair flying into her face. "Once I have what I need, he can die. By then, my teams will have located the old woman and the child, and they'll be dead, too. We'll harvest what we need from Constantine's corpse."

"Does that mean we need to take Jaden Trinn alive? Because she has—"

"Quiet!" Lutz shouted. "Not in front of him!"

Seventeen glanced at his quivering patient. "He's not listening. Not now."

"Nevertheless. Don't say it." Lutz opened the private door. "Don't even think it."

* * * * *

In the hotel, Trinn covered the phone and stared at the computer screen. "What's he talking about?"

"Alexander," Helena said. "Doctor Lutz appears to be concerned that if she mentions your...

411

situation, that Hamilton will hear. Hamilton still doesn't know, correct?"

Trinn sighed, stepping away. "I… I should've told him. He could die without knowing."

"No, dear." Helena adjusted her chin strap. "We're not going to let that happen. Are we, child?"

"We certainly are not." Constantine pulled her bonnet off. "I told you, Alexander is strong. So is our father. Your baby and I will be good siblings, Miss Jaden."

Trinn went to the window and put her hand to her abdomen.

You'll be good siblings, but will you have both of your parents?

Sighing, she put the phone back to her ear, forcing herself to refocus. "Okay, Doc. We set the stage for you. The patient faked a seizure, and the technician jimmied all the displays to make it look real. Now, you're on."

Doctor Shrinidhi maintained a calm speaking voice as she worked to diagnose DeShear's situation over the phone. "As awful as it sounds," Shrinidhi said, "if we can keep a victim out of shock, most people can survive quite a while with gunshot wounds. Even severe ones."

Trinn nodded.

I know.

Her fingers brushed across the scar she'd received courtesy of a sniper in the Bahamas. Holding the phone away from her face, Jaden glanced at the computer. "I'm putting you on speaker, Doctor Shrinidhi. Constantine, write fast and try to show the cards when it's just the technician looking."

"Okay," Constantine said.

"First," Shrinidhi said, "is the patient alert?"

Trinn nodded. "Yes."

"How is the airway?"

"I believe it's good." Trinn glanced at the screen. "He's been talking and hasn't said anything about breathing issues."

"Okay." Static came over Shrinidhi's line. "When a bullet strikes a person, tissue is crushed. We may have secondary missiles, such as bullet and bone fragments, which can result in additional damage. Assume fragmentation until we can get an x-ray. Do we have any exit wounds?"

"Uh…" Trinn glanced at the screen. "I'll have the technician check, but I don't think so."

Constantine scribbled on the pad and held it up. The pad appeared on the technician's monitor back at the lab. Seventeen shook his head.

Constantine turned to Trinn. "No exit wounds."

"Okay," Doctor Shrinidhi said. "I want updates on respiratory rate, pulse, and blood pressure. Let me know if he drops anywhere close to a systolic BP of eighty. And let's see about exposing the patient to allow a complete visual inspection of the body."

Trinn winced. "That's a no go on the exposure. We can't access him, and I don't think we can undress him without alerting his captors."

"Captors?" Shrinidhi asked. "Have the authorities been alerted?"

"You're talking to the authorities right now." Trinn ran a hand through her hair. "I have a medical technician with the victim. Just tell me what to tell him."

Seventeen typed the blood pressure numbers and pulse rate on his screen, then immediately deleted it, giving a thumbs up.

"He's hearing us!" Constantine bounced up and down in her seat. "Keep talking!"

"Okay, good." The doctor cleared her throat. "Have him try to evaluate the extremities for other wounds, any sign of hemorrhaging, crepitus, deformity and mobility. Tell me about any potential circulatory compromise and neurological impairment. Remember, we'll need constant monitoring and reassessment of vital signs. And do we have a cardiac monitor and pulse oximetry?"

Trinn nodded. "Affirmative on the heart and pulse monitors. They're stable."

"Impressive. He's a tough cookie, this victim. Let's give supplemental oxygen and start an IV. We'll manage the open extremity wounds with direct pressure and bandaging."

"He has an IV." Trinn paced back and forth across the room, her eyes never leaving the computer screen.

Seventeen typed, *"I'll see about getting O2,"* then deleted it. Trinn relayed the message to Shrinidhi.

"Okay," the doctor said. "What are the fluid options?"

Seventeen typed on the monitor in the lab; Trinn read his reply out loud. "Crystalloids, colloids and blood substitutes."

"Mm-hmm." Shrinidhi took a deep breath and let it out slowly. "Let's stay with colloids for now, and definitely start the blood substitutes, since he's been bleeding. Keep the patient warm."

Seventeen gave them a thumbs up.

Trinn smiled, leaning against the wall and closing her eyes. "You rock, Doc. Thank you. I'm going to buy you a brand-new Mercedes when we're finished here."

"Just get the old one back to me in one piece," Doctor Shrinidhi said. "Then, please leave Canada."

* * * * *

Hollings had one stop to make on his way to the cave laboratory of Doctor Atria Lutz—a stop with an illegal gun dealer. He parked his rental car and strolled up to the shop that had supplied him with advanced weaponry for years.

Happy Time Toy Center.

"Right, mate." He threw open the door and stepped inside the toy store. "Let's get some noisemaking toys."

The gray-haired man behind the counter peered over his reading glasses as he hovered above a blue train engine. A young boy and a stocky man on the other side of the counter glanced at Hollings, then returned their attention to the locomotive.

The old shopkeeper nodded at Hollings. "Be right with you, Mr. Rupinski."

"Aye, Jonas. Take your time." The fat Brit sauntered around the little shop, whistling quietly and scratching his chin stubble. Jonas' accent sounded of home to Hollings.

Well, we'll be there soon enough.

The obese Brit stopped by the door to the back room. "Would it be all right if I go ahead and have a look 'round whilst I wait?"

"Go ahead." The shop owner handed the blue train engine to the boy. "Bob's inside, and you usually know what you want."

"Right you are." Hollings nodded, opening the door. "Cheers."

In the back room was a trap door leading to a cellar. In decades past, beer and wine had been stored there—and untaxed whiskey bound for Great Falls, Montana, during the American Prohibition years. But for almost a decade and a half, toy seller Jonas and his brother Bob had decided that moving illegal weaponry out of their back door was far more profitable than selling toys out of their front door.

As Hollings descended the creaky wooden stairs, Bob clapped the dirt off his hands from their most recent purchases—two cases of AR-15s and a truckload of surface-to-air missiles.

"Mr. Rupinski." Bob grinned, extending a hand. "How nice to see you again."

"And you, old friend." Hollings shook hands, glancing around at the latest arrivals. "I could do with a load of these." He went to the crate of AR-15s and picked one up, sniffing the sleek semiautomatic weapon like it was a glass of fine wine. "How much?"

"Ah, sorry, mate." Bob shook his head, taking the gun from Hollings and placing it back in the crate. "These have been promised to a drug dealer looking to make inroads into a new casino being built just south of the border. But I could show you something in a very nice Uzi."

"No, it's these I want," Hollings said. "Lots of firepower and a look to scare church out of a preacher." He leaned on the edge of the crate. "Now, how much?"

"I've told you, friend—they're done promised away. But look here." Bob pointed to other crates around the small cellar. "I've got shotguns, machine guns, land mines... A very nice bolt action Israeli number. What type of vermin are you needing removed today?"

"Mate, that AR-15's a two-thousand-dollar rifle, tops, even at smuggler's prices..." Hollings pulled a stack of hundred dollar bills out of his coat pocket and slapped it onto the crate, followed by another, and another. "I've got a hundred thousand U.S. dollars on me, in cash." He dropped another bundle of bills onto the crate. "It's all yours in exchange for just ten of them big scary rifles, some sundries, and help with loading them out the door." He dropped wad after wad of bills onto the crate until there were ten of them. "For that kind of money, you could convince Al Capone to wait a week for a new delivery."

"A hundred thousand?" Bob asked.

Hollings nodded. "Cash money."

Bob picked up the stacks of currency and stashed them under the counter. "Pull your car around, Mr. Rupinski. We've got rifles to load." He smiled, pulling a toothpick out of his shirt pocket and wedging it between his teeth. "And what about ammunition, friend? You do intend to shoot off these magnificent firecrackers, don't you?"

Hollings' jaw dropped. "Oh, yes. Of course!" Tugging at his collar, he waddled toward the ammo counter. "Guns are no good without bullets, are they? Uh… probably a box of shells for each rifle."

"As you wish, sir." Bob nodded, counting out the boxes. "Not that it's my business, but when does this fireworks show start?"

"Soon." Hollings glanced at the door. "I've one or two more stops to make first."

Slapping the ammunition on the counter, Bob smiled. "Here you go. Use in good health. Lastly, just so's I know what to deny if the coppers come sniffing 'round—what audience will be on the receiving end of this entertainment, mate?"

"Close friends, of course—as always." Hollings picked up one of the rifles, peering down the barrel. "A female git by the name of Jaden Trinn what's been a pebble in my shoe for months, her unborn child, a wanker named DeShear, their brat Constantine, and an extremely irritating little old lady named Helena."

He squeezed the trigger, the click of the empty weapon filling the small cellar.

"In a few hours," Hollings said, "I'll have settled all my unfinished business, and they'll all be stone dead."

He smiled, setting the rifle down and heading for the stairs.

"The best part is, the mangy bird thinks I'm working with her." Hollings laughed. "She'll never see it coming."

CHAPTER 43

As Atria Lutz settled back into her chair, she gazed at the monitor next to her patient. The screen showed DeShear walking along the rows of books, the warehouse growing darker. He wrapped his arms around himself, exhaling to send a thin cloud into the air as a draft lifted his hair.

The sound of a wooden stick on concrete echoed through the warehouse. As DeShear turned around, Doctor Hauser limped forward, leaning on his cane.

The wind grew stronger, blowing leaves from invisible trees through the air.

"What's all this?" Lutz asked. "Where are the files?"

Seventeen shook his head. "I'm not sure what's happening. Maybe it's a reaction to the loss of blood."

"Get DeShear to the records!" Lutz hissed.

"I'm trying." Seventeen adjusted the dials on the computer. "He's not listening to me."

* * * * *

A dark sky painted itself onto the library ceiling.

Hauser stopped walking, leaning on his cane and glowering at DeShear. "You know why you're here."

DeShear stared at him.

"You must come with me." The old man held out his hand. "You must allow the inevitable to occur. It's the only way."

DeShear's hand lifted, moving toward Hauser's as if DeShear couldn't control it. He summoned his strength and pushed it back down.

"It's the only way," Hauser said. "If you don't, your daughter will die. You will render unto me that which is mine."

A ripple of fear went through DeShear. This was the trap. He knew it, he anticipated it, and now here it was.

A black door appeared behind Hauser, cold and hollow, the winds rushing past DeShear's face and disappearing into the dark void. It pulled DeShear forward.

Hauser stared into DeShear's eyes. "I must have what is owed me. You know this is the only way."

"No." Heart pounding, DeShear stepped back, shaking his head. "I don't know that."

"Of course you do." Hauser smiled, extending his hand as he inched toward DeShear. "I implanted a device in Constantine's head. It will soon expire—and Constantine will expire with it. We both know you'll do whatever's necessary to keep that from happening."

DeShear took another step backwards. "I won't let you revive your consciousness and use me to foster your evil."

"There's no other way. This had been your destiny all along. I brought you into the world to perform this task, and you *will* perform it."

Panting, DeShear moved backwards. The floor under his feet turned to dirt, the walls of the library warehouse becoming a dark, windy forest. "I'll die first."

"Will you?" Hauser leaned his old frame on his cane, creeping forward. "Then Constantine will die. Is that what you want? Haven't you killed enough children? The embryos in Indonesia, the ones in France and Ukraine..." The old man chuckled. "Where does your pain live, Mr. DeShear? There? With the children you've murdered?"

"They were birthed!" DeShear trembled, backing away. The wind grew stronger, howling through the black silhouettes of the trees. "I saw the adoption records from the U.N."

"And what about your own child? A girl, I think it was, years ago. After so many miscarriages, you and your wife still insisted on having a baby— only to have the child dwindle and die in front of your eyes. Nature was telling you no, but you wouldn't listen. You had to know by then that the two of you couldn't have children, but you proceeded anyway. That's practically the same as murder."

The images of the hospital flashed through DeShear's head. The waning little girl, attached to all those machines…

"Stop." DeShear squeezed his eyes shut, a giant ache clutching his heart. "That's not true. You're lying. You're trying to manipulate me through my thoughts."

"She was not to be." Hauser crept closer. "You killed that child by the stubborn act of bringing her into the world." He pointed to the ground. "*This* has always been your destiny. Turning your physical body over to me so *my* consciousness could inhabit it!"

DeShear curled over in pain. "Stop!"

"You, then Constantine. I *will* have my plans unfold before me."

Thunder rumbled through the sky. The wind gusted, sending dust and leaves through the air.

"Hamilton." Helena's voice swept through the forest, thin and low, like it was being carried on the wind. "You must work to *not* think of what is suggested. He's pulling you in. Keep your mind on something else—anything else. A red elephant. A Ferris wheel. A birthday party. Remember what I told you."

The wind howled.

"You must do as I did when I was in the warehouse in France," Helena said. "And you will feel powerless, but you must force yourself to not envision what is requested. Make yourself see other images. You can do it. You must."

Groaning in pain, DeShear looked around. The riveted, metal doors appeared all around him, rippling with translucence and showing watery glimpses of what was on the other side.

One door opened into a room full of test tubes. The next, books. Another was a cave.

* * * * *

In the lab, Seventeen shook his head, staring at the monitor. "What is he doing?"

"I'll tell you what he's not doing," Lutz said. "He's not going along with Hauser. That's good. We need him to find the selection process first."

"And the regeneration records."

Lutz looked at her technician out of the corner of her eye. "Just help him find the selection process files. What can we do for him?"

"He's getting fluids…" Seventeen rubbed his chin. "Maybe oxygen? That's standard protocol in the treatment of a gunshot wound."

Lutz looked at him. "How would you know that?"

Seventeen recoiled, a jolt of fear going through him.

"Doctor Lutz." A tansuit stepped to her side

"Not now." Lutz turned her gaze back to the monitor.

"Ma'am," the tansuit said. "It's Mr. Hollings. He's at the front entry and he says he's got the AI for you. He wants his payment authorized."

Lutz wheeled around, her eyes wide. "The AI is here? Pay him and grab the machine! I'm on my way." She glanced at Seventeen. "Give DeShear oxygen and try to steer him toward finding the selection process files. If he won't comply…" She waved her arms at the medical devices attached to her patient. "… then shut this all down."

Seventeen looked at her, his jaw hanging open. "Ma'am?"

"If he won't play ball, pull the plug and terminate him." She got up from her seat. "The AI is here. We don't need him anymore."

"But…" Seventeen bit his lip. "That would leave us with no plan B."

"Fine. We'll activate the AI while you keep going." Lutz headed for the cave. "Give DeShear what he needs—for now. I'll be back as soon as I can."

* * * * *

Hauser leaned on his cane, the wind blowing his gray hair. "Where does your pain live, Mr. DeShear?"

DeShear flashed again on the child in the hospital room and the folder on his home computer with letter G, then to the black door. A knot formed in his abdomen.

"Hamilton." Helena's voice echoed over the treetops. "You must fight. You don't have to do what they say."

Hauser scowled, looking up at the dark sky. "Shut up, Keeper 27! This is none of your affair."

"It is," Helena said. "You know it is. You above all others know that it is."

The sky flashed white and the library walls returned, replacing the forest. An image of a younger version of Helena appeared on the wall, like a movie projector had focused it there.

A woman in green hospital scrubs wiped young Helena's brow as she leaned back on the ward room bed.

"And here is your baby." The woman handed a red-faced newborn to Helena, wrapped in white blankets. "Congratulations, Keeper 27!"

"Goodness," Helena said, her eyes weary but filed with joy. She gazed at her newborn. "Hello, Constantine. Welcome to the world."

DeShear's jaw dropped. He looked at the stacks of books beside him. The Delta records opened to Helena's page.

He stared at the book, unable to move.

Her voice came to him from overhead. "It's all right, Hamilton. There were things we dared not speak of in the château, for fear of what might happen, but it's time you knew the truth."

Another image appeared, one of Helena and Constantine. The child sat on the old woman's bed, lifting her injured knee onto a small pillow.

"You have lots of pictures taped to the back of your door," Constantine said.

"I do." Helena busied herself with the edge of the covers, folding them and unfolding them, again and again. "Have you... looked at them?"

"I have." Constantine nodded. "There are quite a few of you with the other children, but most of the pictures are of you and me."

"Oh?" Helena looked at Constantine out of the corner of her eye, continuing to adjust the covers. "I hadn't noticed."

"You did," the child said. "You put the others up so they'd obscure the fact that there were so many of us."

"Did I?" The old woman clasped her hands in front of her, kneading her fingers. "Well, I suppose…"

"It's okay." Constantine lowered her voice. "I know why you did it. We have a secret we mustn't tell. We could be in danger if we do."

Helena's fingers trembled. "And what secret is that, dear?"

"It's the best secret ever." Constantine smiled. "That of all the children in the chateau, I am the only one with a mother—and she's the best mother ever."

"Is she?" Helena's cheeks turned red. "Well…"

Constantine slipped her hand into Helena's. "She is. You are. I know it. I feel it—and I feel it from you, so I know it's true. But I won't tell. It will be our secret, always."

Tears came to the old woman's eyes. "You… you understand why I couldn't say anything, child?"

"I do." Constantine hugged her mother. "One day, we'll leave here. Then we won't have to hide anymore."

DeShear smiled, the wind blowing his hair over his eyes. "I guess the clues were there for anyone who wanted to see them."

On the wall, young Helena turned on her side in the maternity bed, snuggling baby Constantine close to her heart.

"We were afraid for the truth to get out," Helena said. "In the château and afterward. The endless harmful possibilities were too much to risk."

DeShear stood in the library, the walls sending gusts of wind down onto him.

Afterward? Why would you be afraid to mention it after you left the château?

He looked at the old man with the cane. "Helena is Constantine's mother. Why would she be afraid to mention that fact *after* she left the château?"

Hauser stared back at him, his jaw clenched, the wind pulling at his clothes.

"Why did that have to be a secret?" DeShear advanced on the doctor, anger building inside of him. "It threatened you? An old woman and a little child? What could they do to…"

DeShear stopped in his tracks, the wind howling past him.

"…to hurt you?"

He stared at the frail old man.

Helena is Constantine's mother.

Your prized protégé and the person you hand-selected to take over for you isn't even from your vaunted genetic engineering program. Not really.

DeShear clenched his fists. "You're nothing but a fraud, Doctor."

Hauser stepped back, stumbling as he leaned on his cane.

DeShear narrowed his eyes. "Constantine's existence is testament to the weakness of your program—your life's work." He looked down, shaking his head. "It's all been for nothing."

Thunder rolled over their heads, the room darkening again. The ceiling disappeared and the dark forest returned.

DeShear pointed at Hauser. "Where does *your* pain live, Doctor Hauser?"

Everything flashed white, like lightning had struck.

A teenager in a suit stood on a stage, next to another boy who was dressed nearly identically. A man in a navy blue suit stood behind them with a hand on the shoulder of each.

Out of sight, an announcer's voice echoed over the stage. Lights shined into the young man's eyes.

DeShear peered into the image. The face was unmistakable.

It was Hauser as a child.

"And finally," the announcer said, "our last award of the evening. For achievements in Science and Medicine, recognizing his advancements in the study of gene splicing, I am proud to present this award to... the valedictorian of the Princeton Excelsiors Academy, Lucius Hauser!"

The crowd of students broke into raucous applause. The young man next to Marcus Hauser stepped forward, the adult behind them glowing with pride.

"See, Marcus?" The man patted Hauser on the back. "If you study hard, you can achieve anything." He leaned forward, smiling. "What do you want to be in life, son?"

Hauser's memory turned dark. He saw himself a year later, at a freshly dug grave, weeping.

The same man in the same navy blue suit patted him on the back again, but it had an entirely different meaning.

"He'll always be with us, Marcus." His father choked on his words. "Your brother was a fighter, and we need to remember that about him. The cancer was just..." A tear rolled down his father's cheek. "It was just stronger than he was. That's all."

As Marcus Hauser watched his brother's casket lowered into the ground, the question his father asked him a year before at the award ceremony came to him.

But he never told his father the answer he'd decided on. Instead, he watched a different cancer kill his father over the next six months.

And when the doctors finally came to him in college, explaining his own diagnosis and informing Marcus that it was just bad luck—bad genes—and that his family had a predisposition to carcinomas, he remembered what he wanted to achieve in life.

He remembered his father patting him on the back, leaning over as his brother won the award. "What do you want to be in life, son?"

His answer was simple.

"Immortal."

DeShear looked at Doctor Hauser now, a frail old man leaning on a cane, his white hair blowing in the wind as thunder rumbled across the trees. Cold, heavy raindrops hit the ground around the two men.

"I should have been a hero for my work," Hauser said. "If I had been an actor advocating for stem cells that were derived from aborted fetuses, I'd have been lauded. All I did was terminate the cells when they were a little older."

DeShear glared at him. "You did a lot more than that."

The wind picked up, pushing Hauser's now-baggy pants and oversized shirt. His skin hung away from the bones, thin and weak.

The old man gripped his cane like he might fall down.

DeShear squared his shoulders. "You do know that you're dead though, right?" The gusts rushed past DeShear. "That I'm basically talking to an algorithm that you had someone write."

"Yes." Hunched over and holding his cane with a shaking hand, Hauser looked down. "Yes, I suppose I am."

"We part ways here, Doctor. It's time." DeShear looked at the black door. "That door isn't here for me."

The wind grew stronger, pushing everything behind Hauser into the darkness of the door, and swallowing it. As the rain increased, the old man turned and peered up at the empty black rectangle, then lowered his head and stepped through it.

The wind and rain stopped. The library returned. The rows of books looked new. The warehouse, clean and shiny. Everywhere DeShear turned, bright light filled the space.

He looked over his shoulder for the black door.

It was gone.

CHAPTER 44

Atria Lutz rolled up to the entrance gate in her ATV, shutting off the motor and glaring at the guard. A cloud of dust drifted past her as he came forward, a cardboard box in his hands. "What's this?" she asked. "Where's Hollings?"

The guard handed her the box. "I authorized his payment, as you said. It downloaded, and he left."

Lutz pried open the cardboard corner. Small pieces of rusty sheet metal fell out, along with dusty circuit boards connected by old, frayed wire—and a lot of dirt.

"You paid him?" Lutz threw the box on the ground. "For this? He screwed us! Find him and kill him, or I'll kill you. Put a team together and track him down. He can't have gotten far."

"Yes, ma'am!" The tansuit looked over his shoulder. "But... Doctor, if Hollings turned on us, others may be coming. We might need to keep all of our people here, to protect the lab."

She screamed, slamming her hands onto the ATV's steering wheel. Leaning back, she pushed her hair out of her eyes. "Fine. It's fine. We have a plan B. I'll kill the ugly Brit bastard later." She started the vehicle. "I need to get back to the lab. DeShear is our only chance now."

* * * * *

As Lutz entered the lab, one of the tansuit guards rushed forward. "So? Do we have a working AI?"

She reached into the pocket of her lab coat, pulled out her gun, and shot him.

The tansuit fell to the floor and lay still, blood seeping from his chest and back.

Lutz looked around at the others, scowling. "Does anyone else have a question?"

Her workers resumed their duties. Lutz plunked herself down in the seat next to her medical technician. "What progress has been made, Number Seventeen?"

He swallowed hard. "DeShear is back in the library. He just started going through the records again."

"Good," Lutz said. "Nice to see I still have *some* control over somebody around here."

On the monitor, a row of gray binders glowed with a white light, shimmering behind a steel door as its exterior came and went from view. The volumes were marked *Gene Selection Procedures.*

Lutz sat forward. "Yes! That's it! He found it."

Beyond the binders were dirty vials and stained test tubes, the walls lined with decaying children's corpses.

Lutz pounded the armrests of her chair. "What's he waiting for? Tell him to open the binders!"

On the monitor, DeShear turned to face her. "I'm not going to open it."

"What!" Lutz slapped the screen. "Give me that microphone." She grabbed the mic from Seventeen, holding it to her chin. "You will open those binders and read me Hauser's gene selection process for controlling the hybrid prototypes, DeShear! Give me the information I need for my lines, or your daughter will die. I will explode that device in her skull right now. The stent in Helena's chest, too."

DeShear stared at the monitor, slowly shaking his head. "No."

* * * * *

Trinn peered over Helena's shoulder, biting her nail as she looked at the computer. "This could get dicey."

"What should I tell him?" Helena kneaded her fingers in her lap.

"I don't know." Trinn glanced at Constantine. "What do you think? Any ideas?"

The child turned to the screen, her eyes not wavering from the image of her father. She swallowed hard, shifting in her seat. "He's weak. Something's draining him, and he needs help. I feel like… like I want him to go to the pages—to the books of the lines. But he's already been there."

"He may be weak from the blood loss. What do we do, dear?"

Constantine took a deep breath and let it out slowly, closing her eyes and envisioning DeShear. She pushed everything else out of her thoughts. Trinn and Helena spoke, but it was merely faint echoes from far away. Her sole focus was her father.

You could go to the pages, Hamilton. But you did that already. What was there?

She replayed the vision of him walking to the books and opening them.

Something inside of you is telling you what to do, or... it's pushing you. I feel it. It's... it's a thought. A piece of information.

What is it?

She squeezed her eyes tighter.

You looked at your page in the book, and you looked at Helena's. What information was there that changed things? What did you see?

Or what didn't you see?

Constantine sat upright, her heart racing.

Take me through it again! Remember. Look at the pages.

She saw DeShear open the Delta book.

I sense it, now. You do, too. Something's missing.

Images raced through Constantine's mind of the prior book, of Gammas, with grade school report cards, finger paintings, a boy in a Little League uniform...

What is it? What was there?

An Outstanding Officer award. Citations from the Mayor. Newspaper headlines.

Where is it? Where?

He moved to the Delta's book, flipping the pages toward Helena's information.

It's close, Hamilton. I feel it. Push on.

The page recorded her baby's length and weight at birth, Helena's subsequent promotion in her position at the château, details of her annual medical physicals, her hobbies, the foods she enjoyed most, her allergies, a note about a lengthy bout of bronchitis, a record of cuts and bruises she sustained on the grounds while tending to the children…

Go. Keep going.

Constantine scanned through the pages. Helena's life, as Keeper 27, from inception to the last days of the château, it was all there. Every detail, no matter how small or insignificant.

Almost.

Constantine's breath caught in her throat.

Hamilton didn't read all this. He didn't have time. This is a memory of Doctor Hauser's that he implanted in Hamilton!

She read further. Even the information on Constantine's skinned knee was there, and that she was allowed to recover in Helena's bed.

But the stent operation wasn't mentioned.

A jolt went through the child.

Because it never happened!

Constantine pulled herself from the daydream, her hands trembling as she looked at her father on the computer. "Hamilton! I looked at Helena's page. There's no notation about an operation to implant a stent in her aorta."

He looked up at her from the monitor. "They didn't record it?"

"It never happened! They recorded every detail about you and me and every other person, but not that one detail about her?"

DeShear cocked his head. "How do you know that if we didn't read all her pages in the book?"

"You're accessing Doctor Hauser's memories," Constantine said. "And I can see it all. There's no stent in her! Think of Doctor Hauser and ask him! The truth will flash on the screen before there's a chance to make a lie!"

DeShear looked down and closed his eyes, imagining Hauser next to him. The image of the old man flashed on the screen. DeShear narrowed his eyes. "Doctor Hauser, think about the surgery you performed on Constantine."

Constantine's image flashed on the screen.

"The surgery," DeShear said. "Show me the surgery where you implanted that fatal device in her head."

The monitor displayed scenes of Constantine playing in the fields at the château.

"The surgery!" DeShear shouted. "Show me when you did the surgery on her head, or when you ordered it to be done!"

A vision of Constantine hugging Helena appeared as they kicked a soccer ball.

"There isn't one, is there?" DeShear gritted his teeth. "You didn't do it."

The old man next to him slowly lifted his head. "I... did."

"Then why can't you remember doing it? What *did* you do?"

Hauser faded from view. The library wall showed a scene of an office.

"That's in the château!" Constantine shouted. She quickly lowered her voice. "It was a forbidden place."

Hauser walked across the room to his desk, leaning on his cane. A man in clean surgical scrubs came in, followed by a young woman carrying a notepad.

Sitting down, Hauser rested his hands on the desk, peering at the man. "You will perform an elective surgery for me today, Doctor Arham. Put an incision on the patient's head, near the hair line. Make your cut twenty-five millimeters long, but do not penetrate the periosteum, and do not scratch the bone layer." He handed him the patient's chart. "Understood?"

"Yes." The surgeon looked over the paperwork, his hands trembling. "But why? Constantine is your best student, and a role model. Why would you—"

"I pay you a lot of money to do what I say, Doctor, not to ask questions." Hauser frowned. "Go. Do it now, and report to me when you are finished. And make sure there will be a visible scar afterwards."

"A scar? You... you want her to have a scar? A child of that age would heal without one."

"Leave a scar. It's an insurance policy." Hauser opened a drawer, rifling through the files inside it. "That's all you need to know."

The surgeon left the room. The young lady glanced at the door, holding her notepad in front of her.

"Come." He looked at her and pointed to a chair at the front of his desk. "Sit."

She nodded, lowering herself into the seat.

"One day soon, you're going to be in charge of your own facility." Hauser opened a file and leafed through it. "You have to learn that bending the rules, and sometimes breaking them, is necessary to achieve the great things that would otherwise remain unimaginable."

"Yes, Doctor."

"These are the blueprints for a new facility." He handed her the folder. "It's off the books, so no one will know about it—another insurance policy, if you will. Look the plans over and give me your thoughts before you leave."

"Leave?" She cocked her head. "Am I going somewhere?"

"You're going to Canada. Tonight." Hauser got up from the desk, tapping the cane on the floor as he walked. "The new facility will be in Quebec. We break ground on it tomorrow."

The young woman stood. "A facility... for me to run?"

"Of course." Hauser smiled. "Your goal should be to exceed the existing horizons in genetic research—and I have no doubt that you will do so, Atria."

The vision faded. The walls of the library returned.

* * * * *

In Atria Lutz's lab, she clenched her teeth. "He's communicating with someone through the reception grid—and I bet I know who." She turned to one of the guards. "Follow the signal and nail down where it's coming from. It's got to be Constantine and the old woman. Don't worry about addresses or anything else, just follow the signal. It will take you right to them. If we move fast enough, we can find them and kill them all!"

The guard ran to a large piece of electrical equipment at the far wall, grabbing the dials and reading the screens. A moment later, he bolted from the room, clutching his gun.

DeShear stared out at Lutz from the monitor. "Hauser didn't implant a device in Constantine's head, so you can't kill her that way. It's all been a game, and I'm done playing it."

Lutz swallowed hard. "You'll do as I say or... or..."

"Or nothing." DeShear shook his head. "It's like a dream. I can wake up anytime."

"The morphine!" Lutz glanced around wildly. "The morphine will keep you down!"

DeShear glared at her. "What morphine?"

She looked at his IV. The morphine drip valve was shut off. "What?" Gasping, she put a hand to her mouth.

DeShear sat up on the gurney, pulling his headphones from his ears and dropping them onto the gurney.

Lutz pushed her chair away from him, recoiling.

Swinging his bloody legs over the side of the gurney, DeShear grabbed her arm. "Now we'll see who dies at Dark Hour."

Lutz screamed, twisting out of his grasp. She jumped up and ran toward the private room.

Limping, DeShear followed her. Blood dripped from both legs.

Pulling the handgun from her lab coat pocket, she turned around and fired. The upper part of DeShear's shirt sleeve exploded in a puff.

Lutz opened the private door, turning back and reaching for the alarm button.

"DeShear! Put on your headphones!" Seventeen shouted.

Eleven and Seventeen crouched down, shoving their earphones onto their heads.

Lutz slammed her hand into the button.

Seventeen grabbed DeShear's headphones and tossed them to him. The alarm sounded as DeShear slipped his headphones back on and dived to the floor. The Omicron tansuits and the others grabbed their heads, wincing and flailing. One by one, they crashed to the floor, writhing in pain.

Lutz smiled, opening the door to the private room.

"It's not affecting her!" DeShear looked at Seventeen. "What do we do?"

"Just wait," Seventeen shouted. "It's a macrosonic pulse—350 decibels for ten seconds. It bursts the eardrums and blood vessels in the inner ear. The sudden influx in fluids sets off a chain reaction that liquifies the brain."

"And it's been coded at a frequency that only we can hear." DeShear frowned. "So, she's immune."

Lutz casually disappeared into the private room, the alarm blaring. Moments later, the tansuits stopped moving. Blood seeped from their ears as the alarm stopped.

DeShear pulled his headphones down around his neck, racing to the guards and taking their rifles. He handed one to Seventeen. Eleven stood nearby, panting.

DeShear glanced at Seventeen. "Does he get a gun?"

Seventeen nodded. "Please, sir."

"Okay, then." DeShear thrust a rifle into Eleven's hands. "She went in there. Is that a door to the outside?"

"It's her office and another lab room," Eleven said. "I don't know if it goes outside from there."

DeShear gritted his teeth. "Okay. I'm going in after her. Eleven, you stay here and holler if any more of her friends show up. Seventeen, you come with me." He clutched the rifle to his chest and faced the private door. "We'll have to take our chances that she doesn't have an arsenal locked up in there."

CHAPTER 45

Hollings raced down the hallway of Helena and Constantine's hotel, his hired thugs trailing him. "Right, you lot. The room's just here. Weapons out, boys, if you will."

The six men with him pulled their AR-15s from beneath their long, heavy coats.

Hollings walked to the door and put a finger to his lips. "Ready…" he whispered. "Steady… Go!"

One of them ran from behind him and kicked the hotel door in. The others raced inside, weapons out, scanning the room.

Hollings stuck his fat snout inside the doorway.

The room was empty.

"Bugger!" The fat Brit frowned. "That manky tart Trinn had them leave after I did."

One of his men patted him on the shoulder, shoving a thick wad of tobacco into his cheek. "They don't trust you, Hollings. Can't say I blame them. But we'll be taking our fee just the same."

"What fee? The job's not done, mate." Hollings walked around the room, lifting the sheets with the tip of his rifle and pushing back the shower curtain. "They'll be headed home to their house in Virginia soon. We'll go and wait for them there."

"Virginia?" The man's jaw dropped. "What, in the United States? Are you daft?"

"Double the fee for a few days wait. Not bad if you ask me." Hollings looked at each face of his hired hands. "Who's in, then?"

A tall, thin hooligan slipped his rifle over his shoulder. "What about security? You said they hired that firm what uses retired Secret Service agents to guard their plucky estate."

"Bah." Hollings waved a hand. "DeShear fired them a'fore he left town. It's an open house. We'll go in and wait, easy as you please. Once they walk inside, we'll pop out of the bushes and gun them down, all unsuspecting like. Then, we're off. Now I won't ask again—double the wages, lads. Who's with me?"

Every hand in the room went up.

"Aye." Hollings nodded. "That's more like it. Off we go now."

He walked to the door, throwing it open as he stuffed his rifle back inside his coat.

In the hallway, the crew headed toward the elevator at the end of the corridor. Halfway there, a *ding* went off as the elevator arrived on their floor. The doors opened, and a tansuit dashed out, his cheeks red and his brow sweaty, running at full speed.

"Hello." Hollings raised an eyebrow. "What's this?" He waved to the tansuit, pointing at the prominent mole on the man's cheek, just under the left eye. "Mate, you're an Omicron with Lutz's crew, ain't that right? Come for Helena and Constantine, have you?"

"That's right." The tansuit slowed his pace, nodding. "I tracked them to here."

"As did we. They're in the car park now, boy." Hollings pointed. "Spotted them from the window. If we hurry, we can catch them before they escape!"

"The car park?" He turned around, sprinting back toward the elevator.

Hollings and his crew opened fire, killing the tansuit.

As the smoke from their rifles drifted toward the ceiling, Hollings turned to his men. "Best be leaving now, lads. This little bit of business is sure to attract attention." He tucked his rifle back under his coat, heading away from the elevators. "Down the stairs and out the back, lads, calm as you please. Then, get in the van. Trinn and her group will be heading home to Virginia soon—and we'll be waiting there, locked and loaded when they arrive."

* * * * *

Trinn gripped the steering wheel of the Mercedes as it hurled over the mountain trail, bouncing off of moguls and banging into every pothole. Helena held onto the dashboard with both hands, jolting with every bump the car hit. In the back seat, Constantine jolted back and forth.

Jaden peered out the window at the rushing river, the vehicle slamming into another rock. "I may still have to buy Doctor Shrinidhi a car after this."

"The turn is coming up, Miss Jaden," Constantine said. "You know, when we were in the room, I had a sense of your conversation with Mr. Hollings. You paid him twenty million dollars to deliver a broken AI to Doctor Lutz? That was your deal?"

"That was part of it." Trinn swerved to avoid a boulder. "Stop looking at my synapses."

"Turn here!" Constantine shouted.

Trinn spun the wheel, the Mercedes' tires sending up a cloud of dirt.

"Drive to that big tree." Constantine pointed to a massive pine. "The entry is up the path and down a trail."

Trinn drove the car into the brush just past the pine, letting the thick forest swallow the SUV. "Okay." She put the vehicle in park and shut off the engine. "You two get out and hide in the hills. I'm going into the cave via the entrance DeShear used." She put her elbow on the center console, turning to gaze at her passengers. "Stay still and stay quiet. If I'm not back in half an hour, get in the car and drive to the closest airport that's *not* Calgary. They'll be looking for you there. There's plenty of cash in the spare tire cavity. Fly to a safe city, like we talked about."

Constantine reached out and patted Jaden's hand. "You'll be back."

Pursing her lips, Trinn nodded. "Thanks. Keep the phone on vibrate. If it's safe, I'll come back and tell you. Do not answer that phone."

They exited the vehicle. Trinn looked at the rocky mountainside, pointing to a bushy outcrop of rocks. "There's plenty of cover over there, and a wind blocker."

Constantine ran to Jaden, throwing her arms around her. "I love you, Miss Jaden. Are you upset that you found out about Helena being my mother?"

Trinn patted the girls' head, sliding her hands down to pull her close. "No, never. How could I be? I love you, and I love her. And I love that you have her as your mother. You were right, she's the best mom ever." She squeezed Constantine tight and kissed the top of her head. "I'll see you very soon. Until then, stay hidden."

Trinn went to Helena and gave her a hug. "I mean that."

The old woman blushed. "Thank you, dear."

Trinn trotted off in the direction of the cave. Constantine and her mistress went to the outcrop, crouching down in the brush.

When Jaden had passed from eyesight, Constantine stood up and peered over the rocks, tiptoeing toward the cave entrance.

"What are you doing?" Helena whispered. "Miss Jaden said to stay here."

"Hamilton's in danger. We need to help him." Constantine peered at Helena. "We can't do that from here."

"Oh, dear." The old woman got to her feet. "I was afraid you'd say that."

* * * * *

DeShear kicked the door in on the private room of the lab. The lock splintered as the door swung opened and crashed into the wall. Squatting low, he pointed his gun into the room.

It was a small, empty space with two other closed doors.

"Help me out." DeShear looked at Seventeen. "What am I looking at here?"

"There was a separation," Seventeen said. "The females of our line were removed. We don't know where she took them, but since she spends so much time back here…"

DeShear nodded. "They're probably here, too. Okay." He stood up, inspecting the two doors. "These women—they're your… sisters?"

"Some. Others were from different parentage. So they were wives, girlfriends… and children."

DeShear winced. "Children?"

"The separation only happened recently, when we moved here." Seventeen sighed. "Doctor Lutz wanted no unauthorized regeneration of the lines. Of course, being humans, we are prone to human tendencies, so…"

"So there were children."

"Correct, sir." Seventeen walked to one of the doors, putting his ear against it. "Many were taken offline, but there was hope that a few had been allowed to survive."

DeShear made a fist.

Does this woman ever get tired of killing?

He banged on the first door. "Anybody in there? Can you hear us?"

From the other side came shouts from the women.

"Is Lutz in there?" he shouted.

A thunderous cry of "no" pierced the door.

"Sir…" Seventeen leaned close to DeShear. "They could be saying that because she has a gun on them."

Sighing, DeShear stepped back and looked at the door. "Thanks for that." He shook his head. "Well, we'll have to risk it. Ready? I'll kick in the door, then we go in with our guns ready just like last time."

"Yes." Seventeen gripped his rifle. "Sir, does it hurt to get shot? I mean… a lot?"

"Yep. Try not to let that happen."

He kicked in the second door, leveling his weapon as he rushed inside.

Lutz wasn't there.

Half a dozen women in lab coats cheered from the other side of a glass wall. Blondes, brunettes, redheads—tall, short… They waved from their prison laboratory.

As Seventeen flipped a switch on the wall, the glass door opened and the women ran out. A short brunette wrapped her arms around Seventeen, holding him and rocking back and forth.

She called out to DeShear. "Doctor Lutz went through that door. Be careful. She has a gun."

Nodding, DeShear aimed his weapon. "So do we." He approached the egress. "Are there any weapons behind door number two?"

Seventeen turned to him. "There might still be some locked up, back in the guard's area."

"Okay." DeShear held his hands up. "Ladies, number Eleven is outside in the main lab. Go check out the guard area with him and grab any weapons that are there." He turned to the door. "I'm going after Lutz. If she gets past me, make sure she doesn't escape."

Seventeen stepped to his side. "I'm coming with you."

He glanced at the short brunette, then to Seventeen. "You sure?"

"We started this thing. Let's finish it." He ran at the door, lowering his shoulder and breaking it open.

It was another empty room with another door.

DeShear frowned. "What is this place, a hall of mirrors at the state fair?" He went to the door and tried the knob. It didn't turn. "We made three left turns since we came in here. This has to go back to the main lab."

The sound of gunshots echoed through the hallway.

DeShear sprinted back, entering the main lab as Jaden curled up and hit the floor. Raising her hand, Trinn fired her weapon as Lutz ran to a closet and disappeared inside.

"Hank!" Trinn said. "I'm hit."

DeShear ran to her, dropping to one knee. "Where did it get you?"

Trinn rolled onto her side, hiking up her shirt. Blood dripped from a gash in the skin over her lower left ribs. "I'll live." She groaned. "But I'm going to be sore in the morning."

"Me, too," DeShear said. "Seventeen, take care of her. I'm going after Lutz."

Constantine raced to Trinn's side, Helena following her. "We can do that." She looked at Seventeen. "You go with Hamilton."

Trinn frowned. "I told you to stay hidden outside."

"And then you went and got yourself shot again, didn't you?" Constantine inspected the wound. "Now shush and let me administer first aid."

Helena glanced around the lab. "There are many medicines here, Miss Jaden. We'll fix you right up."

* * * * *

DeShear opened the closet door, revealing another corridor. As he and Seventeen ran inside, Seventeen pointed at the floor. "There's a blood trail."

"That's my girl." DeShear grinned.

At the end of the hallway was another door, open an inch and dark on the other side.

DeShear hugged the wall, pushing the door.

Shots rang out, muzzle blasts illuminating the inside of the room.

DeShear ducked, returning fire. Lutz shot again as she opened another door and fell inside, her feet blocking the door from closing.

"Let's go, Seventeen."

Seventeen slumped into the wall, blood soaking through the front of his shirt.

The women returned with guns, Trinn appearing with one arm over the shoulder of a redhead.

"We'll take care of him," the short brunette said. "Go get her."

Sweating, DeShear ran forward, shoving the door and pointing his weapon at Lutz's head. He kicked her gun from her outstretched hand, sending it across the floor. "Don't move! Don't you even blink!"

Lutz lay still on the floor.

DeShear checked for a pulse. He found none.

The women came forward, shouting and cheering.

"There they are!"

"Hello! Hello!"

They rushed toward glass cage after glass cage that lined the far wall, pulling out babies and toddlers and hugging them in a joyous reunion.

"It's been months!"

"I missed you so much!"

In the middle of the room was an oval conference table filled with paper plates and a cake. A monitor on the wall played a video of the children gathered around the table, filling several chairs and high chairs. The room on the monitor dimmed, and a cake with candles appeared, carried by two slender hands.

"Happy birthday to you, happy birthday to you!

"Happy birthday dear Megyn, happy birthday to you!"

On the screen, Atria Lutz set down the massive cake, going to each child at the table and hugging them. She picked up one after the other, holding them close and snuggling them. "Mommy loves you. Yes, I do. Yes, I do! You're my babies and I love you so much!"

The walls were filled with framed prints of Lutz and the babies from the glass cages, cuddling each one of the stolen infants as if it were her own.

Stunned, DeShear gazed at Lutz as she lay dead on the floor in a pool of red. The video restarted its loop, playing again in the background. DeShear sighed, leaning against the wall. Onscreen, Atria Lutz picked up the children again.

"Mommy loves you. Yes, I do. I love you all so much…"

* * * * *

Seventeen lay on the gurney in the main lab, his brunette wife and Eleven tending to his wound. The others helped clean up DeShear's injuries and those of Trinn. Two female technicians dragged the body of Atria Lutz into the room and covered her with a sheet.

DeShear looked at Seventeen. "There was a lot of talk about the regeneration records. Do you still need those?"

"No." He winced, sitting up on the gurney and taking his wife's hand. "We have what we wanted to find from them—where Lutz hid our loved ones. That's all the records really would have shown us."

The short brunette came over to DeShear, extending her hand. "I am Omicron Endius Nine. I want to thank you—and ask you a question."

DeShear shook her hand.

Endius Nine looked around the lab at her family members and friends—genetically engineered human hostages that had been created and imprisoned by Atria Lutz using the corrupt methods and the DNA of Marcus Hauser.

Lowering her voice, she peered into DeShear's eyes. "What happens now?"

Taking a deep breath, DeShear glanced at the newly-freed prisoners and shook his head. "A lot of tragedies happened in this lab, just like in every one of Hauser's other facilities. Illegal research, smuggled drugs, cold-blooded murders... The authorities will probably want to do an investigation of the lab and then they'll tear it all down."

"I wasn't asking about the lab," she said. "I'm wondering, what happens now—to us?"

"Yeah..." DeShear nodded. "I don't know. The tansuits in France were allowed to stay on and farm the château property. Most of the babies in Indonesia and Ukraine were placed with adoption agencies, and that's still ongoing..." He shrugged, glancing around. Every Omicron was looking at him. "I don't know what would happen in your situation. Scientists, working in an illegal genetics lab..."

"Forced to, under the constant threat of death," Enduis Nine said.

"I'm just saying, it may not be a smooth ride." DeShear rubbed his chin. "Governments can be... tricky."

Constantine sat upright. "Must we tell the authorities?"

"They already know, sweetie." Trinn patted Constantine's hand. "I work for the U.S. Government. They authorized my actions."

Helena clasped her hands in front of herself. "Miss Jaden, could they just... leave?"

Endius nine strolled toward Trinn. "The government may come looking for us, or Mr. Hollings may decide to return... And when any of them find us, maybe they'll cage us up again, as Doctor Lutz did. Fear is a strange motivator. Now, I've been led to believe that a new identity can be purchased for about ten thousand dollars. We probably have enough in petty cash around here somewhere to hide us all. And whoever we are, or whatever name we go by, we can just disappear. Omicrons still age a year for every month that we are alive, so we'll only be a problem for about five more years." She stopped at Trinn's side. "I think we can stay out of trouble for that long. We'll just... quietly live our lives, like anyone else."

"I can understand wanting to disappear," DeShear said. "Hauser's people keep coming after us."

Trinn sighed. "He's right. Your situation has been hard, so I won't tell you what to do. I'd like you to stay here and speak with the authorities, but... for the next few minutes, I'm going to be busy making some phone calls and arranging to get my family home to Virginia. If you were to, say... slip away and disappear while I was distracted, that would be a little embarrassing for me, professionally. But I'd get over it."

"Yes, ma'am." Endius Nine smiled. "Thank you."

CHAPTER 46

Trinn reclined in her first-class seat as the commercial aircraft rocked gently back and forth. She closed her eyes, laying a small pillow over her head, a thick wad of bandages sticking out from her side. "Let's fly this way from now on—no more cargo planes or military jets. Just luxury."

DeShear settled back into his seat. Under his jeans, two large lumps of gauze covered the top of each thigh. "I gotta say, I could get used to this."

Constantine bounced up and down in her seat. "I can't wait to get back into our house! The bun-buns must be starving by now!"

"I'm sure they're fine, dear." Helena patted Constantine on the leg. "We gave them enough hay and water to last a week. The horses, too."

"Oh, I do hope so. I've never been away from them for this long. I'm certain they've missed me terribly."

Helena smiled, leaning back into her seat and closing her eyes.

"Champagne?" The flight attendant held out a tray of bubbling fluted glasses.

"Absolutely! Thank you." DeShear took two glasses, holding one out to Jaden. "Cheers, lover."

Trinn smiled at him, then took the glass and set it back on the tray. "I, uh… can't have alcohol right now." She placed her hand on her abdomen.

"No?" DeShear sat up. "Why not?"

Helena and Constantine grinned at him.

"Well…" Trinn swallowed hard. "I've been meaning to tell you…"

"Yeah?"

"I… was having some nosebleeds," she said. "And I had passed out—"

"I remember. You passed out on the fishing boat in the Bahamas. They were shooting at us, and you said you didn't know if you got shot and hit your head as you fell, or if you passed out and hit your head and then got shot…"

Jaden squirmed in her seat. "Uh, well… really, it's just the meds." She took his glass. "You and I can't mix alcohol with our antibiotics—doctor's orders. Sorry." She placed his glass on the flight attendant's tray, glancing at her. "Thank you, though."

Constantine frowned, folding her arms over her chest. "Aww…"

The flight attendant moved on to the other rows.

DeShear smiled at Trinn. "Are you sure there's not something else I should know?"

"There is." She closed her eyes and patted his arm. "But it'll keep. It's a long flight, and the doctor said you'd lost a lot of blood so you shouldn't get excited."

He glanced at his travel companions. They were all smiling at him.

"And what you have to tell me would make me excited?"

"It will." Yawning, Jaden turned her cheek to the pillow. "But in a good way. Now get some rest and we'll be home before you know it. We have a lot to talk about before we get there."

* * * * *

Hollings glanced at his phone before shoving it into his pocket and walking into the living room of his Virginia hotel suite. "Listen up, lads. I've just gotten word that they've boarded the plane. Let's have a few pints at the corner pub and then we'll head over to the DeShear estate when it's dark, so's nobody sees us. We can sleep it off in the bushes and be right as rain in the morning. The whole family will be arriving come first light."

He picked up his AR-15 and patted the barrel.

"And we'll be right there to kill the living daylights out of every single one of them."

* * * * *

The sun peeked over the tall trees of DeShear's Virginia estate, casting a golden-orange glow over the pastures. The horses walked slowly over the green grass; the black and white bunnies nibbled hay from their feeder.

In the thick bushes around the house, Hollings' phone pinged with an incoming text.

He slid his AR-15 over his shoulder and checked his phone. Lifting his binoculars to his eyes, he stared at the approach road to the house. "Here we go, lads. The moment of truth." He let the field glasses fall to his chest. "No messing about. Two shots in the chest apiece. They'll be tired from a long flight and distracted by their injuries, so we'll be able to walk right in behind them."

DeShear's vehicle turned onto his street.

The thug crouching next to Hollings licked his lips, smiling. "This has been a long time coming for you, eh, mate?"

"It surely has." He looked out over his team. "Look smart now, you lot. These AR-15s have a kick to them, especially with the special ammunition I bought. Aim well—and kill without mercy."

CHAPTER 47

President Brantley sat behind his massive desk in the oval office, frowning. "So, what happened?"

"It's all here, sir." FBI Special Agent Matt Eicholtz stepped forward, placing a tablet on the desk. "This is from ViewPoint Security." He pressed a button, and a video played.

Brantley reached for his reading glasses.

The grainy security camera footage from the DeShear residence showed the four family members enter the house, followed almost instantly by a swarm of armed men.

The family turned to see the intruders. The gunmen's rifles jerked against shoulders as puffs of smoke blasted from the gun muzzles. Clothing became covered in splashes of red.

DeShear fell first, with two red splashes spreading over his chest, then Helena. Constantine was knocked off her feet by the shots that hit her.

Trinn reached for a cabinet, pulling out a handgun, but the assassins overwhelmed her. Three or four shots found their mark, throwing her backwards into the couch, where a large fat man walked up to her and pointed his rifle directly at her chest.

The weapon jerked twice. Two more red stains spread over Jaden Trinn's torso.

The leader waved a hand, and the assassins left, disappearing through the back of the pasture and escaping. The four members of Hamilton DeShear's family lay still on their backs, blood covering their bodies.

Agent Eicholtz reached over and shut off the video, then stepped away again. The members of the national security team and the President's traveling secretary, Naomi Harding, sat in what could only be described as stunned silence.

Brantley removed his reading glasses, pinching the bridge of his nose as he closed his eyes.

"I'm sorry, Mr. President," Agent Eicholtz said. "ViewPoint Security's official position is, DeShear had ordered them off the property. By the time they saw what was happening on the cameras, it was too late to do anything." He sighed. "I understand that Jaden Trinn was a friend of yours. I knew her, too. Her death is… a great loss."

Nodding, Brantley scowled. *"Official* position. Seems like everyone in Washington has an official position to cover their butt in one way or another." He glanced at Naomi, tears welling in his eyes.

The traveling secretary jumped up from her seat. "That will be all, everyone. Thank you for attending this special briefing."

The members of the President's staff filed out of the room.

"Agent Eicholtz," Brantley said. "Would you stay with me for a moment?"

The room cleared. Only the President and Eicholtz remained. Naomi reached into the office and pulled the doors shut from the outside.

Brantley rose from his desk, adjusting his suitcoat. "I appreciate you delivering this news to me. I'm sure it was very difficult. Jaden was... almost like a daughter to me."

"Yes, sir." Eicholtz nodded.

The President sighed. "Yesterday, I had to sit down with the parents of an F-15 pilot who was recently killed. He was on a top-secret mission, with a member of the U.S. government who was under cover, and it cost him his life. But he died a hero, and I wanted his parents to *know* he died a hero."

Brantley put on his overcoat.

"It's the worst part of this job," the President said, "but I refuse to shove it off on someone else."

He walked to the door of the oval office.

"I wonder if you'd be free to come with me for a short visit to another parent who will be getting bad news about their child? I have an old friend who needs to hear about Jaden Trinn."

Eicholtz straightened up like he was standing at attention. "It would be my honor, Mr. President."

The nursing home in Arlington, Virginia, took only fifteen minutes to reach, thanks to the

Presidential motorcade. Rain dotted the windshield as gray clouds covered the skies. When the motorcade arrived, there was a flurry of activity as members of the nursing home staff gathered to see the President of the United States visiting their facility.

In a small room on the second floor, a once broad-shouldered, strapping young man now sat in a wheelchair as a frail old man, stooped by time and crippled by a stroke. He rested firm in his seat, his eyes on the small window that looked over the grassy courtyard.

The nursing home staff brought two chairs into the room and closed the doors, ensuring that the President and their resident had privacy. Special Agent Eicholtz was the only other person in the room.

Brantley glanced at Eicholtz, whispering. "They aren't sure how much he hears or understands these days, but I think he hears and understands everything just fine."

He leaned forward to the man in the wheelchair.

"TJ, this is Special Agent Matt Eicholtz. Today, he is being afforded the honor of meeting Thomas Jay Trinn, a former member of the United States Central Intelligence Agency, former All-American college baseball star, and my friend for over thirty years." Brantley sighed, pursing his lips. "You're going to hear some stories about your daughter soon, TJ, and… well, I came here to tell you that they aren't true."

Brantley leaned back in his chair, swallowing hard.

"Here's the truth. Even as a little girl, Jaden was always an amazing person. As an adult, she distinguished herself time and time again, willing to sacrifice everything for her country, and when her country called, she stepped up like the hero she has always been. Most of all…" He cleared his throat, his voice wavering. "Most of all, I will miss her. She was as much a friend to me as you were, and people like that are worth their weight in gold."

Tears welling in his eyes, the President looked at his friend.

The man in the wheelchair didn't speak, didn't move, didn't show his recognition of the words being spoken in any way. He remained rigid, in the same position he'd been in when the two men entered his room, his eyes fixed on the window.

"Anyway," Brantley said, "I'm sorry how this has turned out. I did all I could." The President looked down. "I hope as my friend you can understand, and that you can forgive me for allowing it—and forgive her. One day we might see things differently. Things have a way of changing with time." He sniffled, forcing a smile onto his lips as a tear ran down his cheek. "Heck, I'll be out of office soon. Maybe I can come by with a New York pizza and some beer and we'll have a laugh like in the old days."

TJ reached a trembling hand out to his friend, patting his knee, his gaze staying on the window. "It's raining."

"Yeah." Brantley looked to the small pane of glass, his voice a whisper. "It sure is."

* * * * *

The presidential limo drove over the wet roads, motorcycle cops out in front and behind, carrying the passengers back toward the White House. Several other cars were part of the motorcade, but on this trip the sleek black limousine only carried its driver and two others.

Brantley leaned back on the leather seat, pushing the button to raise the partition between him and his driver. Next to the President, Eicholtz gazed out the window at the passing landscape.

"Thank you, sir," Eicholtz said, "for letting me meet your friend."

"My pleasure. TJ was a hero and so was Jaden." Brantley smiled. "The apple sure didn't fall far from the tree in that family. Boy, TJ was something back in the old days. I could tell you some stories about him."

Eicholtz nodded. "Will you be staying at your ranch sir? After your term finishes?"

"I haven't decided yet." Brantley adjusted his overcoat, pulling it up to cover his knees. "There's something to be said for moving away from Washington once you've served your time."

"I've seen pictures of the ranch. It looks very pretty. Good weather, beautiful scenery…" Eicholtz glanced at the President. "Nice neighbors."

"Yes." Brantley fussed with the hem of his overcoat. "Nice neighbors."

Eicholtz returned his gaze to the window. "Any thoughts about what *really* happened to them?"

The elder statesman stopped adjusting his raincoat, turning to face the young FBI agent in his vehicle. "Well, of course *officially*, they were killed, weren't they? We watched the video—some disgruntled British national hired a team of murderers and killed Jaden Trinn and her entire family. But I heard a rumor that it was all staged, and that the vaunted member of the Bureau of Diplomatic Security now lives on a farm in Iowa somewhere. Supposedly, the whole family took assumed names and moved to a nice little spread, with a couple of horses and their two little bunnies, out where no one would ever think to look for them. Iowa, or maybe it was Nebraska. I can't remember."

Eicholtz shrugged, a smile coming to his lips. "I guess it doesn't matter. I'm just sorry to see them go. I'll miss them."

The President nodded. "Me, too."

The car crossed over the Potomac River, swollen to the brink from the recent rains.

A ping came from Eicholtz's phone. He took it from his pocket and read the screen. "Mr. President, you requested an update on an informant we have in Canada—a gun smuggling operation that fronts as a toy store. The owners confirm they sold ten AR-15s to a British national, along with a small amount of ammunition. However, a different confidential source in Canada confirms that a Mr. Hollings acquired several cases of special ammunition from a different dealer—buying blanks, basically, that shoot red paint balls." He looked up from his phone. "Apparently, on video it looks very realistic."

"Apparently." The President nodded. "I guess Jaden had it all figured out."

"Yes sir." Eicholtz smiled. "She sure did. But you added a nice touch with her father, giving him that New York pizza reference. Think he got it?"

"Oh, he got it. Spies never forget code names. I know TJ was glad to hear his daughter is safe."

* * * * *

The Lucas Jones family of Nebraska was a direct descendant of the state's earliest settlers. Their farm spanned close to two thousand acres, having been pared down over the years as improvements in farm machinery made a bigger spread no longer necessary, and as the Joneses grew older and closer to retirement age.

Mr. Jones drove up the long dirt road to his home, parking the car and ambling up the sidewalk. His wife Betty greeted him from an open kitchen window as she worked on some baked goods.

Lucas smacked the dust off of his jeans and entered the house, the sun sinking closer to the horizon. "Looks like we got some new neighbors."

"Yes," Betty said. "I made them some friendship bread earlier when I got home. I went ahead and took it over because I wasn't sure what time you'd be getting in."

"Well, there was no sense in staying at the auction. Wasn't much in the way of good breeding stock this time around, so I decided three days was enough." He kissed his wife. "They seem like nice folks?"

"Very nice. He's some sort of retired law-enforcement and she apparently worked in the tech industry or something. There's an elderly woman living with them—one's mother or grandmother, I guess—and they have a darling little girl."

"Oh good." Lucas opened the refrigerator and took out a pitcher of lemonade. "Maybe Lily would like to go over and play with her the next time she visits."

"I'm sure. I think they said they lived in Iowa for several months before they moved here, but the wife says this is their new permanent home."

"Well, I'm glad they're settled in. I'll be sure to stop over tomorrow. Don't wanna bother them too much while they're unpacking."

"That's a good idea."

The old man walked toward his bedroom. "What were their names, anyway?"

"Macintosh, I think she said. Or Macinley. One or the other." Betty put her pie on the counter and took off her apron. "You can find out tomorrow when you visit. The grandmother's last name is Montenegro, I know that. They seemed very nice. I think they'll make good neighbors."

* * * * *

DeShear leaned back in his wooden bench, propping his feet up on the railing of his front porch. As he closed a homeschool math book, he gazed out at the setting sun. The smell of fresh baked pie wafted over from the neighbor's house across the way. In the front yard, his six-year-old daughter played with her two fat, black and white rabbits, her elderly matron looking on.

Jaden came outside, taking a seat next to him and nuzzling his ear. "Are you enjoying yourself, Mr. Macintosh?"

"I am, Mrs. Macintosh." He put his arm around her and gave her a kiss. "It's a nice evening."

"It certainly is. It's a nice life."

Trinn's phone buzzed in her pocket. She took it out and checked it, keeping it close to her chest before sliding it back into her jeans.

Cocking his head, DeShear glanced at her. "What was that?"

"Nothing." She slipped lower on the seat, pulling his arm close around her and closing her eyes. "I told you, I'm on hiatus."

"Hiatus? I thought we retired."

"Well, we did, but…"

"Yeah, yeah…" DeShear looked over the railing at his daughter. "It's been months and I still can't believe it worked."

Trinn shrugged. "You said you wanted to disappear. I was listening. I figured Doctor Hauser's people wouldn't keep coming after us if they thought we were dead. Neither would anyone else."

"But you got Hollings to play along." DeShear shook his head. "He hated you."

"In the end, Hollings was about the money— and he played his role well. He put together a small group that bought into the plan. You fire a gun, you see a splash of red on your target and they drop to the floor… Your boss says, 'Well done, lads. Let's go!' so, you go. You cash a big check and you move on— and if you opened your mouth later about what really happened, nobody'd believe you."

Nodding, DeShear closed his eyes and nuzzled Jaden's hair with his nose. "You made everyone believe something that was completely staged. You saved us."

"Mr. Macintosh, the first rule of the Bureau of Diplomatic Security is, if you're going to put on a show, make it elaborate." Jaden wrapped her hands around his. "And I'd say we saved each other."

Constantine looked up at them from the yard. "Miss Sarah, the baby's crying."

Trinn groaned, looking at DeShear. "I may never get used to that name." She sat up, calling out to Constantine. "No, sweetie, he's—"

From the nursery, the sound of a baby crying reached their ears.

Constantine smiled.

Trinn wagged a finger at her. "Stop reading people's synapses." She got up and went to the doorway. "Are you coming? Diapers are an equal opportunity offender."

"Yep, I'm coming." DeShear set the math book on the stack of other homeschool texts and grabbed his cane, leaning hard on it as he walked to his beautiful wife. They strolled hand in hand to the nursery, baby Alexander kicking and grinning in his onesie as his parents entered the room.

Trinn went to the changing table, lifting a diaper off the stack. DeShear unsnapped Alexander's pajamas and cleaned him up.

"You like changing diapers, don't you?" Jaden said.

"No." DeShear sighed, gazing at her. "But I like what a clean diaper gives me. A happy family."

Trinn stepped to his side. "The diaper doesn't give you that."

"No. You do." DeShear slipped his arm around her, kissing her ear.

When they returned to the front porch, their daughter was eager to hold her baby brother.

As Helena sat down on the bench with her, Constantine cradled Alexander in her arms. "You and I shall be good siblings." She tickled his tummy through the onesie. "And best mates."

DeShear stood behind them, his arm around his beautiful wife. He smiled at his family as the setting sun painted the sky a gold yellow before slipping down past the horizon.

THE END

Note to Readers

If you liked this story, please pop over to Amazon and Goodreads to say so. Just a few words from you helps other readers find a new book they'll love.

Thanks,
Dan Alatorre

If you'd like to know what comes next for these or any of my other characters, keep tabs by going to DanAlatorre.com. Click the "contact me" button, and give me your email address; I'll give you periodic updates about my upcoming thriller novels, the story lines I'm considering, and fun behind-the-scenes looks at the story writing process. I promise I won't spam you, and you might get to read my latest book months before anyone else!

AN INTERVIEW WITH DAN ALATORRE
ABOUT THE GAMMA SEQUENCE SERIES

Thank you for reading Dark Hour and the other books in The Gamma Sequence series. Readers always seem curious about where I get my ideas and what my writing process is, so I decided to share some of it with you in this interview conducted by my author friend Colton Berman.

Colton Berman: Thanks for sitting down with me today, Dan. Readers want to know - How did you come up with the idea for The Gamma Sequence series?

Dan Alatorre: Hi, Colton. Thanks for having me. The Gamma Sequence came from a conversation I had with an author friend. She had read some of my murder mystery thrillers and suggested I give medical thrillers a try. We kicked around some ideas, and since I'd always enjoyed TV show reruns like Quincy ME when I was a kid, and more current shows like CSI, I thought it'd be fun to explore that genre and give it my own unique twist. Some people say this series is partly sci fi, too, but there's nothing mentioned in The Gamma Sequence books that isn't currently being practiced or researched in laboratories around the world.

With any book I write, I try to figure out a really compelling idea to base the story around. For example, we know the average human lifespan, more or less; in The Gamma Sequence, I thought, what if you had an *actual*, predetermined age you'd die, based on your genetics? What would you do differently if you knew about something like that? As we see in the first book, one character takes a very negative course. So that got my wheels turning, and that is why it was originally called Kill Switch - a genetic switch clicked at age X, and you died. Then you get to research all the reasons why genetic switches actually happen, like puberty and menopause, and you start to see it's not such a far-fetched idea.

Colton: Did you plan for The Gamma Sequence to be a series?

Dan: No! When I wrote the first book, it was one novel, and when it finished, the story was over. I went back to writing murder mysteries. But as The Gamma Sequence (book 1) became more and more successful, people wanted a follow up book. The more I said no, the more they asked. I decided I'd only write a book 2 if it could be better than book 1. Then one day I was on the treadmill, and I saw a news story that said part of the reason why the USA doesn't remove brutal, oppressive foreign dictators is because the people *under* the dictator are often even worse, and they would take over. And I was like, Wow, if that happened in my book, that would be a cool story – Dr. Hauser's underlings might be worse than he is. And also, when we left off at the end of book 1, DeShear was about to start dying. I thought it would be intriguing if the hero of a story had to hunt down the bad guys *while he was dying* – and Rogue Elements was born.

Now, even as I was writing Rogue, I would occasionally think about ideas for book 3, but nothing big - and again, my rule: no book 3 if it's not better than book 2. And eventually I had an amazing idea for book 3 (and I planned to end the series as a trilogy). Terminal Sequence, where they shut down all the illegal genetics labs and all the computers sharing the illegal information, became the idea. But what really drove that story was thinking about what life was like for the people actually living *in* the genetic program facilities, like Helena and Constantine (two characters I really loved), and the wheels started turning for another book featuring the two of them more - we were off again!

Colton: How long did it take you to write The Gamma Sequence books?

Dan: Everybody asks that, so here it is. **The Gamma Sequence** book 1 (original working title: Kill Switch) took just over 5 weeks to write. That's pretty fast. I started the morning of February 26, 2019, by kicking around medical thriller plot ideas with some author friends. By 8pm the next day, I'd written the first chapter of the story. 15 days later, I had written 17 chapters and 36,969 words, with roughly 12 plot points to go. I finished writing it on April 3 at 11:15pm, so that's a little more than 5 weeks. (I write pretty clean in my first drafts, too, which I'm proud of.) I get excited, and the words just flow.

Rogue Elements was written between August 18, 2019 and October 4, about 46 days or 8 weeks. (Why did I take so much time between those two books? I was writing *another* book but for a different series.)

Terminal Sequence was started November 22, 2019 at about 9am and finished on January 18, 2020, about 8 weeks.

The Keepers took around 7 weeks, and

Dark Hour took almost exactly 7 weeks. Like, to the day.

I say "almost" and "around" because when I'm writing a book, I'll get ideas for other books or scenes or characters. I write them down and stick them in a folder on my computer. Some will go into the book I'm writing, some would be better for a different story, but I capture them and stick them away so I can finish what I'm working on. Then, when I'm ready to start the next book, there are a lot of ideas in the folder (most don't ever get used, by the way), so technically you could say I started writing the book prior to when I actually start.

But each author is different in how fast they write, and I respect that. I have author friends who've been working a single book for more than five years, whereas I know that certain famous authors give themselves 90 days to finish a first draft of a new novel. It usually takes me 6-8 weeks to write a book. Most of my books are around 80,000 words; some are as long as 125,000 and some are shorter, coming in at around 65,000, but I mentally plan on the book coming in at around 85,000 or so. That will take me between 6-8 weeks to do, averaging about 2,000 words per day.

Colton: There is a lot of technical medical information in the books. Do you have a background in medical technology?

Dan: No, I have an imagination. I also have access to medical people. My father was a physician, and I've become friends with lots of other doctors, nurses and medical technicians. I was also inspired by TV show reruns I watched as a kid, like Quincy ME, which opened my eyes to the kinds of detailed analysis that was possible in a coroner's world, and newer shows like CSI. Characters in those stories use science and lab analysis to solve the case, not guns, so that was interesting to me. Another idea was to go with a House-style physician, keeping the setting mostly confined to a hospital, and unraveling the mysteries behind patients' puzzling ailments. I also loved the book (and movie) Coma, and I thought the idea of nefarious elements at work behind the scenes at medical facilities was very intriguing. As readers know by now, my series The Gamma Sequence is a combination of all of the above.

Colton: How would you describe your writing style?

Dan: I try to do three things: (1) write characters you'd want to spend time with, (2) create a fascinating dilemma for them to solve, and (3) tell their story at a fast pace. That's the kind of story I want to read, so that's the kind of story I want to write. Some of my favorite books, movies, and TV shows start out by gripping the reader on page 1, usually in paragraph 1, maybe even sentence 1. I try to do that. As a kid, we watched the Sunday mystery movie reruns like Colombo, and they tended to start right off with the villain doing some horrible deed. Because I loved those stories, I try to combine a gripping opening with the villain doing an awful act. Then, I usually bring in the heroes in chapter 2 and we start in on solving the mystery. But a lot of work goes into that opening. I may work for weeks on the opening *sentence*, just so it has the right feel! (I mean, not all day every day, but sporadically during the writing. Although, if I'm honest, I'm usually kicking it around a lot when I'm doing other things that don't appear to be writing. Lots of good ideas come to me when I'm on the treadmill or mowing the lawn. Agatha Christie said the best writing happens when you're doing the dishes. Your mind relaxes, and poof, a great solution to a story's problem comes to you.) I really try to grab the reader with the very first sentence of a story, which is not easy!

Colton: Your medical thrillers definitely aren't confined to a hospital. Your characters go everywhere.

Dan: I like having my story go to exotic places that readers would like to visit, but still have the medically relevant reason to be there. Because I have traveled a lot, I found ways to take my characters to places I've been - France, Hawaii, Banff Springs in Canada, the UK, the Bahamas... on and on. I worked hard to make these amazing settings relevant to the story, and I hope I have been able to make my readers feel as if they are in these places, too.

Colton: Aside from fun locations, a fair amount of technology and research has gone into the books, as well as foreign languages. For example, most of the books in The Gamma a Sequence series involve someone who's not from the United States, occasionally speaking in *their* language.

Dan: Yeah. Without making it hard on the reader, I always tried to bring the flavor of that character's language to the story. Because I've met so many people from exotic lands, I know that when they speak English, they tend to speak it either more formally than we Americans do, using fewer contractions and occasionally getting a word wrong or out of place. With foreign countries where English is spoken, like the UK, I might have a character use some of the fun expressions that my British friends use and that I've heard when I was there, like calling people a "git" or saying "you lot" when Americans might say "you guys" or "you folks" or "you people," referring to a gang of individuals.

Colton: Who is your favorite character in the books?

Dan: Well, it's Constantine, for sure, but let me expand on that. Readers always ask who my favorite characters are or if I have a favorite book in the series. I do. But you have to have an intriguing bad guy or you don't have much of a story, so I've tried to keep the main presence of the evil character around while introducing different partners or coworkers or disciples that the evil main character may have had. That's fine but it's also a lot of work because I don't want to read the same story time after time. (But the bad guys aren't my favorites; the good guys are.) I've tried to have each different book in the series feature a different good guy.

While Constantine wins out overall for the series, I like different characters in the different books, so here's a breakdown:

In The Gamma Sequence, everything gets set up, and I really enjoyed the banter between DeShear and Lanaya. I think she steals the show a lot of the time. I liked the story arc of where they didn't really like each other at first (mostly it was her not liking him) to finally at the end feeling like they had become good friends. That repartee, evolving slowly over time, is something I will try to do again in a different book series, with different characters. My favorite scene is when he discovers the mass graves in Indonesia.

In Rogue Elements, I love, love, LOVE the character of Jaden Trinn being a kickass warrior *who keeps getting in the way of DeShear's plans!* That was fun, and then having the completely unscrupulous Mr. Hollings backstabbing and double crossing everybody. Both of those were fun characters to create.

In Terminal Sequence, it was originally planned to be the third (and final) book of a trilogy. And when I was doing it, I introduced two additional characters that I absolutely fell in love with, Constantine and Helena. The addition of the 4-year-old/5-year-old to the story as a main character and as a *smart* one, was especially fun for me because my daughter had been that age not too many years before I started writing that story. And there were just so many neat things kids that age do, I wanted to bring some of that to the table. Additionally, I love the idea of Helena (Keeper 27 in that book) appearing somewhat meek but still a force to be reckoned with. My favorite scene is when Helena is getting Constantine ready to meet with "him." My second favorite is when Dr. Hauser got rid of all the children during Rituals, which was hard for me to write, believe it or not. I still cry every time I read it. Surprisingly, fans expected that sort of thing from Hauser, so they weren't as upset as I was!

The Keepers featured Helena and Constantine, while introducing Kitt - and Kitt basically drives half of that book, which was a lot of fun, because she is so different from everyone else in the story. She's not a cop/detective like DeShear, she's not a badass like Trinn, she's not privy to inside information like Helena. She has her smarts and not much more, and she was a terrific character to take the lead in that book. This one starts out more mysterious than the others, which I like, and my favorite scene is when Constantine is escaping over the cliffs.

Dark Hour allowed me to return to the main players again, and feature more of Jaden Trinn while still having almost all of the fans' other favorite characters play major roles. I introduced another interesting villain, Atria Lutz, and put together a very tight combination of stories and subplots that all converge for one final amazing climax. My favorite character in this one was Trinn again, and my favorite scene is probably the Happy Birthday scene. I hope that worked as well for readers as it did in my head. I'm sure readers will prefer the reveal between the FBI Agent and the President, though, when they see our heroes are all safe.

My favorite scene out of *all* the books is probably at the end of Terminal Sequence, when they are trying to launch a trojan horse device to destroy the computers, and the poisonous gas is getting let into the Château. One of my author friends was reading an early draft and said, "The tension here is insane, I can't stop reading." That was nice.

Colton: Tell us a little about your writing habits, and the creative process by which you make your books.

Dan: I'm just like the readers, here - I always want to "peek behind the curtain" and learn about how a great movie director does his or her magic, how a brilliant writer like Ernest Hemingway (or James Patterson or Stephen King or Aaron Sorkin or JK Rowling, etc.) goes about creating an amazing story, how the best comedians build the plot of a joke and make it universally appealing, or how great actors build a timeless character. I want to learn how they do what they do, like how they got me to be scared at a certain point in a story, or how they made me like a character so much. That's hard work and it always looks effortless when it's done by a master, so I want to always learn more about their methods. I'm always watching interviews about the creative process in its many forms. Here's mine.

I like to get up early to write, a habit that came when my daughter was a baby/toddler/infant and would wake up in the middle of the night. When she was a baby, I'd struggle to go back to sleep after giving her a bottle at 2am, so I'd stay up and write for a few hours. Today, I still like to get up at 4am or 5am and write before the rest of the house is awake. It's a very productive time. If it's a school day, then I wake my daughter up around 6:30 and I go make her breakfast and pack her lunch, take her to school – then I'm usually right back to the writing. The short break helps my batteries recharge. A lot of time, that break also allows me to think of a solution to a problem I've been working on, so you'll see me doing a talk-to-text message in the car, capturing the solution and emailing it to myself so I don't forget it. Other writers have their methods; that works for them. Mine works for me. (I know that 4am stuff isn't for everybody!) I try to write characters that I'd want to spend time with, doing things I'd like to do, in places I'd like to go – but knowing they'll come home safe when it's done. And I try to open my soul and put it on the page – because readers can sense it when you do, and they connect with it, even though they may not know why. So the key for me is being open and honest with the reader and not holding back.

Colton: And finally, what's next?

Dan: Oh, man. Lots of stuff. I have several series I'm writing:

the Double Blind murder mystery series features Tampa police detectives Carly Sanderson and Sergio Martin, partners and best friends whose stories follow them becoming experts at stopping serial killers;

the Jett Thacker mystery series is about a former-lawyer-turned investigative TV reporter, now solving mysteries with her brain and by drawing on her legal background and the many TV stories she's done over the years;

The Gamma Sequence has concluded, as we know, and it involves genetically engineered humans and artificial intelligence, and the repercussions of those medical sciences in our world. There may be another book in that series one day, though, because I really like those characters.

So what's next is this: as long as fans keep reading my stories, I'll keep writing them.

If you liked this story, please pop over to Amazon and Goodreads to say so. Just a few words from you helps other readers find a new book they'll love.

Thanks,

Dan Alatorre

A REQUEST FROM THE AUTHOR

Dear Reader,

I hope you enjoyed Dark Hour. It's always fun to bring your favorite characters back in a new story, and for me to try to find new (and dangerous) situations for them to get into, and then to return them safely home again.

Readers always ask me what's coming next. Well, I have been kicking around the idea that Trinn and DeShear are *not* going to sit idly in retirement, so they'll be going off on some adventure... But it occurred to me it *might* be fun to see Constantine grow up a few years, and since she's always had an advanced IQ, it didn't seem out of the realm of possibility that the government might come to her and ask her to join an agency, especially if it's the one her new stepmother worked for.

Trinn had a big role in Dark Hour, and it was fun letting Helena take the spotlight in The Keepers, so it seems like a good idea to let someone else step up and see what they can do. Constantine has had bigger and bigger roles since her debut in Terminal Sequence, so let's see how she does in future stories. I have a feeling that whatever comes next will be a lot of fun.

Remember, YOU are the reason that I will explore the future of these characters! So, tell me what you liked, what you loved, what you hated… I'd love to hear from you. You can write me at DanAlatorre.com.

Finally, I need a favor, please. If you'd be so kind, I'd love a review of Dark Hour. Love it or hate it, I'd really enjoy your feedback. Your honest review will help readers who like what you like to find my stories, and help those with other tastes to not pick up a book they won't enjoy.

You can find all of my books on Amazon, on the Dan Alatorre Author Page.

Thanks a bunch for reading Dark Hour and spending time with me. It's an honor to know you enjoy my stories.

In gratitude,
Dan Alatorre

ABOUT THE AUTHOR

   USA Today bestselling author Dan Alatorre has published more than 50 titles and has been translated into over a dozen languages. His ability to surprise readers and make them laugh, cry, or hang onto the edge of their seats, has been enjoyed all around the world.

   Dan's success is widespread and varied. In addition to being a bestselling author, he achieved President's Circle with two different Fortune 500 companies, and mentors grade school children through his Young Authors Club. Dan resides in the Tampa, Florida, area with his wife and daughter.

   Join Dan's exclusive Reader's Club today at DanAlatorre.com and find out about new releases and special offers!

OTHER THRILLERS BY DAN ALATORRE

NOVELS

Jett Thacker Mysteries
Tiffany Lynn Is Missing, *a psychological thriller*
Killer In The Dark, *Jett Thacker book 2*

The Gamma Sequence Medical Thriller Series
The Gamma Sequence, *a medical thriller*
Rogue Elements, *The Gamma Sequence, book 2*
Terminal Sequence, *The Gamma Sequence, book 3*
The Keepers, *The Gamma Sequence, book 4*
Dark Hour, *The Gamma Sequence, book 5*

Double Blind Murder Mystery Series
Double Blind, *a murder mystery*
Primary Target, *Double Blind book 2*
Third Degree, *Double Blind book 3*
Fourth Estate, *Double Blind book 4*

OTHER THRILLER NOVELS

A Place Of Shadows, *a paranormal mystery*
The Navigators, *a time travel thriller*

OTHER BOOKS
The Water Castle, *a fantasy romance novel*
The Italian Assistant, *a very funny, very sexy romance novel*

Dan Alatorre Short Story Horror Anthologies
Dark Passages
Dark Voodoo
Dark Intent
Dark Thoughts

Short Story Horror Anthologies With Other Authors
The Box Under The Bed
Dark Visions
Nightmareland
Spellbound
Wings and Fire
Shadowland

Family Humor
Savvy Stories
The Terrible Twos
The Long Cutie
The Short Years
There's No Such Thing As A Quick Trip To Buy-Mart
Night of the Colonoscopy
Santa Maybe
A Day for Hope

Illustrated Children's Books
Laguna the Lonely Mermaid
The Adventures of Pinchy Crab
The Princess and the Dolphin
Stinky Toe!

Children's Early Reader Books
The Zombunny
Zombunny 2: Night of the Scary Creatures
Zombunny 3: Quest for Battle Space

Writing Instruction
A if for Action
B is for Backstory
C is for Character
D is for Dialogue
E is for Emotion
F is for Fast Pace

Made in the USA
Las Vegas, NV
04 October 2022

56553040R00298